WINIFRED HOLTBY

(1898-1935) was born in Rudston, Yorkshire. In the First
World War she was a member of the Women's Auxiliary Army
Corps, and then went to Somerville College, Oxford where she
met Vera Brittain. After graduating, these two friends shared a
flat in London where both embarked upon their respective
literary careers. Winifred Holtby was a prolific journalist,
writing for the *Manchester Guardian*, the *News Chronicle* and
Time and Tide of which she became a director in 1926. She also
travelled all over Europe as a lecturer for the League of
Nations Union.

Her first novel, *Anderby Wold*, was published in 1923,
followed, in 1924, by *The Crowded Street* (both published by
Virago). She wrote five other novels: *The Land of Green Ginger*
(1927, to be reissued by Virago in 1983), *Poor Caroline* (1931),
The Astonishing Island (1933), *Mandoa, Mandoa!* (1933), and
South Riding (1936), published posthumously after her tragic
death from kidney disease at the age of thirty-seven. She was
awarded the James Tait Black prize for this, her most
famous novel.

She also published two volumes of short stories, *Truth is Not
Sober* (1934) and *Pavements at Anderby* (1937); a satirical work,
The Astonishing Island (1933); two volumes of poetry, *My
Garden* (1911) and *The Frozen Earth* (1935); a critical work,
Virginia Woolf (1932); a study of the position of women, *Women
and a Changing Civilisation* (1934), and numerous essays.

Winifred Holtby's remarkable and courageous life is
movingly recorded in Vera Brittain's biography, *Testament of
Friendship*, published by Virago.

If you would like to know more about Virago books, write to us at Ely House, 37 Dover Street, London W1X 4HS for a full catalogue.

Please send a stamped addressed envelope

VIRAGO
Advisory Group

Andrea Adam	Zoë Fairbairns
Carol Adams	Carolyn Faulder
Sally Alexander	Germaine Greer
Anita Bennett	Jane Gregory
Liz Calder	Suzanne Lowry
Bea Campbell	Jean McCrindle
Angela Carter	Cathy Porter
Mary Chamberlain	Alison Rimmer
Anna Coote	Elaine Showalter (USA)
Jane Cousins	Spare Rib Collective
Jill Craigie	Mary Stott
Anna Davin	Rosalie Swedlin
Rosalind Delmar	Margaret Walters
Christine Downer (Australia)	Elizabeth Wilson
	Barbara Wynn

Winifred Holtby

MANDOA, MANDOA!

A Comedy of Irrelevance

With a New Introduction
by Marion Shaw

Virago

TO
VERA BRITTAIN
V.S.V.D.L.
IRRELEVANTLY

Published by VIRAGO PRESS Limited 1982
Ely House, 37 Dover Street, London W1X 4HS

First published in Great Britain by Wm Collins Ltd 1933

Copyright © Paul Berry, The Literary Executor
of Winifred Holtby 1935

Introduction Copyright © Marian Shaw 1982

Virago edition offset from Cedric Chivers 1971 edition

Printed in Finland by Werner Söderström Oy,
a member of Finnprint

British Library Cataloguing in Publication Data
Holtby, Winifred,
    Mandoa, Mandoa!—(Virago modern classics)
    I. Title
    823'.912 [F] PR6015.05
    ISBN 0-86068-251-X

CONTENTS

CONTENTS

Book Two
THE LOWER RACES ACQUIESCE

Book Three
MANDOA IS MADE

CONTENTS

RECESSIONAL

AUTHOR'S FOREWORD

Certain events mentioned in this book, such as the General Election of 1931, have, I am told, occurred in the world of fact. Certain persons, mentioned in its pages, such as Queen Marie of Roumania, have, I understand, really been born, though the actions which they are here regarded to have taken are completely fictitious. But the firm of Prince's Tours, Limited and its directors, the constituency of North Donnington and its associates, and the principality of Mandoa and its inhabitants, unhappily cannot be traced in any reputable work of reference. I therefore think it desirable to mention that the only map of Mandoa with which I am acquainted, is in my possession, and to express my gratitude to Miss K. Gilchrist, M.A. (Oxon), for her researches into the geographical, historical and ethnological peculiarities of the country. I should like also to acknowledge my irreparable debt to Herr Otto Martens and Dr. O. Karstedt for the material which I have purloined from their admirable *African Handbook and Travellers' Guide*, and to acquit them of all responsibility for any use I may have made of it. In the story, I presume, perhaps prematurely, that the regulations prohibiting night flying over the Sudan have been abolished by 1933.

INTRODUCTION

Winifred Holtby began writing *Mandoa, Mandoa!* towards the
end of 1931 during the aftermath of the October General
Election. It was a time of national disillusionment; a succession
of economic disasters and rising unemployment had forced the
collapse of the Labour Government, and its replacement by a
National Government at the October election marked the
beginning of an era of hopelessness when the Depression
seemed to settle inexorably on the country, and when timidity
and expediency were to dominate the political scene. And for
those who listened, "the angry noise of history" could already
be heard in ominous unrest and aggression abroad.

The end of 1931 also saw the onset of Winifred Holtby's
serious and ultimately fatal illness, kidney failure. Its symptoms
must have seemed an internalisation of the disintegration
around her. In one of the poems in her sequence, "For the
Ghost of Elinor Wylie", she described what it was like to have
abnormally high blood pressure:

> . . . in the abysmal hour,
> When angry pulses leap,
> And black blood lashes its frustrated power
> Against tall cliffs of sleep . . .
> The fear, the pain, were mine.

Mandoa, Mandoa! is perhaps a surprising response to these
events and circumstances but in the light of what is known of
Winifred's personality, not uncharacteristic. She worked on
the novel in the loneliness of a rented cottage at Monks
Risborough, near Oxford, where she had been sent to rest, and
it was written, Vera Brittain tells us, "mostly in bed when her
body was tormented by pain and her mind had to struggle,
often after wakeful nights, against impairment by heavy drugs".
But there is no doubt that at this time, and in varying degrees
throughout her life, writing was an escape from unhappiness,
from the ultimate distress of knowing that she who was still

young and had much to give to life, was likely to die soon. She later wrote: "Sticking to *Mandoa* and to other work with me is not courage. It may be a kind of superficiality. Pain, sadness and regret bore me so that I would rather think of anything else. I welcome work as something positive and real that we can get a grip on." But if *Mandoa, Mandoa!* was an escape from the circumstances of her life, an "irrelevance", as she subtitled it, it did not become escapist as a literary work but something much more substantial and hard-edged: a novel of political comedy.

Yet the novel's origins lay in an escapist dream of flight from a present world of suffering and tedium to a remote world of beauty and happiness. The name "Mandoa" surely derives from the title of a poem which had been much in her mind during her tour of South Africa in 1926, Sir Walter Raleigh's "Manoa":

> Over the silver mountains
> Where spring the nectar fountains,
> There will I kiss the bowl of bliss
> And drink mine everlasting fill
> Upon every milken hill.

She had used these lines to preface her earlier novel, *The Land of Green Ginger*, named after a street in Hull which represents to the eight-year-old heroine the "dark, mysterious road to Heaven, to Fairy Land, to anywhere, anywhere, even to South Africa which was the goal of all men's longing". This dream of Africa was Winifred's own: "I had always been interested in Africa, partly because the only one of my forebears who ever did anything at all distinguished became one of the first governors of Uganda – and he was only a distant connection; but my mother told me stories of him when I was a child on my father's farm."

But the romantic origins of Winifred's involvement with Africa were overlaid by her developing social and political concern for the country, particularly after her six-month visit to South Africa in 1926. By the time she came to write *Mandoa, Mandoa!* she had a large experience of African affairs and a deep knowledge and understanding of the country's racial composition. Although she was, she said, "a passionate imperialist by instinct", who found in enlightened colonialism a nostalgic parallel with the paternalistic farming community of her youth, she recognised that the most hopeful future for South Africa lay in the constitutional advancement of the black population. Her political sympathies for black people found their practical issue in her commitment to the growth and organisation of trade unionism among the urbanised black population of the Transvaal. As a reformer throughout the rest of her life, she lectured and wrote to raise funds for this cause; as a novelist, her imagination was stirred by the changes in African life such reforms would necessarily bring. What interested her was "the struggles of a bewildered black race confronted by the phenomenon of twentieth-century industrialism. . . . During all my contact with Africa, I had felt that one day I should want to write a novel about the contrast between the two ways of life – African and European."

But although *Mandoa, Mandoa!* draws much of its material from Winifred Holtby's African experiences, and satirically invokes South African history in its depiction of a black population as the potential victims of white commercialism, the novel is not precisely about South Africa:

> I did not want to lay the scene in South or East Africa, because, knowing a little about them, I felt I did not know enough. I preferred to take an imaginary place, so that errors of factual accuracy could not divert me and my readers from the human story. I wanted to take as my Africans a race of Portuguese–Abyssinians rather than Bantu, because, in the first place, I felt they would be more articulate, being more highly developed in social civilization and less drawn in upon themselves, and therefore better exponents of comedy. In the second place, the more I saw of Bantu, the more I realized that I could not yet hope to portray the working of their minds, the effects of tribal experience and the corporate symbolism which forms so important a part of their consciousness. In the third place, I wanted an independent, proud and unconquered race, without the psychological complications which emerge after white rulers have enforced their superiority upon their black subjects.

The occasion which gave her the plot for her African novel, and its element of fantasy, was the coronation in 1930 of the

Emperor of Abyssinia. Even the *Times* accounts of the ceremonies and celebrations make colourful reading: "The service
was of extreme liturgical interest and was conducted throughout the night until 7.50 this morning amid continuous chanting,
beating of drums, and the brandishing of brass rattles." A
banquet, attended by 30,000 people, comprised "large joints of
raw, freshly-slaughtered beef . . . Each man carved for himself with his own dagger . . . The meat was raised to the
mouth with the left hand, and the piece taken between the teeth
was then severed by an upward slash of the dagger." During
the feast military bands recited "with the utmost animation
and much gesticulation, verses, partly humorous, partly
inflammatory".

Winifred Holtby never visited Abyssinia. She heard an
account of the coronation, which seems to have captured
Western imaginations, from an acquaintance, and she read
extensively about the country where traditions of court intrigue, slavery, fierce independence and distorted Christianity
were, not without violent tribal dissent, under pressure from
Western influences introduced by Haile Selassie. It seemed to
her that the transitional state of Abyssinian culture, and the
bizarre events of the coronation, could most appropriately be
drawn on to expose the contrasts and conflicts between African
and European ways of life, and that they were such as led
inevitably to a comic, even satiric, exposure.

The comic possibilities were not missed by a novelist who
was present at the coronation and whose considerable African
experience had also given him a desire to write a story which
"deals with the conflict of civilisation, with all its attendant and
deplorable ills, and barbarism". Winifred wrote that she was
"conducting a literary steeplechase of the kind I thoroughly
disapprove of and despise – because Evelyn Waugh is bringing
out a novel with the same plot . . . so mine has to be rushed
through". In the event, his *Black Mischief* was published in
October 1932, three months before *Mandoa, Mandoa!*

Both *Mandoa, Mandoa!* and *Black Mischief* belong to a line of
imperial novels of which Kipling, Conrad and E. M. Forster
were the most distinguished exponents and which Paul Scott
and J. G. Farrell, amongst others, have continued into the

present. What interests these novelists is not imperial achievement and adventure as such but the problems of communication imperialism thrusts into prominence and the challenge to Western values it invites. Intrinsically interesting in these respects, imperialism also provides an image of the problems of communication between all people, even those who attempt to know and care for each other. Forster's humane advice, "only connect", is as appropriate to the inhabitants of North Donnington as it is to the visitors to Lolagoba, and as difficult to put into practice. In Waugh's case, the emphasis of his comedy is on the hopelessness of making such connections: "I just don't want to hear about it, d'you mind?" says one of his characters, and this is a logical response to a world in which events are arbitrary and people deluded or self-interested. Life is indeed mischievous, and the wit of Waugh's writing does nothing to conceal the pessimism of a novel based on this conception; it is as if Conrad's *Heart of Darkness* has been rewritten as a farce.

Mandoa, Mandoa! acknowledges the near hopelessness of the task of constructing right relations between people of different cultures, and by extension between all people. Its conclusion is reminiscent of the end of *A Passage to India* where Forster's vision of communion between East and West must be postponed: "'No, not yet' ... 'No, not there.'" In one of the most powerful passages of *Mandoa, Mandoa!* the four Europeans of the International Humanitarian Association, in danger and discomfort, in turn silently express the sense of isolation that undermines all human intercourse: "there's no liking, no friendship, no love ... There is no real companionship. We each live in a private, distorted world ... how alien we are. Not two people in the world share the same thought, the same mood." As societies, both England and Mandoa are shown as equally, though differently, corrupt; decadence and exploitation amongst Europeans are matched by the cruelty and treachery of the Africans, and the respective miseries of capitalist and pre-industrial societies are paralleled in the fog of North Donnington and the mud of Mandoa, and in the dole queues outside the labour exchange on Remembrance Day and the annual slave train from Mandoa to the Red Sea. But the novel is saved from the nihilism of

Waugh by its joyful engagement with the political intricacies of the central situation, and its view that, on the whole, people are probably likeable, and certainly that their behaviour is to be enjoyed without cynicism or malice. When the heroine, Jean Stansbury, says, "I like the sense of things happening all over the world – and feeling the contact with curious enterprises," she expresses the author's own enthusiasm for "things happening", her delighted awareness of the complexity which constitutes a historic moment. In fictional terms, the wedding of La'gola is such a moment more publicised than most and more motley in its constituents; it can therefore the more vividly be employed to demonstrate the diversity of human behaviour and motivation and the connections and causal relationships that can be discovered within that diversity. It is in these terms that *Mandoa, Mandoa!* can be classed as a political comedy.

Like other such works – *Gulliver's Travels* and *Animal Farm* come to mind – *Mandoa, Mandoa!* is less interested in psychological and social realism than in the creation of characters who typify human attributes and of situations which show those attributes in action. With schematic thoroughness it assembles a large cast of cultural and class types and draws them into a complex situation by means of a narrative which is simple – a wedding to which many guests come – but a brilliant focus for the interaction of the economic, racial and personal forces involved. Much of the humour and satirical thrust of the novel depends on the incongruities which arise from such interaction, for example, those caused by the impact of technology on a primitive people. Winifred Holtby's comic penetration is well illustrated in the instance of Talal's infatuation with motor cars, cocktail shakers, telephones and steamboats, which is not only amusing, and even absurd, given the absence of technology in his country, but sharply questions the benefits civilisation bestows. Do such commodities represent the summary of Western achievement, and is Talal's susceptibility to them an avenue to his and his country's exploitation? To Winifred Holtby's contemporary readers, themselves precariously embarking on an era of the mass production of consumer goods as well as of colonial contraction, such questions must have seemed doubly relevant.

But *Mandoa, Mandoa!* is more of a hybrid work than, say, *Animal Farm*; it has ambitions other than single-minded political satire, and, as contemporary critics noted, occasionally shifts gear from caricature and near-fantasy into realism. This is particularly true of the two main English characters, Jean Stanbury and Bill Durrant. Jean Stanbury is brought into the novel not for her usefulness to the plot but as a foil to the extravagant characters around her. Admirable, hard-working Jean, who is so much a projection of Winifred Holtby herself, provides a standard of common sense, practical dedication, and liberal tolerance, what is good, in fact, in Western society, against which the excesses and idiosyncracies of other characters, both European and African, can be measured. She is a figure of enlightened English ordinariness: "We have to work for the world as we know it as best we can ... we have to go on," she says at the end of the novel, and this is the belief *Mandoa, Mandoa!* adheres to and which underlies its political satire and also its racial and cultural assumptions. The "world as we know it" is one in which the values of Jean Stanbury are considered if not superior then certainly the standpoint from which those of other cultures are viewed. Inevitably, therefore, the African characters are portrayed as comic or barbaric and Mandoa itself as a fantasy country in which types, even stereotypes, can flourish without too much regard for cultural accuracy or neutrality. As Winifred Holtby said, her concern was not with "tribal experience" but with "the human story" of her imaginary place. *Mandoa, Mandoa!* is only superficially an African story; its main purpose is with the variousness of political and social behaviour defined in Western terms. Although it would be too crude to say that *Mandoa, Mandoa!* is peopled with English eccentrics, some of whom have blackened faces, there is a sense in which, like Swift's Lilliput, it is less the people and conditions of Mandoa that are of interest than what they tell us about English society.

Bill Durrant, Jean's male counterpart, and a negative version of the values she upholds, is likewise "realistically" depicted as a type of Englishman only too likely to have found reluctant employment in an African country during this era of th⌐

tail-end of imperialism and its replacement by commercial development. It is interesting that Evelyn Waugh's "hero" in *Black Mischief* is a similarly disillusioned, penurious Englishman who is superfluous to the advanced industrial society which has so expensively reared him for a role it can no longer afford. Bill Durrant's usefulness in England has expired with the war which he feels should logically have destroyed him; his only escape from the nightmare of his own and England's history is as the rueful and doubting bringer to a "primitive" people of the "three great gifts of civilization – Profit, Power, Pity".

Winifred Holtby invariably drew on her wide circle of friends and acquaintances to populate her novels; *Mandoa, Mandoa!* is a gallery of such fictionalised portraits. Bill Durrant, for instance, is based on Harry Pearson, the charming, inadequate friend she had loved since childhood. As characters, Bill and Jean are successful examples of such autobiographical quarrying; thematically and structurally they are constructive to the novel. But the relationship between them is another matter and although so closely based on the author's own experiences and feelings, its presence in the novel is uneasy and incompletely realised. Winifred Holtby backs away from a committed portrayal of the emotions these two characters have for each other, and at any such attempt the language she employs is stale and evasive:

> She laid her hand on his arm.
> That startled him. He clutched her hand, crying, "My dear – !"
> She felt the strong shock of emotion flow through her. For a moment anything might have happened.
> "Good heavens, he loves me. He feels ... '
> They waited.
> Every instinct, every memory, hung between them. Their past and their future stood balancing on a breath.
> Then long-trained habit intervened. Jean drew away.

But of course, the story of Jean and Bill is not about lovers; rather, it is Winifred Holtby's stoical and supportive valediction, in what must have seemed likely to be her last book, to a man whom she had come to realise could offer her neither passion nor comfort: "She was laying aside physical and emotional adventures; she was laying aside her husband and her children." In the novel Jean marries solid Maurice: disappointing, perhaps, but a movement back from an introspective digression into a fictional realisation of the novel's major theme: "we have to go on". It is fitting that Jean Stanbury, "strong and maternal", should be a vehicle, in all respects, for this commitment to life.

The story of Bill and Jean *is* a digression, and its unsatisfactoriness is not detrimental to the success of the novel. It is, in any case, crowded out by the ideas the novel is concerned with and by the comic and political ramifications of the situation it is centred on. This is also true, to some extent, of the friendship between Bill and Talal. Talal is Winifred Holtby's colourful and sympathetic fictionalisation of another man she knew well, Clements Kadalie, "a magnificent native of Nyasaland, educated at a Scottish Presbyterian Mission . . . [with a] boundless confidence in his own importance", who was the general secretary of the Industrial and Commercial Workers' Union, the union for South African black workers which Winifred Holtby helped to support during the last eight years of her life. The figure of Talal is no simple caricature; his depiction is much fuller than that of the characters of comic or satiric singularity like Sid Granger, Mr Gish and Felicity Cardover. But he is extraordinary, and it is an impressive achievement that he is credible whilst being so much larger than what we normally think of as life, so much of a convincing contrast to what Jean and Bill represent. His characterisation is an imaginative acknowledgement of the vitality and variety the human personality is capable of. The relationship between him and Bill is an attempt, rather in the manner of the friendship between Fielding and Aziz in Forster's *A Passage to India*, to provide an emotional, personalised focus to the themes of the novel. But perhaps because as characters Talal and Bill are in different registers, the affection between the two men, and their incompatabilities, are left disappointingly undeveloped. Perhaps given the ambitious scope of the novel, there was simply not enough time or space to develop the realism of personal relationships, and it seems that it was almost with a sense of impatience that Winifred Holtby broached such an activity at all. For, as she made clear, her purpose in *Mandoa, Mandoa!* was largely an intellectual one: "I want to do something hard, muscular, compact, very little emotional, and with the emotion hammered into the style. Metalwork, not water-colour."

In this respect *Mandoa, Mandoa!* is different from Winifred Holtby's other novels. Whilst not "water-colour", they follow conventional patterns of the nineteenth-century realist novel in their concern with the details of parochial, domestic and personal issues. This is the mode she returned to in her final novel, *South Riding*, which is in the tradition of George Eliot's *Middlemarch*. But *Mandoa, Mandoa!* is an expression of the political acumen and acerbity of mind which made her so good a journalist. Indeed, *Mandoa, Mandoa!* is the novel of a reforming journalist, the fictional *jeu d'esprit* of some-one who could not, she said, "get out of my head my responsibility for contemporary affairs . . . I am a publicist and a darn good one when I exert myself." *Mandoa, Mandoa!* is much more than the publicisation of a progressive view of imperial conflict, written "to make old girls sit up", as one of her friends put it, but more than her other novels it does represent a compromise between the self-acknowledged divisions in her energies: "I shall never quite make up my mind whether to be a reformer-sort-of-person or a writer-sort-of-person."

It is also an unusual novel for a woman to have written. Several of its reviewers remarked on this: she showed "an almost masculine appreciation of practical issues", L.P. Hartley wrote, and, with some surprise, Graham Greene likened the strength of her writing in *Mandoa, Mandoa!* to that of Waugh and Conrad. Indeed, the novel can be seen as the antiphonal voice to that of a work which was being written alongside it, Vera Brittain's highly personal and "feminine" *Testament of Youth*. There is a certain irony in that the only book Winifred dedicated to Vera, the Very Small Very Dear Love of the inscription, should be so different from anything Vera wrote herself. "Hard, muscular, compact" are the last adjectives one could apply to *Testament of Youth* but they are, for the most part, true of *Mandoa, Mandoa!*, as is Winifred's later description of it as "vital and gay". The endeavour and achievement of *Mandoa, Mandoa!* was for Winifred Holtby a form of control over her illness, her fear of death, and her grief at the failure of love; it is as much a Testament as Vera Brittain's book. But with an interesting defiance of traditional modes of female writing about such subjects, Winifred Holtby chose an escape into what is generally regarded as a masculine form, the novel of political comedy. As she remembers the suffering and tedium of the occasion of Rollet's death, Jean Stanbury voices the rationale of the novel: "be brave ... be stoical, be helpful". To this might also be added an earlier comment: "She could not give herself away."

Marion Shaw, Hull 1982

PROCESSIONAL

CHAPTER I

MORNING had come. From the jagged pillars of the Eastern hills the sky hung like smooth dun-coloured silk above the squatting huts. One by one, through black, gaping doorways crept the people, stooping beneath the lintels, stretching their cramped limbs, sniffing the grey air that was flat rather than cool, then making soundlessly for the vast square before the palace. Behind the men came the women, behind the women, the donkeys. The deep dust of the roads was pocked by a thousand footmarks. The smallest children, strung behind their mother's backs, crowed or whimpered; bangles tinkled; the accoutrements of young warriors rattled as they strode; now an old man grunted as he upheaved his crippled body from a pile of skins and dragged himself out from the warm stench of the hut; now a girl, wide-eyed and shuddering, uttered one coughing sob, and then was silent. But for the most part the crowd assembled quietly. The hour was holy and terrible. Implacable spirits of fortune and misfortune were abroad.

The square was already crowded. Before the high stockade the priests had gathered. The six hundred and seventy-nine archbishops of Mandoa stood like statues, their dark hands folded upon the staves of their tall crosses, their white robes as still as marble, till, growing weary of an unfamiliar discipline, one sneezed, another spat, a third scratched hopefully in his hair. Yet their massed figures remained solemn and portentous.

Long before daylight the travellers had been stirring. They stood now, a great uneven caravan, awaiting dismissal. In front, out of sight of the watchers by the stockade, were their bodyguard, Arabs, Somalis, gigantic Turkanas and Abyssinians, armed with rifles; four stout donkeys bearing a dismembered and unusable machine gun patiently submitted their flanks as propping-posts for their Abyssianian drivers, their long, sensitive ears and

13

brown velvet nostrils twitching as the insects woke with
the rising sun. Behind them a string of prisoners, bound
wrist to ankle by thongs of hide, drooped limply after a
sleepless night of terror. Their impotent misery evoked no
pity from the onlookers, who for the most part had eyes
to spare only for the voluntary adventurers. These were
young men from the drought-stricken villages, insubor-
dinate sons from the rich eastern valleys, town-dwellers
tired of the tyranny of the priests, rebels against the old
order, warriors dissatisfied with the routine of the army, all
the youth and restlessness and initiative which Lolagoba
was too small to hold. These did not crouch like the
prisoners, smeared with ashes of humiliation. Proudly
they stood, their limbs polished and oiled, their hair
stiffened with clay, frizzled with combs, or bound with
copper, their weapons in their hands, their hearts beating
fast behind their hairless chests. Behind them lay the
familiar life of unvarying tradition, the life of their fathers
and of their father's fathers, the cooking pots beside their
mother's huts, the winding, trodden paths between the
thorn-bushes, the secret discipline of their church and gods ;
around them arose the admiration of the crowd and the
exhilarating strangeness of the royal city ; before them
stretched the unknown future, terrifying and splendid.
Being young, being ignorant, being trained in a school that
honours courage, they were ardent for action ; they desired
glory ; and since they were going far, they dreamed that
they must be going gloriously.

The girls who followed them had no such fancies. Though
here and there a bold wench simpered before the watching
crowd, twisting her body so that her short kilt slapped her
swinging thighs, ogling the men and boys with brazen
indifference to all time beyond the present, for the most
part they huddled together like scared antelope, their
great eyes liquid with apprehension. The familiar world
being so hard for women, they had little to hope from the
unknown.

The procession straggled back towards the city. Dishonoured priests and landless nobles, gamblers who had
staked and lost even their bodies, artisans who had out-
worn their skill, brought up the rear. They, too, had little

to hope ; they knew that neither in Mandoa nor Ethiopia nor Arabia would life be good to the dishonoured and defeated. Yet waiting there in the dawn, expecting the sacred blessing, they too were touched by a faint exhilaration.

The only travellers unmoved by expectation were the captured slaves. Torn from villages beyond Mandoa, driven and bullied across the inimical hills, starved, beaten, dazed and terrified, they stood like herded beasts. The tall Mandoans in their bright cotton tunics appeared to them as devils. Their unknown destination could be no worse than this.

Awed though it was, the crowd surged this way and that. " Oh, let me look ! " " Stand back ! Stand back ! " " Can't you see you're crushing the lady—and she great with child ? " " Aha ! Father of Twins ! I suppose that you'll be off next ? " " Oh ! the gods be good to him. Good fortune go with him. Oh, my dear, my dear, farewell." An old woman, whose youngest and late-born son stood among the stragglers, a tall soldier, who had failed in his third year tests for the Royal Bodyguard, waited till the Arch-archbishop emerged from the Cathedral door and all hope of respite passed ; then, without a sound, she slid her tongue back into her throat and died, as the crowd pushed on over her to see the final ceremony.

For the time had come.

A dull suffused radiance spread from the east above the city. Into the open space before the stockade stepped six young men, in the red robes of acolytes, bearing the polished copper shield.

The crowd ceased its scratching, fidgeting and pushing. The hearts of the waiting travellers paused on the beat.

The Arch-archbishop strode three paces forward. As the first arc of the sun leapt the black terraces, he raised his golden cross and smote the shield. As though his staff were a torch, the circle broke into glowing light. The sky took fire. The strong arms of the sun tore away the grey morning. From huts, bodies, weapons and stockade, warm shadows flowed like blood along the powdery sand.

The sun was up.

Then the priests raised their brown arms in prayer, and from the waiting city a great cry responded.

" The Lord be with your going," the priests shouted.

" And with your home-coming," answered the people.

" Walk accompanied by angels," cried the priests.

" And so find peace."

" May the lions of courage guide you."

" The snakes of danger flee from you."

" The saints of heaven accompany you."

" The glory of holiness surround you."

" From Mandoa, Mandoa ! "

" To Arabia, Arabia ! "

" From poverty to plenty."

" From labour, from suffering."

" To the home-coming, to the journey's ending, to the life everlasting."

" Amen ! "

And with that final cry, the donkey drivers cracked their whips ; the young warriors raised their spears ; the girls lifted their bundles to their heads ; the old men slung their blankets about their withered limbs ; the prisoners slid their thongs up to the knee that they might walk more easily ; the bodyguard in front uttered a harsh command ; and with a rattle, with a groan, with a cry, with a shuffle, the annual slave-train from Mandoa to the Red Sea went forward.

CHAPTER II

THE DISSATISFACTION OF A LORD HIGH CHAMBERLAIN

SAFI TALAL, Lord High Chamberlain of the Independent Christian Principality of Mandoa, stood in the great square of Lolagoba, disliking the Cathedral.

It was incredible to him that he had once admired it.

He observed its walls, plastered with muddy clay, and saw that they were clumsy and ill-proportioned. Its bulbous dome rose tipsily above its spreading bulk. The copper studs and fruit and flowers upon its wooden doors

were roughly made. As for the saints ! With hatred, Talal
stared at the slanting eyes and polished cheeks of the wooden
images that made a human garland above the western door,
Saint Paul, Saint Thomas, Saint William Wilberforce (in
a collar), Saint John Bright (with a round paunch), Saint
Byron (with flowing hair). Great and good men, whom Mr.
Guerdon had taught Mandoa to revere.

Remembering how the American women had laughed at
his recital, Talal's brown hand slid to the knife at his belt.
He had felt himself insulted through his country.

Yet, until he had crossed the mountains to Addis Ababa
to attend the coronation of the King of Kings, he, like his
fellow-noblemen, had thought the Cathedral miraculous
in its height and strength and beauty, though he did not
share the common belief in its divine origin. Other Mandoans declared that God had made it, God who made all
things : hills and sand and water, the silvery tropical grass,
the verdure breaking like soft green flame from the sun-
blasted trees, the lice, the lions.

Mr. Guerdon had thought otherwise. It was true, he
had told his brightest pupil, that God made everything.
But sometimes He employed human agency. Poking his
head—for he was short-sighted and lost his spectacles in
the swamps—he conjectured cautiously that the building
dated from the sixteenth century when Lolagoba had been
founded. The dome was a possible relic of some forgotten
Moslem visitation.

Talal believed that. He liked to reflect upon the ingenuity
of his ancestors. Not that he believed everything told him
by the Reverend Robert Guerdon, M.A. The little white
man had been the oddest mixture of innocence and knowledge. A missionary teacher, setting out from Khartoum
to found a school for chiefs' sons in Uganda, he had been
swept from his course by the flooding of the Nile, lost in
the Sudd swamp, and carried to Lolagoba by a raiding
party, the first white man seen in the city for four hundred
years.

All human treasure-trove in Mandoa belonged to somebody. Mr. Guerdon was handed over to the Arch-arch
bishop and persuaded to establish in the Mandoan capital
the school intended once for Pagan Negroes. It took him

two years to realise that he was preaching to the Converted.
He never realised until his death that he was legally a slave.
As for the Mandoans, they could not understand the sup-
posed connection between their own Catholicism and
Mr. Guerdon's Evangelical Christianity.

For the Mandoans called themselves Catholic.   They
simply had forgotten that Catholicism claims to be Christian.
Mandoa itself had been founded as a Catholic colony of
Abyssinia.   In the sixteenth century, after a brief missionary campaign, three Jesuit priests and two Portuguese
traders had been driven out and fled, with a little company
of Ethiopian converts, their cattle, their women, their
donkeys and their slaves, through the south-western hill
country, down the steep face of the sun-baked Escarpment ;
and thus, upheld by God the Father, God the Son, and the
Blessed Virgin, had arrived, with only a trifling loss of
slaves and women, on the flat table-land that was Mandoa.
Barren it might be ; it was safe.   Between the Sudd-
swamps and the hills they dwelt secure, building, under
the shadow of the jagged cliffs, their church and capital,
and founding a brown-skinned, straight-haired, swarthy,
handsome race, the Ethopian-Portuguese Mandoans.

They were proud people.   In their veins flowed the blood
of the Lord's highest servants, the Portuguese, whose
empire ran along the world, and the Ethiopians, who were
sons of Sheba.   They were a ruling people.   Mandoans
never, never, never would be slaves.   Nor were they.   They
enslaved the lean, fierce Dinkas of the marshes, the handsome Gallas, the Kikuyu from beyond the lake, the Somalis
and Sudanese.   They raided the southern highlands of
Abyssinia, capturing whole tribes, which they sold back
again at a high profit.   They crept by night round the shores
of Lake Rudolf ; they leapt from shadows upon sleeping
villages ; the flames from huts afire marked their triumph.
Showers of spears pattered against their shields from
ambushed warriors.   Curses of vengeance mounted against
them to the sky.   But they were doubly armed, by white
men's cunning learned from their Portuguese ancestors,
and by their Catholic faith, against which heathen curses
died.   No Mandoan had ever been enslaved.

They grew and prospered.   They dug gardens round the

sparse water-holes ; they pastured their goats and cattle.
They built their city, made their laws, and traded. Their
main exports were labour-power and ivory. Each year
they sent across the eastern mountains their train of slaves
and freed-men who sought slavery.

It was a simple solution of a universal problem, and,
until he had gone to Addis Ababa, Talal imagined that thus
every nation disposed of its own surplus population.

Until he had gone to Addis Ababa.

Twitching his white tunic over one lean brown shoulder,
Safi Talal called for his slaves and donkey. The slaves
uncurled themselves from the sand where they had waited
and brought the beast. Their master mounted and rode
broodily across the market square.

To his left stretched the long stockade of the Royal
Palace ; to his right rose Hollywood Hall.

Critically he surveyed them.

It was true that they were not so fine as the best buildings
in Addis Ababa. But there was no reason why they should
not become so. If Mandoa were visited by kings and princes,
by representatives of all the nations of the earth, it too
could blossom into wealth and splendour. It too had an
interesting history. The American and English gentlemen
had hung upon his words when Talal explained the constitution of his Principality.

Why only a Princess ? They had asked. Because, Talal
had explained, Princes and Princesses were obviously
cheaper to keep than Kings and Queens, and theirs was a
poor country. Were they *always* Princesses ? Always.
Women were easier to manage, being, Talal explained,
only sub-human (and he quoted lines from Alfred, Lord
Tennyson, to prove it). They must be respected ; but they
need not be obeyed. In fact, they never need give orders.
A Royal Princess was kept in the Palace Precincts and used
for state occasions. She opened and closed High Council ;
she provided an excuse for fine processions ; and she gave
birth to more Princesses. " But what if she doesn't ? "
demanded the American. She always did. " But if it's a
Prince ? " It never was. " But who is the father ? " Talal
had piously crossed his hands and answered, " God, God
the Universal Father Almighty." " Yes—— But—— ? "

Then, seeing that they were all men of good birth together, Talal explained. All Royal Princesses were virgin mothers, in compliment to the Queen of Heaven. But nine months or so before a new Princess was born, an archibishop entered the Palace and prayed for God's blessing on his Sovereign. If, in due time, a girl arrived, the archbishop then became an Arch-archbishop, head of the Church in Mandoa. In any other circumstances he disappeared. It was quite simple.

" Does the—er—child also disappear—if it's a son ? "

" There never *is* a son," Talal had said.

" But tell me, are there many archbishops ? "

" Six hundred and seventy-nine at present." There had been jealousy at first, when some ecclesiastics were humble priests and others raised to this splendour of Catholic dignity ; but after deciding to make all priests archbishops, the difficulty had disappeared at once. As for the Arch-archbishop, a candidate's survival chances being about 25 per cent., the competition was less inconvenient.

Safi Talal had gone to Abyssinia a proud man. All true-born Mandoans were hereditary aristocrats. They looked down from the height of their power and nobility upon their hybrid Negro inferiors, savages and slaves and heathen. They were proud of their race and their religion. Talal also had been educated by the Reverend Robert Guerdon. With twenty other sons of nobles, he had learned English. He had read Tennyson, Cobbett, Samuel Smiles, and *The Pauper's Testimony* ; and had remained well-pleased with his own country.

But in Addis Ababa he had seen another way of life. He had talked to American tourists, British officials, Dutch and Germans. And he had learned of a civilisation enriched by baths and cocktail shakers, by motor cars that ran more fleetly than the priests' camels or the best Arabian ponies. He had used cutlery from Sheffield ; he had conversed by telephone ; he had bought handkerchiefs and blown his nose upon them ; he had listened to music from boxes, which could be varied indefinitely by changing flat black plates. And, still more important, he had read English and American magazines. He had gazed, enthralled, upon illustrated advertisements. He had seen, as in an Apocalyptic vision, a new Heaven and a new Earth.

Then, the coronation of the Emperor achieved, he returned to Lolagoba and its unchanging life, to the perennial wrangling of noblemen in the High Council, to the monotonous law suits about nothing at all, argued interminably with the insincere rhetoric of tradition. He had returned to a diet of rancid goats' flesh and cakes of sodden grain ; to the whining music of slave girls ; to the lamentations of his third wife who had just became the mother of twins ; to the long routine of the year's ritual, with its appointed feasts and ceremonies.

And he was bored. He was bored beyond endurance. He was homesick for a civilisation that he had never known.

He looked about the squalid huts, and hated them. He thought of the life in the Royal Palace, and was repelled by it. He remembered the chaos and discomfort of his home—the finest in all Mandoa—and despaired.

There was no place on which his thoughts could rest in comfort. In the precincts behind the Cathedral his friend Ma'sull, the Arch-archbishop, once the most daring mountaineer in all Mandoa, fretted against his ritual confinement. In the Royal Palace, the little fool of a Princess, Um'bola, wept at the arrogance of her heiress daughter. Why could she not marry Ma'sull whom she adored ? Why could not La'gola, her daughter, take her place ? Talal was revolted by her feminine supplications. If she had been an ordinary woman, he could have ended them soon enough. Tiresome women were easily disposed of in Mandoa. But she was the Royal Princess, and he, as Lord High Chamberlain, was compelled to listen to her sorrows.

Sometimes he thought of throwing over the whole business and becoming an archbishop, or even of leaving Mandoa. But the Church had nothing new to offer him ; and beyond Mandoa, he was nobody.

It was not the season when a nobleman could leave the court ; and even if he defied custom, what novelty was there for him in the country ?

He was tired of hunting hippopotami, and drinking sispri. He was weary of plotting with his warriors against Ma'buta. He was tired of huts and dust and donkeys and slave girls.

He had drained Mandoan life of its emotions. He had
raided five villages in Kenya ; he had entered the single
monastery of Mandoa, and whipped himself all night,
through six desperate vigils, almost dying of exhaustion
on the seventh day ; he had known over fifty virgins ;
when he had inadvertently broken sacred etiquette and
treated a freedman as though he were a slave, he had submitted to an Honour Flogging, sucking a fierce enjoyment
from the pain. When his own eldest daughter committed
indiscretions with a Somali slave, he had buried her alive,
according to the custom. As a young man he had been
rapturously devout. He had flooded himself with the
ecstasies of the dance, the hymn, the penitence, the prayer.
In his maturity he had lived as fully as any man in Africa.

But rapture was not enough. Pain and pleasure faded.
The sweet lust of life lost flavour. Long before strength
waned, went the will to use it. There was no longer profit
in killing a man or mastering a beast, or holding a
woman in one's arms. Sensation endured for a night, but
disillusionment came with the morning.

A motor car, an aeroplane, a dictophone, an electric
refrigerator or a speedboat—these were real. These did not
vanish with the dawn.

Oh, level pavements under dim, grey noons, and hurrying
traffic down the city streets, and high-piled buildings,
rising floor on floor, cranes swinging silently against the
sky, steamships, electric lifts, smooth ordered days, quiet
and intellectual talk in clubs, commissions to Geneva, files
of documents, little dinners in restaurants, padded chairs ;
these were the goal of any true man's longing.

Had he not read it in the magazines ? In *Harper's* and
The Tatler, in *Good Housekeeping* and *The Saturday Evening
Post*?" A civilised life demanded exquisite little houses, clean
and orderly, with electric light and central heating, hot and
cold water laid on in every room, and all modern conveniences. It demanded puddings made from custard
powder, exotic soups and vegetables out of tins, gas
ovens that cooked the meals unaided. It demanded the
eternal youth of women, who by face creams and corsets,
hair tonics and massage, could remain for ever beautiful.
There were motor cars and aeroplanes ; trains and cruising-

steamers like hotels ; health could be bought in tins and tubes and bottles, beauty hired on the instalment system ; intelligence was the gift of institutions ; personal magnetism could be learned by correspondence courses.

Ah, why had Mandoa prided itself upon its isolation ? We have been fools, fools, fools, thought Talal. In the whole country there was one man alone who shared his dreams ; and he was offal, an ex-slave, a Galla freedman, whom Talal had taken with him to the coronation.

The man was clever with his hands, and oddly quick at learning. When Talal conceived the magnificent idea of buying a car and taking it across the mountains home with him, it was the Galla whom he had trained as his chauffeur. Then he discovered the disastrous fact that cars are delicate creatures and require roads. Trying to take his down the goat path over the hills it got out of control, fortunately when empty, and tipped quietly over a ravine.

But the training and talents of the Galla were not wasted. Talal returned to find his city agog with new excitement.

An American cinema company, making a talking film called, " The Siren of the Swamps," in the South-East Sudan, had been caught by the floods. A small group, including Jane Crossgill the star, the cameramen, and a mechanic, with all the apparatus for trying out dialogue and pictures, had been, like the Reverend Robert Guerdon, taken prisoner and brought to Lolagoba. Talal had been delighted ; with joy he seized upon them, bought them from their captors, built a small bungalow for them, as nearly as possible like those he had seen in Abyssinia, besought them to leave as ransom their apparatus in Lolagoba, to train the Galla as an operator, and grant to the Mandoans and their subjects the inestimable benefit of the Talkies.

And so it happened.

They had four specimen reels, " Hollywood Parade," " Diamond-set Divorce," " College Girls Must Love," and " Red Hot Momma." The Galla transformed himself almost over-night, as it were, into Byron Wilberforce Gish, and, in the enthusiasm of the first show, was honoured by the official title of Lord High Culture Promoter. The largest

free hut in the city—part of a derelict monastery—became
Hollywood Hall, and before the Americans left with the
next slave train for Jibuti and the Red Sea, every small
slave-boy in the streets was replying to his orders with
" O.K., chief," " Yes-*sir*," and " I don' say mebbe."

To-day, Hollywood Hall was the chief rendezvous of
Lolagoba.   There, nobles and slaves alike tasted the same
delights.   One, two, three, four, night after night in rota-
tion, Byron Wilberforce Gish displayed his films ; the voice
of civilisation brayed its rasping phrases.   College cuties,
blonde sweeties, weeping stars in close-ups with immense
tears on their synthetic lashes, enraptured half Mandoa.
Thither, when weary of barbarism, the Lord High Chamberlain retired.

This evening, he was weary of barbarism.   He waited to
see the sunset flare beyond the squatting huts.   He knelt
as a religious procession passed along the street, the nodding
statues of saints and virgins followed by acolytes who beat
drums and sang an old Mandoan hymn to a tune from the
great all-singing, all-talking film, " College Girls Must
Love,"

" Oh, Dinah !
You're the belle of Carolina !
There's not a girl that's finer !
Sure thing."

He noticed a refractory slave being driven to execution,
and observed that the hawkers, whom he ordered his
servants to drive away, were leprous.

He could not bear it.   What was more, he would not bear
it.   He was a man of destiny.   Was it for nothing he had
gone to Addis Ababa ?   No, a thousand times, no !   He
would find some way to end this isolation.   He would bring
visitors to Mandoa as the Abyssinians had brought them
to their country.   He would have streets and baths and
gramophones and cocktails.   By the Holy Saints, by the
Gods of old Mandoa, by the Sisters Gish and Mary Pickford,
so he would !

Some day—some how.

He tossed the bridle of his donkey to a groom-slave, and
announced that he was going to the pictures.

BOOK I
AN IMPERIAL PEOPLE PROPOSES

CHAPTER I

MAURICE DURRANT WINS A VICTORY

JUST before midnight on October 27th, 1931, Maurice Durrant, followed by his mother, his agent, the chairman of the local Conservative association, his defeated opponent, and a small group of supporters from both political parties, emerged from a French window on to the balcony of the Town Hall, North Donnington, overlooking the Market Square.

This was his hour and his triumph. He had experienced success at other times, at school, at Oxford and in Prince's Tours, Limited ; but nothing that he had ever known before had been like this. At last he had overcome his fear of crowds and his nervousness on public platforms ; he had wrestled with recalcitrant committees and over-ruled officious officials ; he had used asperity as well as tact in dealing with the Ladies' Canvassing Club, completely against the advice of his advisers, and he had, after his first experience as a parliamentary candidate, carried a notably unsafe seat by a majority of eleven thousand eight hundred and fifty-seven votes.

He glanced at his mother's rapt, beaming face. Her grey hair was just a thought dishevelled ; her nose a trifle less immaculately powdered than usual ; her hat lacked its habitual perfection of adjustment. But she was happy, radiant. No doubts, he thought, qualified her satisfaction now. Maurice imagined her repeating in her mind, " Maurice Durrant, M.P. Sir Maurice Durrant, Bart. The Rt. Hon. Sir Maurice Durrant. Lord Durrant of Donnington." Why not ? Why not ? Was he not the youngest director of Prince's Tours, Limited ? Was he not the most efficient candidate that North Donnington Conservative Association had ever known ? Did not good luck arise mainly from good management ? Was there anything that he had really tried to do that he had failed yet to

27

achieve—except——? But the exception would now be remedied. This was his night, his triumph.

The balcony was flooded with light so that when Maurice and his friends appeared, they were like actors on a stage, brilliantly conspicuous. But they in their turn could see nothing of the crowd below, for under them rolled a billowing sea of yellow fog. The roar that greeted them was as incohate and anonymous as the roar of the tide.

"Democracy," whispered Maurice to his mother. "A voice from the fog."

Somebody pressed his arm. "Go on. Now, Mr. Durrant. Speak to them."

Maurice went forward, and with his hands on the deathly chill of the balustrade, leant down towards the rolling clouds of fog. Fog floated round his face. Fog caught his throat. When he spoke, his voice was muffled in fog. "Friends. Electors of North Donnington—my constituents," he began. But the huge uproar below him drowned his carefully composed speech. The shouting hardened into intelligible words, the raucous melancholy of "The Red Flag," and the clatter of wooden rattles.

"Richards! Richards! We want Richards!" shouted the electors.

Maurice waited. He stood calmly and easily, his hands in his pockets, a faintly derisive smile on his handsome face, confronting the impotent hostility of the unseen mob, his triumph all the sweeter because those whom he had beaten could not even take defeat like gentlemen.

"Stick it, Mr. Durrant, stick it," prompted his agent.

"Cads! Cads!" snorted Mrs. Whittaker, chairman of the Ladies' Unionist Club.

"Friends—if you will listen!" Colonel Westwood bellowed.

Maurice shook his head.

The Socialist candidate stood beside him. A shout of approval greeted his burly figure, but he lifted his hand and bawled, "Now, come on, comrades. Fair play. Here's your new member. Stick to him. You voted for him, not I, mind you. I don't mind telling you I did all I could to put a better chap in his place. But since you've got him, you'd better listen to what he has to say for himself. Next time you can put me in, an' then you can hear me talk."

There followed a yell of delighted laughter.

It was not the introduction that Maurice had intended while, during the tedium of the count, he had prepared his victory message. But the noise subsided. He began to speak, driving his tired voice as far out into the fog as he could send it. " I know perfectly well," he said, " that it is not I for whom you have cast your votes to-day."

" Quite right ! Hear, hear ! " laughed his auditors, with good humour.

" The electors of North Donnington were faced by a choice between a united nation and a party ; between the spirit of imperial unity and a class-war ; between the freedom of a great democracy and the dictation of a trade-union Caucus. They have chosen, as all over this country of ours to-night other constituencies are choosing—they have chosen to vote for freedom, unity and Empire. They have dared to answer the sneers of the anti-patriotic in-tellectuals, the cynical defeatists, the humanitarians who bribe their way to office, the dreamers who promise what no statesman could perform. They have dared to be realists, to be patriots, to be British. We are, I believe, on the eve of a great national revival. Torn by faction, intimidated by doubt, our nation, since the war, has hesitated, unable to assert her former faith or to stride forward to her great imperial destiny. It is over : the doubt and the division ; over, the flirtation with Bolshevism. Over, the feeble inter-nationalism ; the anarchy of pauperism is at an end. You have been told that the imperial idea is dead. It isn't. We believe that the British race has something still to give to the world. We believe in the responsibility of our great possessions. We believe that this civilisation which we have inherited, this little island that is the heart of a vast commonwealth of nations, reaching from Adelaide to Nova Scotia, from Toronto to Singapore, has a destiny before it which has not yet been fulfilled. We have fought hard. We have fought straight. We have fought clean."

Maurice had other things to say about their manner of fighting and the significance of the victory achieved. But at that moment, a sharp gust of wind, blowing down the

High Street, tore the curtain of fog below the balcony. Through the gap he could see for the first time the crowd in the square ; and in the crowd, one face, his brother's. Bill was there, standing against a lamp-post, hatless, his longish brown hair blowing across his forehead, the Socialist colours of red and yellow pinned to his coat, his arm round these shoulders of a young woman who waved in her free hand a small wooden rattle. He looked ill, shabby, dissipated, yet Maurice knew that the irony of family likeness had given to both brothers the same tall, wiry figure, the same finely-drawn features, the same light, curving smile. He could watch, as though in a mirror, his own expression on his brother's face down in the crowd. As he had smiled at the unsportsmanlike antics of the mob, so Bill smiled now at the victor's complacent rhetoric.

Maurice heard his voice falter. He recalled Bill's last ribald comment upon National Unity and upon fighting straight, and, whether the crowd was already tired of his words, or whether, by faltering, he lost his hold on its attention, he was, in either case, unable to proceed. The shouts redoubled. Again there was the cry of " Richards ! Richards ! " And as Maurice withdrew to make way for his opponent, the fog closed in again and obliterated all signs of his brother's presence.

" Well, friends," cried Richards. " your new member's a 'great traveller, and he's won his seat on his United Empire stunt. It's a pretty picture, but I tell you, what's wrong with his Empire isn't that it's too big but that it's too small, not that it's united, but that it divides—bosses from workers, white from black, Britons from the rest of the world. When it does good, it does it by accident, and you can't run a complicated civilisation upon accidents. Well, we who believe in international socialism may have lost the trick, but we shall win the rubber. We've been beaten by the big battalions, the big purses and the big illusions. But you can't defeat a living movement by a dead tradition. This Empire business may have won to-night, but to-morrow, the dawn, is ours ! "

Maurice drew his mother's arm through his and smiled down at her.

" Tired ? "

She shook her head.

" It won't be long now."

᾽ His agent prodded him again. " Will you have your photo taken with Mr. Richards ? "

" Come along, mother. We've got to sacrifice you just a little longer." Maurice turned to his opponent, and the ceremony of personal friendliness and good fellowship proceeded.

CHAPTER II

SIR JOSEPH PRINCE CONTEMPLATES ENTERPRISE

WHILE Maurice Durrant was reminding the electors of North Donnington of their great Imperial Responsibilities, Sir Joseph Prince, Chairman of the firm of Prince's Tours, Limited, rose in an ascending elevator past floor after floor of an immense Oxford Street emporium.

The counters were shrouded ; the long aisles lay empty ; yet the lift was crowded with a voluble and vivacious company. As he stepped out on to the top floor, Sir Joseph heard a handsome woman in a backless bronze garment, declaiming to the world in general, " I've been spending the *whole* evening with Charlie Chaplin. He's so rococco. Ah, *dear* Sir Joseph ! *Have* you seen Charlie Chaplin ? I was just saying to him that this is a turning point in British history. *Too* rococco ! "

All around them swayed, pushed or gyrated a crowd of men and women in elaborate evening toilets. The high-pitched scream of their voices competed with the saxophones and percussion instruments of a band which, at one side of the first room Sir Joseph entered, was attempting to provide a rhythm for those whose efforts to dance led them to push their way in couples instead of singly through the crowd. As a method of penetration, this had its points.

Sir Joseph, ever a man of resource, seized a glorious young creature of eighteen from her mother's side, and, with his arm about her, pushed her before him down the room.

"Forgive me. It seemed the only way. Tell me, my dear Nancy, everything."

"Well. The band's here. And the champagne's in there. But we won't be able to get in for years. There's a double queue being pushed through by perfectly bee-autiful commissionaires in uniform, and there's to be a cabaret. And the Aga Khan's in that corner, and mother hasn't seen Charlie Chaplain, and there's to be a boxing kangaroo, or was that last time ? It doesn't really matter, because you can't see anything, anyway."

Sir Joseph looked about him with appreciation. He liked crowds. He liked parties. He liked young creatures with bright, starry eyes and delicately rounded bodies dressed in white. White, the colour of virginity, was charming for the young. Nancy Penoyre, whom he had torn so unceremoniously from her mother, was a delicious creature.

"I am so dreadfully hungry. I was canvassing for quite two hours right in the slums this afternoon, making all those women come out and vote, you know. It was frightfully thrilling, up miles and miles of stone staircases, just the sort where they find the body on the third floor, the throat cut from ear to ear, *you* know. And we had the most frightful old cronies of Daddy's for dinner ; and really I was too exhausted to eat anything, and Mother was *so* upset because some one said that we shan't be able to go to Cannes this Christmas. So do, *do*, darling Sir Joseph, get me through to the supper-room."

Nancy was right about the double queue. With endless courtesy and patience, the uniformed officials, trained to discipline the equal enthusiasm of White Sale hunters, pushed relays of guests through a short corridor into a room prepared as a buffet, the tables laden with chicken, galantines, jellies, pâté de foie gras, truffles, vols-au-vents, trifles and champagne. Particularly champagne.

Thither, at length, she and Sir Joseph made their way. He found a chair for her, and prawns in aspic, and pâté.

"You're a lovely person at parties," she sighed contentedly, as he filled her glass. "You always know what to do."

"I have had practice. I have lived for a long time," he replied.

He made no secret of his seventy-five years. He was proud of them. He knew himself to be a strikingly handsome, distinguished, sociable, and interesting person. He perfectly appreciated his beautifully-trimmed imperial, his well-manicured hands, his upright, youthful figure, and his white abundant hair. He was aware of the flattering attention invariably provoked by his picturesque presence.

"There's Sir Joseph Prince." "Oh, my dear, isn't he an *angel*?" "I always think he looks like Don Quixote, only well-*fed*, you know." "A terrible old roué." "Yet how *young* he looks on it."

Sir Joseph himself cultivated a reputation for rakishness. He enjoyed informing acquaintances that at his age one was, like Nietzsche's super-man, beyond good and evil. Having built up a public legend of excess, he preserved it by private asceticism that kept his digestion good, his figure boyish, and his eye clear as running water. He had done so much, seen so much, travelled so far, known such diversified periods of fortune and misfortune, and yet remained as little blasé as a schoolboy mounting Wembley Stadium to see his first cup-tie final.

Nancy regarded him with open adoration.

"And the results?" he asked, in his deep voice. "Have you turned your attention at all to the results? I suppose that at some time, somewhere, somewhere, there are announcements being made?"

"Oh, it's *too* monotonous. We're just sweeping home. I didn't stay long in the results room because one knows already. The Reds are simply melting away. Poor things, I felt quite sorry for them! I wish I'd been here in 1928 when they say the crowd outside roared like the French Revolution."

"Ah, you were in the nursery then."

"Not at all. I was in the fifth form at St. Angela's."

It was some time before Sir Joseph found his way into the third room, where on gilt chairs several hundreds of British citizens sat facing a wall hung with small placards bearing the names of parliamentary constituencies. From time to time a man in evening dress mounted a small platform and through a megaphone shouted election results, while uniformed officials scaled ladders and nimbly set beside the shouted names, cards bearing the number of votes received.

The watchers on the chairs had been provided with booklets like dance-programmes, from which hung silver pencils on silken cords, and some even went to the trouble of marking down the results as they were announced by megaphone. But this occupation soon grew monotonous, and most preferred to talk, applauding with mechanical joy each almost uninterrupted victory of the government.

" Splendid ! Splendid ! " murmured Sir Joseph, gazing down at the voluptuous flesh of a magnificent blonde seated before him. Her dress of pale peach-coloured satin hung from a collar of brilliants round her neck, and left her back, shoulders and arms generously exposed for his delight.

" It's the industrial North. That's what is so surprising. Going solid against Labour. Solid."

" Splendid ! " repeated Sir Joseph, as the lady moved. Her hair was soft and light as floss, her profile when she turned her head, adorable.

" You say Splendid ? " murmured a Welsh professor of physiology. " Splendid ? "

" Don't you ? What do you think of it ? " asked Sir Joseph.

" I think," sighed the little man, drawing a frayed cuff over his meagre wrist, " that I shall henceforth abandon myself to a life of sexual pleasure. I see no hope to be anticipated from the development of human intelligence."

" That's just what I *do* see." Sir Joseph's eye wandered to a tall, knife-thin brunette in black chiffon. He liked her rich vermilion-painted lips and finger-nails. " What could you want better than this, eh ? "

The physiologist did not see the brunette. His eye ran over the names and figures. " The writing on the wall," he sighed. " Landslide, panic, the negation of reason. Democracy at its worst."

" You need a drink. Come along, man," Sir Joseph rallied him.

" No drink can drown my deep depression. Besides, if you knew all I know about the action of alcohol on the liver . . ."

" I know its action on mine. It's grand," declared Sir

Joseph stoutly. He took at most two mild whiskies-and-sodas a week; but he disapproved of temperance on principle.

"Then it must be alcohol which makes you see any matter for encouragement in this nauseating spectacle."

"Why? Whatever's wrong with it?"

"Wrong? You are the creator of the most enterprising of all travel agencies. It is to your interest that people should journey uninterrupted from Mexico to Madagascar. You need a stable monetary system, and encouragement of international trade."

"Just why I didn't want these Socialist fools to monkey with the pound."

"Which has already fallen, thanks to certain unfortunate naval occasions following upon the ridiculous attempts of this hybrid government to save it. You need good international relationships, and you are delighted at the prospect of a Nationalist reaction. You need money in the pockets of the people who will travel adventurously, and you applaud the victory of idiots prepared to sacrifice the young professional classes to the older stereotyped *rentiers*. How many of your clients last year were school teachers?"

"About thirty-five per cent. we reckoned, but, of course, that was because of our reduced scholastic rates."

"My dear Sir Joseph—the more commonplace agencies could send parties to Lovely Lucerne and Ostende. You specialise in precisely those less comfortable, less accessible quarters of the globe to which only the young, the enterprising, the intelligent or the eccentric wish to go. And yet here you are shouting with glee at the worst catastrophe youth, adventure, innovation and enterprise have suffered since the war. Within a few months, the professions will have wilted beneath government discouragement; nobody will go abroad, owing to a Back-to-Britain movement; the rage for Protection, exaggerated by the unequal exchange rates, will make foreign travel as difficult as it is unpopular. In short—in short, you are applauding the men who are about to cut off your nose to spite your face."

"Poor Hugh! Is he being terribly dismal, Sir Joseph?" Mrs. Davies, mother of the physiologist, a large conversational lady, approached the travel agent and linked her well-covered bare arm through her son's skinny one. " Of course what I always say is—what do politics matter ? Science is the only thing that counts. In fifty years we shall be content to put the expert in control." She beamed in proprietary affection on the little man beside her, as though having produced one scientist, she was privileged to speak for his entire profession.

" Unfortunately," said her son, " politics matter a good deal, my dear mother, as you would know if you were an unemployed girl of seventeen with a cut in your dole and every prospect of the Rent Restriction Act coming off."

" Girl of seventeen ? Let her go into domestic service. I'm sure that kitchen maids to-day . . ." began Mrs. Davies, who, when not undertaking to speak for the whole academic world, was much like other middle-class house-wives. " Until the girl of to-day learns that domestic work is as dignified and important as clicking a type-writer——"

" I didn't expect to find you a Socialist, Davies," said Sir Joseph hastily, long experience having warned him to beware of discussing the servant question with leisured ladies of over forty.

" A Socialist ? God forbid ! Have you ever tried to make a trade union official regard a new technical regulation from the physiological point of view ? A plague on both your houses, say I. But—you—you incorrigible optimist— I wash my hands of you."

" Oh, now, isn't he Dismal Desmond ? " Mrs. Davies patted his arm fondly ; the couple were borne away on the crest of another surging wave of newcomers.

Sir Joseph was only a little disturbed, but he disliked prophecies of evil. He wanted, now that he felt no longer young enough to wait indefinitely for the millenium, to be assured that already all was for the best in the best of all possible worlds. He wanted to think that all humanity was progressing through stormy but not ignoble perils towards a hopeful and happy future. He liked the sound, the savour, the feeling of prosperity.

This man Davies croaked like a raven.

All encouragement of enterprise, patriotism and progress must be good for Prince's.

He would not believe that national recovery could be long delayed.

He would find some new, swift, dramatic satisfaction for his pride to feed on. He would snatch one more victory from time, before its hurrying chariot overtook him.

" Sir Joseph ! "

He turned to find himself accosted by a young brunette in the early twenties, pretty as a flower, pert, fresh and confident. She took both his hands.

" You don't remember me."

" You were in the nursery . . ." he hazarded. " And you have grown so beautiful."

She grimaced.

" Mother told me to come and ask how you were and why you cut her."

" My answer to the first question is that I am immortal ; I am always well." He defied his consciousness of time's implacable pursuit. " To the second, that I have been so ravished in soul by all this display of charm, brilliance that . . ."

" Splendid ! I love you. My name is Brenda Harrison. My mother is Constance Harrison, née Bradley, with whom you used to flirt outrageously. You couldn't possibly remember me because you've never seen me before. But I accosted you because I want to introduce you to a perfectly lovely friend of mine who wants to meet you."

" No friend could be more perfectly lovely than you——"

" I know—I know, but you're to come and meet Jane Crossgill. Yes. The movie star. Do you go to the movies ? "

" I have not done so for many years. . ." He was conjuring his brain for a gallant remark to match the glittering liveliness of the young woman, when his eye was caught by a languid, wraithlike sylph, floating towards him in a cloud of pearl-grey drapery.

" Oh, Jane. Here he is. He's longing to meet you," cried Miss Harrison. " Sir Joseph Prince—Jane Crossgill. The Siren of the Swamps—a shooting star who has travelled even further than you."

The sylph inclined her head. Her large gelatinous cow-like eyes rested for a moment on Sir Joseph's face, then

fell wearily. She said, " Do you mind if we sit somewhere ? "

" Oh, darling ! You've had no supper," cried Brenda,
and once more Sir Joseph escorted his ladies through the
shifting crowd.

Again they found a table.

" Sir Joseph, would you believe it—Jane's only been
back two months from Africa—she's had the most *hair*-
raising adventures—making a film called " The Siren of
the Swamps "—only they're going to do it in California
now because real swamps are too agitating to photograph
really well. And they were caught in the floods, and some
of them got separated—Jane was with the camera-men,
weren't you, Jane ? And they put her and a whole lot of
apparatus on a raft . . ."

" My dear, Henderson's out ! "

" Too amazing. A perfect landslide."

" And the Dingo caste. . . ."

" Dinkas, dear, not Dingoes," sighed Miss Crossgill.

" Oh, Sir Joseph, *there* you are ! " Nancy Penoyre was
back again.

" Hush, my dear, I'm just hearing a story of wild adventure. Sit down and listen."

" . . . And they came to some high ground and found
themselves cut off from all the others—didn't you, Jane ? "

" Oh, where was this ? I've missed the beginning ! "
cried Nancy, helping herself lavishly to lobster pâté. " *Do*
begin at the beginning."

" In Mandoa. And they were taken to an extraordinary
town called Bolabola——"

" Lolagoba," corrected Jane. " The capital."

The couple on Sir Joseph's right were launched into a
political argument that for a moment drowned all other
conversation.

" I tell you, there'll be revolution before Christmas.
The unemployed'll never stand it."

" Oh—the Old Country isn't done yet."

" And it was too extraordinary," Brenda continued,
" the native chiefs spoke English because . . ."

" Look how they took the General Strike. We don't make
revolutions here."

" And they actually set up their talkie apparatus in a hut—didn't you, Jane ? "

" Hollywood Hall," sighed Jane.

" I've had too much champagne, I think," observed Nancy pensively. " Or is every one really talking at once about something different ? "

" Anything, anything, to get away from that terrifying Sudd," moaned Jane.

" Ellen Wilkinson's out."

" No—not *possible* ! "

" So now you know why I wanted you two to meet," Brenda cried. " How many people are there in this country who have actually been *inside* Mandoa ? "

" Five," answered Sir Joseph promptly. He really did know his business. " Yourself, Miss Crossgill, your engineer, Hakenkratz, with whom I lunched last Friday, a junior administrator from the Sudan called Holloway, Captain Bartlett from Abyssinia, and Jerry Sanders the flying man."

" Oh, then it's no good. I've lost my bet ! " Brenda lamented.

" I am desolated. What have I done ? "

" I bet Tim Willoughby I'd introduce you to some one who'd been in a part of the world that you knew nothing about. And you know everything ! "

" Oh, no, I don't. There are a thousand things I want to know. Please tell me, Miss Crossgill. Is it true that you taught the Mandoans how to speak the best Chicago *patois* ? Jerry Sanders said that when he landed outside the town and asked two ferocious-looking natives for water, making signs with the usual optimism of a monolingual Englishman, they looked at him and said, ' O.K. water, baby—sorry we ain't gotten gasoline.' "

Jane laughed.

" If it's not true, it's credible."

" Oh, we *must* go." Brenda seized Sir Joseph's hands. " Send an expedition there, dear, darling Sir Joseph. Build one of your hotels there. It sounds all too lovely. Jane says there's a perfectly adorable sheik called Safi Talal who *loves* the English. Couldn't you ? "

" I'm having a Moth for my twenty-first birthday present,"said Nancy. " I'll fly there—it sounds marvellous."

" We'll all fly there. We must *do something*. Can't we
start a new Imperial Airway or something ? What's the use
of me telling my Girl Guides down at Wroxley every
Tuesday evening that they've got to be enterprising, if
we don't have enterprises ? "

Sir Joseph smiled. He enjoyed their pretty pleadings.
Jane Crossgill's languid grace concealed an unquenchable
audacity. Sir Joseph knew more about her reckless history
than she guessed. Brenda was vivacious and innocent as a
kitten, Nancy white and gold with the metallic precision
of the débutante of autumn, 1931. He liked them all. He
liked the shrill sweetness of the young girls' voices, and
the low, dove-like tones of the movie-star's slow speech.
He liked to feel about him the atmosphere of pleasure and
excitement, of people satisfied with a good day's work
well done.

The National Government was in beyond all question.

An hour passed most pleasantly before a minute vis-
countess smothered in purple orchids tore Jane Crossgill
away from her party.

" Now—did we, or did we not, come to listen to election
results ? " asked Brenda suddenly.

They decided that they did.

Just as they reached the doorway, the impersonal voice
of the megaphone blared at them :

> " *Number* 79. DONNINGTON NORTH.
> Durrant (Conservative)   .   .   15,989
> Richards (Socialist)   .   .   4,132
> ─────────
> Conservative majority   11,857
> Conservative gain."

At so decisive a victory, even stinging hands clapped,
even hoarse voices shouted. Sir Joseph's heart leapt with
pleasure.

" That's one of our directors," he told his attendant
nymphs. " The youngest. Maurice Durrant. Good lad.
Very."

" Oh, splendid ! Let's send him a telegram of congratulation. You can do it free here," Nancy declared. " There's

a choice little booth along there. I've sent twenty-three already. One gets so few free gifts in this life."

So Prince's had been victorious all round.

The national crisis had meant only a moment's pause in its triumphant progress. Youth, daring, adventure were still lovely things. A hotel in Mandoa ? A holiday centre in the only remaining part of Africa unexplored, yet fit for European habitation ? A new enterprise to defy the march of time ?

Durrant in—a link with the new National Government—Foreign Office support—shortening the air-route to East Africa—another service rendered by Prince's to the Empire ? Was he old, was he tired, was he done for ?

Never !

Gripping the soft arms of the two young girls he went to telegraph congratulations to his youngest director.

CHAPTER III

MRS. DURRANT IS A GOOD MOTHER

Two hours after making his victory speech, Maurice Durrant sat with his mother in their private sitting-room at the Donnington Station Hotel. He drank hot whisky and lemon ; Mrs. Durrant sipped hot milk.

There seemed no need for words between them. Both were pleasantly exhausted ; their throats and limbs ached ; they could hardly speak above a whisper. But they smiled at each other from time to time, Maurice triumphantly, Mrs. Durrant with fond affection.

Maurice bathed in satisfaction as in a warm, smooth sea. His victory marked his conquest of more than Richards. He had not spared himself, dashing backwards and forwards between the London office of Prince's, and his constituency. Coming in late at night from political meetings, he had dictated business letters. After difficult tussles with foreign agents, he had motored north to speak about the export trade, about currency, about Socialist extravagance and the abuses of the dole.

He had kept his head. Everywhere Mrs. Durrant had
gone, canvassing, sitting on committees, dining with local
Conservatives, she had heard his praises. It was impossible
for her not to be proud of him. It was his success which
had elated her, his reflected glory in which she moved. He
had won her at last.

It had been hard work. Maurice had started life at a
disadvantage. When he was just eighteen months old, his
father had been killed in the hunting field. Mrs. Durrant,
left with a small but adequate income, conscientious and
grief-stricken, decided to devote herself entirely to her
young children. She moved to Wimbledon, took a small
house with a garden, dismissed the nurse, sent Bill, then
nearly six, to a kindergarten, and announced her intention
of looking after Maurice herself.

Her relatives praised her sensible decision. What could
be more consoling to a widow than the constant companionship of her little sons ? Unhappily for Maurice, Mrs.
Durrant, like many other women, was bored by babies. She
did not acknowledge this. Indeed, the suggestion would
have horrified her. But the fact remained that the more
time she spent with Maurice, the less she really liked
him.

At eighteen months old, no child is a civilised companion.
Maurice was messy. His meals were a nightmare of spilled
milk, smeared jam and spattered gravy. He was ubiquitous.
It was no longer possible to put him to sleep in his pram for
hours at a time. He needed constant attention, entertainment and supervision, and neither his looks, his manners,
nor his monosyllabic conversation really compensated his
mother for her sacrifice of those activities to which she had
been accustomed and which she heartily enjoyed.

Mrs. Durrant, during her husband's lifetime, had been a
popular young hostess, an impassioned novel-reader, a
player of bridge and tennis, and an ardent member of the
Ladies' Unionist Association. The sudden and drastic
exchange of these agreeable occupations for the daily
washing, feeding and amusing of a delicate and rather
difficult small boy affected her profoundly. She grew weekly
more depressed and irritable, but, being completely convinced by current theories of the maternal instinct, attri-

buted her depression to her bereavement, and accepted it as inevitable. Her depression affected her temper. She found herself less and less able to suffer equitably the accidents and annoyances of the nursery. Maurice caught cold ; he ran temperatures ; he acquired the major as well as the minor infantile diseases. Mumps, measles, whooping cough and scarlet fever had only to be thought of, and the child had them. Bored, weary, exasperated, Mrs. Durrant pursued with a martyr's querulous devotion, her self-appointed task.

But she could not help the sudden change of expression that illuminated her face when Bill, escorted by the young housemaid, rode on his tricycle up the garden path after his day at school and poured forth a dramatic recital of woes, triumphs and adventures into her sympathetic ear. Mrs. Durrant liked men. She liked their strength, their intelligence, their contact with an exciting unfamiliar world; and Bill, even at six, possessed some quality of manhood. He was a charming, handsome, fearless child, precociously independent, very little trouble while in the house, and out of it most of the day. His health was excellent. He enjoyed all the usual boyish amusements and added to this an enormous literary appetite. There may be educational advantages in that theory which would prevent a child from learning to read till it is adolescent, in order that it may acquire first-hand experience of life ; but there is nothing to be said for it from a domestic standpoint. Bill, at six or seven, could be set down in a chair with *Rupert of Hentzau*, *The Boys' Own Paper*, *The Swiss Family Robinson*, or a bound annual of *The Ladies' Realm*, and remain silent and absorbed till bedtime. No obstacles of fatigue or irritation came between Mrs. Durrant and her love for him.

Maurice, watching the weary, reproving face he knew to be his mother's, transformed by radiant and adoring love for Bill, learned too soon the peculiar torments of jealousy. Mrs. Durrant tried to be impartial ; when she scolded Maurice, she would unjustly include Bill in her indictment ; she gave presents equally, if possible spending a trifle more on Maurice than on Bill. When she opened her arms, she drew both sons to her soft, violet-scented bosom. Maurice had the greater share of her time, her devotion, her thought, and her caresses ; but he never doubted for a moment that it was Bill who had her heart.

Just because it was not his, he wanted it. Bill, whose easy affections strayed to cooks, villagers, school friends, the doctor's groom who let him hold the reins in the high gig, and the young curate who could vault the garden gate, repaid his mother's adoration with an easy, confident love. Maurice, shy, delicate, nervous of other people, distrustful of the world outside his nursery, responded to her dutifully parental caresses with hungry violence.

But as he grew older and so less of a nuisance, she found her rôle of devotion more supportable, and her affections became more evenly divided. It is possible that when they were both at school or the university, and Maurice was winning by dogged industry the prizes that Bill had lost by careless brilliance, Mrs. Durrant might have gained equal pleasure from both her sons.

But when Maurice was fifteen and Bill nineteen, in his first year at New College, the war broke out, and Bill went straight into a cadet corps. Then, indeed, Maurice passed through the Valley of Humiliation. Bill became an officer ; he went to France, faced death, led men, saw horrors undescribable. He was proving his manhood at the risk of his life, and God was to be thanked who watched him with that hour. If he returned safely, he would be a hero, if he fell, his name would live for ever more.

Mrs. Durrant, vibrating with pride and fear and glory, threw herself into the profession of a soldier's mother. She packed parcels, sewing them up in linen and addressing them with indelible pencil ; she rolled bandages, knitted socks, organised recruiting meetings, took stalls at Red Cross bazaars, and gave bridge drives for Belgian refugees. Her drawing-room reflected from shelf, piano, mantelpiece and table, Bill's photographed features.—Bill as a cadet, slim and boyish, Bill as a second-lieutenant at Folkestone with the first shadow of hair on his upper lip, Bill home from France on his first leave, with a mature moustache, snapshots of Bill on horseback (radiantly handsome), in camp (manly and careless, a glass in his hand), home on leave in the garden, playing tennis—Bill, Bill, Bill, Bill.

Meanwhile Maurice at school crammed Latin prose and slid about the muddy playground, drilling with the O.T.C., his fingers swollen with chilblains, his complexion hideous with the pimples of adolescence. His school days had all the discomforts and deprivations of war time, and none of its queer compensations, its added intensity, its drama and its sense of great issues at stake.

He prayed nightly with fervent passion that Bill should not be killed, not because he loved Bill (though through all this be believed himself to harbour normal brotherly affections), but because a hero's death would set the seal finally and irrevocably on Bill's triumph.

His suffering was morbid and irrational, but no less agonising ; for it is an error of judgment which discounts the pain of that grief which cannot be justified by reason. He bore it in secret, which made it all the worse. The news of an offensive in the daily paper, lectures given to the O.T.C. by patriotic colonels, the refrain of " Good-byeeee " thumped on the recreation-room piano, the poems of Rupert Brooke, popular amongst the Bookish Set at school, tore him with rending anguish. Its first mitigation came when Bill, who had transferred from the infantry to the R.A.F., crashed—in England, not in France.

It was the first sign of fortune's reversal of awards.

After that, life became more tolerable for Maurice. At eighteen he left school and entered a cadet corps. When the war ended, he was in uniform, though not in France. He was growing out of the spotty hideousness of an overgrown delicate schoolboy, into the slender immaturity of his later good looks. After the Armistice he refused to enter the university. He assumed that Bill, like so many undergraduate officers, would return to Oxford and he determined to avoid competition with him there. To the surprise of every one he insisted upon going straight into business, and a place was found for him in Prince's Tours, Limited. The true reason, which he confessed not even to himself, was that by this policy he had stolen a march on Bill. Bill could still be in tutelage, subject to deans and proctors and penalties, dependent on his mother for pocket-money, while he, Maurice, was an independent business man.

Fortune outwitted him. Bill, who had been on light duty

in England, rejected the chance of returning to New College. The air crash had temporarily disabled his body, and permanently deranged his nerves. He walked with a slight limp, talked wildly, drank too much, looked nearly forty instead of twenty-three, expressed the most outrageous opinions about war, politics, morals and the academic life, and announced his intention of commuting his gratuity, and of taking over, with an ex-officer friend, the lease of a fruit-farm in South Africa.

Mrs. Durrant, infinitely perturbed by his conduct, distressed by his health and dazed by the transformation of his character, was less sorry than she thought to see him go. She loved him still, but her love was no longer happily confident nor proudly tragic. It was painful and apprehensive, the love of a mother for a son who has become a stranger, and whose presence could make the entire house uncomfortable. He had come home one night from London, where he had been presumably buying his kit for South Africa, shamefully, brutally, sordidly drunk. Mrs. Durrant had found him in the hall and had gone at once for Maurice, begging him to put Bill to bed before the maids or visitors should see him. Maurice dealt with Bill, made effective excuses to the visitors, and consoled his mother with a new tenderness.

He had never been happier in his life.

Since then, if justice had been done, Bill's star should have declined and Maurice's risen. Bill lost his money on the farm ; tried other jobs in Cape Town ; went to the Argentine ; married disastrously ; and finally became accepted as a ne'er-do-weel. Maurice rose steadily at Prince's. Sir Joseph liked him. The pain of his frustrated childhood had taught him both sensitiveness and tenacity. He applied the first to his personal, the second to his business relationships with his employer, and at twenty-nine found himself a director ; at thirty-one, a member of parliament and successful man, the advisor, protector and comforter of his mother.

" Isn't your boy splendid ? You must be fond of him," people said to Mrs. Durrant, leaving her no doubt about which boy they praised. Indeed, Wimbledon had nearly forgotten Bill ; North Donnington had never heard of him ;

and what London knew of him, the sooner forgotten, perhaps, the better for every one.

So Maurice came into his own, and sat glass in hand, leaning back in the green plush chair of the hotel sitting-room and smiling at his mother.

She spoke first.

" Maurice."

" Well, Mums ? You ought to be in bed."

" I was thinking."

" Bad habit at this time of night——"

" I want you to do something for me."

" Sure."

" Promise ? "

" Well. Within reason. You've been quite a good canvasser."

" It's very reasonable. It's self evident. I know you'll do it."

" Well, if you know, you know, and that's that. What is it, darling ? D'you want Lord Irwin to dinner, or an invitation to Chequers ? "

" I want you to speak to Sir Joseph about Bill again. No. Don't stop me. I know you've said you can't, but it's not as though you were just an employee at Prince's now. You're a director yourself. You should have power. And after to-night they'll be pleased with you. Sir Joseph told me how important it was for you to be in the House. You can do a great deal for him, and I'm sure you've always worked very hard, dear, and never asked anything for yourself. . . . And I haven't asked *you* for much, Maurice."

Maurice said nothing. He swallowed off his whisky with a gulp and set down the glass.

So this was what she had been thinking of. This was what his victory meant to her. Something for Bill again. Bill. Bill. Bill.

He might have known.

Mrs. Durrant went on.

" Did you see him to-night ? "

" I hoped you didn't."

" Oh, Maurice, what's the use of my trying to deceive myself ? He's my son." Her weary voice was more moving than a cry of anguish. She really cared. She cared horribly.

Maurice rose and stood beside the fire, so that she could not look directly into his face.

She spoke again, forcing herself to make confession for her beloved. " Do you know he's been working for the Socialists all the time ? "

" Not for Richards."

" No, for a man called Darton at Perynn. But that's not twenty miles away. There was a photograph of him speaking there in the Donnington *Free Press.*"

" I didn't see it."

" I know. I burned it. I didn't want to worry you."

" Mother *dear* ! "

" Well, it's no use pretending you don't mind what Bill does. I know you do. We both do. And it wouldn't have got into the local papers at all if it hadn't been for that girl —the one he was with to-night. She works on the *Free Press* as a reporter or something. She was round at the Central office one night when I was there."

" I've seen her at meetings."

" Mrs. Halliday says he's living with her," Mrs. Durrant said with extraordinary bitterness, then dropped her head on to her hands and began to cry.

" Mrs. Halliday had no business—— Oh, mater dear. Don't *worry*. Don't get upset like this. It probably isn't true. And if it were true. . . . After all. Bill's gone his own way for years now."

Damn him and blast him ! Couldn't he even let them alone for one evening ? Must he intrude his squalid adventures right into the middle of their happiness ? Bill had no shame, no taste, no decency.

" To bring her with him ! " moaned Mrs. Durrant. " To stand there under the light, where every one could see. Such a common little thing, too. To get his name into the papers. Maurice, I can't bear it. I can't . . ."

Her voice died away. Her shoulders shook.

" Don't worry, darling. You're tired. You're all worn out. In the morning . . ."

Maurice was tired, too. But who bothered about that ? His triumph that had been so sweet now tasted bitter as gall. It could never compensate his mother for Bill's failure. Nothing he did, no pleasure he could give her,

would outweigh the incalculable burden of his brother's
shame.

There was no reason in love. She had loved Bill first
because he brought her pleasure ; she loved him now
because he brought her pain.

" I thought I couldn't bear for him to leave the country,"
she said at last, in a small, dead voice. " Last time he went
abroad I slept so badly. But now I can't bear him to be in
England if he's going to behave like this. Get him away,
Maurice. Please, dear. Please get him away."

" Oh, my dear—don't. Don't, mother dear. Don't,
little one."

But of what use was comfort ? Comfort is cheap coinage.
He was down beside her now, his arms about her.

" Don't, darling. Don't cry. I'll do something. I'll
try—I promise. I'll speak to Sir Joseph."

Even as he promised he savoured the irony that his
promise should be to send Bill away from her, knowing
that neither in presence nor absence, in life nor in death,
would Bill relax his hold upon her.

At last he acknowledged to himself his hatred of his
brother.

Next day he was in bed with laryngitis and a temperature.

CHAPTER IV

MAURICE DURRANT KEEPS A PROMISE

THE day after his return to the office, Maurice lunched
with Sir Joseph at Lavalli's. These luncheons took place
regularly once a month and conformed to a pleasant ritual.
When Sir Joseph pulled the menu towards him and fiddled
with it in his brown, pointed fingers, he invariably asked,
" Well, d'you feel up to hot lobster to-day ? " And Maurice
invariably answered, " Rather ! " But usually they ate
sole. They were both fastidious eaters, careful of their
digestions.

The joke, however, had worn well. It dated from the
first day of their intimacy.

Maurice had entered Prince's in a spirit of defiance, but he remained there for love of the work. Naturally quick, diligent and adaptable, he soon displayed qualities of initiative and intelligence undreamed of by his schoolmasters or family. For the first time in his life he was free from the shadow of his brother's competition, and his natural abilities sprang forward from release.

Virtue, however, is not invariably rewarded ; and had it not been for one happy accident and for the peculiar circumstances of Sir Joseph's life, Maurice might have waited years before reaping the fruits of his devotion.

It happened that Sir Joseph, popular, honoured and privileged as he was, was lonely. His son, to whom he had intended to hand on the business after his retirement, had been killed in 1915. His daughter, a disappointingly commonplace and tiresome woman, collapsed into domesticity in Northumberland and had no thought beyond school-reports and servants. The reports were so dull that Sir Joseph had little hope of adequate succession from his grandchildren.

A successor must be found. Sir Joseph, for all that he had turned Prince's into a limited company, remained a benevolent despot with controlling interests in the firm. It was his personal creation, his pride, his love, his child, his life-work. It meant far more to him than a successful and agreeable means of making money. If he had been losing as much yearly on it as he made, he would have gone forward till his capital was drained to its last shilling.

His attitude towards his work was quite innocently romantic. His youth had been wild and roving. He had even performed the sadly hackneyed feat of running away from school and going to sea. He had been a cabin boy, trader, porter, reception clerk to a shady hotel in the Bahamas, stable-lad in Melbourne and hunter in South Africa. It was this last activity which gave him his first notion of business. He had been employed as safari-manager and hunter to a rich Australian in Uganda. Later he had done a little ivory hunting and trading on his own, and finally he set himself up as advisor on equipment for other men's expeditions. He loved adventure. Travel was his religion, and with the practical and concrete imagination common to most mystics, he would foresee before it set out all the emergencies likely to overtake an enterprise, from blistered heels to broken bridges, floods and fever. It was upon this combination of romanticism and common-sense that he founded Prince's Limited ; but with him the practical sense was almost subconscious ; it was the romance that filled his thoughts.

The work was more than a business. It was a crusade. He wanted men and women to live dangerously. Afflicted by the ignoble security of modern urban life, he saw a positive virtue in discomfort. He was convinced that a society unaccustomed to risk and hardship would decay. He gloried in the records of past adventure, and urged forward new generations to emulate their ancestors.

The business had grown prodigiously, and beyond all his early visions of it. It controlled now a great store of sporting equipment in the Strand, travel offices in London, New York, Sydney, Toronto, Cape Town, and Calcutta, with fifty-seven subsidiary branches all over the world. It organised mountaineering expeditions and polar expeditions. Its clients crossed the Sahara, explored Thibet, and negotiated the Upper Reaches of the Amazon. From organising isolated expeditions for the adventurous, it proceeded to the arrangement of original holidays for the enterprising. Prince's agents scoured the globe for strange, romantic and unexpected places, whither Prince's hotels might lure the strenuous, the hardy, and the sophisticated, weary of convention.

But among his subordinates, Sir Joseph found few who shared both his dreams and his abilities. He knew good business men and brave explorers. The few who combined both characteristics preferred for the most part to work on their own. It was Maurice Durrant, the docile and methodical clerk, who unexpectedly gave signs of under-standing the complete significance of Prince's Limited. An illness of Sir Joseph's secretary had brought young Durrant first into his private office. Among the letters which had to be answered was an invitation from the B.B.C. asking Sir Joseph to give a series of travel talks to young people. Sir Joseph was for refusing. A bad bout of rheumatism had prevented him from fulfilling a cherished

plan of making a personal tour of his hotels and bureaux
in the Far East. He felt petulant and contra-suggestive.

" Why should I ? Waste of time—lot of nonsense. Boys
who have any stuff in them don't need travel talks. Bilge."

There was no confirming reply from his substitute
secretary. He looked round with a snort and saw young
Durrant's eyes fixed on one of the pictures adorning the
office—" The Boyhood of Sir Walter Raleigh "—a senti-
mentalised conception of the future imperialist listening
to an obvious " travel talk " from a ragged seaman. It
was the type of picture that appealed to Sir Joseph's
taste.

" Did you hear what I said ? " repeated Sir Joseph.
" Bilge, isn't it ? Eh ? Lectures ! Eh ? "

" Do you really mean me to say what I think, sir ? "
asked Maurice politely. " Or shall I just take down your
answer ? "

" Eh ? What ? You don't agree with me ? You've got
an idea up your sleeve ? "

Maurice met the older man's snapping blue eyes with his
own solemn hero-worship.

" Well, sir," he said, " If you really want to know what
I think, I think it's a thundering good idea of the
B.B.C.——" and gasped at his own daring.

" Do you ? The devil you do ! And why, pray ? "

" Well, you see—when you're at school you hear a whole
lot of poppy-cock one way and another from the vicar
who'se been to Palestine, or from some one who went with
the Hellenic Travellers to Greece. Just occasionally an
airman, or an explorer comes down—and he's a blazing
success. But most of us know we can't fly the Atlantic or
be the first man to take a canoe up the Amazon—so it just
ends in smoke—like a wild-west film—or a war lecture now
that the war's over." Maurice paused.

" Go on. Go on," urged Sir Joseph.

" But what *you* could do, sir, would be to put the thing
into their grasp. Prince's has made exciting travel practi-
cable for ordinary people. You could show them not just
what other people had done, but what they could do
themselves. You could tell 'em about prices and equipment
and time and training, and all the things that Prince's

provides for travellers, and see what happens. When a fellow's at school," said Maurice, all his memories of frustration and bitterness seething within him, " it's the hopelessness of ever getting anywhere that defeats him. It's the sense that it's all so far away and . . ."

" Go on," Sir Joseph repeated, in a changed voice.

He was listening to the articulation of some of his own unexpressed conclusions. He drew Maurice out and found that here at last was a junior who not only shared but contributed to his dreams. Maurice at twenty-four was already an imperialist. He saw in Prince's a training ground for the Cecil Rhodeses and Clives and Raleighs of the future. He saw it as a weapon against skulkers and Little Englanders. His own experience was, as he admitted, armchair experience. He had not travelled further than Dieppe. He had suffered no hardship worse than that of Salisbury Plain in October, 1918. But he was in love with the minutiae of travel. His mind already contained an encyclopædic knowledge of climates and altitudes, ethnology and roadways. When his colleagues in the office were playing football, falling in love, and educating themselves as men of the world, Maurice had been reading about the world, consuming travel books with passion, devouring atlases, and working out details for the equipment of expeditions which he had neither the physical stamina nor psychological taste to share.

Not all of this came out during the first conversation about travel talks ; but enough emerged to make Sir Joseph say at length, " H'm. Well. We must get a move on. Can't spend the whole morning over one letter," which flattened Maurice to the depression his pessimistic mind habitually anticipated. " You'd better come and lunch with me to-day and continue this edifying lecture," which raised his spirits to such a pitch that he almost lost his head. Almost, not quite.

Sir Joseph was like that. He was not " office-trained." If he wanted to continue a conversation with a junior clerk, he carried off the clerk to lunch and had it out over hot lobster and roast duckling.

Maurice was more than a junior clerk. His diligence and initiative had already been commended to Sir Joseph's

attention. It had not been quite by accident that he was
sent to deal with the chairman's correspondence that
morning. That he did not know. What he did know, as he
heard with rising apprehension Sir Joseph's orders to the
waiter, was that he could not eat hot lobster. He could
not eat safely any shell-fish ; but hot lobster followed by
roast duckling would be fatal.

Sir Joseph chose the menu out of kindness, remembering
his own exotic tastes as a robust and impecunious young
man. Being abstemious in his appetites, he hardly touched
the dishes himself, and had his junior's plate piled with
food enough to make a city alderman blench.

Maurice turned pale ; he turned faintly green ; but he did
not falter. Sir Joseph was accustomed to dealing with brave
men. What would he think of a poltroon who wilted merely
at the prospect of an indigestible meal ?

Maurice ate everything set before him ; but his subsequent memories of the interview were obliterated by its
gastronomic violence. He held out until the end, and reached
the cloakroom just before the lobster had its revenge.

Sir Joseph never noticed. He was delighted with the
young man; and though for several months he showed no
special indication of his favour, from that morning he
determined to have young Durrant with him on the Board.

During the following year, Maurice became his private
secretary, and travelled with him in comfort, on an Empire
voyage round the world. Four times during that journey
they ate lobster, and after the fifth time Maurice's stomach,
bullied into submission, ceased to revolt. Later, when he
had become a director of the firm, he told Sir Joseph the
story. The older man was amused. He insisted upon maintaining the legend, and the joke. Durrant became the
Man who Made his Fortune by Swallowing Hot Lobster.
It was a good story to tell.

When they sat together at Lavalli's, Sir Joseph put on
the huge horn-rimmed spectacles which he had just acquired and of which he was inordinately proud, and looked
at his junior.

" Well, young man, and what does it feel like to be an
M.P., eh ? "

" Uncommonly like being a schoolboy with the measles,"

laughed Maurice. " I've been in bed ever since the night
of polling day with laryngitis. The confounded fog, and
yelling against iron-lunged street orators and municipal
trams, were too much for me."

" H'm. You look about as fit as a sick cat. Can't have
that sort of thing if you're going to be of any use to us.
I tell you, we're in for a hard fight. Prince's and the country
and the rest of us."

" Oh, I'm all right now."

" You don't look it. Come. What sort of work did your
brother last—er—fail to do ? "

" Good God ! You know, then ? "

" I guessed. I know your mother. Fine woman, your
mother. Always a warm spot for the prodigal—ye—es."

" I don't think you've met my brother, Sir Joseph."

" No. No. So far as I remember, he was not anxious
to meet me."

Maurice writhed. There had been one monstrous occasion
when Bill failed to turn up at a lunch arranged, after
labyrinthine diplomacy, entirely for his own benefit. At
Simpson's in the Strand. Oh, he was hopeless. Hopeless
and shameless.

" Smashed up in the war, wasn't he ? "

" An aeroplane—but it was in England. He'd been in
France, of course. Two years."

" He's older than you ? "

" Four years."

" And he's never really done much since ? "

" Nothing permanent. He was in South Africa for a bit
—on a citrus farm. But it failed. Then he got a job on a
Cape paper and was doing rather well, I believe. He has a
certain flair for writing. But he quarrelled with the editor
over policy—colour question or something—he gets bees
in his bonnet. Then he went to the Argentine. But he left
that—on his wife's account. Rather a bore, that, because
it was quite a decent job and I think he liked it. But, of
course, it was a rotten place to bring up children."

" I didn't know he had a family."

" He hasn't. Cynthia divorced him over a year ago and
she's married again now. She took the child, of course.
Between ourselves, I think it was rather a put-up job, but

I don't blame her. He never could have kept her—not in the way she was accustomed to. Very decent family, the Hardy's. He met her staying with some people in the Argentine—riding. But, of course, it never did. It never would have done."

" I see. And he's never held a job since ? "

" He's tried. Mostly duds."

" Now, what do you honestly think yourself of his capacity ? "

Maurice drew his fork in patterns along the table cloth. Just because he knew the extent of his jealousy, he goaded himself to scrupulous justice.

" He's the sort of fellow who'se a complete gamble," he said at length. " He's got any amount of ability—much more, for instance, than I have. He could always beat me hollow at anything if he wanted to. The trouble is, he doesn't always want to. I suppose it's the war. They always say it's the war. I wish to God, sir "—Maurice suddenly heard himself cry out—" there'd never *been* a war. It makes life pretty intolerable for some of us who weren't old enough to be in it. They'll never forgive us. Never."

" It made life impossible for some who were in it," replied Sir Joseph slowly, and Maurice flushed, aware that he was thinking of his son.

Sir Joseph sighed, helped himself to more turbot, and asked, " Is he straight with money ? "

" So far as I know. But I don't know enough of him nowadays to take my oath on anything."

" Drink ? "

Maurice shrugged his shoulders.

" How does he get on with other people ? "

" Can do—perfectly well. Unusually well if he chooses He's supposed to have—charm."

" Could he take a position of responsibility—put a thing through—use his own judgment ? "

" Depends what it was. I really can't say. He *could* do anything."

Sir Joseph's next question was unexpected.

" Have you studied the Cairo-Durban air routes ? "

Maurice had. He had studied each projected enterprise

of Prince's Tours in Africa. They came within his department.

" What do you think of Lolagoba ? "

" Geographically handy. Right place for a rest camp, filling station and all that. But a bit primitive, isn't it ? "

" Exactly. That's what make me consider it. We'd have a free hand. No competition. Perfectly possible site for an aerodrome and hotel. We might wake up the town a bit— native government and all that. It should be easy to get a sphere of influence. I don't know." Sir Joseph, contemplative, sucked his moustache. " It might be worth while sending an agent there. Does your brother fly now ? "

" Afraid not. He got his ticket in 1917, but he's lost his nerve since the smash."

" Pity. Does he know anything about the conditions necessary for ground work, and so on ? "

" That's possible. As a matter of fact, in the R.A.F., he was doing that kind of work, I believe. When he was on light duty."

" Do you think it would be a good idea to try him out on Lolagoba ? Let him go to the place, see the queen or whatever she is—hunt round a bit—have a look at the ground and so on, and make a report ? Could he do that kind of thing ? "

" He—just—might."

" Of course, there are half a dozen men that I could send. And I don't know whether it's worth while sending any one. But it's an idea that had occurred to me. And it just might suit your brother."

" He might make a prodigious ass of himself."

" He might. He probably will. The point is, it wouldn't matter much to any one but himself if he did. If I want to take a risk with a man, I send him to a native state where there are nothing but blacks. He can cook his books, drink himself to death, blow his brains out, do any damn thing he likes, and it's his own funeral. If I let him go where there were other white men, the reputation of the firm might get damaged."

" Yes. I see."

" Well ? "

" It's most uncommonly decent of you."

" Nonsense. I may be doing a good day's work for myself.
Send your brother round some time and let me have a look
at him."

" Send him ? " Maurice smiled wryly.

" Oh, ho ! Like that is it ? Well, bring him. Ask him—
beg him. Anything you like so long as you don't expect me
to go to him."

They left it at that ; but Maurice at dinner that night
in the new flat which he had taken for his mother in
Knightsbridge, was able to say that he had kept his promise.

CHAPTER V

SID GRANGER REBUKES A PRODIGAL

THE scudding rain struck the faces of the waiting queue
like an insult. Some men turned their backs to it, huddling
their coats close round their ears. Others shrank into the
shallow doorway.

" Roll on Christmas ! " said Mick, apropos of nothing.

Sid Granger twirled a mangled cigarette between his lips,
inhaled furiously, encountered a deposit of grit, spat it out,
and swore.

" Christ, what a life ! Thirteen years after the bloody
war's over. Thirteen years after the—— Hell ! Who'd'you
think you're shoving, eh ? "

" Keep a civil tongue, mate. I didn't make the war—
nor the weather." The old builder's labourer twisted the
metal watch chain, from which no watch now hung, and
made room in the doorway.

" Who said you did, grandad ? The capit'lists made the
war. They made the bleedin' peace. And they made this
bleedin' Labour Exchange an' all."

" I wish they'd made you shut up, Sid Granger," interrupted a thickset young man in a plum-coloured sweater,
shabby plus-fours, a bowler hat and black sand shoes. His
eccentricity of attire may have been due to his personal
taste ; but it was an act of God which had given him his

ferocious squint, and an act of the king's enemies that had
deprived him of two fingers on the left hand.

" Who are you to talk ? " retorted Sid. " You're all right.
You got a partial disablement pension for being a traitor to
your class, I *don't* think. Look at you ! All dolled up like
a cinema star. We all know you, Ronald Coleman. You're
the bad boy of the family, you are—and they kill the fatted
calf every time you go home crying to mother."

" Oh, stow it ! "

But Sid would not stow it. He, like the others, was cold,
damp and disheartened ; but he was not subdued. His
spirits rose as his tongue ran like the engine of a well-oiled
car. " You say stow it ! " he cried to the more recent
interrupter, a thin, respectable-looking young man, with
the slightly superior air of a clerk. " And we all know who
you are. You're the good boy of the family, mother's little
joy an' comfort. When you want to leave the room, you
say ' Please, teacher ! ' and if she asks ' Where are you going
to, Tommy ? ' you *tell* her. You salute the Union Jack,
and sing the National Anthem, and you wear your cap
like the bleedin' Prince of Wales to show your loyal senti-
ments, and you vote Tory at every damned election just
to spite the rest of us. Old comrades of the Great War—
yah ! "

The clerk looked for a minute as though he were going to
strike Sid. His grey face flushed ; his weak lips parted
from his clenched teeth. But the habit of docility was too
strong.

" Look at you. A bleedin' poppy in your button hole,"
continued his tormentor. " How much did you pay for
that ? And as for Blossom-face here"—turning to the ex-
soldier in plus-fours—" he's gotta couple. Grandad's got
one too, but you can't blame him. He's in his second childhood, he is. I suppose you got yours from a stuffed duchess
all togged up to kill—thought it an honour to touch her
lily-white hand. ' Oh, please, Mr. Man, won't you buy a
poppy for the poor soldiers ? ' ' I'm a poor soldier myself,
mam—always ready to help my old comrades. Here's a
penny. I'm out of work because my boss found a new way
of saving overheads and sacked me an' half my mates,
and we've been on the dole till we came off it, and now

we're waitin' at the Labour Exchange queueing up for
Paradise—in blessed hope of the glorious resurrection of
the Socialist Party, now lately buried by your class and
that bloody traitor Ramsay MacDonald. But I'll buy a
pretty flower for old sake's sake, thank you ! ' "

" You shut your ugly face," growled the plus-four man,
who had, indeed, paid a penny for his poppy from an
ordinary-looking young suburban miss, who truly had
appeared to him as the very flower of youth and freshness,
with her cheeks glowing in the sharp wind, her shy smile
and her fashionable synthetic fur coat. " You shut your
ugly face, or I'll shut it for you."

A loud hooting resounded from the street corner and a
motor bicycle scraped and staggered up to the queue, then
died with the spluttering surrender of its species, and sank
sideways as its rider dismounted and kicked down the foot-
rest. A lean young man in a belted leather coat, consider-
ably the worse for wear, hatless, but wearing worn gauntlet
gloves, came forward to the queue.

" Hallo, Captain. What are you doing here ? " cried Sid,
with malignant pleasure. " Come to give us a nice little
Armistice Day chat on Socialism ? A fat lot of use Socialism
did us in the last election ! Turn-coats. Bourgeois ! "

" Captain nothing," said the newcomer. " I didn't expect
to see you here, Granger."

" Captain Durrant, friends. One of our brave heroes we
all fought to make homes for." Sid tapped his forehead
meaningly. " Not at home now—there anyway. Thinks
Mister Arthur Henderson can save us from *Mister* Mac-
Donald and *Mister* Baldwin." The spite of his hissing
" *Mister* " was terrific.

" You'll have mist an eye in a minute if you don't watch
out," grunted Plus-fours.

The motor cyclist put his hand in his pocket and produced a battered metal cigarette case. He offered it to Sid,
" Have one ? "

Mr. Granger took it with a sneer.

" Anything to oblige." Plus-fours took one too. Grandad
shook his head, coughing.

" Now, honest, spit it out, Captain. What are you doing
here ? "

" I can't understand," murmured Bill Durrant, bending
into the shelter of his mackintosh to light a cigarette, " why
you should persist in calling me Captain. In the first place
it is not, as I have pointed out several times, any longer
my correct title. In the second place, I thought you were a
Communist and bound therefore to call me comrade."

" Comrade ? Comrade be b——. When you're standing
here waiting for a job with the proletariat, I'll call you
comrade."

" Call away, then, Comrade Sid. The hour has come."

" I *don't* think."

" I do. What are the prospects ? Do you think this wind
is likely to blow us a good fall of snow that will require
sweeping away ? Is there any chance of a burst in a main
water pipe that might cause a little flooding ? You're an
expert, Sid, in the manœuvres of the wicked capitalists
and the economies of Tory municipalities. What do you
think ? "

" Go on—Captain."

" Comrade."

" Mister Durrant. You're not really out of a job."

" I am."

" Honest ? "

" Honest."

" Then it's a damn shame to take the bread out of the
mouths of the working class. There's grandad there trying
to keep a sick daughter with four—or is it five—kids,
and Tuppy up there been off benefit four months, and
me——"

" With an ever unslaked thirst—I know it, Sid."

" Why can't your fine relatives keep you ? Driving about
in their Rolls-Royces and getting into parliament ! "

" Ah, why, indeed ? Family feeling, Sid, is not what it
used to be. The *Daily Mail* says so. And the *Daily Mail* is
always right."

" Now, look here, Mr. Durrant. What's the game ? "

Sid had drawn the newcomer a little apart from the
others and questioned him with genuine curiosity.

" There is no game. Like you, I am unemployed. Like
you, I am genuinely seeking work. At least, I think I am ;
the question is, are you ? "

" I thought you were private secretary to old Darton,
ex-Power Minister."

" You may not have observed in your assiduous perusal
of the press, my dear Sidney, that George Darton, like
several other members of the late ministry, is no longer in
office ; nor is he in parliament, nor is he even in a job. It
may not be long before he, like his late secretary, is
standing in a queue waiting to shovel non-existent
snow."

" Rot ; you don't tell me Darton didn't feather his nest
while he was consorting with dukes an' royalty. All those
pale pink Socialists did pretty well out of the pockets of the
working man before they let him down."

" To my knowledge, Darton had a fairly sound job, in an
insurance office in Glasgow, which he gave up when he
entered parliament—for £400 a year. He can't have been
a rich man when he took on the Power job. And that's
only worth £1200 a year. Come, come, Comrade Granger,
it's not easy to become a great capitalist on that. Remember
the heavy expenses involved in being a minister. He had
to employ me among other things."

" Where's that little reporter girl who used to keep
hanging round ? Can't she get you a job in her office ? "

" Alas, no. Provincial newspapers seem to have a singular
prejudice against supernumeraries."

Sid Granger looked at the tall young man beside him and
then at the group straggling round the Labour Exchange.
Old men with fumbling, toothless mouths and useless
hands ; self-respecting, highly-skilled artisans, loathing
their new humiliation, shy, awkward, and suffering ; young
boys who had never done a week's work since leaving school,
and on whom the deterioration of idleness and malnutrition
had set its mark ; middle-aged fathers of families, grown
callous from impotence to relieve the misery of their
emptying homes ; loafers to whom the anguish of society
provided an easy excuse for their individual tastes. These,
Sid thought, were admirable company for the disdainful
gentleman with the satirical tongue.

" Is this your first experiment ? "

" More or less."

" You think you're here on terms of equality with the

rest of us, I suppose ? " Sid's shrewd face had the intelligence of a malevolent monkey.

Durrant shifted his heavy leather coat.

" Not entirely."

" Oh, yes, you do. Look at those boys. See ? you know
what happens to them ? " Sid indicated two pretty pink-
faced youths. " Make 'em join up in the Flying Corps—
make men of them, eh ? Can't be a man of the world until
they've seen the world ? A nice fairy-story they'll find
that in the army ! " In reply to the other man's raised
eyebrows, he persisted : " You know it's true."

" It might be."

" No stamina. Bread and margarine. What d'you
expect ? "

" Aren't you being a little sentimental ? Homosexuality is not necessarily due to malnutrition by any
means. On the contrary——"

" Now, then, Durrant. Don't you be so bleedin' clever.
Did I ever say it was ? No. What I say is, those lads have
no stamina because they've got no guts, and they've got no
guts because they're got no physique, an' they've got no
physique because they're permanently underfed, and they're
underfed because they've never done a day's work, and their
fathers haven't done more'n three days' work since they
were school age. And they've lived on the dole and they'll
die in jail if they're not in the bug-house—and they're
unemployed an' unemployable. And if that's not the result
of your blasted capit'list system, I want to know what
is."

" It's not my system. If you'd once really listened during
these meetings at Perynn, you would know that. But it is
as I feared. My best eloquence is wasted ! "

" Why must you always talk in that damned
satirical way ? You've got brains all right. So have I."

" I never denied that."

" But you've got ten times my education. You're the
gentleman. I'm a worker—*and* not ashamed of it. But I
tell you this. You call yourself a Socialist. You come down
here and wait with us for a job at the Labour Exchange.
And you think you're not taking an advantage of your class !
Look at you. Motor bike. Clothes. Look at your hands !

Every time you talk you give yourself away. You can't suddenly get rid of all those things your class give you. If you and I were up for a job—who'd get it ? "

Jumping up and down with a sort of dancing motion in his broken shoes, Sid Granger confronted his acquaintance. He had heard Durrant speak for the Socialist candidate at Perynn. He had enjoyed more than one half-friendly, half-antagonistic encounter with him. Partly from genuine resentment, but still more from a temperamental impulse which made him always prefer conflict to boredom, Sid challenged him. It was something to do. The unexpected encounter brought drama into a situation only too familiar and wearisome, and Sid lived for drama.

He observed also that his words were not entirely without effect on Durrant. That young man leant with his back against the wall, his coat collar turned up round his ears, his gauntlets tucked beneath his arm, while with one bare, slender hand—the hand that so much outraged Sid's sense of equality—he turned over the coppers in his pocket. His lips were pursed for a soundless whistle, but his grey eyes ran over the little crowd. At that moment the door opened, and the men began to shuffle forward into the Exchange.

" Are you coming in ? Coming to take the bread out of some poor devil's mouth ? " gibed the little man. " Oh, I know your argument. You amateurs think you've got as much right to work or maintenance as the rest of us. And if this was Russia you'd have not more chance, but less— see ? But as it is, if you really want to benefit the working classes you'd better go back and live on your mother an' brother an' not come competing with us."

" I like you, Comrade Sid," Durrant replied contemplatively, " because you don't sit down under ready-made situations. You always create your own. You intrude yourself——"

" No—that's you. Intrusion's your middle name." Sid grinned. The morning had become unexpectedly entertaining. The two progressed as far as the inner entrance to the exchange. A match-boarding partition, painted white, cut off the large room from the door into the street, leaving a small lobby from which Sid and his companion could watch the grey comedy played within. The men drearily slouching up to the tables, replied to clerks who drowsed or snapped according to their individual natures.

" ' Too unhappy to be kind,' " murmured Bill Durrant.

" What's that ? "

" A quotation from a very true poem by a Cambridge don who called himself a Shropshire lad. The clerks also have received a cut in pay. Some of them joined the Civil Servants' Protest Procession. We're all in the same boat, Sid. They're a spotty-faced, spiritless lot, I think. Don't you ? Not much hope of revolution yet ; eh ? "

But at that moment, something happened.

The long melancholy moan of a siren swelled, not so much into a sound, as into a vibration in the air. The clerk at the nearest table glanced up at the office clock, then wearily pushing a weight over his papers, rose and stood to attention. The others rose too. The unemployed gathered themselves together as though remembering with difficulty their indvidual relationship to society. As citizens and soldiers, Oddfellows, Freemasons, bandsmen, and fathers of families, they emerged for two minutes from the annihilating twilight of the Labour Exchange and stood upright. The ugly, merciless room became the chapel of a devotional cult, as the living saluted the memory of the fortunate dead.

A car, passing along the street, stopped with a squeal of brakes.

Sid glanced quizzically at the ex-flying officer beside him. " Down-and-out officer in Labour Exchange on Remembrance Day," he muttered. Thin, damp and dishevelled, his longish brown hair lank in the rain, a mud-splash on his cheek, Captain Durrant hardly looked as though he had profited greatly by his thirteen years of peace. Sid wondered if he was thinking about his experiences in France, his dead friends, and his ruined life. Gossip in Perynn said he was divorced. Good for him ; it was better to be divorced than tied to a woman.

Christ ! what a farce. Two minutes' silence. Remembrance Day. Poppies. " Their name liveth for evermore." Unknown warriors. Sid looked down the long, hideous, hopeless room. Unknown warriors. Casualties in the class war. Fools. Driven sheep. Sid wasn't a sheep, anyway.

He'd rather be a wolf than a sheep. Earwig. That was what
one of those fellows had called him. " Dirty little earwig."
Well. He knew a thing or two. He'd like to march the whole
pack of them down Whitehall into that tremendous and
glittering ceremony round the Cenotaph, with its massed
bands, and gleaming accoutrements, and the white surplices
of the choir boys fluttering. That would show 'em. After
thirteen years. Some fools believed that if you took photographs of the Cenotaph crowd during the silence, you could
catch spirit-forms on the negative. Sid would like to show
them physical forms. The killed ? Here were the Fallen.
These were the Casualty Lists of peace—the yellowed
records fluttering now on the clerk's desk. " Albert Taylor
—ex-private, London-Scottish. Tuberculosis contracted
after gassing in 1918. Detected eighteen months too late
to be called attributable to war service. Tried light employment for three years, but health constantly breaking
down. On the dole." " Reg Batley, aged twenty-two.
Engaged on leaving school as errand boy to grocer. Dis-
charged for sake of economy after passing insurable age.
Never employed since." He composed his own case-paper.
" Sidney Rex Granger—of no definite occupation.   Ex-
weigh-clerk, night watchman, labourer, anything, ex-
corporal in the Fourth West Yorks (God forgive him for a
born fool !). Unemployed since 1923, owing to foreign
competition in the British coal industry after the development of the Ruhr." Fine their names would all look on the
Cenotaph. Here was a nice tomb on which a Prince could
lay his pretty flowers.

A dog barked. As though in answer, the buzzers, hooters
and sirens called to each other across the silent city.
" The All Clear," sneered Sid, as the rigidity of the tension
relaxed, and the men crumpled into their familiar postures.
Bill Durrant flicked out into the street a cigarette end that
he had been holding throughout the silence and that had,
for the last few seconds, burned his fingers.

" Well ? " sneered Sid. " Coming ? "

" No. I don't think so. As you say—why not induce my
mother to kill the fatted calf ? "

" Would she ? "

" Only too readily."

Sid's face twisted unexpectedly into a benevolent grin. " More luck for you. Hope it tastes good. Get on out while the going's good. Stop outside——" He indicated the doorway. " Abandon hope all ye that enter here. Stop outside. Keep in your own class while you've got one."

" And after the revolution you'll hang me on a lamp-post ? "

" You've said it."

Bill Durrant smiled.

" Bribery any use ? " He produced a handful of silver from his pocket. " When you've done your business, will you come and let us have a last drink together—so to speak ? Drink to the Revolution ? I'll wait here for you."

Sid glanced at him quizzically.

" Still the squire, condescending kindly to the bright working man ? " he teased. But there was no venom in his sneer. He and Durrant understood each other well enough. They were the only two men of spirit in that hole. " All right—I'll come. Better not wait in the wet. I'll come across to the Duke's Head. So-long."

" Don't be too long." Bill Durrant went off whistling into the rain.

" Rum chap. Now have I really made him change his plans ? Can I send him home to mother ? "

To change the life of so remote, and even shabbily splendid a creature as Captain Durrant, brother of the M.P. for North Donnington, was an achievement. It lifted Sid from the desolate group about him. It filled his morning with drama. He had exerted his personality, vindicated his principles, impressed his will upon the outside world. A good morning's work.

" Hurry along now," yapped the weary clerk. " We're late. Get a move on."

CHAPTER VI

JEAN STANBURY URGES ADVENTURE

JEAN STANBURY entered her cottage, loving it. No place in the world could possibly please her more, she thought, setting down paper bags on the clean kitchen table, lighting the gas fire in the big upstairs sitting-room, and changing her clothes in the dark little downstairs room where she slept.

After years of sharing bedrooms in her parent's house, of " making do " on sofas, and awaiting invasion at all hours, she had a home of her own, into which she could shut herself night after night, and remain confident of privacy, blissfully undisturbed. These were her possessions. The honey-coloured walls, the rows of books, the beech leaves in great earthenware jars, the jade dragon that George had sent her, represented her taste.

It was not a particularly original taste. Dozens of other sitting-rooms in Chelsea were carpeted with the same brown whipcord and curtained with the same green linen. But Jean never professed originality. All that she asked of a home was privacy and restfulness, and the exquisite welcome given her by her own treasures at the end of a long day. There they were : the dragon that her brother George had sent her from China ; Robert's Algerian rug ; Martin's kaross from Nairobi—the tributes presented to her by the brothers whom she had brought up and sent out into the world ; but not a stick, not a cup from the house in Highgate. Nothing, nothing, thank Heaven, to remind her of those days.

Jean was assistant editor of *The Byeword*, a weekly review devoted to the exposure of our more purulent national and international evils. Its editor, Hubert Hailebury Carter, was a man of such sensibility that he was forced, for five days in the week, to mitigate his suffering from these offences by drinking whisky in his Sussex home, and writing acid little satires against Imperialism or Fascism, or ill-treatment of minorities. During his absence from the office, Jean, for a salary of three hundred and twenty pounds a year, expended upon the paper the energy and devotion that she had once concentrated upon her large and helpless family. A father crippled by rheumatoid arthritis, a mother who collapsed after her seventh confinement into hypochondriacal neurasthenia, and five younger brothers, had given Jean experience in tending difficult and precarious lives. How she had scrambled through her degree course at London University, she never knew. But when at last her widowed mother failed to recover from the shock of her favourite son's death in China, after three others had been killed in the war, and the fifth gone off for ever to East Africa, Jean had given a great sigh of shocked relief, sold the house in Highgate, taken her Chelsea cottage on a thirty years' lease, and locked the door against domestic intrusion for ever and ever.

" I'll never do anything for any one again in all my life," said she. It was the resolve, not of a selfish person, but of a naturally obliging one, satiated by a career of altruism. " Ah, Jean, wait until you marry ! " her friends had said with the coy assurance of all friends suggesting matrimony.

" I do not intend to marry," Jean declared. " I have seen enough of family life to last for several generations, thank you. All I want now is a steady job, a latch key to my own cottage, and undisturbed sleep at night."

Because she was intelligent, friendly, and as attractive as any young woman with these other qualities can be nowadays, if she so desires, her friends continued to laugh. She always got on well with men, they said. Her brothers had trained her admirably. She was so capable in the house. She'd make a splendid mother. All modern psychologists warned us against the frustrations of an abnormal sex life. Marriage and motherhood. . . . Jean listened politely. She did not like to consider herself abnormal and incomplete. But she could not honestly discern any inconveniences in her virgin state, and its conveniences were congenial to her.

She had lived alone for six years now, and liked it as well as ever.

Thus she was not entirely pleased when, just as she was

washing her hands in the backyard-bathroom, she heard the
telephone bell, and answering, recognised Bill Durrant's
voice. He asked her to dine with him in Soho. She refused.
She was too tired to set out once more towards Bloomsbury,
she said. " Then the Chelsea Grill ? " " Oh, *no*, Bill. Not
to-night." " But I must see you. I must have your advice.
It's vital." " Oh, dear. Then you'd better come and feed
here. But you'll have to do with eggs," and she hung up
the receiver, growling to herself over her wasted evening,
reluctant, but docile.

Why was it, she wondered, that men always seemed to
want so much advice ? They never took it unless it was a
confirmation of their own desires, but they liked to have it.
They liked to march fortified by feminine approval as well
as by masculine initiative. Would women, she mused
while in the kitchen, opening paper bags, laying out plates
and knives and spoons on trays, cutting tomatoes, grating
cheese, and scraping the remnants of ham from a knuckle
bone, would women have done better through life if they
had more consistently demanded from men the toll of
daily council ? If, instead of merely doing things, they had
waylaid friends, lovers, husbands, and brothers, and set
before them this plan and the other, crying dramatically,
" This step will make or mar me ! " Or, " If I go wrong here,
I'm done ! " Or, " But in spite of God and the devil, I'll do
it yet ! " Women, reflected Jean, too often knew that, as
likely as not, they would never be done till dead. Their
personal obligations rarely admitted the drama of finality.
Nor did they see God and the devil as their adversaries.
Their own shortcomings and the limitations of circumstance
they commonly found to be sufficient handicap. It had
been, she decided, very stupid of them ; they were the
sufferers. But long-formed habits are difficult to change ;
and Jean, bred in the ancient school of feminine solicitude,
felt too old to acquire a wiser code.

Her meditations about men and women were general, but
her feelings towards Bill Durrant were particular enough.
He had been her brother Stephen's friend. And Stephen
had been killed in the air crash which Bill insisted upon
attributing to some carelessness, some failure of responsibility, in himself. Bill had come first to Jean as her

brother's self-confessed murderer. She had been forced to lay aside her own sorrow and comfort him. They had stepped straight from their first meeting into intimacy, the strange maternal-penitential intimacy of a not too imaginative woman and a nerve-racked, hag-ridden, and tormented man. Since then he had returned to her a hundred times, as though the injury he had done her (which she still declared to be all nonsense) constituted a valid claim to her sympathy, her patience and her sheltering strength. There had been a time before he went to the Argentine and married Cynthia, when she had felt herself carefully warding off his proposals to her, and she had even toyed with her image of him as her husband, and found it, apart from her antipathy to family life, not too displeasing. Then he had returned, in the throes of his matrimonial disaster, introduced her to his handsome, ego-centric, intolerant Cynthia, and placed ever increasing reliance upon her disinterested friendship.

He would absent himself for weeks together, without a word or a postcard. Then he would ring up, as he had done to-night, peremptory and impatient ; or she would lift her eyes from the kitchen table as she prepared her solitary supper, and see his slim figure outside her window, and his impish, irresponsible smile. And always her heart jumped a little; her hands on the cheese grater shook just for a moment, until she reminded herself how tiresome and selfish and unreliable he was.

When Bill arrived this evening, he found her in a characteristic attitude, seated at the kitchen table, beating eggs in a basin on her knee, and reading *The Economics of Agricultural Revival*, propped against the coffee machine. He called to her as usual through the window, and when she had let him in he greeted her with, " You know, Jean, the real reason why I never finish any of my projected literary masterpieces is because I always picture you propping the wretched volume against the cruet and deciding, between breaking an egg-shell and reaching for the fork to beat it with, whether it's worth a signed review or a short note done in the office."

" The real reason why you never finish anything," said Jean, severely, " is because you're bone idle. You've never done a real day's work in your life. Pass me the slicer, please."

"Work? Good Heavens! Haven't I helped you to get the supper a million times? And don't you make me slave like a dog?"

"The truth of the matter is, that like most men you enjoy doing things in a house because you've never *had* to do them." She bent over her omelette pan.

"Hark at her! Never *had* to! This, to me—of all people. How do you think I got on at Rinderkloof?"

"Very badly, from the way you've always complained about the hardships you endured."

He gave her the sidelong glance she knew so well, mocking, ironic, yet in some queer way, admiring, as though he were amused at and proud of her contentious spirit. And as ever, she felt the unwelcome excitement which made her immediately assure herself of how unsatisfactory he was and always would be.

He looks ill to-night, she thought. How tiresome of him. I suppose he's come again to pour out his yearning for Cynthia. Why can men never keep their sorrows to themselves? She turned the omelette with a peevish slap.

"That is *not* the way to cook an omelette, my dear girl," he observed.

"Do it yourself, then," said she crossly, and seizing the tray, carried it upstairs to lay the table, aware of his laughing eyes that followed her. His lashes were far too long for a man, she had decided, and she was glad that he would have to eat his own spoiled omelette.

But it was not spoiled. He had found the right dish and warmed it and borne it up in triumph.

Good Heavens, how could any mature, adult woman endure for half an hour the absurd egotistical childishness of men?

"Well," she said at length, for she respected justice. "It's not so bad as it might be. . . . And what's your trouble? What have you been doing?"

"Among other things, standing in a queue for a job at a Labour Exchange and getting snubbed by a drunken little Communist," said he. And with considerable humour, vivacity and exaggeration, he narrated the episode of Armistice Day.

He told her that he had really been quite desperate. He had changed his last ten shilling note, and was in debt to his landlady, to the grocer, to the laundry. He had the loan of an army friend's motor cycle, but could afford no more petrol. He knew that there was money in his name at the Earl's Court Bank, but he would not touch it. To accept an allowance from his brother, he considered, robbed him of all self-respect. He could not be both dependent and defiant. Maurice scoffed at his Socialism; he hated Maurice's smug Conservatism; their mother sided with Maurice because she secretly loved Bill. Jean knew all this without being told. She nodded at the account of the motor bicycle and held her peace.

Bill described the queue. He described the place. He described Sid Granger—" a dark, spiteful, black-eyed, crooked little fellow, dirty as an earwig. But, somehow, I like his pluck. I like his protests. There's a sort of perverted public spirit about him. You might turn a Sid Granger into a decent citizen. You can do nothing with sheep. When Sid called me an amateur I was insulted. When he claimed that I had an unfair advantage over him, he told the truth. When he ordered me home to my mother, I went. Like a whipped schoolboy. Can you explain it ? "

Jean smiled.

" Pride, Bill. You couldn't bear to hear a Sid Granger say you were taking the bread out of his mouth because you've still really got the feudal attitude. You'll do good to the poor. But you won't take favours from them. You were scared stiff of finding yourself under an obligation to any of those men. Now weren't you ? Call yourself a Socialist ? You're far more at home among Pukka Sahibs and whatnot. You ought to go overseas, to India or somewhere, where you can live like a white man, maintaining a benevolent feudal interest in the natives. Do you know what I think is really wrong with you ? You're the administrator manqué, with nothing to administer. You're one of the few men I know who are really interested in people. That's why you get tied up with so many Sid Grangers and such."

" Well, for once in your life, you and my excellent
brother Maurice appear to think alike."

" What do you mean ? "

" He's offered me a job to go out and look after the
poor natives."

" In India ? "

" In Africa. In a place called Lolagoba."

" Never heard of it."

" I'm disappointed in you. You know all about war debts
and transitional benefit and the taxation of land values. I
felt sure you'd know all about Lolagoba."

" I suppose it's one of Prince's right-off-the-map-
holiday centres."

" It isn't yet. And I can't think, as he's talking of sending me there, that he ever means it to be. I'm not very
clear yet, to tell the truth, where it is myself. It's somewhere near the Sudan, and it's the capital of a native state.
And Sir Joseph has got one of his romantic notions that it
might make an air port for the mails to East Africa.
Generally, Maurice manages to curb the old man's less
practical notions, but this time he sees a chance in it to get
rid of an incumbrance."

" Meaning you."

" Well, Jean—dash it all, a man must think of appear-
ances—you know—jolly awkward—ex-service brother on
the dole—Socialist and all that . . . not quite the thing,
is it ? " Bill caricatured not so much Maurice's speech as
the idiom of his thought.

" What's the idea ? "

" That I should be taken out by air and dumped down in
Lolagoba as agent of Prince's to the queen or whatever she
is, of Mandoa, to negotiate for rights to make the air port
and to see where's the best ground for it, and so on."

" I see. You *do* know something about aerodromes,
don't you ? "

" Yes. It's all very plausible." His voice had suddenly
grown bitter. His face had clouded to dramatic gloom.
She cried, " Bill !—you don't really mean it's a plan to get
rid of you ? "

He shrugged his shoulders.

" I don't know. I don't really care. If you mean has

Maurice any criminal intent ? Of course not. He's the soul of honour and respectability. But if you mean, would he be sorry if anything happened to me ? Well, really—he'd be more than human if he were. I'm an embarrassment to him. I'm pretty much of an embarrassment to myself. The world hardly seems to tumble over itself in the rush to make use of my services. On the other hand, my mother yearns to see me doing ' a man's job,' expanding the Empire, making Africa what it is, and so on. On looking back," he continued musingly, " I seem to have spent a considerable portion of my life going out into the great open spaces, so to speak, to please my mother."

" But you've always come back," said Jean brutally, for she hated self-pity and disliked Bill when he spoke bitterly of his mother who had, she thought, been very generous to him.

" I know. That's true. It's odd, isn't it, that I never seem able to make a success of things ? I'm not a fool. People like me all right. What is it ? What is it, Jean ? Am I really cursed ? Sometimes I think I am—that I've been cursed so that I can never do anything successfully. So that everything I touch crumbles to ashes. I might as well oblige my family by removing myself gracefully."

When he was in this mood, Jean definitely detested him. She admired decision, strength, intelligence, and their logical consequences—success. She could not help thinking that men and women brought their own failures upon themselves. If Bill had pulled himself together after the war, if he had returned to college and taken his degree, if he had really intended to succeed instead of drifting and finding excuses for himself, he need never have been dependent on his brother's patronage. Her face hardened. She had suffered too, fought too, faced disappointments and renunciations. Yet her cottage closed about her like a sanctuary. She had, in her limited field and to a certain stage only, won through. Further conquests lay before her. She was heartily thankful now that Bill had married Cynthia, not her. She could never love him. Love must be based on mutual respect. She had exhausted all her pity long ago.

She looked at his bent head, at the dishevelled waves of his soft, brown hair, at his strained face, too thin, too

old, too much lined, for his age. She judged him beside the
contributors to *The Byeword*, and found that with far
greater talents and advantages, he had done far less.
Other men had been through the war without making
it an excuse for every subsequent failure. If they had
suffered from " nerves," they had learned to hide their
suffering.

Bill had been spoiled. That was what was wrong with
him. His mother had spoiled him. Women had spoiled him.
Every one spoiled him. Even Maurice, in a way, spoiled
him just because he was jealous, and, being Maurice, had
to get even with his conscience. Bill had been given chances,
exceptional chances, again and again, and made no use
of them. He was saying, with the ironical air with which
he masked self-pity, " The possibilities are endless. I may
get killed on the way. In fact, nothing is more probable. Or
I may die of fever. Or I may drink myself to death. Or I
may be knifed by a merry Mandoan. Or stung by a
scorpion. Or bitten by a snake. In fact, the opportunities
for a picturesque and heroic exit almost equal those better-
advertised ones of the Great War."

But Jean was the wrong audience for this type of
humour.

" What's wrong with you, Bill," she said at last, " is that
you're far too clever at making excuses for yourself. You
blame your mother. You blame Maurice. You blame
Cynthia. No, I *will* speak." For he had winced, with an
exaggerated self-conscious display of sensibility, as though
she had stung him. " You asked my advice. You shall have
it. You're too quick at making gestures and going away in
heroic tempers, and cutting off your nose to spite your face.
All this childish running away—like a sulky schoolboy.
And now Maurice has offered you a most suitable and really
frightfully exciting job in Prince's, that a man who was
half a man would jump at, and you go about whining that
it's a polite family invitation to suicide. I've no patience
with you."

He really was roused now. But he had self-possession
enough to give a little sarcastic laugh, and say, " I see.
It's the great opportunity to make good, is it ? So glad to
know."

" Don't be so *stupid*," she retorted. " Can't you behave
for once like an adult human being instead of a tragic
cinema star ? It won't go down with me. I've known you
too long. I know Maurice, and he's a straight, decent,
honourable fellow, who shows more courage in half an hour
of his ordinary routine work than you've shown in your
whole life. Oh, I dare say you were brave enough in the
war. So were a million others. But you've shown jolly
little heroism since. How *dare* you sneer at your brother ?
He knew what he wanted to do, and he did it. What if he
has less imagination than you have ? What use has your
imagination been to you or to any one else, I should like to
know ? You've let it control you, instead of controlling it.
You've made a fetish of it. What if you did kill Stephen by
your own damned carelessness ? No. *Sit* down. It's time
some one made you face up to the truth. It's highly probable that you did kill him. You've been irresponsible ever
since, so why not then ? But what of it ? What *of* it, Bill ?
Thousands of officers after the war must have realised that
owing to something that they had inadvertently done or
left undone, other men had lost their lives. But they haven't
gone mooning about, excusing every other inefficiency by
saying, ' There's a curse on me.' They've tried to do something useful in the world to make up for the harm they once
did. If you were a man now—instead of—whatever you are
or think you are—you'd go and take this Mandoan job and
make something of it. What if it is a wild-goose chase ?
Catch your wild goose. What if Maurice doesn't think you
you can pull it off ? Show him he's wrong. Get your concession. Construct your air port. Build your hotel. . . .
But, of course, you won't. You'll come back in three months
very pathetic and devastated, drinking like a fish, shaking
with malaria because you were too slack to keep up your
mosquito net, and too self-indulgent to take enough
quinine ; and we shall all be very sorry for you ; and your
mother will welcome you, like the returned prodigal, as
usual. " Oh, go away. I've got no use for you. Nothing I
say can possibly penetrate your complacency. You wrap it
up in cheap cynicism, but we all know that you're so
damn pleased with yourself——"

She could not continue. Tears and fury choked her. Oh,

why were women cursed by this infirmity of tears, when all they felt was anger ?

Bill showed no signs of any inclination to weep. He had risen and stood with his back to the window, very stern and dignified.

" If you have finished telling me what you really think of me, perhaps you will excuse me," he said quietly.

It might have been Jean who deserved the reproach of hysteria.

" Go—for goodness' sake ! " she cried.

" Then I will wish you—good evening."

She tried to laugh at his pose of superiority, but the laugh broke on a sob. She heard the door close and his steps on the creaking stair. The familiar banging of the front door told her that he had really gone.

She sat up and saw her room empty, the green curtains blowing against the open window, the supper unfinished on the table.

She dropped her head on her hands, and remained for a moment, abandoned to humiliating tears.

Then, briskly, she pulled herself together, raised her head, blew her nose, cleared the table, arranged her papers, and sat down to finish *The Economics of Agriculture*. It was a better book than she had expected, and really deserved a long review. If Jenkins would do it for current rates ? She made a note.

CHAPTER VII

MAURICE DURRANT INVOKES AUTHORITY

MAURICE DURRANT'S attitude towards parliament, as towards a number of other institutions, was unconsciously but incorrigibly romantic. Some members enter the House already disillusioned. Not even their first recognition by the policemen at the doors stirs their pulses. The worn brasses on the pavement of St. Stephen's Hall mean no more to them than the advertisements in a station waiting-room. Legislation is a business like any other business, more tedious than some and less remunerative than most, but useful as a means to an end ; and that is all there is to it.

To others, and Maurice Durrant was among them, age cannot wither nor custom stale the infinite variety of Westminster. When he spoke to the electors of North Donnington about the iniquity of a trade union caucus dictating to the British cabinet, he actually saw treason striking at the heart of the mother of parliaments. His references to the heritage of England, her noble traditions of justice, and her imperial responsibilities, were utterly sincere. To him the monarchy was a sacred trust, disloyalty blasphemous, and the British constitution (so oddly compounded of anomalies, impossibilities and fortuitous convenience) an incontrovertible sign of political genius. The precincts of parliament covered holy ground. The brightly-coloured frescoes in the lobby (all but the tempestuous King John which he mistrusted), represented to him decisive incidents in a story of freedom slowly broadening down from precedent to precedent. Membership of this historic House was an honour for the honourable. Maurice himself was now a member. He intended quite humbly to be worthy of it.

All this he felt rather than thought. Certainly he never spoke of it except on platforms, where the rules of conventional English reticence are laid aside. His natural romanticism was overlaid with an acquired sophistication, and his ordinary acquaintances thought of him as a worldly-wise and well-informed young man, rather exceptionally intelligent and alert:

He did not fall into the usual errors of the unsophisticated. He did not dream of holding the House spell-bound by his eloquence in a dramatic maiden speech. Aware that the flower, Influence, rarely grows in public places, he set himself to cultivate it during little dinners, in small acts of service to members of the treasury bench, and in assiduous attendance at committees, institutes, and associations. He spent many hours in the bars, restaurants, subterranean alcoves and other unofficial meeting-places of the House exploring abstruse problems of the technique of success, the art of putting one's personality across, and the importance of contacts.

His mother was his confidante. Nightly he explained to her how he had lunched with so-and-so to " put across " such-and-such a policy. He and his friends were continually engaged in " pulling " something " off," " putting " something " over," or " knocking " something " on the head." Mrs. Durrant soon acquired the exhilarating notion that the lobbies buzzed with world-shattering intrigues. Luncheons were of greater importance than divisions—a fact hardly surprising in a House dominated by an unshakable majority. One lunched with a man over Manchuria, or the gold standard, or the Rent Restriction Act. Every encounter had its hidden purpose. No primrose by the river's brim was less simple to Wordsworth than a card for an " At Home " to Maurice Durrant. Whenever two or three members of a political party were gathered together, there the unholy ghost of oblique manœuvre was in the midst of them. Conversation with an under-secretary uplifted Maurice as intimacy with an archbishop uplifts a fervent Catholic ; but he never thought of seeking such interviews directly. If he wanted to make a suggestion to a cabinet minister, he approached a colonel whose sister had married a professor who was friendly with a peer who had sat on a committee with the man whom he desired to approach.

Thus life became immensely complicated, fatiguing and exciting. His work at Prince's now fell into its place in an intricate plan of campaign, the ultimate object of which he never quite acknowledged even to himself.

Indeed, he had no simple objective. Maurice was not by any means merely a self-interested careerist. He sincerely desired to promote the good of Prince's, of Sir Joseph, of the Conservative Party, of the Empire, even of his brother. Bill did him wrong. Maurice had no intention of putting an inconvenient relative quietly out of the way. He wished nothing but good to all men of good will. But, conscious of the truth that it is more blessed to give than to receive, he desired to be in a position to confer rather than to accept benefits. He wanted to be the business genius through whom Prince's was spared the worst effects of the financial crisis. He wanted to prove that the victory of the National Government had been an unmitigated boon to travel agents. From the purest motives in the world, he desired power.

Among other subjects which he sought to " put across " was the Mandoan affair. He needed the benevolence of the Foreign Office, to support him in encounters with the government of Mandoa ; of the Air Ministry, to encourage trans-African transport ; and of the Colonial Office which should be grateful for British enterprise so near Uganda.

The man to help him, he decided, was H. M. Warrington. H. M. knew every one. If H. M. saw possibilities in Mandoa, the blessing of the treasury bench was practically assured.

Henry Marchant Warrington was one of those quiet, slow-speaking, slow-thinking persons whose influence on public affairs is as unquestionable as it is inexplicable. Officially he was parliamentary secretary to an under-secretary. But unofficially he was a doorkeeper in the House of Israel. Formal, pompous, reticent, he bridged a deep gulf of natural stupidity by an obstinate belief in his own omniscience and a dogged application to detail which almost justified that faith. Having inherited immense wealth, he married in a moment of youthful indiscretion the daughter of a prominent peer, and found himself committed to the embarrassment of being announced at parties as " Mr. Warrington and Lady Muriel Warrington," and of seeing his photograph in the *Tatler* described as " the husband of the lovely Lady Muriel."

It was his sense of decorum rather than his masculine

vanity which was outraged by these solecisms, and he proceeded immediately to work for the peerage which alone would restore the perfect ritual of address. This pursuit, though discussed openly by his friends, was neither acknowledged by himself nor suspected by the leaders whom he served so diligently. Maurice, however, recognised him as a master of technique, admired his sure plodding progress to authority, and coveted the advantage of his co-operation.

He secured, after elaborate manœuvres, an introduction to him. He invited him to lunch, but, wishing to make a good impression, asked also Sir Joseph, whom as a notable character, most people were pleased to meet, and a distinguished Italian publicist who was passing through London and whom Maurice wished to please. The conversation at luncheon was, therefore, general, and never got nearer to Mandoa than a passing reference to Italian ambitions in North Africa.

Next, Maurice waylaid Warrington at a reception, and spent ten minutes in friendly discussion of the pound, American architecture, and " Cavalcade." So anxious was he to avoid the appearance of interested motive that he deliberately shied off from a possible opening by way of the effect of the Exchange on foreign travel, and fled to the universal sanctuary of anecdote.

After that, he hardly liked to suggest another meal. He did not even care to cultivate Warrington too assiduously in the House. The thought of going straight to him and asking his opinion of Sir Joseph's proposition never entered his head.

His pursuit was undeviating but so subtly masked that, even with his quarry before him, he was helpless.

At last, however, he found him in the Harcourt Rooms, seated alone at a table, finishing his coffee. They exchanged greetings, and Maurice slid into the vacant chair, accepted a cigarette, agreed with a comment of Warrington's on the futility of the Socialist motion then before the House, told a new anecdote about George Lansbury, told several anecdotes about Jews and Indians, agreed with Warrington's rather banal remarks on the Round Table Conference, and felt increasingly desperate about his Mandoan scheme.

The tape on the wall clicked and passed on, recording the speech of another, and of yet another member. Silence like a blight settled upon Maurice and H. M. Warrington. Maurice twice cleared his throat to speak, turned a contemplated sentence over in his mind, and dismissed it as unsuitable. Then, as from a long distance away, his companion's voice asked astonishingly, " By the way; you're a man who specialises in outlandish quarters of the globe, Durrant. I've been meaning to ask you for some time and did not get a chance. Have you ever heard of a little spot called Mandoa_? Somewhere not far from the Sudan ? "

Maurice choked, but he succeeded in turning the choke into a cough, and in observing nonchalantly, " Why, yes. Mandoa. As a matter of fact, I'm rather interested in it. Are you by any chance thinking of going there ? "

" No. But I met a very charming woman the other day who told me a most romantic tale about being stranded there with an American movie company."

" You mean Jane Crossgill ? "

" Ah. You've met her ? "

Maurice had not, but Sir Joseph had reported her conversation, and it came, he considered, really to the same thing.

" She is delicious," he countered. " Have you seen her on the screen ? A very finished artist, I understand."

" I have never yet been able to acclimatise myself to the cinema," said Warrington. " Foolish, I know. My more progressive friends tell me how much I miss. Now, tell me, is this Mandoa really a perfect medieval state—a sort of uncorrupted Abyssinia ? It sounds fantastic."

" From what I have heard it is fantastic ; though not as fantastic as an uncorrupted Abyssinia. If there is anywhere more corrupt than the Christian Empire of Ethopia, I have yet to find it. The Crown Prince is coming over—I dare say you've heard ?—No—Mandoa's a little place. A few hundred square miles, mostly dry tableland between the marshes of the White Nile and the hills ; completely shut away from any one approaching by road or boat, but quite accessible by air. Jerry Sanders, the flying man, landed there, you know. He tells me that there's an open

space near Lolagoba, the capital, that makes an almost
perfect natural aerodrome. God obviously intended the
place as a station on the Cairo-East African-Durban route.
Much better than Juba. But God proposes and waits for
man to act."

" Is man going to act ? "

" I don't know. What's your opinion ? Here's a little
native state—run as the blacks do run their states—
slavery, priesthood—they call themselves Christians, but
in Mandoa every priest becomes an archbishop, so you can
imagine the mess—a kind of grossly tyrannical feudalism—
plagues, poverty, stagnation and all the rest of it. But
certain natural resources. A perfect air port. Water quite
easily accessible, Sanders thinks, by artesian wells and so
on. Heaven knows what undeveloped resources. But no
one will go there because there's nothing to go for. I believe
every single European who's ever been in Mandoa, went
there by accident. Yet I'm pretty sure—from all I've heard
—that there are possibilities——"

" Are you thinking of going there ? "

" My brother is. He was a flying man in the war. Smashed
up a bit and hasn't done much since. We thought at Prince's
we might give him a chance. He's rather an expert at
aerodromes and surfaces and so on. Of course there *may* be
nothing in it. But on the other hand—— Well—you know
better than I the British position both in the Sudan and in
Abyssinia. You heard Mackenzie's allegations about slave
raids into Kenya and Uganda across the frontier. Now,
would it, or would it not, be a good thing if a British firm
could secure a concession from the Mandoans to make an
air port there ? Centre of European trade, stepping-stone
to East Africa, civilising influence—all that kind of thing ? "

Warrington hummed and hawed. He had reduced non-
commitment to a fine art.

" I should have to consider a good many things before I
expressed an opinion. Are you really serious ? "

" Up to a point. That is, my brother really is going to
see what the possibilities are."

" Have you discussed the matter with the Foreign
Office ? "

" Not yet. I rather thought . . ."

In short, Maurice needed Warrington's help.

" The permanent officials are your men. Get them on your side and you're safe. The Air Ministry's all right. Always enterprising where it costs them nothing. But you'll have to be careful with the Foreign Office. It has the Sudan *and* Abyssinia under its wing."

There followed technical details ; but Warrington was a man of resource. The establishment of an air port at Lolagoba really depended on the relationship of a certain high official in the Air Ministry with another high official in the Colonial Office ; it involved the playing off of an under-secretary against the Minister of another department. It could be expressed in tactical advantages which lay wholly within the boundaries of Whitehall. The possible complications with Abyssinia ; the hypothetical minerals of the Mandoan escarpment ; the cultural influence of a Prince's hotel set down in Lolagoba, were all counters in the game of Westminster chess.

Warrington's mind ground slowly, but it ground exceeding small. It reduced all Sir Joseph's grandiose designs of imperial scope to minor moves in this departmental game.

" The important thing," he concluded, " is to get Griffin on our side. Griffin's the man. But he's been thoroughly well inoculated by the anti-slavery bug. You say there's a danger of slave raids from Mandoa ? "

" A danger ? They happen."

" Ever since Griffin went to Geneva and handled that anti-slavery convention he's not been quite sane on the subject. That may be just as well. We'd better see Griffin. Yes. Certainly. Griffin's our man."

Before Maurice left Warrington they had agreed to lunch Griffin on Mandoa—and lunch him well.

CHAPTER VIII

" THE BYEWORD " ADVERTISES PRINCE'S LIMITED

"THE BYEWORD" went to press on Wednesday. On
Tuesdays the titular editor, Hubert Hailebury Carter, if
he felt well enough, came up from his Sussex home and
appeared in the office at about half-past eleven. In order
to reach his own sanctum he had to pass through the room
where Jean sat dictating letters to the typist. During
Thursdays, Fridays and Mondays she had the paper to
herself, and by Tuesday mornings it was usually running
smoothly enough, but the moment that heavy tread resounded along the corridor and the editor flung open the
door and strode in, chaos was come again.

The extent of the chaos, which lasted till late on Wednesday night, when Mr. Carter caught his last train home,
depended upon a number of variable conditions—the state
of his nerves, the amount that he had drunk the day before,
the behaviour of the almost non-existent advertisers and the
follies of a distracted universe. Unfortunately for herself,
Jean had no influence over many of these accidents. She
could only keep her head and hope for the best.

On this particular Tuesday, just after the Christmas
holidays, she felt unusually impotent. The manuscript of
the heavy article, already advertised the previous week,
had not only failed to appear, but, on telephoning to the
house of its author, she found that he had, according to a
singularly stupid maid with adenoids, " God away."

" Where's he gone ? "

" I dōant knaŏw."

" Oh, but he must have left some instructions. Has he
gone for long ? "

" I doānd knoŏw."

" I mean, is he coming back to-night ? "

" Oh—doa." Then after another bout of questioning,
" They say he's god abroad."

That told Jean nothing. He might have flown to Paris for

the night, or he might have boarded the *Leviathan* for New York. The fact remained that his article on " This Manchurian Business " had not arrived, that his maid was a half-wit, and that the Lord alone knew what they were going to do about it.

At the most hopeless stage of the telephone conversation, when the voice at the other end dwindled into the inanity of a nightmare, and the more Jean questioned, the less she learned, the door opened and the editor appeared.

He was a heavy, white-faced, black-haired, round-bellied man in the late forties, who walked with a limp from a pre-war cycling accident, cultivated the picturesque by an Inverness cape and raven side-whiskers, and glared at a disappointing world malignly out of round, rather prominent, intelligent, unamiable black eyes. Convinced that society had failed to appreciate his really substantial abilities, he repaid it by perpetual doubt of its good faith on all other matters. His original and genuine Liberalism of outlook had developed into the perpetual grievance of the irreconcilable. Nothing was right, nothing fair, nothing honourable. Politicians bought office ; judges misused their power ; democracy was duped. The government, whatever its party pretensions, did those things which it ought not to have done and left undone those things which it ought to have done, and there was no health in it. Even worse was the behaviour of private individuals. They cherished a secret but bitter and undeviating grudge against Hubert Hailebury Carter ; they envied his ability, frustrated his ambitions, and deliberately set themselves to undermine his influence.

But Carter returned their malice handsomely. In *The Byeword* he had a superb instrument of revenge. His reprisals were not petty. If a lecture agent hummed and hawed over his proposed American tour, but seized with joy upon a cherub-cheeked young novelist, Carter replied by a smashing exposure of " Americanisation " in *The Byeword*. For weeks his " Americana " ridiculed the inanities of Hollywood, and the savagery of Chicago. From Wall Street to the White House, from Pittsburg University to the sea-coast of Florida, he pursued with venomous ferocity the political and cultural defects of trans-Atlantic civilisation. When the B.B.C. committed the indiscretion of omitting his name from the symposium on " Journalism of To-day," *The Byeword* rang with denunciation of the Mussolini of Savoy Hill. If an individual lacked respect for Carter or his paper, confessed his ignorance of the former's literary work, or declared his preference for a rival of the latter, the shadow of the editor's anger darkened Europe. The " Notes of the Week " bristled with warnings, condemnations and reproofs. France was manhandled, Spain castigated, Germany admonished, Russia and Italy thrown into outer darkness ; Mr. Baldwin was mocked indulgently, Mr. MacDonald openly defied. The entire world was drawn within the circle of Carter's displeasure, and had his Table of Contents that week included an article on astronomy, no doubt the stars also would have paid the penalty for human insolence.

Jean knew her editor pretty well, humoured and tolerated him, and tried to soften, whenever possible, the impact of his mighty discontents. She thought him a rather tragic figure, so cross and lonely and uncontrolled, like a bad-tempered little boy who breaks his toys to satisfy his anger against the weather. She loved her work. She was grateful to him for leaving her so much alone. She would not have exchanged him for half a dozen more estimable employers whom she knew.

That morning he began without formal greeting.

" What's the matter ? Some fool sent his stuff in late ? "

He towered above her, immense, atrabilious, vindictive, as she bent over the telephone.

" Who is it ? Who is it ? "

Unable to cope with an imbecile and a maniac at once, Jean put down the receiver and said quietly, " It's Dermond. He hasn't sent his article on Manchuria."

" He hasn't ? Then tell him to send it at once."

" His maid says he's gone abroad."

" He's what ? Gone where ? When did he go ? What arrangements did you make about his sending the article ? I suppose you did not make it clear that it was *this* week we wanted it. It is the most extraordinary thing that women never can understand the importance of practical punctuality. Get on to him please at *once* and say we

must have his copy before twelve o'clock, and come into
my office and bring the dummy with you."

With Olympian disregard of possibilities he strode into
the inner room, his cloak floating out on the storm of his
wrath, the door banging behind him.

The typist raised intimidated eyes to Jean's face.

" Just finish that letter to Rosalind Bruce. Tell her we
are delighted to know she is willing to review for us and
will let her know directly anything of her sort comes our
way . . . with kindest regards, Yours——" Jean referred
to a letter. " Sincerely. No—*very* sincerely. Don't forget
the *very*, because we probably shan't be able to use her for
months, if ever, and we can't afford to quarrel with her,
because her husband's a director of Stokes Current and Co.,
the publishers, and we've lost enough advertisements lately
in all conscience."

The typist was an old and loyal ally.

Jean gathered the dummy, her block, and pen together
and went into the editor's room, prepared for tempest. He
attacked her at once. " You knew what Dermond was like.
You should have got on to him last week. You should have
had a messenger waiting for the manuscript."

" He promised it for this morning and he's never let us
down before. It may still come by the second post or by
messenger. And if it doesn't come, I suppose we could use
that financial article of Drew's. It's good stuff and topical."

" Drew ? That man writes like a public actuary. He'd
kill the whole issue. It's inconceivable to me how absolutely
nothing is done when I'm not in this office. Have you seen
that thing of Rollet's on slavery ? "

" No. I saw he had sent something, but I haven't read it
yet."

His withering glance told her that she could not have
read it ; he never expected her to have read it ; it was too
much to have expected any woman to have read it.

" It might do. Slavery isn't much in the news just now
—but you'd better have it set up to use in case the other
thing falls through. Now where's the dummy ? "

The morning's tornado of discussion, arrangement,
telephoning, cancelling and contrivance began. At three
o'clock, Jean was able to glance through the pulls of the

substitute article on slavery. The first word her eyes lighted upon was Lolagoba.

It was very strange, she thought, how all her life she had gone without hearing of the existence of Mandoa, and suddenly she was unable to escape it.

Arthur Rollett, a fanatical and unflinching champion of Liberty, spent his time in tracking down its enemies. Any assault against free thought, free speech, free voting, free motherhood, free trade or free love stirred him to fiery protest. His drawback as a journalist was that his conclusions were foregone, but his asset was a dramatic and scorching brevity of eloquence, as though his ardour had burned out all impurity from his style. Carter published his work because it invariably took the form of denunciation, and Rollett accordingly honoured Carter as the most fearless editor in England—an opinion which the editor of *The Byeword* shared, and which raised his own estimate of Rollett's judgment.

This week he had discovered that Mandoa was the centre of an immense intrigue against the Slavery Commission of the League of Nations ; that a British commercial firm was proposing to enter into alliance with the corrupt mockery of government at Lolagoba, and to exact from it economic concessions of vast profit to absentee capitalists, in return for helping to hookwink the placid idealists of Geneva.

" Really, really, Mr. Rollett," Jean murmured as she read it. " I suppose you mean Prince's Tours, Limited, and Sir Joseph and the Durrants. This is a little too far-fetched."

She was not alone. On Tuesday afternoons her office hummed with business. A middle-aged journalist, rather deaf, and wearing a huge white muffler, sat on the arm of a chair finishing a survey of the Licensing Commission's Report. A bright young man, in tweeds and a Fair-isle jumper, was reciting limericks about Dean Inge to a tall drooping novelist in a tiger-skin coat, engaged upon searching the bookshelves for something to review.

" I'm putting in Gilbert Frankau with Wassermann and one of these Russians," she was murmuring. " So chic, I think, don't you ? To mix the rococo and the primitive."

" There once was a cleric called Inge,
    Whose pen had a notable stinge . . ."

persisted the bright young man.

" You'll have to let me have another two hundred words,
Miss Stanbury," grumbled the muffled gentleman. " I
have not dealt with clubs. We must mention clubs."

" Please," said a messenger girl, appearing breathless and
rosy-faced at the door. " Have you the pulls of the first
heavy ready for the printer ? He says . . ."

" Look here, Miss Stanbury," interrupted the novelist's
languid voice. " I won't take the Russian. I'll have the
Frankau, the Wassermann and this thing by Yegohudi.
He's a terribly pure Jugoslav, and they're *so* refreshing.
He writes about rape and tortures as though they were
faux pas at a Jane Austen tea-party."

" Yes, that's terribly funny, Mr. Dawson. . . . I'm
sorry, you *must* cut it down to eight hundred. . . . No, the
pull's not ready yet. . . . Certainly, Mrs. Coutts-Beaton.
Have the Jugoslav if he's more amusing." Jean rose with
the copy of Arthur Rollett's article and knocked resolutely
on the editor's door.

He had a habit of muttering " Come in," or " Who's
that ? " so indistinctly that it was impossible, through the
shut door, to hear a word, and then of scolding whoever
waited, for not entering immediately. Jean knew his habits.
She went in.

" What's that ? What's that ? I'm busy just now."

" I know. I'm very sorry." He was writing his leading
article, which he always reckoned to do on Monday nights ;
but which he almost invariably left until Tuesday or
Wednesday afternoons, holding up the mechanism of the
paper, swearing with rage when interrupted and trying
Jean's patience to the utmost.

" Mr. Carter, I expect you'd like me to get this article
of Rollett's glanced over by McKisach before it goes back
to the printer, wouldn't you ? " McKisach was the paper's
lawyer.

" What on earth ? Why d'you come and ask me a silly
question like that ? What's wrong with the article ? "

" Well—it's rather libellous, isn't it ? "

"Libel? Nonsense. Rollett's as careful of his facts as the Bible."

"Quite," said Jean, thinking the simile only too apt. "But I believe that this time his righteous indignation may have led him astray a little. As a matter of fact, I happen to know what he's referring to. Prince's Tours, Limited, are sending out a man called Durrant—brother of the new Conservative M.P. for North Donnington—to see whether there is anything in the idea of an aerodrome at Lolagoba for East African air transport. But I can't see old Sir Joseph Prince intriguing to hoodwink the League of Nations."

"Can't you? A lot you know about Sir Joseph. A charming, picturesque old scoundrel who gets at the soft spot of all the women. I assure you, Miss Stanbury, if you knew all I know about the past history of Prince's Limited, you'd be less ready with your assurances of virtue."

"But I'm sorry. I do definitely know the man they've sent out, and I'm sure there's nothing in it."

"Indeed? You are so fully informed of his movements?"

"He's an old friend of my brother's. I've known him for years."

"Then he knows you're a journalist on the staff of *The Byeword*. Naturally he would tell you all the secret intentions of the firm. Or perhaps you want me to think that you're so greatly in his confidence that he could not fail to tell you *everything*? No, no, Miss Stanbury. There's such a thing as being too clever."

"That's just what I'm afraid Rollett has been this time. The thing's a mare's nest, Mr. Carter. It won't stand a moment's sensible investigation. If you'd read it again you'd see for yourself. Rollett's got into such a habit of suspicion that he'd think it an Imperialistic plot if his egg was underboiled. He would really."

"Miss Stanbury—are you editing this paper or am I?"

The true reply to this question not being the one expected by Mr. Carter, nor one that Jean could herself well make, she left it unanswered. "I'll thank you to let me judge for myself on Rollett's merits. . . . He is one of the few first-rate men writing to-day. He has courage, which is more than ninety-nine out of a hundred of the half-witted, white-livered nincompoops who call themselves journalists have to-day. Of course he twists people's tails. That's what he's there for. It does them good. Creates interest. I've got absolutely no objection to his twisting that old humbug Prince's tail—Prince is a hypocrite and a liar. He's always pretending to be interested in Liberal and progressive movements. But it's all eye-wash to get a little more popularity. If he had an ounce of sincerity in him, he'd prove it in a practical way—the *only* practical way."

Jean knew that the editor was referring to an old quarrel with Prince's over his failure to renew an advertising contract. Jean shared his desire. If she had her way, every firm in England would take weekly pages in *The Byeword*. But she could not share his habit of judging the entire morality, competence, and honour of business houses by the simple test of whether they did or did not advertise in her paper.

" I dare say," she said soothingly, " that he is a bit of an old scallywag. But he's rather clever. And it obviously would not be worth his while to fall foul of the League of Nations people, when so much of his business lies in organising tours to mandated countries, and these ' Inspect the League's Inspections ' journeys. He's always boasting, you know, that he is the man who's making the League popular by associating it with adventure. After a few school teachers have fallen off donkeys in Syria, or been mauled by lions in Tanganyika when looking at mandates, or got knived by opium smugglers in Shanghai, or done in by white slave traffickers at Marseilles, the League will be as fashionable as winter sports. I simply can't see him playing the double game Rollett suggests, and he's too simple to try to advertise by opposition."

" I really am rather busy, Miss Stanbury. Your analysis of Sir Joseph's motives may be interesting, but it is hardly opportune."

" I'm sorry to be a nuisance, Mr. Carter. But I feel I must say what I think. We've done rather too much of this wolf-crying lately. There was the Hatton case—and Lord

Quantock. We can't go on like this or we shall lose our influence."

Indeed, she knew and Carter knew, that much was already lost. Carter's idyosincrasies were too well known. His perpetual assaults on the good faith of his political opponents grew monotonous. The waning brilliance of his own style seemed to affect his contributors, and, as for his paper, its bitter intransigence had made it a Byeword indeed.

The editor knew this. He knew also that he and the paper lived only from week to week. It was losing more money than the proprietors could afford. Three times he had been solemnly warned of his precarious position. He knew that Jean knew this, and loathed the humiliation of her knowledge as much as he disliked his dependence on her reliability.

His white face grew whiter. His black eyes protruded ferociously. His plump, rather dirty hand trembled.

" You think you know better than I do the law of libel ? "

" I'm afraid that this article is libellous. At least, I feel sure McKisach ought to see it."

" We're insured against libel."

" Only up to twelve hundred. Prince's have endless resources, and Sir Joseph's a fighter."

" And you suggest I'm not a fighter, eh ? "

She was too desperate to be amused. " Oh, no. It isn't that. But dare we risk it, just *now* ? "

He took her " just now," which referred to their general financial and political crisis, as a personal allusion to his carpeting by the proprietors. His anger choked his speech. He could only glare.

" You see Prince is so frightfully popular just now," she pleaded. " I know a libel action's good publicity, given the right cause and time. But is this the right time ? Prince is fashionable. He's making the best of both worlds by advertising British adventure, which gets the Nationalists, and international travel, which gets the rest. We've been losing readers because we're supposed to be defeatists and pessimists. An article like this gives us the worse of both worlds. It implies that Prince, the Nationalist, is a knave, and that the League Slavery Commission are fools. We should antagonise every one."

" Miss Stanbury. I think you have said enough. I have no more time to waste. Kindly send this article to the printers—as it stands."

Jean's mind was a turmoil of conflicting impulses. Uppermost and most constant was her long discipline of feminine acquiescence. She was naturally inclined to, and had re-inforced by practice, the docility that suffers long and is kind, even at the cost of undefended principle. First in her home and then in her work she had learned through agreement and disagreement to hold her tongue. Her reputation for sense and tact had been founded upon silence.

But already she had broken her old habit. Her outburst to Bill Durrant, before Christmas, had done violence to her tradition of restraint, and had let loose all her long dormant combative instincts. Her will was not weak ; it had been deliberately subordinated, and a lifetime of control had strengthened rather than destroyed it.

She was utterly convinced that the editor was wrong. His irresponsibility could ruin the paper. If he published the article, provoked the challenge and then weakly gave way, he would become a laughing stock. If he fought the case, he must be beaten, and that would mean beyond all hope of recovery—the end.

All her loyalty, her ambition, her protective passion, and her taste for bringing things off were centred in *The Byeword*. It was her child, her toy, her achievement and her justification. Her friendships arose from it ; her interests centred in it. Even her satisfaction with her cottage was largely derived from the contrast of its peace with the stimulating tumult of the office.

That Rollett's article incidentally slandered the Durrants, meant nothing to her. She would have been glad to think Bill capable of the positive effort of political intrigue. But that a rash impulse of abuse, a momentary gratification of *amour propre*—accidental too, since Dermond's article might have arrived in time—should risk the entire survival of the paper, seemed to her monstrous.

She faced her editor, now white, now blushing, her voice choking her.

" I'm very sorry . . ."

She was at a loss for words.

" I'm very sorry, Mr. Carter, but please—I beg of you—reconsider the article. Modify it a little——"

" Did you hear what I said, Miss Stanbury ? Will you send this to the printers ? "

" No, I can't . . ."

" You mean you won't ? "

" As you please. But——"

" You know what that means ? "

"I—you—I——"

" Are you going to carry out my request or not, Miss Stanbury ? Because if not, I am afraid I shall have to ask you for your resignation. I cannot possibly retain a member of the staff who is deliberately disloyal."

It was Carter, not Jean, who retained his dignity. There is a technique of opposition, and Jean had not acquired it. Experience rather than rectitude enables people to come through scenes such as this with credit, and Jean had no experience. She simply did not know how to behave. She tried to be reasonable.

" I know what you feel, but . . ."

" Will you please stop arguing ? "

That checked her.

" Now, for the last time, will you send through that article ? "

" Oh, don't you see—I——? "

" Then kindly accept the two months' salary in lieu of notice which is your due. And go at once."

" Go ? "

" At once. I prefer to see the issue through without you. I am sorry it has come to this, but you seem to have lost your head. I cannot do with hysterical women in my office. I will see that the cheque reaches you early next week. Now please go at once."

Still she was incapable of realising what she had done. Her heart leapt from side to side in her body. Her pulses banged. She stared stupidly at the editor's face as at a white moon through mist.

" But this issue ? The letters not sent off—the . . . ? "

He lost his temper then. " *Will* you please get out of my office and let me manage my own affairs ? "

" I'm sorry—I——"

" Be quiet. I *will* not have all this argument. Since you cannot behave like a rational adult, I must ask you to leave the place at once ; at once, do you hear ? Or you will drive me to the humiliation of having you put out ! "

She went then.

She went out into her little room and saw the usual Tuesday afternoon crowd awaiting her. Messengers, note-writers, reviewers, advertisement canvassers pressed round her, bombarding her with questions.

" Hi ! Jean—I want your sage advice a second——"

" Please, Miss Stanbury . . ."

" Miss Stanbury, look here."

" Miss Stanbury, Colonel Maldon's on the 'phone about the India notes . . ."

" Miss Stanbury, please. Is the first heavy ready now for the printer ? "

" Is the editor free now, Miss Stanbury ? "

She pushed her way through them to the curtain behind which she kept outdoor things. Without a word she began to put on her hat and coat. She did not even notice their expressions of amazement.

She returned to her desk and gathered her personal possessions together ; her pen, an old piece of red india-rubber, a comic calendar, a dictionary. But having collected them, she did not know what to do with them, and stood looking helplessly at her small leather bag, as though it should remind her of something she had forgotten. It did. She removed from it her office keys and laid them on the blotting pad.

" Miss Stanbury . . ."

" Miss Stanbury . . ."

Their voices buzzed in her ears, annoying her.

She spoke at last.

" You'd better ask the editor. I'm going out."

And she went, down the familiar curving steps of the stone stairway, through the entrance hall past the circulation and advertising offices, out into the road.

The precocious January sunlight caressed her face. A

woman with a basket on the pavement cried, " Buy a bunch of white heather, pretty lady. White heather for luck. All good luck, dearie."

She looked up and down the street as though she were a stranger.

A taxi crawling along the curb, paused ingratiatingly. She stepped inside.

" Where d'you want to go, lady ? "

" Anywhere—just drive. No." Her unbroken habit of economy overcame her distraction. " No—go to 18 World's Walk, Chelsea."

Though her stunned brain still failed to record the consequences of her folly, and she was yet unaware that, by acting out of character for five minutes, she had cut herself off from her work, her security, her career, her pride of achievement and her opportunity to save *The Byeword*, she was conscious of an intolerable anguish of bereavement. She sat, staring in front of her, swaying as the taxi turned, her gloveless hands clutching her leather bag, and her lips repeating stupidly, " I have lost everything. I have lost everything. I have lost everything."

CHAPTER IX

PRINCE'S LIMITED IS DULY GRATEFUL

BILL DURRANT left London for Mandoa at the end of January.

His departure was merely one of the routine activities of Prince's Limited. Every month, it seemed, young men set off from the great Kingsway Buildings for Malaya or Bolivia or Thibet. Sometimes they returned. Sometimes they did not. Sometimes their adventures were favoured by chance and resulted in new hotels, new travel concessions, new contacts. Sometimes they resulted in nothing but a loss of so many pounds, dollars, marks, rupees, yen, to be duly recorded in the large calf-bound ledgers. The doors swung softly to and fro ; the lifts floated up to the thirteenth floor ; the clients changed their money in the cool marble hall adorned with flowers and fountains, or sought advice in the Research Department, or bought tickets in the Travel Bureau. It was all just as it had been before, except that on the huge map down in the foyer, another little flag— green for " Projected Centre "—had been stuck somewhere in Africa, and those whom curiosity led to read it, could see in white letters the unfamiliar names " Mandoa— Lolagoba."

Maurice, Mrs. Durrant, Sir Joseph, Sid Granger and Jean had managed it between them. It was they who had planted that flag, assisted by Jane Crossgill, Henry Marchant Warrington and the electors of North Donnington. But they hardly recognised their achievement.

Maurice certainly thought it was all his doing.

After his lunch in the autumn with Sir Joseph, he had written to Bill's old lodgings in Earl's Court, had written to the bank where his account stood, and had even written to Jean Stanbury. But nobody could tell him where Bill had gone.

Then one cold November morning at about half-past two, he let himself into the Knightsbridge flat, longing for hot whisky and bed and sleep, after his first late sitting in the House, and heard the astonishing sound of voices in the drawing-room. Not knowing what to expect, he opened the door, and saw his mother, radiant, talkative, seated beside the fire, hand in hand with the shameless scapegrace, Bill.

She looked up at Maurice, first, for a second, as though he were a burglar. Then joyfully she called, " My dear ! Look who's come ! "

" Hallo, Maurice," grinned Bill. " Have you brought me the fatted calf ? I've got the robe and the ring."

He had.

He was wearing his father's signet, reclaimed from pawn after selling his wardrobe, and an old dressing gown that belonged to Maurice.

" He just came in this evening after dinner as though he'd never been away," cooed Mrs. Durrant, blissfully.

" I don't know how you expected me to come, my dear. As though I'd never seen you before ? Congratulations on your victory and all that, Maurice. I should have written, but you know what it is. Of course, I was all for your opponent. But I must say you made a pretty good effort. I'd no idea you could speak so well."

" Thanks," said Maurice—the first word he could interpolate into the conversation.

It was, he thought, typical of their relationship that Bill should be seated in the best armchair, welcoming him home, as it were, to his own flat, and patronising him, as though Maurice were the stranger and Bill the son of the house. And Maurice had to say " Thanks," damn it, as though it were he who should be grateful. " I've been looking for you all over London," he added gruffly.

" Yes, dear. Bill's been explaining. He changed his rooms, you know, and he was trying to find work, and couldn't, and that poor man he used to work for is out of a job himself. You know, though they *are* Socialists, you can't help feeling sorry for them." Into Mrs. Durrant's face stole that benevolent pity which commonly results in soup kitchens and hospital subscriptions.

" I've come," said Bill. " To lay my bones among you. Sorry to be a bore—but the mater says there's a spare room. And I don't suppose I shall be here long, anyway."

" That's all right. Have a drink ? " suggested Maurice. The rights of hospitality were his at last.

Not till next day did he learn the extent of Bill's capitulation. Bill was not only restored to the bosom of his family. He had come because he was penniless. He preferred, he said, to sponge upon his brother rather than to fall back upon the untender mercies of the state, even if it came to the same thing in the end.

Besides, to sponge upon Maurice was more comfortable. He was sick of the husks the swine ate, he said, of dirty sheets in cheap lodgings, of economising over laundry, and of coarse tasteless food. He hungered for the flesh pots of Knightsbridge, for Turkish baths and eau-de-cologne shampoos. If Maurice had a job for him, he'd take it. Mandoa ? Rather remote and primitive and all that, wasn't it ? Still—three months—and good pay—and possible pickings——

Condescendingly, he decided that he might try it. He consented to go daily to the Kingsway office. He submitted placidly to interviews and instructions. He discussed with the air-staff the details of landing grounds, and with the research staff such facts as were known about Mandoa. He adopted towards his brother an air of ironical gratitude which Maurice found exasperating, and towards his mother a graceful devotion which made her feel as though he had given her the sun, moon and stars to play with. Night after night when Maurice returned from the House, from committee-meetings, from speaking in dull provincial constituencies, he found Bill and Mrs. Durrant just back from some jaunt to the theatre, to restaurants, to supper-and-cabaret shows, paid for by Mrs. Durrant, out of her younger son's hard-earned money. Never since the war had Mrs. Durrant looked younger or more gay. Bill waited on her, teased her, scolded her, and even danced with her at the Savoy, courting her with a debonair charm that Maurice had neither time nor energy to imitate. It was Maurice who provided the flat, the dinners, the stalls and flowers and taxis, Bill, who reaped the loving gratitude, the rapture, the welcoming adoration in his mother's eyes.

Maurice, who had initiated the Mandoan business in good faith and honesty, now indeed began to wish his brother dead, dead and defeated preferably, dead and dishonoured most of all. The motives that Bill had once falsely imputed to him, now became really his. But the worse he wished Bill, the more wretched he grew. His conscience, pampered by a career of singular integrity, was quite unaccustomed to those adjustments and revaluations in which more ex-perienced consciences are well-skilled.

He kept on repeating to himself that he had done all a brother could do. He had not suggested Mandoa. The pro-posal was Sir Joseph's. Bill had gone to Africa before. Other agents and investigators went to still wilder places. The Mandoans had been reported friendly. Well, then? Well, then? Well, then?

It was Mrs. Durrant who first expressed misgivings. A week before Bill was due to sail she came into Maurice's bedroom where he was sitting up in bed, after three late nights, eating his breakfast. He noticed her pretty new rose-coloured wrap (bought for Bill's gratification), her polished nails, her fine and delicate air, and knew that never for him had she taken so much trouble. She had always been fastidious ; but for Bill she had grown young.

She sat down on his bed, twisting the rings on her white fingers.

She talked of this and that, of North Donnington, the new cook, of a dinner party planned for the following night.

Then she came to her point.

" Maurice, *must* Bill fly ? "

" Fly ? "

" To that place—to Lolagoba."

" Why not, dear? There's no other way at present of reaching it, unless he somehow gets down over the Abyssinian hills, or goes right round by Kenya—and there are no roads. Why not fly ? "

" Because, I think I've discovered something. I believe —he'd never acknowledge it, of course—but I believe he's terrified. He's suffering, Maurice. He's never been up since then."

" He's not piloting the machine, Mums. He's only got to be a passenger."

" But you don't understand—it's torture to him. I'm *sure* it is. We went to that air-war film last night. He *would* go. And he was trembling all over. After the crash— it was horribly real, Maurice. Such things should not be shown on the screen—he went absolutely *grey*. I thought he was going to faint. I think he *was* sick afterwards. He spent ages in the cloakroom. He pretended the fish at dinner was bad. He's been awake all night. I could hear him tramping up and down his room."

" So *you've* been awake all night ? "

" Maurice—I——" Her mouth trembled. " Can't you find something else for him ? Somewhere so that he can keep on the ground ? "

" It's all fixed up, Mater."

" You're a director. You can unfix it."

" My dear, I can't. Bill's never complained to me. He knows just what it will involve."

" I can't *bear* it."

" Did he discuss it with you ? "

" Oh, no, no. He never would, you know. Maurice, you're his brother. You *can't* force him to do this."

" Force ? Oh, God. Mother—*when* have I forced Bill ? *Who* asked me to get him a job at Prince's ? " Maurice lost his patience.

There followed a scene that strained his weary nerves to snapping point. Mrs. Durrant, after a sleepless night of worrying, was hysterical. Maurice, tortured by jealousy, exasperation and fatigue, was intolerant.

He ended it by jumping out of bed and going to his brother's room, to find that Bill had already gone virtuously to the office.

Maurice had put himself in the wrong again. He had been rude to his mother and lost his self-respect. He had exposed his enmity towards Bill and lost her confidence. He was defeated all round and completely wretched. Neither H. M. Warrington's support nor Sir Joseph's favour could restore his peace of mind, and it was no comfort to him that the only person attempting to reassure him was his brother.

Maurice could not bring himself to question Bill, but he told young Houghton, who was to be his pilot, about the air crash, and suggested that he should sound his future passenger. Houghton reported a very jolly conversation, everything O.K. Durrant Senior seemed good sport, and that was that.

Nevertheless, when Maurice sat at the first board meeting of the year, in February, he wished that Bill had been sent to Gleneagles, or Cannes, or anywhere nice and safe. He heartily wished the whole business over, and could not refrain from thinking how typical of their situation it was that Bill should add to his other injuries the insult of making him think less well of himself.

He paid little attention to the formalities of minutes and reports. The early stages of the meeting were indifferent to him.

Then he heard Lord Woodcock ask, " What's this proposal to open up a branch in Mandoa ? Where's Mandoa ? "

Sir Joseph chuckled.

" Better ask Durrant. It's his brother who's gone."

So it was Maurice who had to explain the possibilities of the new air port and the reasons for sending an agent of the firm to spy out the land.

" I thought we were retrenching," grumbled Lord Wood-cock. It was a thought he always cherished. " I don't call it good economy to send out men on wild-goose chases after new countries when we've already got our hands full."

Maurice looked at his chairman, hoping to be spared the discomfort of justification ; but Sir Joseph, who saw no cause for discomfort and believed in delegation of labour, only nodded, urging him to continue.

" It hardly is a wild-goose chase," he protested, miserably. " The initial outlay is insignificant. This man Houghton was flying to Kenya anyway, and quite glad to take my brother as passenger. He'll call for him on his return journey. That only means travelling costs and three months' salary—at the worst."

" And the best ? "

" Considerable prospects. I've talked to the Foreign Office and the Air Ministry about it." This was true, thanks to H. M. Warrington. The reference soothed Maurice's vanity. " They seemed to think it might be a first-rate idea. There was some anxiety about Mandoa. The Italians once had a shot at claiming it as a Catholic state and asking for a mandate over it ; then the Abyssinians have made eyes at it, because it could be a very useful blind for the slave trade. As a matter of fact, you know, it really ought to be part of the Sudan. But we can't walk in and annex new territories nowadays. If we want to clean it up we have to establish a sphere of influence, and get the League of Nations behind us. The French built railways in Abyssinia. There's no reason why we should not built an air port in Mandoa. Possibly an hotel. Possibly roads from the Sudan to the hotel—or a light railway over the mountains to Addis Ababa—but air's the thing. If the reports that I have had are correct, it was made by nature for an air centre. Of course there may be nothing in it. But I do not think that I am exaggerating, gentlemen, when I say that the National Government looks to Prince's Limited for a lead in directing and initiating British enter-prise. Mandoa, undeveloped and isolated as she now is, might prove a new centre for investment and our export trade. Believe me, the government looks very favourably, *very*, at the proposal. If there is nothing in it, we are no

worse off. We have made an interesting, and—I think—
an honourable experiment. The cost will have been trifling."

"That's all very well. But I should like further facts
and figures. When do you say your brother proposes to
go?"

"He left last Friday. He'll be nearly at Cairo by this
time. He's flying from there."

"Oh, I see. *Fait accompli*, eh?" Lord Woodcock
shrugged his shoulders. "The government trusts us. All is
fair, and above board. Then would you mind telling me
why nobody seems to have replied to that?" And he
threw down on the table a copy of *The Byeword* containing
Arthur Rollett's article called "And Why Mandoa?"

"What's this? What's this?" asked Sir Joseph, putting
on his horn-rimmed spectacles.

"It's a peculiarly scurrilous piece of work, implying
that we're going to Mandoa to line our pockets with un-
specified concessions, in return for winking at the slave
trade. Who's this man Rollett?"

"A Radical crank—not worth our notice," snapped
another director.

"I don't know. He's got a following," said Sidforth.

Sir Joseph asked for other copies of the paper, remarking
petulantly :

"I always detested that man Carter. He looks like a
slug."

"Clever fellow, but wrong headed."

"Yellow. Yellow to the core."

"I hope very much, gentlemen," continued Lord Woodcock, "that you will see your way to answering this fellow.
I don't know how you take it. I take it very seriously. I
do not like these attacks on the honour of Prince's, and I
think there is too great a tendency nowadays to let slander
go unchallenged."

"D'you want us to take it to the courts?" asked Sir
Joseph. He dearly loved litigation, though he would have
preferred a duel. But usually his fellow directors curbed his
combative tastes.

"Isn't that going to mean a lot of rather undesirable
publicity?" suggested Maurice.

"Undesirable? Undesirable? Since when has publicity

become undesirable ? " retorted Lord Woodcock, who
thought the youngest director a prig and enjoyed snubbing
him whenever an occasion arose.

" Nothing is known yet. We may have to let the whole
Mandoan scheme drop. We really have decided nothing yet
but to investigate. Are we certain we want to turn the
limelight on to a scheme that may prove abortive ? "

Maurice rarely spoke as strongly as that. He was the
youngest and most recently promoted director. He was one
of the few who were also salaried servants of the firm. His
forte was efficient work and loyal service rather than the
exercise of a dominant personality. He understood Sir
Joseph's warm affection for him, but he also knew his
place. He had not been invited to that famous mahogany
table to oppose his elders.

Sir Joseph was sniffing battle like a retired colonel of
volunteers. He had been reading Rollett's article with fury.
" There's no doubt at all—we have a perfectly clear case.
A man like Carter needs exposing. It's time his filthy little
rag came to an end. In a national crisis like this, it poisons
the public mind. I consider it our duty, quite apart from
anything else, to teach Carter and anti-patriotic cranks of
his kidney a lesson. Eh ? Eh ? "

The Board, as a whole, agreed. Maurice was powerless.
But the more he thought of a possible libel suit the less he
liked it. If Bill made a hash of things—as twenty-to-one he
would—Maurice would look a fool for recommending him ;
and if the adventure ended in disaster, he might look like
something worse. On the other hand if Bill achieved anything, a blaze of publicity would be turned upon him and
he might come out of the absurd affair an acclaimed hero.
It was all maddening, ridiculous, and a little dangerous, too.

Maurice went to Sir Joseph ; but Sir Joseph could see
nothing in his half-articulated misgivings. He went to the
firm's solicitors ; but the legal mind was convinced of a
clear case, and spoiling for litigation. Whichever way he
turned, he was defeated.

Then he thought of Jean Stanbury, a sensible girl, and
on the staff of *The Byeword*. He would go to her, and persuade her that the case must not come before the courts.
Her editor must withdraw and apologise, or be ruined.

He rang up the office to find that she had left a month ago. He rang up her cottage to find that it was let. He wrote to Cynthia, with whom he still sometimes communicated ; but she, secure in her Westmorland retreat, affirmed that she had not heard of old Jean for donkeys' years, and had not the remotest idea where she could be.

Too late he tried to approach Carter. The editor of *The Byeword* refused to apologise. With heroic folly he stood by his contributor, and Rollett proposed to rally the forces of Truth, Liberty and Humanitarianism in his defence. He wrote a terrific onslaught against Sir Joseph, headed " The Prince of Darkness," insinuating that already on his account slaves toiled under the lash of Arabian drivers, and forced labour augmented the profits of the Kingsway firm.

But before it was published the catastrophe which Jean Stanbury had foreseen occurred. The directors of *The Byeword* took fright, commanded Carter to apologise, and when he refused, requested his resignation, and closed the office.

The Byeword was dead.

CHAPTER X

LORD LUFTON IS NOT WILLIAM WILBERFORCE

In the early spring of 1928, Rupert Lufton married Selena Askett, took an Elizabethan farmhouse in Buckinghamshire, and transferred his attention from politics to horti- and other cultures. A man, he considered, who has given the best years of his life to a cause, who has fought hopeless constituencies, laboured at petty secretaryships, contributed hundreds of thousands of unpaid words to unread memoranda in party files, who has attended conferences, committees and summer-schools for twenty odd years, has earned his leisure.

Besides, Selena had three thousand a year of her own. Stoney Ridge Farm was, strictly speaking, hers.

They suited each other admirably. Both were humanitarians, vegetarians and Socialists. Selena was also a member of several organisations which recognised women's special interest in peace, world fellowship, and the freedom of the individual. Both enjoyed gardening, nature study, classical records on the gramophone (Rupert preferring Mozart while Selena worshipped Beethoven), old furniture, book-collecting and the preservation of the countryside. Rupert was also interested in photography, while Selena joined a club for folk-dancing. She was a large-bosomed, tranquil, comfortable woman, who wore cretonne dresses, a good deal of home-made jewellery, and her abundant dun-coloured hair in plaits coiled round her ears.

Rupert lay back on her personality as upon a richly upholstered Chesterfield sofa, which, indeed, she somewhat resembled in appearance. But though he had abandoned an active political career, he was not without ambition. He found, however, a new and agreeable road to its fulfilment. While immersed in the rough and tumble of Labour politics he had known many snubs and hardships. It is not easy both to make a living and serve a cause, and Rupert had found himself exploited as a voluntary worker, sweated as a paid official, and awarded little credit in either capacity.

But as the host of a charming house, he blossomed like his own hyacinths. So soothing were Selena's excellent beds, so restful the broad matured garden, that Rupert had only to prune his roses, talk learnedly of crops and chaffinches, and change the gramophone records with tact, for his week-end parties to become affairs of state. Trade union leaders, under-secretaries, publicists, and distinguished foreigners took tea on his southern terrace. His hollyhocks and begonias received confidences about the Premier's temperament, the Chancellor's health, the problems of Geneva and the hardships of Downing Street. In order to secure immediate attention, ambitious young men had only to murmur casually in the lobby of the London School of Economics or the dining-room of the National Labour Club, " Oh, I went down to Stoney Ridge last week."

Central heating, log fires, succulent salads curling from large porcelain bowls, and shelves opulent with first editions, proved more effective assets to prestige than years of labour over blue books, agenda, and the propagandist's uneasy life.

" The world," Rupert would tell his guests, waving a plump and generous hand at the timbered walls, the tiled lawn and the Downs beyond the garden, " the world has been too much with us. Man must sometimes practice the Humanities. Peace—we need peace, and beauty. *Il faut cultiver nos jardins.*"

The over-worked secretaries and back-benchers would look up from their temporary haven in Selena's excellent armchairs, and wistfully, unavailingly, agree.

Certainly Rupert, by cultivating his garden, prospered. By the spring of 1931 he had become, for political and social services, Lord Lufton of Stoney Ridge.

Almost immediately, his health failed him. He became afflicted with high-blood-pressure, and its attendant discomforts of headache, nausea and fatigue. His Labour friends attributed his breakdown to years of over-work, and declared his recent honours well-deserved.

Thus, throughout the disquieting events of 1931, he lay sequestered, nursed by Selena, shielded from the emotional disturbances of the Crisis, the election, and the lamentable divisions in his party.

When he re-emerged into public life, and Selena again wrote notes of invitation to week-ends at Stoney Ridge, the winter crisis had passed. Lord Lufton, it appeared, was in both camps, or in neither. He had cast from him the works of controversy, and put upon him the whole armour of philosophic tolerance. He was sorry for poor Ramsay, who was such a charming fellow and who would certainly kill himself from over-work. He was sorry for the dispossessed ex-Labour ministers, frustrated in their fulfilment of the inevitability of gradualism. He was sorry for the unemployed, the martyred Chinese, the persecuted (if misguided) Indians, the unseated and even unemployed Socialist members, the miners of South Wales, the Kikuyu of Kenya, the child slaves of Hong Kong and the proletariat of all countries. He embraced in universal sympathy all suffering humanity, and wandered about his terraces in the furtive summer sunlight enjoying Selena's constant injunctions that he was on no account to stoop, and the solicitude of his guests who had been cautioned by Lady Lufton to avoid " all controversial questions."

Most questions being, in 1932, controversial, it seemed preferable while at Stoney Ridge to devote one's whole attention to horticulture, birds and botany, to symphony concerts, the Camargo Society, and the tapestry work which Lady Lufton had recently added to her repertoire of accomplishments. Noble, serene, and large, like a Demeter in home-spun, she sat in her loose blue gown, pulling the coloured wools in and out through her canvas, while her harassed trade union secretaries and I.L.P. propagandists declared wistfully, " Of course, you people really know how to live "—an opinion shared by the Luftons, who were, however, too kindly to express it, with its implied criticism of the bustling, laboured, contentious lives of their guests.

So, on one warm Saturday afternoon in May, Arthur Rollett, the journalist, rounding the corner of the house, heard a noise which he failed to recognise as the second movement of the 7th Symphony in A minor, and saw, seated about the large cabinet gramophone on the paved terrace, his host and hostess, Danielson from the London School of Economics, Marlow, an American sculptor who specialised in proletarian subjects, their respective wives, and a tall woman, lying on a pile of cushions, whose face was vaguely familiar.

Lady Lufton put her finger to her lip and motioned vigorously towards the instrument. Rollett, who disliked gramophones and knew nothing about music, drew back with a faint sensation of rebuff, and stood at attention while the record spun to its core and died into a faint whirring of the needle.

As though released from a spell, the listeners roused themselves. Lady Lufton rose, dropping a cluster of wools from her ample knee.

" I _knew_ you would understand," she breathed. " I always feel that one must be polite to Beethoven. Even on a record. Like clapping a film." She took both his hands. " You know all these people—Arthur Rollett—Paul and Rita Danielson, Ivor and Sophie Marlow—Jean Stanbury." She had adopted the Quaker custom of calling acquaintances by their Christian names.

" I've met you before," Rollett said awkwardly to the

tall woman. Her name conveyed nothing to him ; but, looking at her face, he felt sure that somewhere he had received from its owner friendliness and courtesy. A small, fierce, sensitive, incorruptible little man, he had not found the world over-generous with either commodity. The conflict between his unsleeping conscience and his natural kindliness daily tormented him, for the former drove him to tell unpleasant truths which caused reactions desperately painful to the latter. He had come down to Stoney Ridge to summon Lord Lufton back to the political duties he had deserted, and his reception left him with little hope of success, and none of comfort. Perhaps this young woman would help him.

" I think," said Lord Lufton, " you knew Miss Stanbury on *The Byeword*. You used to write for *The Byeword*, didn't you ? "

" Write for it ? You were its executioner, weren't you ? " smiled Danielson, malicious and knowledgeable, always knowing far more about the inside history of events than the people most concerned in them.

" Ah, *The Byeword*," sighed Lady Lufton. " A very clever paper in its way. But I was never sure that it really gave enough attention to the things that matter."

" The things that matter " was one of her favourite phrases ; vague and uplifting like " love of the beautiful," " our better natures," " pursuit of the highest," and " world fellowship." She rolled serene blue eyes round the enfolding landscape, and the shortcomings of *The Byeword* lost themselves in agreeable consciousness of the Beethoven symphony, her husband's return to health, the new tulips that were doing so well, and the late, ridiculous cuckoo, see-sawing his two notes somewhere on the beech trees behind the house.

" Poor Carter," said Lord Lufton. " That was a bad business. Jean here lost her job, of course. As a matter of fact, the directors appealed to me when the paper was in its death-throes ; but I told them I was not a rich man. And with all the calls one has in these days. . . . Besides, it never was Socialist, though there was good stuff in that old Radical school."

"Thank God," thought Jean, "that nobody seems to know when I left the paper, or why."

At that moment she thought she cared more for Peace, the Lufton's god, than for Truth, which was Rollett's. Since leaving *The Byeword* she had passed through a strange period of desolation, bereft of her cottage, her work, her friends, and even of herself. For, without savings, she had not dared to stay in London, and had wandered about the provinces, visiting relations, who demanded, as the price of their hospitality, that she should not be "clever," nor "contradictious," and that she should adapt herself, her views, her standards, and her entire personality to their habits.

At last, when she could bear it no longer, she took the small sum she had collected from her cottage rent and returned to London, to face three weeks of growing terror as her resources dwindled, and new work evaded her. Then Evelyn Raye had told her of a job at the London office of the International Humanitarian Association, to start the following month. Lady Lufton's invitation came almost at the same time and she went down to Stoney Ridge for peace before facing her new battles, still shaken, still breathless and only half alive. And now Rollett had come, the author and begetter of her recent tribulation, and her frail fabric of tranquility tottered.

She sighed and temporised. "It was very bad luck for Carter. He had put a lot of good work into the paper."

"Bad luck? I thought it was bad whisky," said Danielson. "Miss Stanbury. . . . Is it true that he only came to the office once a week, to write a leading article? And brought a bottle of whisky with him, and by the time he had finished the leader, he had finished the bottle too? Weren't there endless rows with the directors? The paper was losing about twelve thousand a year, wasn't it? It wasn't just the Mandoan affair that killed it. It was dying of D.T.'s anyway."

"The Mandoan affair?" echoed Marlow. "You mean this royal wedding?"

"Ivor and I thought of flying over," interpolated Mrs. Marlow. "He thinks those Mandoans should make wunnerful models. It all sounds *too* romantic. I *adore* Sir Joseph Prince."

"Rollett doesn't," smiled Danielson, his shrewd, dark eyes glittering with amusement. He loved situations like this, and watched with cat-like pleasure Rollett's blinking misery as his conscience goaded him towards explosion, Lady Lufton's vague apprehensions, the Marlows' round-eyed interest, and Jean Stanbury's increasing pallor. Of all the party, he alone guessed that Jean had left the paper as a protest against Rollett's article. He wanted to see what she would say. But Rollett had his opening. Turning upon his host with a ferocity that masked profound discomfort, he plunged into his protest.

"Look here, Lufton. It's precisely that Mandoan affair I came to see you about. I meant to talk it over in private ; but I have nothing to say I would not say in public. You're a well-to-do man. You have influence. You have leisure. I know you've been ill ; but I've particularly inquired about your condition from a number of medical men and they all agree with me that a little political activity couldn't possibly hurt you now." The pretty German parlourmaid brought out the tea-tray, and Lady Lufton attempted to use it as a weapon of defence, stirring herself and asking every one about milk and sugar. Her husband, no less eager to escape, rose with unusual demonstrations of infirmity, to hand the cakes ; but Rollett went mercilessly on :

"You know I wrote the truth in one of the last issues of *The Byeword*. Prince's Limited is attempting to boom Mandoa. Sir Joseph is a corrupt old cynic. He has thrown dust in the eyes of every respectable philanthropist, or he couldn't have preserved his public reputation so long. In my article I said that he had bought his immunity in Mandoa by conniving at the most iniquitous practice of slave-raiding in the world. Liberian and Abyssinian records are spotless, compared with what goes on in Lolagoba. Sir Joseph thinks he can stage-manage this royal wedding, attract tourists to the spot, and use the incident as a jumping off ground for commercial advantages."

"Mrs. Marlow—excuse me, Mr. Rollett—but *did* you say lemon and no sugar ? " cried Selena desperately. But

Danielson was enjoying her distress too much to permit its subsidence.

" I entirely agree with you, Rollett," he said, in his soothing, intimate voice. " I wouldn't put any villainy past that suave old devil, Prince. But what I *do* wonder is, what he thinks he is going to get out of it financially."

" Jean, dear. You're eating *nothing*. Try this oatcake," Selena pleaded. But Rollett was implacable.

" Potentially," he continued, " Mandoa is a rich country. Cotton—minerals—possibly tobacco and coffee in the highlands. Thanks to its peculiar contacts with the outside world, it has a certain appetite for progress. Like every other African country. And why not ? Ultimately, it may become a useful market. But at the moment, its wealth consists in man-power—arms, legs, heads, bodies. Slaves. Slaves and raided ivory. Mandoa as a country is wretchedly degradingly poor. But its nobles grow rich and fat on blood-money, and Prince is out to profit from it. The slave-owners want motor cars and gramophones and Paris gowns for their wives—and Prince will see they get them. The country will be drained dry—squeezed till the pips squeak—for this royal wedding. And the profits from the squeezing will go into Prince's pockets. Can't you *see* what he's doing ? If the country were allowed to develop its commerce in an ordinary way—healthily— from the bottom, European contacts might prove the greatest blessing. But what's going to happen now is ruin—blind, bloody ruin. And we're letting our government connive at it ! I should not be surprised if a quarter of the population were wiped out by the time Prince has finished with the place ! "

" But, look here, Rollett. Look here, Rollett," fussed Lord Lufton. " We've got no evidence—we've got no evidence."

" Evidence ? " Rollett laughed. " Do you know that *after* my article was published, fifty Mandoans were caught burning a village in Kenya, and a letter was found on the body of the leader quite definitely implicating Prince's agent at Lolagoba ? "

" How shocking," murmured Lady Lufton serenely. " More tea, Mrs. Danielson ? "

" In what language," asked Danielson, stirring his tea, " was the letter ? "

" I can't tell you. I'm not at liberty yet to give any details. But my informant is a man of proved integrity. I'll tell you something else. The Colonial Office knows what's going on. The Air Ministry knows it. The Foreign Office knows it. And they muffle it up. They want to keep it quiet. Why ? Because Sir Joseph Prince has friends in the government. Do you know," Rollett stared round about him, as though collecting attention before launching his master-evidence, " do you know *who* the agent for Prince's in Lolagoba is ? The elder brother of a director of Prince's called Maurice Durrant, who is the new Conservative member for North Donnington ! "

" Oh—I know who you mean," said Mrs. Danielson, brightly. " He was one of the new members receiving our *questionnaire*. He's very unsound on birth control. I always feel," she continued conclusively, " that a man who's unsound on birth control would be unsound on *anything*."

" Now, I *do* want you to look at my tulips," exclaimed Selena, knowing that her husband was not only unsound, from Mrs. Danielson's point of view, on birth control, but was growing more and more unhappy at the conversation. " Rupert, dear—*do* show Mrs. Marlow the tulips."

But Rollett refused to be side-tracked. " *No*, Lufton. This is a fundamental matter. This is a question of principle. I need your help. I'm not asking you to do anything that will injure your health. I'm asking, I'm beseeching, you to use your influence to raise the matter in the House of Lords. The public ought to know the exact connection between Prince's and the government of Mandoa."

Even Selena's patience could not survive that direct appeal. Her mild face assumed an aspect of resolution. She turned to her guest with gentle but assured reproof. " Mr. Rollett, I must beg of you to leave my husband alone for the moment. He really is not *fit* to be worried. I dare say that you find this Mandoan affair very important : and I admire your courage, and your—your——" She meant to say tenacity, but could not think of the word. " But we must keep a sense of proportion. There are so many things wrong in this poor, sick world !" She sighed deeply, her ample bosom heaving with universal compassion.

"I'm sorry, Lady Lufton. I have a great respect for your husband. Too much respect to let him lose this opportunity of world-service." Rollett looked round the tea-table. He read in the faces of the company amusement, incredulity, annoyance, fear, and boredom. Was there not one righteous man in Ninevah ? Jean Stanbury alone, her face averted, her tea untasted, plucked at a daisy-flower with trembling fingers that might indicate some decency of indignation.

Arthur Rollett was perfectly well aware that he was ruining a pleasant tea-party. But he could not think a tea-party more important than the Right.

He rose to his feet, his chair legs screeching on the stone terrace, and drawing a pained protest from the pretty, spoiled American woman.

"I know I am a tactless man," he said, looking down upon them. "But I cannot help it. I am unable. I am simply unable, to understand the point of view of men and women who cannot feel the shame, who cannot wish to prevent—even at the expense of interrupting an agreeable week-end—this evil thing. Do you not see that you and I—the British public—on whom the responsibility ultimately rests for what our government does—don't you *see* that we are conniving at one of the most hideous African transactions since the Belgian Congo scandal ? I can't understand it. Do you really care more about your tea and your tulips than about the torture of hundreds of innocent men and women ? "

"My dear Rollett," Danielson's smooth voice answered him, " I shall be enchanted to go into this when I am back in town. If you'll come and call for me at the school one morning, we'll lunch together."

"A sense of proportion—*il faut cultiver nos jardins*," murmured Lord Lufton.

"Our gardens ! Tulips ! Civilisation ! *My God !* I beg your pardon. I appear to have—I——" He turned to go, thought better of it, and again faced the tea-table. "Lufton, you can't get away from responsibility. Don't hide yourself from the world behind a screen of culture.

Don't sell your soul for tulips ! " He waved his hand round the terrace, the mellow red-brick of the house, the spreading shadow of the cedars on the lawn, the gramophone, the tea-table. " Don't let yourself grow too comfortable. You were one of the finest propagandists in the Labour Party. It's not like you to try to *rust* out instead of wear out. Gardens! I tell you—gardens and gramophones are ruining the cause of Socialism in England."

He turned on his heel and went as he had come, rounding the angle of the house.

The company, united in relief, heaved one sigh. Then Selena spoke : " Poor Rollett. You know, some one told me that he had been overworking badly. I asked him down to give him a little rest. But I didn't know it had gone as far as this. I'm so *sorry*." By assuming her responsibilities as a hostess, she seemed to wipe out the responsibilities of all of them as citizens, and to put Rollett in his proper place as a neurotic intruder into their civilised peace. She rose. " I must just go and see to him." But Jean Stanbury was on her feet.

" Dear Lady Lufton—please let me go. I know you haven't finished your tea—and I think I . . . perhaps——" She hesitated.

" Oh, Jean, will you ? Just calm him down if you can. I'll send you *both* some tea into the library. I *know* how clever you are at dealing with——"

She indicated the world of cranks, fanatics and dipsomaniacs. Jean followed the departed prophet.

" Such a dear girl," murmured Selena. " Such a clever girl. The only person, I believe, who could manage poor Carter. She'll soothe him down. Mr. Marlow, please, could you just ring the door bell ? We want fresh tea, I think . . ."

Jean's long legs, pursuing Rollett's short ones, caught him up, half-way down the drive. He was walking, hatless as usual, his longish grey hair standing stiffly on end, his bag in his hand, his head high, a valiant little soldier, marching away repulsed but not defeated, to further battles.

" Mr. Rollett ! Mr. Rollett ! " He stopped and turned. To her dismay she saw that behind his glasses, his eyes were swimming with tears.

" Mr. Rollett. Can you wait a minute ? I want to ask you something."

" Of course."

" Could you come and sit down for a minute ? "

" I won't go back."

" No, no. Here—in the orchard. No one will interrupt us."

He followed her meekly to the seat she indicated behind a wall against which apple, plum and pear trees were richly spread. He was exhausted by his outburst ; there was no more spirit left in him.

" I want to tell you something."

" Yes ? "

" I was on *The Byeword* when you sent in your article on Mandoa. Carter dismissed me because I refused to pass it for publication. He was quite within his rights to do so."

" Why didn't you want to print it ? "

" Because I thought it was libellous, and that a libel action just then would do for the paper completely. I'd nursed it through so many crises—I couldn't bear the thought of letting one article kill it. Of course, in a way, it *did* kill it."

" You cared more for the paper than for justice ? "

Jean reflected for a minute. " I expect I did. But it wasn't only that. I've known the Durrants for years. I could not believe them capable of the intrigue you suggest. Maurice might do it—Bill couldn't. I almost wish he could. Mr. Rollett—are you honestly certain about this conspiracy ? "

Rollett blew his nose comfortably. He no longer felt indignant. Here was some one who at least faced honestly the problems with which he sought to confront society.

To her he could even make a concession.

" I'm not sure that it's a conscious conspiracy," he said " Your friend may hardly know what he is doing. Though that does not excuse him. It's the monstrous *inattention* of people that alarms me. Unconsciousness is almost the worst political vice. We commit crimes like somnambulists slaying in our sleep. I know nothing personal about this Durrant in Mandoa. But I am perfectly certain that—

directly or indirectly—Prince's are profiting from a completely indefensible traffic."

" It will be indirect," said Jean. " Bill's queer. He runs away from life. He pities himself too much. But he's not cruel. He's a Socialist. And he cares for people. And he's never made a commercial success of anything in his life."

" He's making a commercial success of this. Have you seen the new brochures Prince's have issued about Mandoa ? "

" No. I must."

They were silent for a time. The sun poured down through the apple blossom, dappling the rich green grass. Both Jean and Rollett were conscious of an incongruous alliance. They, who had so much reason to dislike each other, were drawn together by a common impulse.

" I've got a job with the International Humanitarian Association. I don't quite know how it's going to work out," Jean said eventually. " But if you think it worth while to send me particulars about the Mandoan business, I might be able to look into it."

" Good. I wanted to get hold of Larsen. He's your chairman, isn't he ? "

" Yes. He's at Oslo. I've never seen him. I'm to work in the London office ; but we generally all meet in September."

" Good. I shall come and see you as soon as you start your work. Your office is in Victoria Street, isn't it ? "

" 387."

" I know."

He rose, picked up his battered suit-case, and stood looking upon her.

He, who usually went about the world enclosed in the monastery of his absorbing interests, suddenly became aware of the very beautiful slender brown hands clasped on her lap, of her waving auburn hair that caught the sunlight, and the candour and comeliness of her quiet face. She was a woman, he decided, who was good to look upon, not disquieting, but honest, calm and grave.

" You're a sensible woman," he declared. " You have a

sense of values. You may have acted stupidly, but at least you *think* ; you care."

She looked up at him with a sort of serene surprise.

" I suppose that's the wrong thing to say. I never have understood what is and what is not permissible in polite conversation. I might say that you have beautiful hands. But I happen to think your sense of values more important. Mark my words, young woman. Mark my words. There's too much of this *beauty* about. It's ruined a lot of good men—and Rupert Lufton's one of them. I must hurry. Catching the 5.50. See you in London. Au revoir."

And he had gone, striding down the drive, his heavy case thumping against his busy legs.

CHAPTER XI

THE I.H.A. TAKES ACTION

It was very hot.

Below, in the deep canyon of Victoria Street, buses roared like water ; middle-aged women waited outside the Army and Navy Stores, and home-going typists in sleeveless frocks complained about their feet. In the offices of the International Humanitarian Association, a bee, strayed in the honeyless desert, blundered among the sun-curled papers ; Jean's damp fingers slithered on her pen and for the fifteenth time that afternoon Greta James powdered her nose.

The International Executive was in session in the big council room below.

" It's a mistake," observed Greta, meticulously inspecting her complexion in the two-inch-square mirror of her powder-box, " to be a blonde in summer time."

" . . . possibly eighteen hundred prostitutes," muttered Jean, trying to turn a forty-page report on social conditions in Hong-Kong into a snappy news-paragraph.

" The only thing is," Greta continued—she was by now

accustomed to Jean's abstractions—" it does keep you thin."

The messenger girl had just brought in their office tea— flat, strong and tepid. Greta leaned back in her chair and reached for a tin.

" Biscuits ? "

" Isn't there any cake ? " asked Jean, pouncing with sudden delight on a new thought for a final sentence. " We shall be here till Heaven knows when to-night. I'm hungry."

" You don't know your luck," sighed Greta, handing to her a large slab of slightly stale gingerbread. " You eat potatoes. You eat bread. You eat cake between meals. And you never grow fat. Whereas, we, poor things, spend half our lives abjuring the joys of the flesh."

" Only some joys," grunted Jean, still deep in the throes of composition.

" Some ? "

" After all "—Jean laid aside her pen and swivelled round in her chair—" what do we keep thin *for* ? "

" Leading question by the press-secretary," commented Evelyn Raye, the third occupant of the office.

" You can't expect me to be philosophical on a hot day," groaned Greta. " Oh, damn ; has any one a gasper ? Don't be sententious, Stanbury." She sang in a deep, burlesque contralto, " A girl's jus' got'ta have love ! "

" Jean hasn't." Evelyn Raye's glance was intimate and quizzical. She had known Jean for years.

" It's all very well for her," grumbled Greta. " I *wanted* to go out this evening. You two don't seem to mind whether you work till five or ten. I believe you really *like* sweating here over reports on child slavery and what not."

" I do. At least I should," Jean admitted, " if only I could persuade our noble masters that they can't expect new subscribers and friends and influence if they will hide their lights under a bushel. If one of you could find me a really exciting personality or a really first-rate scandal, so that we could get the I.H.A. into front-page headlines once a week at least, I'd put on two stones with joy. No wonder I'm thin. You'd be thin if you'd wrestled for three months with twenty-odd highly respectable philanthropists, trying to persuade them that a little drama loosens the purse-strings quicker than any amount of solid good intentions. It's personality that pays——"

" Hear, hear. Lecture as usual by Miss Jean Stanbury, publicity expert."

" I don't care. I'd write it up all over the council room. I'd like to have Larsen rescued from assassination—and Frau von Schelden kidnapped, and young Riccardi shot in Buenos Aires. Then we might *do* something."

" Two stones is a lot," mused Greta.

" Cheer up ! my poor one. Remember Sophie Tucker's song, ' There's lots of sex appeal in the Ong Bong Poing.' " But before Evelyn could complete her gospel of consolation, an electric signal buzzed over Greta's desk. The afflicted blonde groaned, picked up her block and pencil, and went down to the council room. In the intervals between her more serious occupation of finding a husband, she was secretary to Mr. Beaton, the chairman of the English branch.

" Poor old James," commented Evelyn. " She ought to live in the Chinese famine area. I've just been doing a report on it. She'd get down to her precious 7 stone 11 in no time."

Jean had turned back to her papers. Munching gingerbread, she corrected a typed copy of her article on a coming conference to be held by the I.H.A. on slavery. Evelyn Raye watched her with narrowed eyes, affectionate and amused.

" You set us an example of ardour and enthusiasm which shames us," she mocked at last. " No wonder you had to leave *The Byeword*. It's office wasn't big enough to hold you."

" Shut up a minute." Jean deleted a couple of superfluous adjectives, added a missing comma, pondered over a semi-colon (a form of punctuation to which she was particularly addicted), and turned back to Evelyn. " What were you saying ? "

" Have some more tea ? I said that you were probably suffering from repressed maternal instinct, which makes you seize with passionate possessiveness on organisations. You nursed *The Byeword* like a broody hen. You ought to be married and have an immense family."

Jean considered this proposition with her habitual broad-mindedness.

" It's interesting," she observed at length, " how terri-fied we are nowadays of daring to suggest that all our impulses aren't purely biological. We're frightened of being thought intellectual prigs. I mean, if there were a lot of people here, I doubt if I should have the moral courage to say anything but that I was utterly riddled with complexes, and was trying to sublimate my maternal instincts on offices. But as a matter of fact, I've *lived* in a family. I *did* work off my maternal instincts on younger brothers and invalid parents. I've bathed, nursed, cuddled, and rocked babies until I never want to see a human creature under twenty-five again in my life. I may be suffering from reaction against excessive vicarious maternity ; but the fact remains that I actually enjoy this sort of life. It's not a *faute de mieux*. To me, it's fun. I like the sense of things happening all over the world—and feeling the contact with curious enterprises. The reports coming in. The notices going out. I do really happen to hate cruelty and disorder and waste and ignorance, and I do admire the people like Larsen and Schlacht and Millicent Tessing-thwaite who attempt to check them—although they're individually a little odd."

" If you had the whole world to choose from, though, you wouldn't go on with this—would you ? "

Jean struggled between the claims of truth and the solecism of superiority. She compromised.

" I'd rather be on the travelling side. I'd like to have power. I'd like a private income so as to say, ' To hell with you all ' if I disagreed with the committee. I'd like to have a quite different sort of personality, so that when I wanted something, I could make other people want it . . ." She paused, thinking of other honest desires. " I'd like to have more money and my own cottage again. I don't like being in a ' one-roomed flatlet for professional women.' I'd like to have time to read more and go to more concerts. I'd like to know Bernard Shaw, T. E. Lawrence, Siegfried Sassoon, and Virginia Woolf, quite, quite intimately, so that I could ring them up and drop in whenever I liked. I'd like to be on the Board of *Time and Tide*. I'd like to go

to Russia—no, I'd like to *have* been to Russia. I'd like to
have something to work for that I believed in absolutely
and enormously ; something so much bigger than myself
that when I was working for it I should hardly even know
that myself existed. I'd like to know that if I died to-
morrow, I could think, as I was dying, ' Well, anyway, I
have done . . .' But I don't know what."

She put down her cup, which she had been waving en-
thusiastically, and laughed at herself. " And even that
isn't all. The thing I really want isn't to be put into words
—by me—anyway."

" Can't, or won't ? "

" Can't."

" Well," smiled Evelyn. " You're lucky you have so
many desires that you're almost certain to get one of them
before you die." She sighed and Jean suddenly felt de-
flated, ashamed of her naïve declaration.

For Evelyn Raye admittedly only wanted one thing, and
that was beyond all possibility of attainment beneath the
tyranny of time. She wanted her lover, who had been killed
last year in a motor accident, not to have died ; she wanted
to be his wife and to bear a child to him : and she wanted
nothing else.

" Oh—it's impossible ever to tell the whole truth about
anything," said Jean.

" Love ? " asked Evelyn, casually.

" *Quite* impossible." Both, for a minute, were silent.

" It's so much more important," Jean went on, " to
love than to be loved. And my sort of person can't love
without admiring—and the field for admiration is—
limited."

Evelyn smiled, her dark, restrained, tragic little smile,
and at that moment, in came Greta, a bundle of notes in
her hand.

" Well ? Any more empires fallen ? " asked Evelyn.

" They've taken your advice about that Mandoan
business, Stanbury. They're going all out."

" They're—what ? "

" Mandoa. Prince's Limited. Great British Travel
Agency Battens on Slavery. You've got your headlines
all right. They had your friend Rollett up—and your

report on dramatic action—and they've decided to go full steam ahead." Greta slumped down into her chair and fitted paper into her machine. " You'll get your personality all right. Only it's a villain—not a hero. William Harrington Durrant, *Esquire*—Prince's agent at Mandoa—chief accomplice in mass slave raiding. Adored by the wicked nobles — unscrupulous — able — cynical — lived alone for months among the savages—white man gone native. And how ! "

Click, clicketty, click, rattled her nimble fingers, tapping out the resolution that the International Humanitarian Association should investigate the scandal of Mandoa.

But Jean hardly felt like an object of congratulation. She had lost her breath and sat speechless. Evelyn Raye was watching her.

" By the way, Jean. Wasn't it on account of the Mandoan affair that you left *The Byeword* ? "

" Partly."

" I thought that you didn't *believe* in any scandal then ? "

" I didn't believe in killing *The Byeword*."

" You don't mind killing us ? "

" It might make us. That's what Rollett said." She passed a vague hand across her forehead. The situation had suddenly become so complex that she could not readjust her feelings to it. " He said I cared more for institutions than for truths."

" *I* said something like that."

" No. I was thinking that those of us who have been reared in the family tradition—who are always serving a small limited corporation—we can't be uncompromising about truth. I mean, you can't say what you think about Gandhi if it'll upset Uncle Algernon for weeks and be bad for Aunt Ethel's heart. . . . We get used to that sort of perpetual balance between the opportune and the ideal that is most convenient in offices."

She had thought that all out before, so it came glibly, a screen of words to hide her perturbation and to silence the foreboding in her brain.

That was how she explained it to herself.

She had tried in vain to save *The Byeword* by avoiding the Mandoan affair. She would try to advertise the I.H.A.

by cultivating it. The more she saw of Rollett, the more she liked him. Being a humble person, she was inclined to over-estimate the value of fanaticism, having so little of it in her own nature. Bonnets, she thought, were none the worse for a few bees in them.

Rollett's case against Prince's was strong.

Jean, during the next few weeks, studied the advertisements, brochures and leaflets issued by Prince's Limited. She heard, in a press interview with Sir Joseph Prince, his usual trumpet-note of high romanticism. She listened-in to his broadcast talks on youth and adventure. She learned that about thirty parties from England to the royal wedding had already been organised, that a special route down the Nile to Juba and on by air had been arranged for those who disliked the long flight ; that a mule track over the mountains from Abyssinia was being widened, and that it was hoped to bring motor cars through before the spring.

She saw photographs of the hotel in preparation and drawings of its completed appearance ; photographs of the noble, tall Mandoans in their white tunics ; photographs of the royal palace ; photographs of a wild torchlight dance ; and one photograph at which she stared for a long time, sitting very still.

It showed a group of white men on a raised platform, lit by torches, and below them a wild crowd, waving arms and spears. In the centre of the platform, advanced a little from the others, as though he were addressing a meeting, stood Bill Durrant, smiling and self-confident.

It might be a trick of the camera ; but she thought not. Some pose of the light, easy figure convinced and shook her.

So Bill was really the villain in the case—a leading actor, not a figurehead.

She had told him to go.

Not that she set much value on her influence over him. It might mean nothing at all to him if he found that she was one of the enemies of his enterprise. He had never given himself away to her—never really broken through the veil of impersonality let down between them.

And she had almost swept her mind clear of him. Or could have done so.

Had he remained in her mind as the memory of an

irresolute, introspective, self-pitying, dependent creature, she could have forgotten him ; but the I.H.A. with its inquiries and reports and indictments, was erasing that image and replacing it by this other—the image of her enemy—of a man who outraged honour, humanity and decency in public and commercial relationships—who would exchange general advantage for private interest, civilised standards for barbarism, and order for the chaos of unbridled individualism ; and this man somehow became important to her.

The days passed.

Arthur Rollett proved indefatigable, in and out of offices, lobbying members of the House, pestering committees, stampeding editors, yapping like a small but valiant terrier round the heels of the apparently unconscious Sir Joseph Prince.

The great House of Prince's in Kingsway and the offices of the I.H.A. in Victoria Street became the rival headquarters of a yet unacknowledged struggle.

There was no doubt that Prince's were doing well.

The marriage between La'gola, daughter and heiress of the Royal Princess Um'bola of Mandoa, to Prince Anjak of Abyssinia had not only been arranged. It was already an affair of international importance. Mussolini, constant in his determination to lose no opportunity of extending Italian influence in North Africa, had declared his intention of sending to the wedding not only a representative of his sovereign, but a Fascist guard.

The French, thus awakened to the awkward enterprises of their Latin cousins, immediately despatched compliments to the Royal Princess of Mandoa, and offered a Republican envoy and a magnificent, if economical, gift of three canvasses by Watteau (their authenticity had been contested by the best authorities) and a bust of Voltaire.

The Holy See, recognising the enduring vitality of the Catholic faith (however corrupted) in Mandoa, proposed to send Cardinal Gapruzzi to inaugurate a new mission to Mandoa.

By this proposal His Holiness only forestalled the Patriarch of the Greek Church, who was, however, put to a slight disadvantage by the Mandoan tradition that the original colonisers of the country were Jesuit missionaries and their disciples.

The Czechs, Poles and Yugoslavs, responding as usual to the lead of their spiritual master, proposed to follow the French example ; and Queen Marie of Rumania announced her desire to visit Lolagoba in person.

Our ex-allies, the Portuguese, remembering their ethnological connection, expressed their peculiar interest in this ancient independent principality; and the Spanish Republic, stirred by old imperial memories, as well as by new anti-clerical prejudices, determined not to leave the representation of the Iberian Peninsular to the Catholics and Portuguese.

Seeing that the original enterprise had been English, and that the Air Ministry, having granted a subsidy to the civil air stations at Juba and Nasser, would be extensively interested in the development of the Mandoan route, it was only natural that the British Government should consider the possibility of official representation. It was rumoured, in Kingsway and elsewhere, that Sir Joseph, trading on his almost invincible charm, was manœuvring for the Prince of Wales himself.

Jean read of these activities with absorbed interest. She read of a mild and irrelevent debate in the House of Lords when poor Lord Lufton moved for papers concerning Mandoa. Two questions in the House of Commons were answered apparently to the satisfaction of the public. The inquirers, it is commonly presumed, do not expect to be satisfied.

Meanwhile, the I.H.A. lay low and collected evidence. Its idea was to let the Mandoan affair advertise itself ; to make all necessary inquiries, and to launch at the right moment an unanswerable indictment. It was, Jean thought, a serviceable idea. She turned it over and over in her mind, drafting memoranda, sketches for pamphlets and press paragraphs. Her mind worked with unusual facility. Ideas flocked to her. She had never felt so fertile, so ingenious so much master of her work. Whatever emotional stimulus might underlie her interest in Mandoa, it suited her.

She lived in a strange state of exhilaration, frequently working at the office till late evening.

So it happened that one November evening, she found herself still at her desk after the others had gone home. It was about quarter to seven. The typists had left. The cleaners clanked their pails along the stone corridors. Tired, but satisfied, she gathered her papers together. She often took work with her back to Kensington.

It had been fine when she set out in the morning, a warm autumn day, and, having been at a public luncheon, she was wearing her new coat and skirt, and had foolishly brought no umbrella. But when she reached the door to the street, the heavy rain was drumming along the pavement. Sleet blew on her face.

She withdrew for a second into the sheltering doorway, wondering whether to wait, or to risk ruining her clothes. The street was almost empty, but a plump little woman, tottering along the pavement on high-heeled shoes, hailed a taxi, which rushed contemptuously past, just as Jean closed with a bang the inner door behind her.

The woman in the street had turned, saw the possibility of shelter, and panted up the steps, her drenched coat clinging to her round body.

Jean, preoccupied with her own predicament, did not recognise her, but at the sound of her own name, she turned and faced Mrs. Durrant.

" Jean Stanbury ! Well, how nice ! *What* a storm ! Oh dear ! that taxi wouldn't stop. I don't know what they're coming to these days. But where have you been all these months ? Maurice told me he tried to find you ages ago, but you'd left *The Byeword* and you'd left your dear little house in Chelsea. I do hope you haven't been ill ? "

" No—oh, no. I went to stay with some relatives in the country in the spring. Then I got a new job."

" Oh, of *course*—how silly of me ! Such a simple explanation. It always is, really, isn't it ? And there ; I thought of accidents, and of going abroad, and of quarrelling with us all. But, of course, abroad and accidents have been so much in my mind, with Bill in Mandoa. You've heard about him, of course ? He's doing *so* well. I always knew he would, and I know you did, too, Jean, dear. I was always so grateful to you for believing in him in the old days, when he was so unsettled by the war—and, of course,

we never. could *quite* see our way ahead. And then, this.
I always knew he'd find himself."

She was jubilant, radiant. Water poured down from her
little wet hat on to her uplifted face. Her charmingly
waved hair dripped in wet streaks ; but she cared for
nothing but Bill's justification.

" You must come and see us. You're stopping in
London ? "

" I've got a job here. I'd love to, some time—I'm
working rather hard."

" Not every night, surely ? Ah, you're looking tired, I
think. What about a Saturday or Sunday ? Maurice would
like to see you. He'll be quite excited to hear I've met you.
It'll do you good. You must come."

Her kindness, her pleasure, her pride, shone like a lamp
in the dim entrance.

Jean gripped her papers in panic.

" It's awfully good of you," she repeated, stupidly.
" It's awfully good of you."

She did not know what to say. Her resolution, trained
for so long to dependence upon the pleasure of others,
fled before this naïve rapture against which she and her
forces stood arrayed.

She had prepared to fight Prince's, not Mrs. Durrant ;
slave-owners, not this little woman.

" You know, Jean—it's a funny thing to say here, but I
always wanted to tell you—how *much* your belief in him
meant to me—and Bill."

Oh, but this was intolerable, impossible.

Jean had not meant, by serving her institution, to involve
herself in personal treachery.

The word leapt unbidden to her mind. It was from it,
rather than from Mrs. Durrant, that she fled, with a muffled
excuse, down the wet steps, into the shattering rain, the
sleet, and the concealing darkness.

BOOK II
THE LOWER RACES ACQUIESCE

CHAPTER I

SAFI TALAL, Lord High Chamberlain to Her Most Christian Highness, the Virgin Princess Um'bola of Mandoa, rode down the broad central street of Lolagoba to call on Mr. William Harrington Durrant, Mandoan agent for Prince's Tours, Limited.

It was early April in the year 1932 and the rains had not yet come ; so the ass's feet made no sound in the deep powdery dust of the roadway. Talal's bodyguard, stumbling and sweating under the ruthless sun, occasionally evoked from him a sharp reprimand or a more languid direction.

The escort consisted of four Dinkas, in yellow shirts, white kilts and puttees. Two carried rifles, Italian army pattern, smuggled by devious routes from Tripoli. One bore an Austrian percussion musket of the type issued by the Hapsburgs in 1840, and the fourth clutched to his breast, as a mother nurses a child, the barrel of a dismembered machine gun. Machine guns were fashionable in Lolagoba, owing to the influence of the Chicago crook-film, "Diamond-set Divorce," at Hollywood Hall ; but since, like the babe of Solomon's judgment, most weapons had been divided between several owners, they did not add perceptibly to public danger.

Safi Talal was a prepossessing person. His nut-brown skin, fine features and black-pointed beard were legacies from his Ethiopian-Portuguese ancestry ; but his white tunic, draped over one arm, leaving the right shoulder free, was a Lolagoba 1932 fashion, and most becoming.

The house which he sought lay just beyond the main part of the town, and had been used a year earlier to accommodate Jane Crossgill and her fellow adventurers. Its main structure resembled that of most Mandoan houses—a square box of red mud, thatched with reeds, having a low doorway opening to the road ; but, as a concession to American taste, two windows had been cut into the walls, and an extension of the thatch supported by poles shaded the verandah, up which a dusty and wilted creeper trailed.

Talal surveyed the house with satisfaction. Fortune befriended it. One of his slaves had reported the discovery of a two-headed snake gliding from under the verandah, just before Durrant came flying from the west with the young man called Houghton. This was not the first aeroplane Talal had seen, even in Lolagoba. There had been the arrival of Saunders, whom Talal had entertained, as the patriarchs entertained angels and gods unawares.

In that house, Talal thought, lay a typewriter, a rubber bath, and a fountain pen. They were the harbingers of civilisation. One day the typewriter would click its magic orders, the fountain pen would write, and from London, New York, Berlin, Detroit, and Manchester would appear bicycles and sewing machines and loud-speakers and motor cars, plate glass, and steel rails and reinforced concrete, to build a city not made with hands, but with cranes and compressed air and elevators.

As for the young Englishman, Talal loved him. He was a man of culture. He was civilised. He treated Talal with the respect due to his birth, and showed none of that insolent and patronising animosity too often displayed by Americans and Europeans at Addis Ababa. He took serious things seriously, and appreciated the Mandoan need for such amenities of life as soda-water siphons and spring mattresses. He understood Talal's immense and restless boredom. He shared his tastes and interests.

Outside Durrant's house, Talal sprang to the ground, tossing his bridle with a jingle of bells to his senior guardsman. His silver scabbard smacked against the saddle as he dismounted, and he straightened his sword-belt before climbing the steps to the verandah. The little ass, dismissed by a slap on the thigh, minced off, swinging her hips with the self-conscious dignity of a mannequin. The bodyguard flung down its weapons and dropped casually into the sand. Like all other litter in Mandoa, discarded servants lay about the streets till required for further use, and since any freeman owning above thirty acres of land felt himself as naked without an escort as an English gentleman would

feel without his trousers, the street of Lolagoba were
frequently choked by sleepers.

Talal, standing on the verandah, blinked into the dusk
of the doorway, crying, in a voice rich and warm as mulled
claret, " Dominus Tecum. Say, baby, how's tricks ?
O.K. ? "

" Hallo, Talal ! I say, I think I was asleep. Phuh ! It's
been hot to-day. Just wait a second while I tidy myself.
Hi ! Mutt ! Jeff ! Drinks ! Bindi ! "

Two negro boys rolled themselves out of the shadowed
sand and appeared on the verandah, carrying enamel mugs,
a clay water-cooler and a jar of sispri, a fierce Mandoan
spirit distilled from prickly pear and sugar-cane. While
they were setting these out on the wooden table, Bill
Durrant appeared in the doorway.

He had been in Mandoa for over two months, and was
already burned almost as brown as his guest. He was
thinner than ever, but his eyes were clear, his hand steady,
and his smile of welcome to the Lord High Chamberlain
devoid of its old shadow of bitterness.

" I'm glad you woke me. I'd slept far too long. D'you
know, I rather like this habit of dividing the day into the
morning and the evening, like the Lord during the labours
of creation. I couldn't get used to it in South Africa,
but it seems to suit me here." He began to pour out the
sispri—a few drops into his own mug, for he found the
stuff almost undrinkable ; but he knew his guest's ample
capacity and served it to Talal raw.

" Say when, will you ? "

" Er—when. The sanction of alcohol indubitably one
advantage of Christ over Mahomet. And I don't say
mebbe. Here's how ! " With great dignity Talal bowed
to his host above his lifted mug. The extreme gravity of
his voice and gestures, contrasting with the hilarious *argot*
of his speech, never ceased to delight Bill.

" Do sit down. Tell me what you've been doing ? Have
you any news for me ? How's our friend Ma'buta ? Allow
me." Gravely ceremonious, Bill leaned forward and flicked
a tree-tick, fallen from the thatch, off his guest's tunic.
Talal bowed acknowledgment, and sat, with grace rather
than comfort, on the edge of a rickety *chaise-longue* that

one ingenious American had constructed out of sticks and
hides for Miss Jane Crossgill. Bill took his seat on a packing
case. The Lord High Chamberlain produced from his tunic
a small note book, a present from the agent, and consulted it.

"I want suitable dope on highly selected subject,"
said he. "Right now engaged in investigating Report
from League of Nations on Traffic in Women and Children."

"Oh, yes."

Bill had been in Lolagoba for a few days only when he
learned of the important part played by Geneva in the
political imagination of progressive Mandoan statesmen.
While staying at the Abyssinian court, Safi Talal had been
shown, by an obliging secretary, the documents sent to the
government of that country as a State Member of the
League of Nations. Hearing of the annual assembly, so
vastly more impressive even than the Mandoan High
Council of archbishops and nobles, of the multiplicity of
officials, offices, typists, entertainments and speeches in
the city by the Swiss lake, he was enchanted. The League
became to him the centre of the world of culture. Eagerly
he had pleaded for a closer sight of those magic papers, and
had finally secured, by a transaction not wholly uncon-
nected with a couple of valuable female slaves, copies of
papers which had been, indeed, only a source of embarrassment to their former owner. Armed with these, Talal, on
his return, had set to work to study civilised customs, and
when Bill arrived, one of his first duties had been to elucidate
incomprehensible passages concerning the value and
exchange of currencies, the international application of
motor-driving licenses, the statistical requirements of the
Temporary Mixed Commission on Disarmament, the
vaccination of Armenian refugees, the Hague Court
decision on the competence of the International Labour
Organisation to deal with agricultural labourers, and the
administration of the Saar Valley.

All these questions Talal regarded with wondering and
unprejudiced curiosity. Bill had at first been amused by
the naïvety of his conceptions, but after a few weeks he
began to realise that his new friend was a man of subtle
and profound intelligence. Talal really was a remarkable
fellow. Difficult, of course. It was impossible to predict

what next would outrage his amazingly sensitive code of honour. Bill never knew when he would start up with flashing eyes and his hand on his sword, hardly to be reassured by professions of ignorance.

Talal was honourable; and he accepted bribes shamelessly. For all his liberality, he gave gifts with a most lively hope of favours to come. He would have sold his own nieces into slavery, could he have done so without breaking the laws of kinship. He lied on principle, frequently, and with deliberation. In Mandoa, truth was too rare a coin to be used in current exchange. Courtesy demanded that answers should please the questioner, even if a knife awaited him round the corner. Etiquette overruled humanity. Indeed, the thought that cruelty was in any way objectionable never entered the minds of high-born nobles. Talal was known to have buried his favourite daughter alive, and his peers thought all the better of him. He commanded disobedient slaves to be thrashed to death and supervised the execution of the sentence with tranquillity. His desire to introduce modern fashions into his country was intellectual not humanitarian. If he spoke to Bill of hospitals, schools, transport, sanitation and cinemas, he did so from the positive motive of acquiring advantages rather than the more negative and normal one of preventing pain. Pity was a sentiment not merely unknown to him but undesired. The Mandoan code neither cultivated nor allowed it.

Bill, alternately repelled and attracted by so odd a mixture of savagery and refinement, ended by liking its exponent. At least, he was never dull.

Talal took charge of situations. He cared intensely whether he got the things he wanted. Bill had stopped caring intensely years ago. All that he asked of life was that he should not have to make decisions, to take initiative, to spur his dulled and enervated will to action ; and this the Lord High Chamberlain made easy for him.

In return, he had to answer Talal's endless inquiries about sociology, politics, and the working of railway time-tables. He had, at this particular moment, to return to the woman question.

" You know," he observed tentatively. " I don't think

you can take the Expert Inquiry on the Traffic in Women as
a typical introduction to the study of English family life."

" You mean League experts unreliable ? "

" No. Not that. But they deal with exceptional cases.
You see, in England, and in other civilised countries of
Northern Europe, and the United States—not so much
perhaps among the Latin people—women do pretty much
as they like to-day. Their education is as good as a man's.
They play games—hockey, and tennis and all that—they
drive cars and aeroplanes. They're pretty independent,
I can tell you."

" I have seen high-stepping dames drive automobiles
on the talkies," assented Talal.

" Just so." Bill also had seen the four talkies known
to Mandoa and thought them hardly more illuminating
witnesses to Western domesticity than the League Report.
" But English women are darned independent nowadays.
They keep themselves, you know—aren't attached to any
man, a lot of them."

" Hm. Have you known one such ? "

Bill's thoughts strayed with amusement to Jean Stanbury, and her arrogant, independent ways.

" Yes. Quite well."

" How many children has she ? "

" Oh, none. She's not married."

" Is she a virgin ? "

" Certainly—well—I expect so. Yes—I should think she
is." Suddenly confronted by this leading question, Bill
found himself slightly abashed. He had known young
women in London to whom the question, " Are you a
virgin ? " would seem as natural as the inquiry, " Do you
like dancing ? " or, " Have you seen the Academy this
year ? " But Jean Stanbury was not among them. Jean
had her reserves.

" Ah," commented Talal significantly. " We also have
ancient virgins serving the Lord. I understand perfectly.'

" Not quite. She's not a nun. She simply chooses not
to marry."

" Ah. A prostitute. That seems to me a very snappy
institution. What I don't get, Durrant, is why you keep
prostitutes and give frozen mitt to woman-traffic. My

Guerdon taught one red-hot O.K. principle, ' He who desires the end must also desire the means.' "

" I admit it sounds illogical. But we are illogical. We're also possibly hypocritical. Only you make a mistake if you think that prostitution is an honoured British institution. On the contrary. Our police can arrest the women for soliciting, and keeping a brothel for profit is an indictable offence."

" Unless licensed ? I understand you have many thousands of licensed—you call them public houses—in England ? Some, I understand, called Tied, where girls are slaves, yes ? Others called Free. Though why free women should . . ."

" Oh, *public* houses. They're for drinking, not women."

" Women never go ? "

" Oh, yes. Women can go in, but . . ."

" Oh, yeah ? "

Bill made a comic little gesture of capitulation.

" I'm sorry, Talal. It's one of the things that seems impossible to explain. Talking won't do. Words mean different things to us——"

" Ah, English highly corrupt lingo," conceded Talal, gracefully ; but he sat, upright and expectant, awaiting further information.

Conversation between them frequently reached this deadlock. Talal's most inconvenient trait, from Bill's point of view, was his insatiable appetite for knowledge. He was interested in everything, and critical of most things, except the beauties of a mechanised civilisation.

Seeing the Englishman yawn, Talal referred again to his note-book and announced his desire to discuss the League attitude towards Abyssinian slavery. Bill was to explain the English method of getting slave-work done by freemen.

Freemen ? Bill mused, and thought of Sid Granger and his friends. The bleak grey streets of an industrial town stretched before him, its squares of smoky grass, its tanks of steaming water, and half-frozen cabbages in allotment gardens. Half to himself, he began to describe the way in which British industrial work was carried on. The people were not slaves—but they were not free. They

obeyed orders, "clocked in" to factories, downed tools
when the whistle blew, were bullied by foremen, and dismissed at the will of an employer. They allowed their cars
to be stopped by the police at cross-roads, worked eight
or nine hours a day to benefit shareholders they never
saw, and to judge by their votes at the last election,
accepted the system with complacency. While Bill talked,
Talal raised his fine eyebrows and stroked his silky beard.

When Bill described the queue at the Labour Exchange,
Talal countered with the slave train to Abyssinia and the
Red Sea. When Bill urged the mercy of unemployment
allowance, Talal remarked that in Mandoa, if a noble
allowed his slaves to starve, he lost the worth of them.
When Bill conceded that Socialists spoke of the British
system as wage-slavery, Talal shrugged his shoulders and
observed that the attitude of the League of Nations towards
his friends in Abyssinia was all the more incomprehensible.
For Talal, at the court of the King of Kings, had heard a
great deal about the League's inconvenient and fussy pre-
occupation with the subject.

" I guess," Talal affirmed, " you are 100 per cent. slaves
and also slave owners. One of my properties, Kanackrie,
a Kikuyu, once lived in Kenya. Freeman? Oh, yeah!
British subject. All right. No Briton *owns* a Kikuyu.
No, sir ! Britons own government. They own roads. They
own land. They levy taxes. If Kikuyu won't work for
them, they take more land, levy more taxes. Kikuyu must
make money to pay taxes. O.K. Shall they grow coffee
for sale ? Britons say nix to coffee. Only white men grow
good coffee. Shall they make rich farms ? Britons want
land for white men's farms. Shall they sell their crops at
market ? Britons make all roads and railways to white
farms. So. Kikuyu work for Britons to make money for
taxes—but Britons do not feed Kikuyu, do not breed
Kikuyu, make no huts for them. Only pay so much for
labour as they agree among themselves. Now *I* have slaves.
I have bought them. I must feed and clothe and house them.
I must make women fine and strong mothers, must buy
strong breeding men, must feed children till they can work.
What Kanackrie tells me of British system just freezes us
right out."

Bill was not the man to contest Talal's position. He was all too ready to accept opposing points of view, and in this case he did not think that his own standpoint was different. Of course, when it came to thrashing slaves to death, that was going rather far. But there were thrashings in Europe—Lithuanian Jews with crippled feet, white Russians tortured by the Red army, " Red " spies beaten by Whites. . . .

Talal declared that nothing was wrong with public morality in Mandoa. All that he and his countrymen needed were material things. And those Bill could secure for them.

It all fitted in splendidly. Bill had fallen on his feet. There was nothing he need do except report favourably to Sir Joseph Prince when, after three months, Houghton called to take him back to England, or to receive his plans for further action.

He left it to Talal to face the High Council, to propitiate the Conservative isolationist party led by the old Chief, Ma'buta, and to secure the personal safety of the English agent.

Bill had no grave objection to risking his life. The old fear of flight that had haunted him and nearly driven him mad before he left England, was dormant, not dead. If ever he piloted a 'plane again, he intended that hour to be his last ; but he had endured the anguish of flight as Houghton's passenger. Fear had clutched him as the earth fell softly below the rising 'plane. With each pitch and swerve, each check in the steady roar of the engine, his heart had leapt into his throat. But he had survived. He had never given himself away. His grey skin and trembling limbs he had ascribed to air sickness. Houghton had not known.

That effort of self-control had saved him, for a time at least. After that, a knife thrown at him in the dark was nothing. The knowledge that he was the only white man in a city torn by intrigue and festering with resentment, was nothing. He was not afraid of death. It was life he feared, life, and responsibility, and taking decisions upon himself.

So he let Talal fight the High Council. If he wanted Prince's Tours, Limited, to set up an hotel in Mandoa, he must work for it. It was Talal, not Bill, who dreamed of asphalt pavings and ice-cream soda fountains. All that Bill did was to amuse himself drafting grandiose schemes for the popularisation of Mandoa. He discussed a hundred times with Talal the possibility of some sort of coronation like the Abyssinian affair, that might act as a magnet to tourists. The wilder his suggestions, the better the Lord High Chamberlain liked them.

It might not be the traditional rôle of the Pukka Sahib, but that Bill was well content to leave alone. He lay on his verandah smoking, dreaming, sketching out suggestions, talking to his friend, or listening to the Negroes, Mutt and Jeff, who were his chief advisers upon Mandoan etiquette and custom.

But he certainly wanted some sort ot answer to give Houghton, who might be expected almost any day now. Would Mandoa grant the concession to Prince's Limited, or would it not ? Mandoa meaning the High Council of nobles and archbishops. Bill had no means of knowing.

Therefore this afternoon he questioned Talal again, rather more urgently than usual.

" Have you any news for me ? How is my business going ? "

Talal drew his hand through his beard, sipped his neat spirit, and smiled.

" In a few days. In a few days," he said. An expression of rapt brooding stilled his dark features. " The rains may come any day now."

Bill had learned long ago that the concession depended in some way upon the rains ; but there his knowledge ended.

He left it at that.

CHAPTER II

BILL DURRANT INVOKES CIVILISATION

THREE nights later the first rain came, a light fine shower, little more than heavy dew ; but it was enough. It heralded the great May rains ; it reminded the Mandoans that God and the Holy Saints had not forgotten them ; it gave the awaited signal to Safi Talal.

Bill slept little that night, but there were few in Lolagoba who slept at all. Drums beat ; bonfires flared ; from end to end of the city pandemonium was loose. For a few hours Bill had walked the streets, his familiar figure arousing no marked attention among the revellers. He watched groups of black, gesticulating figures dancing round the flames, whose heat entirely destroyed the faint promise of freshness in the air. A procession of archbishops, led by a huge statue of the Virgin, swayed and straggled among the seething crowds. As most of the archbishops, like their lay brethren, had celebrated the occasion with lavish potations of sispri, the order of the ceremony was not conspicuous. Bill decided that there was nothing to be seen worth keeping him out of bed, and went home, followed by Jeff. Mutt had departed for the night on private business.

No sooner, however, had he dozed into a light sleep than he was aroused by Jeff's voice announcing, " Safi— messenger." Starting up, he switched on his electric torch, and its in unsteady circle of light focused an immense Masai, grinning and panting with an odd effect of aimable breathlessness. The newcomer started with shock at the effect of the torch, but composed himself to make the customary salutation of the country, a low bow over clasped hands. Then he produced from his saffron-coloured loin- cloth a paper, already limp and discoloured with sweat. Bill took it.

He was unaccustomed to the receipt of letters in Lolagoba, but the Lord High Chamberlain proved an exception to most Mandoan rules, and the paper, which Bill recognised as the back of a penny exercise book given by him to his friend, was fastened with Talal's seal—a lump of beeswax stamped with a Maria Theresa dollar brought from Addis Ababa. The message, written in a beautiful, delicate copper-plate, ran thus :

" DEAR SIR,—How is it with your life ? I also am well. Make right now copies of air port, hotel, publicity schemes, moneys, men required for levelling ground and all desirables. Thirty-five for High Council, Holy Church, Royal Court and Humble Servant. Rains come. Decision immediate. Step on the gas. Mandoa is Mandoa. Yours affectionately. T."

Bill tried to question the Masai as to the whereabouts and business of his master, but received no answer to his English or his stumbling Mandoan. Jeff's attempts at interpretation were no more successful. Then the man opened his mouth and pointed. Anxious to learn, even from gestures, whether Talal was still in Lolagoba, Bill flashed his torch full on the messenger's face and looked, between his parted teeth, into a gaping hole. His tongue had been cut out.

" Messenger O.K.," was Jeff's easy comment. " Country custom."

The Masai waited while Bill lit the lamps and wrote his reply, promising to make copies of the specifications for the aerodrome, already fully discussed with Talal ; but the other proposals, suggested as a sort of joke in response to Talal's lyrical enthusiasm for the coronation of the King of Kings at Addis Ababa, he declared to be hardly suitable for an official memorandum. If the Lord High Chamberlain seriously wanted to put them forward, he must come and talk over the matter further, and tell Bill precisely how far he was prepared to go.

His note dispatched, Bill returned to bed, but he had hardly fallen asleep again before the Masai reappeared. This time he had ridden. One of Talal's best mules, spattered with foam and dusty sweat, stood panting by the verandah. The messenger made straight for Bill's bedside and returned to him his own note, on the reverse side of which had been scribbled, " My god come clean publicity plans marriage most urgent dear friend talk nix I am leaving capital short business *private and personal*, T."

" Well, well," commented Bill, and reaching for his fountain pen wrote under Talal's message the letters " O.K." The Masai bowed, turned, and was off at a gallop along the now deserted road, in the opposite direction, Bill observed, to the Lord High Chamberlain's house.

Well. Things were happening then. The comedy had begun. Disinclined for further sleep, he called for shaving water. It was not, he considered, his business to question his patron's movements. All this time Talal had worked for him ; it was his turn to make some reciprocal effort. " Their's not to reason why. Their's but to do or die," he murmured, as he splashed in a minute tin basin of tepid water.

The rapid Mandoan dawn had come. Before he was shaven and dressed, wan drab-coloured light flooded the street. The air, after the shower, was almost fresh. Bill sought, in the twilight of the stuffy, dishevelled sitting-room, for his typewriter. He hunted among his papers for the draft agreement already planned and approved by Talal, giving permission to construct, two miles north-west of the city on land now belonging to the Royal House, an aerodrome, with site for a hotel and all the necessary offices, to be built by the firm of Prince's Tours, Limited. He collected paper and carbons, fitted a new ribbon on to the machine, and sat down to his first direct participation in the making of Mandoa.

Tick, ticketty, tick rattled his fingers on the keys. Tick, ticketty, grr. Something was wrong. The space-key was definitely out of action. Cursing softly over his spoiled copies, for paper was precious, Bill began to tinker.

But it very soon became evident that the case was hopeless. Without further tools, he could do nothing. He needed a small screwdriver, wire, heaven knew what—or he must copy thirty-five documents by hand. He sat cursing and tapping dismally.

The solicitous Jeff came with his tea. He looked at the machine and at Bill's disconsolate face.

" Sick ? " he inquired, comprehensively.

Bill nodded.

" You take him to Mr. Byron Wilberforce Gish, eh ? Mr. Gish A.I. mechanic," Jeff continued, touching the disabled machine with a timid finger.

" That's a good idea, Jeff," said Bill, who had never learned the indignity of accepting suggestions from a slave. His interest in human beings as such played havoc with his appreciation of the finer shades of social decorum. Safi Talal or Maurice Durrant would have known that this frank acknowledgment of indebtedness was improper. They might possibly have sought Mr. Gish later in the day, and as though on their own initiative. But Bill, from his first arrival in Lolagoba, had openly depended upon the advice of his two servants, and never realised the solecism.

" First performance now," Jeff observed. He at least was well enough trained to know his place, and threw his suggestions out casually, as though into the air.

" Why, so it is. I should catch him now, I suppose." Bill remembered that during the dry season, when only two periods of the day were tolerable for public assembly, the cinema shows were held at dawn and sunset.

Glad to avoid walking in the heat of the day, he shut the typewriter into its case, told Jeff to carry it, and set off for the cinema.

Hollywood Hall was a long thatched hut near the Great Square with the usual clay walls and floor of beaten mud. When Bill arrived, a little group of countrymen were drifting in through the box office for entertainment before beginning the day's serious business of haggling over their wares in the city market. The townsmen were for the most part absent, sleeping off the effect of their night's excitement.

Behind a raised platform of solid clay, under an overhanging thatch, sat one of the Mrs. Gish with her eldest son. Mr. Gish, senior, on his return from Addis Ababa had dismissed six of his wives, retaining the two most intelligent, whom he christened Lilian and Dorothy. These he admitted to partnership in his activities ; and Bill considered that the arrangement, whereby the wives took turns to assist their husband with his work or to stay at home and look after the children, was perhaps the happiest solution he had yet encountered of the motherhood-and-a-career problem, which used to perturb Jean Stanbury. Polygamy, he decided, had its points. Here was another advantage of the Mandoan system.

A money currency being still imperfectly established in Lolagoba, the audience paid for its floor-space in kind more often than in coin. The Gishes, mother and son, sat at the box office. Master Gish accepted or rejected proffered payments, and Mrs. Gish collected or controlled the takings, giving change with a promptitude and resource which delighted Bill. In a venerable dress of red-spotted cotton and a man's sailor hat, she dominated the queue.

As Bill approached, she was just removing three beads from a string in payment for a mother and two piccaninnies. She bit the gut on which the beads were threaded, ripped them off and returned the string, with the dexterity of an expert London shop assistant tying up a pound of margarine. An egg, carefully shaken and smelled, entitled its owner to two of the best seats for himself and his friend. A parcel of cow-dung, two pomegranates, and half a melon, a handful of peanuts, a strip of cotton, and two razor blades, which Bill recognised as his own castaways, were all accepted and assessed. The clay slab looked like a provision stall after the final day of the vicarage church bazaar, when four young bloods, still slightly inebriated from their midnight celebrations, proffered with such casual ceremony as attends the handing of a five-pound note to the box office of a small provincial cinema, a scrawny fowl, screeching and struggling, its legs tied together with a strip of hide. Mrs. Gish received it gravely, consulted her son, and handed as change a length of cotton, three beads, and a handful of cow-dung. There was some bargaining ; but after throwing in a few ground nuts and a slice from the melon, she gained the acknowledgment of a fair price and the young men went in.

Both the Gishes were delighted to see the Englishman. Mr. Gish, junior, leapt to his feet, holding out a cordial American hand, " Chin ! Chin ! " said he, splendidly. " Meet the lil 'ole' Momma, Mrs. Lilian Gish. Great performance to-day, looks O.K."

Bill explained his errand.

Mrs. Gish nodded. " Call Dad."

Dad was called. Mr. Byron Wilberforce Gish was one of the few men in Mandoa who aspired to European dress. In khaki shorts, a morning coat, patent leather pumps and pince-nez, he was indeed a resplendent figure. The glass of the pince-nez was missing, but the gilt rims encircled his round intelligent eyes with striking effect. In answer to Bill's request, he said simply, " Of course, I am a high-skilled mechanic," and taking the machine from Jeff set it down on the slab. A crowd quickly surrounded them, and, the performance being delayed, the audience appeared at the door of Hollywood Hall, though prudently refusing to come out altogether for fear of having to pay for re-admission.

The Lord High Culture Promoter went down on his knees in order to obtain a better view of the instrument. It occurred to Bill that this might be the first typewriter Mr. Gish had ever seen—unless he had handled such instruments in Abyssinia ; but the attitude of kneeling seemed appropriate to his adoration for all objects held together by screws.

Mr. Gish shifted his pince-nez solemnly. With a tentative finger he tapped the alarming keys, flinching when the hammers came up and hit the roller.

" Ah ! Interesting. Very interesting. The operation of the lever," he observed.

" But the spacing won't work. You see, the words all run together," Bill explained.

" Defect. Ha ! Mechanical defect." Very boldly Mr. Gish lifted the instrument and turned it upside down. The roller, released, fell heavily over the keyboard, shutting up both the instrument and the mechanic's thumbs inside it.

" Ow ! " cried Mr. Gish, dropping it.

" It bites ! " screamed his wife.

Annoyed with himself for ever trusting his treasure to these people, Bill picked up the machine, putting it on the clay slab of the counter, and began lugubriously to drum the keys.

A miracle had happened.

The spacing worked.

" By jove—it's all right again," he cried. He stared at the Corona. Mr. Gish stared. His wife stared. The crowd stared.

" Has any one any paper ? Paper ? " asked Bill, not too hopefully.

" Ah ! Paper ! " With glee the Lord High Culture Promoter produced from the pocket of his morning coat a sheet on one side of which was an entirely confidential letter that Bill had once helped a cousin of Talal's to write to the Royal Treasurer. On the reverse side was printed a handbill advertising the cinema. Bill's slight shock of recognition gave way to his understanding of the refuse problem in Lolagoba which has been solved by having no refuse. A city so poor, where even dung was treasured as fuel, meat eaten when rancid, and dirt left to lie where it fell, needed neither dust cart nor incinerator. As for paper, it was used ten times over.

Bill tapped out a few words on to the letter-handbill. All was well. He turned to thank his benefactor.

" Not at all. Delighted. O.K., baby," beamed Mr. Gish, graciously. " Glad to oblige."

Honesty, Bill had long ago decided, is a co-operative affair. It takes two to tell the truth—one to speak it, and one to understand. Nothing he might ever say—and any such explanation could be unthinkably discourteous—could persuade the inhabitants of Lolagoba that the Lord High Culture Promotor had not, by his exceptional skill, mended the typewriter. Indeed, Mr. Gish was taking every precaution that his achievement should be thoroughly well appreciated. He sprang on to the box office slab, and, with the typewriter in his hands, began intoning a hymn of triumph to the people.

Bill knew very little Mandoan, but Jeff, accustomed to act as interpreter, translated occasional words. The song ran something like this :

" Salutation and honour to Safi Byron Wilberforce Gish,
    For he hath tamed the savage beast of Safi Durrant.
    Safi Durrant brought it in a box.
    The box was opened. The typewriter leapt forth.
    All hail to Safi Byron Wilberforce Gish."

"All hail!" yelled the crowd, "to Byron Wilberforce Gish."

"Safi Durrant spoke to the typewriter and cursed it.
  He said angry words to it. He repeated charms.
  But could it move? Would it obey his fingers?
  It would not. Safi Durrant wept tears of sorrow."

"The devil I did," thought Bill, but he knew better than to interrupt a chant of triumph.

"Safi Durrant came to the Lord High Culture Promoter,
  He found the crowds flocking to the Lord High Culture
      Promoter.
  Offering gifts, offering beads and pomegranates.
  All for the honour of the Lord High Culture Promoter."

"That's a bit of a lie," thought Bill. "They came to see the pictures."
  But the crowd shouted in rapture, "All for the honour of the Lord High Culture Promoter."

"Safi Byron Wilberforce Gish seized the animal.
  Terrified, led by evil spirits, it turned and bit him.
  But at that moment the evil spirits left it——"

"Driven by the powers of the Lord High Culture Promoter," echoed the crowd, screaming and swaying now in an ecstacy of excitement.
  Bill watched the thin uplifted figure of the mechanic. "He's like that fellow who conducts community singing before a cup tie," he thought. He observed the rapt faces of the crowd, and remembered similar scenes that he had witnessed at Twickenham and Wembley. Crowds were crowds, in England or Mandoa. They had their corporate emotions, their mystical experience.

"Now is the typewriter cleansed and docile;
  Cleansed of the evil spirits that possessed it;
  See, it obeys the fingers of its master,
  Tamed and restored by the Lord High Culture Pro-
      moter!"

" Charming," smiled Bill, watching Mr. Gish, his round eyes rolling, beating time with his pince-nez. He remembered advertisements for patent medicines, hair restorers and infant foods. " I was bald ; now look at my lovely hair ! " " Jackie was at death's door. We gave him Flaxol, and now he is a Bonny Boy." What were these testimonials but triumph-songs ? Was there so much to choose between them ?

But the patent food advertisers did not speak of evil spirits. They spoke of anæmia and imperfect elimination and vitamins. " And what," thought Bill, " do we all know about vitamins ? Red corpuscles and white corpuscles, spirits and devils, vitamins and witch doctors ; is there so much to choose ? "

At least the crowd was enjoying its demonstration. Beautifully modulated, the voices rose and fell. White teeth flashed in dark faces ; white eyeballs rolled ; thin, dark arms were raised in the lovely intoxication of excitement. The music of Mandoa was an eery music. Long minor cadences, wailing and curious, rose, trembled, and shook themselves off into silence.

Bill thought of the cup tie crowds singing " Abide with Me," and decided that the entanglement of religion, commerce, beauty and vulgarity was more complex than he had believed.

" Well," smiled Mr. Gish when the song was over, " I sure am pleased to have been of service to you. Now you come right along and see show ? "

He beamed with magnificent condescension.

Bill did not at all desire to see the show.

He had his work to do. The thought of the airless, stinking atmosphere of the movie palace horrified him ; but he knew that to offend Mr. Gish would be unwise as well as impolite. He murmured thanks, and entered.

The hut was full already. The audience squatted thigh to thigh on the mud floor, thick as sheep in a pen, stirring and shuffling with the blind, drowsy noises of waiting sheep. Pushing, grunting, mumbling, chewing ground nuts, dates and pumpkin rind, sat the adults ; the babies sucked and knocked at their mother's pendulant breasts, " like lambs," thought Bill, and half expected in the darkness to see the ecstatic wriggling of lamb's lively tails.

From a hole in the wall, the silver tube of light moved across the hut seeking the screen, found it, and clung there. The watchers groaned with pleasure. The stiff skin-curtain fell back against the door, shutting off the only channel of ventilation. The heavy thatch pressed down the stench and the darkness upon the audience.

With a click and a flutter the mechanised noise began, like the grinding of a worn gramophone needle on a cracked record.

Dancing shadows flecked the silver light on the screen, then slowly coagulated into transient form. Bill read :

```
" Col—   rls—   M . . . v
  Dir     ted     y
  Bi      ly      gess
  Pho             by."
```

The whirring sounds had collected themselves into a shouted chorus of male voices singing an emphatic march-ing song ; but the patched film, omitting this strip, had passed to a shadowy circle of six half-naked girls, photo-graphed in fiery, unreal colours, who danced with a light gossamer veil, throwing it up so that it floated like a captive balloon above them, shaking it till it stirred like ruddy flame and wrapping it round their slender, swaying bodies. Their languid movements made a strange shim-mering counter-point to the rough march of the music, but just as the dancers faded from the screen, the tune changed to the liquid melody of their movement.

It was too late. The film splashed and flickered to the interior of a farcical restaurant ; a fat man in evening dress beckoned a comic waiter. A cutie with dimpled cheeks, her hair tied in an enormous bow, slithered into a vacant chair. With nodding jowl the man stuffed rich-looking food from his heaped plate into his gaping mouth. The dimpled girl caressed him ; her pliant fingers pawed his bulging sleeve.

The exhibition disgusted Bill. He had no objection to the simultaneous satisfaction of two carnal appetites, nor did he despise vulgarity. But this particular film appeared offensively obscene.

To the audience, however, it was simply a part of entertainment, unrelated to experience. They sat in composed and dignified acquiescence, sucking in pleasure, accepting novelty, disconcerted neither by magic nor mechanics.

Bill made his escape as soon as possible and returned to his typing. By curtailing his afternoon rest, he had all thirty-five copies of the agreement finished before dusk, and withdrew to his living-room, where he sat biting his pen, over the more ambitious proposals.

Was he really to tickle the fancy of the High Council by visions of tourists flocking in air-liners to Mandoa, of cars with caterpillar wheels and detachable floats, carrying sightseers from Egypt? All the absurdly impractical schemes that he had outlined to Talal buzzed round his head as the insects buzzed round his lamp.

" Proposals for advertising Mandoa," he wrote :

" 1. Arrangement of spectacular public function, *e.g.*, coronation or royal wedding. *Cf.* Abyssinian coronation ?

" 2. Invite representatives of great powers, who would be probably only too pleased to come, each with the idea of establishing exclusive protectorate over Mandoa.

" 3. Invite tourists. Unique interest of indigenous feudal state, unpolluted by contact with outside world since sixteenth century, with striking evidence of modern cultural contacts through (*a*) aviation, (*b*) the cinema.

" 4. Safaris planned and big game shooting organised."

He had hardly realised that Mandoa possessed so many charms. His pen ran easily and fluently.

" Typewriter sick again ? "

He glanced up to see Mr. Gish peering through the window.

" Oh, no—not at all. Perfectly well. But I always write first in pencil. Come in and have a drink."

Lifting the lamp, he was about to invite the Lord High Culture Promoter to sit on the verandah. His proposals for the High Council, spread all over his table, were as private as anything in Lolagoba could be.

But Mr. Gish had other plans. He bowed his way into

the room and walking up to the light, calmly blew it out.
Bill started, half expecting to feel a knife in his back.

" Better so," observed the Lord High Culture Promoter,
gravely. " Not want to be put on the spot, no ? "

" Why should I be ? "

" Safi Talal gone on business. Oh, yeah ! Bring Englishmen, hotel, aeroplanes to Mandoan coronation. Eh ? Like
Abyssinia ? "

" What do *you* know about Safi Talal's business ? "

" Safi Talal. Big noise. But *not* Cat's Pyjamas. Safi
Ma'buta is Cat's Pyjamas."

" I doubt it, but go on."

" Royal Princess Virgin and Arch-archbishop—you
know ? Now, I want aeroplanes. I am first-rate mechanic.
I want Englishmen, hotels, modern convenience, hot-and-
cold. Sure thing, kid ! But it is *not* safe to sit with lamp in
open window."

" I see." Bill began to grasp the notion that the Lord
High Culture Promoter was warning him of danger. He
remembered the thrown knife. " Do you think some one
might try to kill me, eh ? "

" Safi Talal not here."

" I see. Put me on the spot while Talal's away, eh ?
Well, it's remarkably decent of you to come and warn me.
I'll be careful. Have a drink ? "

He groped about on the dark verandah, finding sispri and
mugs.

" And what do you think of our plans ? " he asked lightly,
curious to discover how much the other knew.

" The saints prosper them," said Gish, piously. " I pray
every day to Our Lady for real dynamo and high-tension
batteries."

" We shall have to see what we can do for you."

" Her Royal Highness prays more ! "

" What ? " Bill was really surprised. " Does *she* know
anything about it ? "

" She wants marriage to Arch-archbishop. No Royal
Princess of Mandoa yet married. All, all virgins save by
grace of Holy Spirit. She is tired of virgin—wants to be
like Mrs. Gish, active modern progressive dame. Paris
fashions, beauty culture, cigarettes, travel. Also free love.

Arch-archbishop fine man—you know ? S.A.—and how ! "

" Really. You amaze me. All this is entirely new to me. I thought that Her Royal Highness lived in complete secrecy, and that nobody knew a thing about her ? "

Mr. Gish raised his mug.

" Women talk," he said. " I am highly modern first-class mechanic. Mrs. Dorothy Gish first-class midwife. We frequent the Palace. Listen. You have a royal wedding here. Princess La'gola marries Abyssinian Prince. O.K. *She* then is Royal Princess. No need for our Um'bola to stay virgin. *She* marries Arch-archbishop. Every one pleased."

" I see."

They sat drinking together in the dark bungalow.

After last night's festivities, Lolagoba was very still. But its silence was not the large, empty silence of the Argentine ranch, broken only by the occasional stampede of a restless steer. It was not the silence on Bill's fruit farm in the Transvaal. It was a city's silence, pregnant with the sense of quiet movement and sounds subdued, just as the darkness was a city's darkness, broken by the red glow from dying fires. Ashes fell ; babies cried suddenly from the black huts ; a blind dog, nosing a red hot cinder, yelped ; from the slaves' quarter, a woman ·screamed. Bill could feel all this crowded, fierce, bewildering life closing in upon him. This was Mandoa. He was Prince's agent. His activities here had been set in motion by a group of elderly Englishmen sitting round a fine mahogany table in a Kingsway board-room. They were directed by another more casual group gathered round a lunch table in Westminster. What had these people to do with the love affair of a royal princess, whom Bill had never seen, and an arch-archbishop, who was a handsome fellow, confined in a miserable yard called the Cathedral Precincts ?

He thought of his mother as the real enemy of the implacable Ma'buta. He thought of Talal as the real agent of Sir Joseph Prince. That was less incongruous. For Safi Talal and Sir Joseph were not so much unlike, though Sir Joseph worshipped adventure and the great open spaces, while the Lord High Chamberlain of Mandoa wanted spats and underground railways and a cinema organ.

As for himself, he had given up wanting or expecting anything. The world was mad. Life was too much for him. One thing or another. He lifted his mug and the burning liquid trickled on to his tongue.

CHAPTER III

A ROYAL PRINCESS INVOKES ACTION

THE Royal House of Mandoa had its constitutional peculiarities which Bill had not taken long to discover. Accustomed to a country in which royalty won its highest prestige by constant assertion of common humanity, by confessing to rotten shots at golf, by drinking tea with elderly cottagers, eating boiled rabbit, and displaying that fortitude in sickness which may be shared by princes and postmen alike, he learned that in Mandoa the contrary principle prevailed. Royalty there was divine, the Palace guarded, the person of the Princess shrouded in mystery. No man save an archbishop had seen her face unveiled. Yet no sentiment of reverence or affection inspired the public, whose duty it was, on pain of death, to kneel with faces to the ground when the royal litter passed. Mandoan humour set princesses and archbishops in much the same place as the older music halls in England set mothers-in-law, honeymoon nights, ripe cheese and twins.

All this was quite amusing. It was something to observe and meditate upon, as Bill lay idly on his verandah waiting for whatever action should result from the papers that he had so arduously copied. The Lord High Chamberlain had been away for nearly a week now, though Mutt reported that he had spoken to a woman, who had a cousin, who was a slave in the Royal Palace, and who knew that Safi Talal had been seen going there by night.

But Talal had sent no word to Bill, who was bored, depressed, and had nothing to do. The rains had not yet come with their full vigour; and, though by day the city burned and the dust blew as usual, at night a damp hot wind blew through the streets, and the mosquitoes went mad with joy. Bill did not feel well. He had, he thought, a touch of fever, and his ancient enemy, insomnia, was returning. Since reaching Mandoa, he had slept well. But for the last few nights, the old fear lurked in the corners of his room, and rustled in the thatch. Suddenly Bill knew that the pleasant coma in which he had lain since he reached Africa, might leave him at any moment. He might wake up one night and find himself ill and desolate, utterly alone in a savage and horrible place, where men killed and hated and tortured each other, where nothing tender nor green nor beautiful had life, and where even Talal, the man he called his friend, touched him with cruel, blood-stained fingers.

He tried to pass the time by talking to Mutt and Jeff ; but even they seemed to become inimical. The few court officials and nobles whom he knew avoided him. The people in the street looked up with surly faces. There were rumours of terrible famine and drought in the hill districts. It was said that slaves were being slaughtered wholesale. The donkeys were too weak to bear their burdens. Any man might catch and keep them as they crawled untended between the huts. To Bill it was all hideous. He felt that if he really opened his eyes and looked at what was going on, he could not bear it. But Mutt said, " It is the drought. Always drought before rain," as though frequency made it more tolerable.

" I shall go home," Bill decided. " I shall certainly go with Houghton. I can't stand this."

And then the fear came upon him that Houghton might never come. He might have met with an accident. Or have changed his mind. Or forgotten. Or the whole thing might really have been a trick to get rid of the English agent.

When he thought that, he would sit up in bed, his arms round his thin legs, staring into the darkness, hating Maurice, hating his mother, hating Sir Joseph. If he lay down, he felt the swirling fall through space before the aeroplane crashed.

He gave himself another week.

It was after one such night that he lay in his pyjamas, shaken by fever, unshaven, in the *chaise longue*, trying to read *Pride and Prejudice*, one of the few novels he had brought with him. Even in his loneliness and fever he drew a mild pleasure from the follies of Mrs. Bennet and her younger daughters, the absurdity of Mr. Collins, the balls, the Parsonage, the pomp of Rosings, and the circumstance of Mr. Darcy's country seat. At the sound of his name, he raised his head and, instead of the shubberies at Netherfield saw, almost with surprise. the blue geometrical shadows on the sand, the red huts, the burning sky, and the brown face of a Mandoan official whom he had met once or twice before.

This man approached with ceremony, and handed Bill a brief message from Talal, requesting his presence immediately at the High Council.

Bill saw no alternative to obeying the summons, and after a hurried toilet, followed the messenger on foot through the sun-cracked streets and across the market square.

Before him rose the long mud wall, crowned with pointed stakes, that encircled the Royal Palace. Towards the south, it was broken by a broad gateway, with double pillars supporting a thatched roof. The gates themselves had come off their hinges and lay propped against the wall, but they had been rendered superfluous by a guard of eight sentries who kept watch night and day. As Bill's escort approached, they crossed their spears, shouting a fierce challenge, which the court-official countered by a low-spoken password. The spears not only fell at once, but the guards relaxed their military attitude and entered into cheerful conversation with the three slaves who had followed Bill and his guide. Trailing their weapons, they joked and gesticulated, obviously enjoying some intimate and ribald joke. Their cheerful informality reminded Bill of the very different behaviour of the horse-guards at Buckingham Palace, and he reflected upon the sensible refusal of the Mandoans ever to let ceremony interfere with natural pleasures.

He had ample time for reflection while crossing the great court, for it was nearly as large as the market square. Its walls were shaded by thatched sloping roofs, leaning to wooden posts and forming an open shelter for the convenience of visitors to the Royal Palace. The natural heat of the day was augmented by four enormous fires, at which joints of buck, goat and ox-beef were roasting, their fat dripping and sizzling into rough clay troughs. Beside the fires women pounded mealies or ground corn between round stones. Fowls pecked, curs scratched for fleas, and naked babies, with protruding stomachs and spindle legs, grovelled for melon-rind among the ashes.

A company of fifty soldiers was being drilled by a big Sudanese sergeant at the outer end of the court. Closer to the palace a group of fine, saucy girls stood giggling and nudging each other, as they exchanged repartee with the slaves holding their master's animals. The liveliness of the courtyard indicated a session of the High Council. The scene was vivid as a flower bed and animated as a school playground. Black shining limbs, and grey or tawny beasts, tunics of saffron, blue and white, long spears with waving pennons, nobles dismounting from their donkeys with a jangle of bells and glittering of gay accoutrements, servants quarrelling with good-humoured violence, overseers barking out emphatic orders, a chattering of tongues, a scurrying of feet, shouts to recalcitrant beasts and sudden spurts of laughter ; these sights, these sounds closed in about Bill as he approached the palace, engulfing him in a bewildering kaleidoscope of colour, noise and odour.

The great palace doorway was guarded not only by men but by machine guns. Moreover, the gunners, Talal had told him, had learned their job in Tripoli. Yet to Bill's mind an even more effective guardian was the stench that greeted him at the mouth of the hot, black tunnel leading from the outer to the inner court. Used as garrison stable, storehouse and latrine, this passage presented to Bill an almost impassible barrier. He suddenly appreciated for the first time the horror and ecstacy of Mandoan dogs who zigzagged whimpering or yelping joyously across the sand, as against their nostrils blew the varying scents of sweat, dust, donkeys, rancid meat, smoke from dung fires, grease and babies. Like a curtain swaying in front of him as he moved down the passage, hung the smells of Lolagoba. His fever sharpened his senses ; he felt sick and giddy. He thought that it would be just like his luck if he fainted before he reached the High Council ; but even while he tried to remember remedies against that humiliation, he found himself again in the open air, standing outside an immense circular hut. His guide went forward, exchanged a whispered conversation with two young warriors, a hide curtain was held aside, and Bill found himself before the High Council of nobles and archbishops.

The light inside the hut, slanting down from a ring of small windows under the thatch, revealed almost a solid mass of ecclesiastical figures in white cotton robes facing a dark phalanx of warriors, naked from the waist upward, who had flung off their ceremonial tunics. Between them both, completely veiled in dingy Nottingham lace, stood an erection which Bill supposed to be the throne.

The hide curtain swung back behind him, shutting him in. He was aware of white eye-balls gleaming, white teeth flashing ; and he knew that he was sweating not only from heat and weakness, but from fear. He did not like being imprisoned in this hut with sinister and ruthless savages. His nerves recoiled against the thoughts of trust or friend-ship which he had formerly cherished toward them. He wished to God that he had his revolver. The hut felt like a trap.

An alarming salutation greeted him. The assembled Council rose, and lifting dark arms, shouted the deep cry, " Mandoa is Mandoa ! " then sank to its former position on the ground. Bill stood, not knowing what to do next, while a seemingly interminable debate was resumed between a small, vehement warrior, and a large, calm archbishop. Bill's inadequate knowledge of Mandoan enabled him to make no sense of their words, and he felt as though the whole episode were a farcical nightmare, impossible to take seriously, and yet terrifying.

Suddenly he heard himself addressed in English, and looking to the right saw, near the throne, the tall form of the Arch-archbishop.

" Safi Durrant. You come as messenger of great English Prince ? "

" Sir Joseph Prince. I am his accredited agent." One Prince or another, thought Bill. After all, Sir Joseph *was* a prince.

" You wish for the Prince to build aerodrome, hotel,

advertise Mandoa, marry Princess Apparent to Abyssinian Consort ? "

" If possible. Yes. That is what we should like."

Evidently a translation followed this brief exchange ; then from both sides arose violent argument. Papers, on which Bill's schedule had been so carefully typed, were crumpled recklessly. In one corner two young ex-soldier-archbishops came to blows. A very old man in a leopard skin, who evidently served as Speaker for the House, beat thunderously upon a drum for silence. Bill waited, dazed and bewildered by the clamour.

Suddenly it stopped. The Nottingham lace curtains about the throne moved a little. A soft voice emerged from their swaying folds.

" Our daughter will marry," it declared, first in Mandoan, then in brave, incorrect English. " We ourselves will abdicate. The present Arch-archbishop will retire with title. Safi Durrant will receive free commission. The High Court is closed. We have spoken."

By a law as old as the principality of Mandoa, the reigning sovereign had the right to issue mandates which, if uttered in High Council, became law. But nobody ever dreamed that under any circumstances a puppet princess would exercise her right. She was a breeder of daughters, a legal fiction, the pivot of an elaborate mechanism of magic, artifice and convenience, which left the nobles and clergy free to act as they pleased. Her only public utter-ance was the formula, " The High Court is closed. We have spoken," pronounced on the prompting of the Speaker at the end of every session. If the walls had spoken, the effect could not have been more electrifying than this first independent royal action for three hundred years.

The assembly broke into confusion and Bill thought for an instant that a free fight would ensue. But from the noble's side rose Safi Talal, dignified and composed.

" I speak for the nobles. The Royal Princess has spoken. Her words are law. Mandoa is Mandoa."

From the opposite side of the hut the Arch-archbishop's great voice silenced his wrangling clergy.

" I speak for the church. The Royal Princess has spoken. Her words are law. Mandoa is Mandoa."

The repetition of the customary formula calmed the Council. Like the National Anthem at the end of a boisterous English meeting, it produced a mechanical reaction. Before dissentients in either party had time to make their instinctive opposition articulate, the confirming cry, " A law is made. Mandoa is Mandoa ! " had sealed the royal words. A bodyguard of eight Galla warriors lifted the throne on its long poles, and carried it down between the packed ranks of Church and State. The hide curtains parted. Bill stepped aside as the Royal Princess was carried out. He had the impression of swaying veils of lace, of creaking poles, of the great shoulders of the bodyguard; and she was gone. An echoing memory mocked him with the words, " Remove this bauble." The councillors stood at attention until, three minutes later, a drum announced that the palace door had closed safely upon the occupant of the throne. Then, still dazed and silent, nobles and archbishops began to disperse.

The *coup d'état* had succeeded.

Nobody spoke to Bill. He saw his friends pass him without a sign of recognition. The Arch-archbishop led his clergy forth. Glad to escape from the suffocating heat of the Council chamber, Bill found his way to a patch of shadow in the Inner Court and stood, trying to summon courage to face again the stench of the black tunnel.

At that moment he disliked all Mandoans, all dark skins, hot sun, strong smells and crawling ants. He wished to be alone in a cool green place, and had a great desire to lie again in a punt on the Isis near Oxford, beneath a wall of reeds crowned by the cream-tossed froth of meadow sweet.

A messenger in royal uniform bowed before him, beckoning. He was a prisoner in this fantastic palace. Wearily, he arose.

He was led between huts, down passages and through stifling tunnels into a small square room hung all round with Nottingham lace curtains. The Mandoan dust had dyed them to a hot, uneven red. Three stools, and a throne-like chair of beautifully carved and polished blackwood, furnished the room. Bill felt suddenly so ill that he sank down on to one of the stools and dropped his head in his hands. The fever sang in his ears.

Presently he heard a woman's voice, " Safi Durrant ;
you sleep ? " and he looked up to see Mrs. Lilian Gish, and
behind her, a smaller figure entirely draped in Nottingham
lace.

" Her Royal Highness Princess Um'bola wished to see
you," explained Mrs. Gish. " Meet the Princess."

Bill rose and bowed to the pillar of lace.

" I am honoured," he murmured.

Mrs. Gish translated something into Mandoan. Bill
waited.

Suddenly the Princess took a step forward and with a
gesture of desperate courage, flung back her shrouding
veils. Bill found himself looking for the first time into the
face of a high-bred Mandoan lady. Her small features were
rounded yet delicate ; her full lips quivered with sensibility ;
her great eyes swam with unrepressed emotion. Mandoan
women aged early. Their hard life and frequent child-
bearing wore them out. But the Royal Princess Um'bola,
with a daughter of nearly sixteen, looked a child herself.

She confronted the Englishman with dumb yet eloquent
appeal, throwing out her hands, beseeching him.

" She wants you to get her daughter married quick,"
explained Mrs. Gish.

" Can she speak English ? " asked Bill, referring to her
as though she were not there.

" Not she."

" But just now ? In the High Council ? "

The right eyelid of Mrs. Gish drooped with cunning
significance. She turned to the Princess and said something
in Mandoan. The little lady dropped on her knees before
Bill, and seizing his hand, began to kiss it with an intensity
of appeal and passion that alarmed him. The tears rolled
silently down her face.

" Look here—she mustn't do that. It's not right."

" She wants to marry Arch-archbishop, see ? Daren't do
it ever since daughter born, for if they had sons, Arch-
archbishop put on spot, see ? Fifteen years is a long time
to love," observed Mrs. Gish, contemplatively.

The Princess began to speak, an unintelligible outpouring
of passionate abandon. Bill cried to Mrs. Gish, " I can't
stand this. For God's sake make her stop."

" I'll do what I can."

The interpretation followed. The Princess raised her eyes to his, adoring him as though he were a god who could bring ease to her tortured soul. Her gestures had a bewildering significance and grace. She seemed to embody all the fear and pain felt by those Mandoan women whose histories were anonymous and obscure as the histories of beasts. He remembered the processions of slave-girls carrying water, the frightened faces of children who were already wives peering from dark thresholds, the stories Talal had told him of frequent suicide.

This was a princess. Her hands, very small and fine in structure, had long, pointed nails, never broken by labour. Her bowed head concealed the face of a distracted child.

He was moved to terrible and helpless pity, and to a shameful realisation of his impotence.

Hitherto he had been separated from understanding of these people, because their speech, their customs and their appearance were intelligible to him only in terms that he had been taught to consider comic. Their extraordinary idiom, their incongruous names, clothing and economics, moved him to laughter, because incompletely adapted importations are commonly associated with comedy.

But the Princess, in spite of her veils of cheap curtain, was not comical. No broken familiarity of dialect obscured the meaning of her appeal. She spoke, as a reigning sovereign should speak, for all her country-women ; and Bill understood for the first time that he was not a tragic, adult personality working out his fate against a fantastic background of comedians, but that he and the Mandoans were human beings together, trapped in an inescapable relationship of destiny.

The interview ended. Mrs. Gish, alert all the time for the sound of footsteps, suddenly tore the Princess away and pushed her out of the hut. Bill was left alone.

He did not know where to go, nor what to do. He sat down again on the stool, and strange images of captivity and power assailed his mind. Time stopped for him. A day or an hour passed.

Presently a slave brought him fruit and milk which he drank greedily, not caring, in his thirst, whether it were poisoned or healthy. But the fruit he could not eat.

Then the court official who had first conducted him to the Royal Palace reappeared, and, beckoning him to follow, led him out through the labyrinthine passages between the huts.

It was late afternoon. Sharp blue shadows bit into the sand, distorting the outline of every tree and thatch, painting their heat in the colour of mocking coolness. For after these summer days, heat slept in the sand, the red mud walls, the stone, the metal. Though Bill rested his hand in the cool cobalt of shadow on the palisade, the hot clay stung his palm.

The square was clamorous with excited life. Bill's fever-quickened eyes saw the dark gipsies, the pedlars hawking eggs and pumpkins, the merchants, the slaves carrying water in round clay vessels, no longer as the picturesque inhabitants of a primitive town, but as men and women like himself, having their loves and anxieties and ambitions. Their bodies could ache ; their mouths could burn with thirst. A leper held out odious white stumps towards him, begging. Two girls, carrying figs on their heads in wicker-baskets, ogled him. A bishop, riding in state under a huge umbrella of plaited palm leaves, greeted him.

These were the people. Their future depended upon his judgment.

He was committed to them.

He thought of the eager smile of Mr. Gish as he said, " I pray every day to Our Lady for new dynamo and high-tension batteries." He thought of the Arch-archbishop, a splendid beast, caught in the trap of state ; of Safi Talal, the wary, untiring diplomat ; and of the Royal Princess.

He wished that they had left him alone. He felt ill and tired. He did not want to be stirred to pity or to action. He wanted to return to England with Houghton—if Houghton ever came. He wanted to be allowed to sleep again, in the soothing unreality of his first vision of Mandoa.

CHAPTER IV

SAFI MA'BUTA REPUDIATES PROGRESS

TRAVELLING three days by easy stages south-westward from Lolagoba, Safi Ma'buta reached his destination. Straight before him reared the stark hills of the Equatorial Plateau. When the rains have passed, their lower slopes are green with verdure and alive with game, but now they were harsh as rusted metal. Tumbled piles of broken stone, granite-coloured and black and red, disfigured their sides like the devastation after a bombardment. A dried water-course which becomes, for three months in the year, a tributary of the Bahr-el-Jebel, wound down a valley desolate as death.

But to those familiar with the place, this skeleton river marks a traveller's rest. Where it touches the plain, lies a hidden water-hole. It is sacred, guarded by implacable spirits of cruelty and revenge, and those who come to it from the pagan south press northward hurriedly, unless extremity of thirst overcomes their fear. The Christian Mandoans are bolder, fortified by the protection of a company of saints included in no calendar recognised by Rome.

Two miles from the water-hole, beyond the influence of its attendant spirits, Safi Ma'buta camped, with nineteen warriors and a few porter-slaves. He awaited the arrival of Talal's eldest son, David Copperfield Talal, coming from Kenya with a hundred and seventy slaves, part of the tribute paid by his father to secure the safety of the English agent in Lolagoba.

Ma'buta had agreed with the Lord High Chamberlain to go south and take over the slaves at the water-hole called M'Biki ; for slave raiding in either Kenya or the Sudan was not without its risks. He was half surprised that Talal had sent his son instead of leading the expedition himself ; but the boy must prove his manhood.

That was understood. He asked no questions.

The first light rains had already come and the caravan was overdue ; but Ma'buta could wait.

He squatted beneath a rude shelter of stones, hugging his lean ribs beneath his zebra-skin cloak and rocking back and forth.

Oh, he could wait. He was old, and had learned patience. He was favoured of the Gods, and knew power.

His mind sang a song of faith and patience as he looked over the bare, sandy plain, quivering in the light.

The Gods, the Gods favoured Ma'buta, the Almighty Christian Gods of Old Mandoa. The Father gave him power, to rule his lands, to over-ride the High Council, to defeat his enemies ; the Father had made him the strongest nobleman in Mandoa. The Son, who was Lord of Hell, having vanquished Death, was with him ; the Son delivered Death into his hands like a folded napkin, like a sash that strangles a slave in the dark when none knows it. The Holy Virgin, who was mistress of chastity, gave him dominion over women, that he might implant his seed of life in their living bodies ; the Mother of Gods had made him fruitful as a rich vine in a watered garden. The Trinity had blessed him. He was its faithful servant.

But now he prayed neither to the Mother for Life nor to the Son for Death ; he prayed to the Father for triumph over his enemies and power to drive forth evil from the land.

Safi Talal and his allies sought to corrupt Mandoa. They brought machinery—a vile and dangerous magic. They spoke an alien tongue. They sought the friendship of white men whose presence meant disaster. What did Mandoans want of white barbarians ?

For generation after generation, Mandoans had subjugated all inferior races, Dinkas, Nubas, Shilluks, Gallas, Hottentots. They had stood aloof from the crafty Abyssinians. They had driven off Arabs and Egyptians with easy scorn.

Masters of cattle, masters of slaves, what had Mandoans to do with men and women who were, by their own representation of their native customs, lecherous, cowardly, impious and irreverent, a people without honour or dignity ?

Ma'buta had attended performances at Hollywood Hall. He had seen the crude shamelessness with which these lower races exposed their folly. He had observed the conduct of the American movie actors. He had heard of the degrading heresies of the Reverend Robert Guerdon.

He knew that an evil spirit had invaded Safi Talal's subtle, ambitious mind. He knew that the old, the sacred, the noble ways were threatened. But he was unafraid.

Had he not already frustrated Talal's attempt to import a fire machine from Abyssinia ? None but Ma'buta could tell to-day who loosed those stones beneath the mountain path that hurled his enemy's motor car into the ravine. The slaves who did the work were silent. " None is so safe a messenger," ran the proverb, " as he who has no tongue."

Hollywood Hall might stand a little longer, flashing and braying its obscenities in the dark. The longer it stood, the more honest Mandoans, men of true, noble blood, came by night to Ma'buta, offering alliance

Durrant, the Englishman, might lie a little longer in his foreign bungalow. For every day of his safety, Talal must pay in slaves—the incorruptible currency of Mandoa. The longer the foreigner stayed, the richer Ma'buta grew, and riches meant power, power blessed by the Father.

Oh, praise to the Father of Power who would preserve unbroken the tradition of Old Mandoan glory ! The sacred springs would yet be unpolluted. The thatch of wickedness would roar to heaven in cleansing fires. The foreigners would be driven forth to perish in the wilderness. Thirst and fear would come upon them. They would run in circles like beheaded fowls, until they fell ; until the jackals came ; until the vultures dropped from the clear sky upon their decaying flesh. Let God arise, and let his enemies be scattered !

The old magic still lay over springs and water-holes. The rain still fell upon the just rather than the unjust. The clouds and tempests, the crops and creatures, obeyed their ancient masters.

And so it would be, world without end, Amen.

So it would be, world without end, Amen.

Backward and forward rocked the old man, till his quick

ear caught a strange sound, before his failing eyes discerned
the rolling dust of a rider.

A camel was coming from the north-east, sidling, loping,
lolloping along the roasted land.

Ma'buta's warrior attendants stiffened.

A messenger lighted down and stumbled with stiff limbs
to the great noble.

" Mandoa is Mandoa."

" Come in peace, my son."

The rider was a Sudanese freedman, who had once been
Ma'buta's slave.

" I have news from Lolagoba."

" Good."

" Say it is good, and good it will be, father of many
spears." And choking, panting, he gasped out the story of
the *coup d'état* in the High Council, the astounding utterance
of the Royal Princess, and the accepted mandate.

Ma'buta said no word. Once or twice he grunted. He
knew now why Talal had chosen this time to send his son
for slaves.

" So." And then, " so."

Finally, " That is all ? "

" If my father says that is all, that is all. But the
Englishman lay sick in his bungalow. And some said, ' He
is poisoned,' some, ' It is the fever.' Then from the sky
came another white man's chariot, and from it the white
man who first came with the man Durrant (may his soul
rot !)."

" Amen."

" And both went together to the Palace, the sick man
riding upon an ass."

" Have they now gone ? "

" The man in the chariot has gone, but that Durrant
remains. Safi Talal has placed a bodyguard round the
bungalow, and he who was sick has recovered from the
fever."

" So."

" It is said that a multitude of sky chariots are coming ;
that white men are to build a mighty palace, and that the
Heiress Apparent (may all virgins bless her !) . . ."

" Amen."

" Is to be married to a Prince of Abyssinia with great
glory."

" So."

Again Ma'buta grunted. His messenger dared to glance
up from his crouching position.

" The news is good," he ventured. " If my father says it is
good."

" It is good. But it has been long in coming and I knew
it all."

He had the messenger thrashed with five strokes of a raw
hide thong for tardiness, and with five extra strokes for
bringing evil news. But he did not have his tongue cut
out, so the man was lucky.

Next morning the first spies reported the approach of
the slave caravan from the south.

Ma'buta did not thrash the messengers who brought that
news. He put on his cotton robe and sat at the mouth of
his shelter, with gourds of sispri and baskets of dried flesh
before him. His slaves rolled cakes of meal in honey and
fried them in rancid butter.

Before noon the slaves appeared at the head of the
valley. First came a small company of riders on mules,
picking their way down the steep track among stones baked
hot as oven-bricks ; then the Negroes, stumbling and
breaking line like foot-stalled oxen, thrashed back into place
by Arab drivers. Talal always employed Arabs or Abyssinians as drivers. They understood their work.

The slaves were men and women and children. Some
carried ivory, some baskets of cotton and ground nuts.
They were forest men and lake men, and they climbed
clumsily down the rough paths of the hill. Hardly one had
not fallen at some time, because the loads were heavy.
Their knees were bruised and torn by stones, their backs
by the whips. The sweat rolled down their faces, breasts
and thighs, as though their bodies wept. Five Nuba girls
from the west, with gourds on their heads, were water-
carriers. They alone were hill-people. Their beautiful
upright bearing shamed the men beside whom they strode.
Some of the lake women carried babies.

When they reached Ma'buta's camp, their drivers halted,
and the counting began at once. The slaves were marched

in companies of ten, past their new owner. There were a hundred and fifty-two, counting children ; but of these three were ill, and unlikely to survive ; two were lepers ; fourteen were babies in arms, and seven too old for value. Ma'buta's face showed no displeasure while these deficiencies one after the other, were revealed.

As etiquette demanded, the young Talal remained apart with two servants until the count was ended. Then, as though unconcerned with the transaction, he approached Ma'buta.

In their grave greeting lay no hint of antagonism, and their talk was of the season, the rains, the hunting. Near Lake Albert, Talal had killed buffalo, buck, and an elephant. He had tracked a lion but it had got away.

They ate and drank as though in friendship. Ma'buta, from his small red-ringed eyes, watched his enemy's son. The young Talal was a light and plausible youth, with his father's agility of mind, but more vanity than arrogance.

When the meal was ended, Ma'buta said :

" It is sad, my son, that I must lose your company. But before you return to fetch my other slaves, you will, I hope, rest till the cool of the evening."

A change of expression, so faint that it might have been only the shadow from a flying bird, passed across young Talal's face.

" So," he said.

In that brief transaction Ma'buta conveyed his decision to have Durrant killed unless the full sum of slaves were delivered to him. He was sending young Talal back to the dangers and uncertainties of a second slave-raid—an almost impossible undertaking, once the authorities had been aroused. And the younger man, who had optimistically hoped to pacify Ma'buta by half-measures, resigned himself to the obligation.

He set off again in the evening. Ma'buta gave orders for the caravan to rest for the night and start next morning for his estate. There he would work the slaves during the rains, reaping full value from them before their sale.

That night his young men feasted on the fruit, the flesh and corn brought with the caravan. After darkness came, they danced round the great fires, singing a hymn of honour for their faith. They praised strong limbs and glittering spears. They praised their mastery over subject peoples.

" Mandoans," they shouted, " never, never, never will be slaves."

They praised their Royal Princess, calling on God to bless her and make her victorious over all her enemies.

But when they came to that verse, their leader grunted. The phrase was intended to be metaphorical. The idea that the veiled figure should herself have enemies or should herself attempt to confound their politics, had no place in their national creed.

They praised the isolation of Mandoa, locked in upon itself by hills and marshes. Mistress of the sudd that blocked the great Nile swamps, she lay inviolate.

" Mandoa is Mandoa."

But as the great cry rose, and the spears were lifted in salute, an outpost rushed from his spy-hole on the rocks.

" Two white men came over the hills with Offal soldiers." Such was the Mandoan nickname for the King's African Rifles. They were strangers no longer to those Mandoans who ventured to raid southward into Uganda or westward into the Sudan.

" How many soldiers ? "

" It is dark, my father. But perhaps ten. Perhaps twenty."

Ma'buta gave a sharp order.

The dance was resumed, the shouts echoed along the hills ; but under cover of that triumphant sound, Ma'buta could hear the shuffling and grunting of the slaves, being pushed back into the caverns and fissures of the sheltering hill.

When a little company rounded the crest of this final path, they saw the fires and the young warriors dancing, and the old Mandoan noble in his robes of state, enthroned on a great boulder.

The African soldiers halted. The two young officers approached the fire. They were brown, hard-bitten, alert, humorous men who chose their peculiarly dangerous and delicate work because they liked it.

They had been saying, as they approached the camp, " These chaps speak English."

" If they're real nobles."

" They may also be the fellows we're looking for."

" If so, they would hardly kick up this hell of a row right on the frontier after burning three villages. They're insatiably cruel, but not witless."

The senior of the two shouted a greeting to Ma'buta. He grunted. It was not true that he spoke no English. Like other nobles, he had been through Guerdon's school; but he refused to degrade his tongue by the hateful language.

He summoned an interpreter.

The Englishmen now stood just behind the range of the firelight. They were taking one of those eccentric risks which belong to the technique of their business.

Through the interpreter, Ma'buta welcomed them politely, and observed that Englishmen rarely strayed into the principality of Mandoa.

" Oh. We are over the border then, are we ? " asked the senior officer.

" You have done us the honour of visiting our country," Ma'buta said coldly.

" Then we should be glad if you could tell us where is the nearest water-supply. I imagine there is some in the district."

" In the dark it is hard to find, but we have water here."

It was produced in skins, harsh and warm, but welcome. Ma'buta sent warriors to refresh the K.A.R. troops. He invited the officers to share with him sispri and dried flesh. No sign of the abundance so recently carried over the hill-path was visible in the circle of firelight.

According to custom, the talk was ceremonious and non-committal. The officers were prepared to play for time and daylight.

They suspected this crafty-faced old Mandoan of some connection with the recent raids, but they had no proof, and Mandoa was still an independent country. They were, and they knew it, over the frontier.

Then Ma'buta surprisingly and imperturbably remarked, " The men whom you seek have gone towards the lake."

" What men ? We patrol the frontier."

" And I await mine enemy's son, with whom I have a
rendezvous." The duels of Mandoan noblemen were common
talk north of the equator. " My spies tell me that he has
gone hunting beside the lake." " Hunting " was the
accepted euphemism for slave-raiding. The younger
Englishman gasped at such bare-faced acknowledgment.
His senior knew that the old man might have good reason
to betray his rival. He was growing old. His hand might
have lost its cunning. He might be glad to see him dispatched by alien justice.

" He hunts by the lake ? That is forbidden by the White
Empeior."

" Our Lord High Chamberlain's son is a young man,"
observed Ma'buta, and he did not lie. " He fears no man
save his father. Least of all, white men. His father has a
white man for a friend, living at Lolagoba. Perhaps
this white man gave him leave to hunt across the
border."

" Ah—your white man—he may be a friend of
ours ? "

" His name is Durrant. He comes from a great prince—
Sir Joseph Prince."

Something like a muffled choke of laughter disfigured
for a second the gravity of the younger Englishman. A
great prince—old Sir Joseph Prince : Prince's Tours,
Limited, in Lolagoba—what fantasy next ?

" They go to build a palace," continued Ma'buta,
imperturbably. " Perhaps my friend Talal needs labour
for the building."

And not another word would he say about the
matter.

He permitted the British officers to sleep near his camp ;
he sent them back with an escort next morning over the
mountains. And, sure enough, in two days, young Talal
was caught red-handed burning a village in Kenya. A
sharp encounter ensued. Eight casualties were incurred
by the Mandoans, two by the African riflemen, and twenty-
seven by the wretched villagers. Among the Mandoan
dead was young Talal, recklessly brave and vain as ever.
Upon his body was found a half-finished letter addressed

to his father, the Lord High Chamberlain of Mandoa. It mentioned the Englishman ; it mentioned the slave-raid ; it anticipated swift return to Lolagoba ; but it did not mention that the major proportion of the slaves were already in the hands of old Ma'buta ; because that particular transaction was too private to be safely committed to paper.

The day after young Talal's death, the rains came in earnest. Safi Ma'buta rode north on his mule, his back bowed to the weather. Before him, in safe detachments, plunged and slid the caravan of slaves. Beneath him the earth responded to the refreshment from heaven.

God had been good. The sharp hoofs of his mule cut into earth that would soon quicken with life. The season of growth would come again. Seed-time and harvest would not fail Mandoa. The thin spears of rain plunged into the churned soil. The thin spears of corn would soon rise to meet the air.

Young Talal was dead. His enemy's son had fallen.

The white men from the south were mad about their slaves. They would know who had raided their villages.

Ma'buta never did work himself that he could safely leave to others.

These white men might be as good instruments of Providence as any other. God had arisen. His enemies would be scattered. Praise be to the Lord !

Over the slippery ground, stumbling, sobbing, sliding, drenched through with rain, terrified and bleeding, the slaves were driven forward to their unknown destiny.

CHAPTER V

AN ARCH-ARCHBISHOP SEEKS RETIREMENT

FROM the Cathedral to the threshold measured thirty-eight paces. From the threshold to the gate of the royal court-yard, measured seventeen. From the gate of the royal courtyard to the hall of the High Council measured fifty-four.

Ma'sull, the Arch-archbishop of Mandoa, was no mystic. His predecessor had enclosed himself within these priestly limits and found himself a king of infinite space. He would squat between the door-posts of his hut, roll back his eyes, and travel far from Lolagoba, from Mandoa, from the end-less shifting of personal relationships and the cramping dignity of inaction. He could call down the rain out of its season; he could blight the corn of his enemies, and set a shadow to follow the shadow of his friends.

Ma'sull had no such powers.

He had been a warrior. He had fought for the honour of his family against the family of Ma'buta. He had been a swift runner, sure-footed as a goat upon the mountains, a useful man with a spear, a wrestler of delicate skill.

When he was consecrated as archbishop, the rhythm of fighting and hunting was enriched by the further obligation of religious ceremony. He walked in procession with his colleagues. His deep voice shouted the antiphonal responses of the service to Almighty God, the Trinity of Father, Son and Mother. He lived in the Consecrated Precincts, feasting with his brethren in the Lord, riding out to hunt by day, wrangling in the High Council, and chasing girls by night in the hill villages, when he paid his pastoral visits.

All this had been good. Then the lot fell upon him to make the Prayer for Succession, and he looked for the first time upon the Royal Princess Um'bola. And in due course, he was told that Um'bola would bear a child.

He knew then that fate held for him only two alter-natives. If she bore him a son, he must die immediately.

If it were a daughter, he would become Arch-archbishop.
A prisoner in the Palace, guarded night and day, during the
nine months of royal pregnancy he waited, as his prede-
cessors had waited, without thought of escape. For if he
eluded his human guards, divine authority would hold
him. If he fled to the mountains, if he hid himself in the
marshes, if he swam the great lake beyond the sacred
boundary in the south-east, the hounds of heaven would
pursue him. The hand of the Father would fall upon his
shoulder. Whither could he fly beyond that power?
Neither above the clouds nor below the earth; no pit was
deep enough, no sudd-grass thick enough, to cover
him.

So he had waited, crowned with jewels, feasted, fêted,
with dance and song and slave girls, until he learned that
his prayers had been accepted; the Princess had borne a
daughter, and he, Ma'sull, was Arch-archbishop of
Mandoa.

Which meant that he was still a prisoner—a highly
honourable, influential and dignified prisoner, confined till
death between the Cathedral, the Royal Palace and his own
episcopal hut. Without political ambition or taste for office,
he had become the most powerful priest, prince, and
magic-maker in Mandoa.

Neither slaves nor feasts nor spells nor sacrifices could
compensate him for the satisfactions of freedom. He wished
to climb again the sheer rock cliffs of the Escarpment. He
wished to hunt lion in the grass country of the south, to
spear buffalo, to raid villages, to dance the sweat out of his
body over triumphal fires.

For sixteen years he had desired these things, yet no
man knew his heart except Talal. And Safi Talal, for all his
power and confidence, his subtle mind, his official authority,
and his cool daring, could not alter the Divine order govern-
ing Mandoa.

Or so it had seemed, until the white man came.

Ma'sull paced from the Cathedral to his house-door. If
he shortened his paces he could make the thirty-eight into
fifty. If he lengthened them, into twenty-nine. The
acolytes, watching, bowed their heads each time he turned,
thinking he wove a spell.

Perhaps it was a spell. Perhaps the magic for which he prayed without hope had indeed been his. Ma'sull had prayed that the unalterable might be altered.

The Arch-archbishop, the Head of the Church, could not abdicate. He could not make unholy that which had been consecrated. The oil which ran down even into the hem of Aaron's garments made him a priest for ever after the order of Melchizedek.

He had been given power over the rain and wind. The stars and the seasons were in his command. While he lived he must draw up the sun from the hills, and call the moon to rise. He must pace out the magic path of the south-west wind and bring the rains and the heat in their ap-pointed order.

These prayers were unchangeable and authoritative. He prayed them at the sacred hours, standing in the Cathedral, the priestly Ephod, heavy with gilt and jewels, upon his shoulders. He prayed them while tramping the rectangle of his priestly court, the long robe of his office checking his eager stride. Though his limbs might chafe against their confinement, though his heart might rebel against his destiny, he was the Arch-archbishop. He had power.

But hitherto that power had only enabled him to do those things which one in his office must do. He had used it only for legitimate desires.

Praying for safety from fire and flood, he was that safety. His outstretched arms gathered in his people as a hen gathereth her chickens under her wings. Praying for power against all enemies, he was power. His muscles swelled on his arms, and on his thighs ; his buttocks stiffened ; his lips ran back from his grinding teeth. Praying for rain the sweat ran from his breast and armpits ; he dissolved in water ; he bent down to refresh the parched soil.

But only when he prayed the annual prayer for safe departure ; only when he struck the copper shield with his cross and lit the city ; only when he raised the cry for the priests, " The Lord be with your going ! " did his whole body and spirit, his heart, his nerves, and his entrails, move within him to a passion of wrestling prayer.

" Walk accompanied by angels ! " he cried to slaves and warriors ; and even as he heard his voice vibrate above the other voices, he felt round him the unseen hosts of heaven.

" May the lions of courage guide you ! "

He heard through the night the terrific barking roar ; he saw through the grass the tawny, brittle flank ; he smelled the fierce wild-animal smell. He was again both hunted and hunter ; the courage of the lion passed into him ; he crouched again to aim his spear deep, deep through the entangling mane, deep to the heart, the heart of a lion that was his heart.

" From Mandoa, Mandoa ! "

From the court of the Royal Palace ; from the hot, sacred darkness of the Cathedral ; from the prison of authority. " To Arabia ! Arabia ! To the home-coming, to the journey's ending, to the life everlasting."

Ah, then he knew prayer that was powerful. Then he felt the magic stir in his hands that touched the Cross that defeated Death, in his feet that trod in the dust that subdued corruption, in his tongue that broke the sacred silence of the appointed hour.

He had been then all the travellers who left the city ; his soul had left his body and accompanied them till the huts of the city ceased in the barren plain, till the path grew steep, till the rocks that he had known so well towered above him.

His prayers had been mighty.

Since he had been Arch-archbishop the slave trains had found their way in safety ; their drivers had returned with immense tribute. Mandoa had flourished.

He knew how to pray for travellers.

But now Talal had put a strange and terrifying thought into his mind.

A man might pray for his own desires.

Ma'sull wished, with that part of his being which was still a man, not a deputy of God, for an end of power. He desired the impossible ; he was divided against himself. The current of his power as a vehicle of divinity flowed back upon itself. In dreams he fought against the very thing he was.

A prayer for himself, a contrary, separate, private, secular prayer had mixed itself with the holy, corporate, ritual prayer of his office. The prayer for the Thing that

Must Not Be, had mingled itself with the prayer for the
Thing that Must Be, corrupting the stream of power. There
had been droughts. There had been floods. The flow of
divinity had been polluted.

In terror of frustrating his own inalienable magic,
Ma'sull had thrashed his rebellious limbs, starved his proud
stomach, and spent nights of anguish stretched cross-wise
on the Cathedral floor.

And now the golden cord might be loosed, the silver
bowl broken. His sundered desires might cleave together
again. He, Ma'sull, himself, the boy who climbed the rocks
with clutching fingers, the man who smelled in the grass
the flesh of the lion, might be at one again with the Arch-
archbishop, the Priest of the Most High Trinity.

So.

This, then, was the thing that Talal said.

White men would come in aeroplanes and build a great
house beyond the city. The Heiress-Apparent, the daughter
of Um'bola and of God—God, who dwelt in the loins of
Ma'sull, his priest—would marry. For the first time in
the history of Mandoa, virginity should be voluntarily set
aside by a princess—not by the Royal Princess, the Virgin
Mother dedicated to government, but by her daughter.

While he paced the courtyard, Ma'sull's slow, positive
mind dwelt on three thoughts, and built from them definite
images of future occurrence, until he saw the Heiress-
Apparent married and heard the shout of the rejoicing
people.

No evil augury appeared to contest the vision. It was
good.

Yet, with the Heiress-Apparent married, with a daughter
born to her, it would no longer be necessary for the Arch-
archbishop to inhabit his holy prison lest the virtue of
birth should depart from him.

He could go free.

He could climb the rocks, hunt the beasts and swim the
rivers.

Urging his mind, goading it like a stubborn camel, he
tried to see himself swinging from steel-hard wrists down
the sheer cliff; his toes fumbled for the cleft in the rocks;
his toe-nails scraped on the hot stone.

The image would not come. He could not feel his freedom. The magic failed him.

Up and down he tramped.

He knew that Lilian Gish, the Galla's wife, had taken Um'bola's place on the royal throne.

He knew that Talal had cheated the High Council.

He knew that the Englishman, Houghton, had flown away in his great air-machine with stamped and sealed letters of warrant to build a white-man's palace in Mandoa.

All this had taken place in order that he might see again the plains and the ravines and the marshes.

He closed his eyes, tramping the sacred rectangle. But the images refused to obey his summons.

A cold sweat broke upon his chest and forehead.

The power of the Trinity no longer flowed clearly through him. He was afraid.

Yet it was too late to withdraw. What he had done, he had done.

Eight red-robed acolytes, the sweat-damp cotton clinging to their limbs, came out to him, bearing the Archiepiscopal canopy.

He raised his hand in blessing and they set round his neck a stole of ochre-dyed wool, embroidered with crosses and lions in raffia. They gave him the long staff with the gilded cross; and, leaning on this, he walked under the canopy to the Cathedral.

There, before the altar on a silver tray, lay four reddish clots of caked earth. They were the turfs, one cut from each corner of the new aerodrome, brought for blessing.

The Cathedral was full. The white robes of the arch-bishops gleamed in the dark chancel. The nobles and people rose as he entered. The familiar scent of their bodies, their closeness, the corporate presence of the church militant here in Mandoa, reassured him. His prayers were their prayers; his will, their will. He was the deputy of God, and his judgment was infallible, being divine.

The chanted hymn filled his ears, calming his nerves, reassuring him.

He felt benediction flow from his breast and down his arms, into the staff with the golden cross.

When the singing ceased and he lowered the staff,

touching the turfs and calling upon the Trinity, he knew
that what he had done was good.

His blessing filled the Cathedral, the air, the city.

When he dismissed the congregation his voice was rich
with benediction.

Away they went, flocking from the darkness into the
sunlight. From his place by the altar he saw them go,
bearing the tray. He heard their voices fade slowly into
the distance and saw, no longer with his bodily eyes, but
with the power of his imagination, their progress across the
square, through the wide streets between the low red huts
and out from the north-western borders of the city.

There stretched the plain which was to be levelled. He
knew how. Safi Durrant had explained. Sandy holes were
to be filled in, mounds cut down, the quagmire that
formed in the rainy season drained the foundation for
the white man's palace, the hotel, dug like a pit. Many
hundreds of slaves would sweat there ; and when they had
finished, the man called Ma'sull, no longer the prisoner
of power, but once more a hunter and warrior, would be
free.

He left the Cathedral and returned to his own house.

In the darkness of the hut a figure stirred. He knew
who it must be.

" Um'bola."

Her shrouding laces brushed against him.

" Soon," she said. " Soon. You have blessed the
turfs ? "

He knew that in her eyes the royal marriage meant only
safety for their union. She had known no man since her
child was born, lest, bearing a son, she should bring death
to him.

Once the heiress had a daughter, the Royal Princess
might bear sons without fear to the Arch-archbishop.

He shivered with the effort of his benediction. Virtue
had gone out of him into the turfs.

" Do you know," she said, " that young Talal was killed
by Englishmen across the frontier ? "

That had nothing to do with the efficacy of his prayers.
He shook off the thought like a fly from his shoulder.

" Ma'buta is collecting slaves. He is three times richer

than Talal. Daily he draws to himself men who will follow him. Lilian Gish has heard that he has also white men whom he has angered against Talal as a slave-owner. Can you not pray against Ma'buta, who is our enemy ? Could not God strike him dead ? "

But Ma'sull pushed away her clinging hands. He had no prayer beyond those given him by virtue of his office, and though daily he prayed against the enemies of the Royal Princess and her country, it was not for him to say on whom that malediction should descend.

Was Ma'buta the enemy ?

Mar'sull had no cunning like Talal's to anticipate action, nor had he a woman's fear of the personal, human thing.

But as the rains fell more and more heavily on Mandoa, he moved through the ordered ritual with increasing effort, unable to be certain whether it was God's will that before he died he would be free again to resume the life his body knew and loved.

CHAPTER VI

TALAL ENTERTAINS THE ANGELS

THROUGHOUT the rainy season, Mandoa laboured. Slaves were plentiful. Streams poured down in torrents. Two quite unprecedented deaths by drowning took place in Lolagoba. Vegetation rioted. Bill returned after ten days in the hills, examining the stone quarries, to find his bungalow swallowed alive by an immense tlagi-vine. Its succulent green arms clutched walls, thatch and verandah ; tendrils plump as water-pipes climbed through doors and windows ; buds like vegetable marrows swelled among the chairs and tables.

It took three days and thirty slaves to cut it clear, and even then Bill sometimes woke sweating from a nightmare in which man-eating tlagi-vines smothered him in a devouring embrace. But he had fever in those days, and was apt to dream.

Before the heat came and while the ground was still soft,

there was so much to do that he dared not be ill for long. He took quinine till his head sang and his feet seemed a long, long way from his red-rimmed eyes. In the days when he was at his worst, Talal nursed him with a mocking devotion that Bill found strangely agreeable.

Drenched, mud-caked, and aching, the slaves drained the huge field of the aerodrome and danced it level with naked feet. They tore an amphitheatre out of the side of the hill. They dug the foundations of hotel and hospital.

The Mandoa nobility, their cotton tunics laid aside, rode naked to the hips among the straining slaves, criticising, amending, suggesting, and sometimes calling out a listless worker to be thrashed. The High Council met constantly, and the Royal Princess continued to visit in secret the Ecclesiastical Precincts.

Toward the end of the rainy season, there are sunsets to be seen from Lolagoba. The rich humid days wane, leaving the city drenched in shadow, while the western sky glows like a fiery furnace. At such times the people leave their huts and walk up and down, excited and uneasy as cattle before a storm. They have never learned to take such transitory brilliance for granted, and will not believe that so much ado of red and purple, streaming light and golden cloud, can be about nothing.

But it was not only the expectation of natural phenomena that drove them this evening to the aerodrome.

Round and round, up and down, they walked, their voices little louder than the perpetual choir of insects.

Twenty days ago Houghton had arrived in his monoplane to inquire how far the preparations had gone, and, finding the row of hangars standing beside the levelled aerodrome, the stones and wood ready on the site of the hotel, and the ferocity of the rains abating, had returned to fetch the directors of the remaining work.

They should arrive at any hour, and all Mandoa would be there to receive them. In the Cathedral, archbishops had spoken of their coming. Like angels they would descend upon Mandoa, bringing prosperity and power with them.

And now they were due.

Bill Durrant walked alone among the people.

When from time to time he turned westward, his whole

body was caught and bathed in light. Beyond the horizon
the dark plain melted in bright splendour, transforming
the commonplace figures of the loiterers into sharply
dramatic groups. An immense significance, a mystery, a
stillness, held them as by a spell.

Then from the heart of the sunset came a soft vibration,
not a sound yet, but as though a nerve detached from each
watcher were twanging outside and yet connected with
him. They looked westward, drilled by the pageant-master
curiosity, and stood hooding with cupped hands their
dazzled eyes.

" Safi ? "

The men round Bill appealed to him.

" I can't see. I'm not sure."

But others, longer-sighted than he, had seen.

" The aeroplane ! The aeroplane ! "

Out of the west it came, at first no more than a black
speck, then a bird broadening against the ruddy light, a
bird with spreading wings. The vibration deepened to a
soft humming, then to a roar, as down from the sunset the
great biplane zoomed over the aerodrome of Lolagoba.

" It's beautiful. Good Lord, it's beautiful," muttered
the English agent. His eyes were dazzled, and when he
looked back at the field, fiery rings expanded and contracted against the darkness.

But all was ready. On white ponies at the entrance to the
field sat Talal and his warriors. Beyond him the archbishops waited with the golden cross.

Three times the huge biplane circled over the crowd,
blackening the sky, roaring above their heads ; then down
it came, smoothly, sweetly, taxi-ing along the field stamped
level by a thousand feet.

The Lord High Culture Promoter and his corps of groundsmen ran out. The nobles and archbishops moved forward.
A circle of warriors with lowered spears held back the
people.

Then Safi Talal, leading a hundred mounted noblemen,
swept forward at the gallop on little Arab horses. Three
times they circled the machine, their bright swords lifted
in glittering salute. Three times they shouted " Mandoa is
Mandoa ! " Then they stopped dead and sat like statues

in a ring, as the archbishops in their white robes walked sedately into the circle that they made.

The golden cross caught all the sunset fires.

" As the Holy Spirit descended upon Mary," sang the vanguard of archbishops.

" So did the sky-machine descend on Lolagoba," answered the rear.

" With blessing to make her fruitful."

" With power from the west to bring prosperity."

" That our souls might be saved."

" And our bodies nourished."

" World without end."

" Amen."

The procession halted.

Fiery cross, ponies with tossing manes, grave brown-armed men, vast crowds and spears uplifted, stood for a moment fixed in golden light.

Then, as though a hand wiped out a drawing from a blackboard, a blue cloud wiped the colours from the sky. The spell was broken. The pageant dissolved with the abrupt irreverence of Mandoan custom.

Nobles dismounted and handed their bridles to the running grooms. Archbishops chatted and swore and, arm in arm, wandered about the field. The warriors had to use all their strength to hold back the curious mob.

The newcomers descended from the big passenger machine.

Bill saw Mason, one of the chief engineers attached to Prince's, Jordan, an architect, Nicholson, a trade commissioner, and three or four of the lesser fry.

He waited at the edge of the circle.

For months he had been living in expectation of this moment. These were his people. He was no longer alone among Mandoans. Henceforward he could enjoy the society of men who spoke his own language and shared his thoughts and memories. The perpetual misunderstandings and cross-purposes of most Mandoan conversations would be at an end. It was to meet such company again that he had nearly run away from Lolagoba, the first time Houghton called. He had been on the verge of throwing up his work, his position and his self-respect for them.

Now he was panic-stricken, afraid of his own expectations.

Here were Englishmen. They were coming to make Mandoa into a modern city to please Talal. They were men of civilisation, mellowed by experience. They shared the secret memories of Europe, memories of Oxford quadrangles by moonlight, and of Bach quartettes played beneath painted cherubs in elegant gold and white apartments, of the smell of coffee and warm baked bread in small Paris streets, and of damp, upturned earth in a newly-ploughed field.

It was ridiculous to be afraid of them. Bill fed his courage upon the reflection that he, after all, had got here first. He it was who had borne the loneliness and the fever. His beard had grown because the Mandoans had stolen both his razors. His shirt was stained and shabby because Mandoa was a bad place for clothes. His hands shook because he had had malaria. If the mud hut in which the newcomers had to sleep was primitive, he need not be ashamed of it. Such accommodation had been good enough for him.

After all, he had done the Mandoan business rather well. He had kept himself alive among these savages. The aerodrome was built, the hangars ready. Even if he himself had contributed little but tactful inanition to the work, the result was satisfactory.

He went forward.

" Ah. So you're Durrant."

Mason's cold eye might have been inspecting a bridge. Bill felt as though his proportions and spans and levers had been measured and disapproved of. The engineer was, he knew, a brilliant technician. Perhaps mastery over inanimate matter gave one this grim and unreceptive self-assurance. Jordan, the pallid, dark-haired architect, looked more congenial ; but he also looked air-sick. Nicholson was already practising the technique of salesmanship, shaking hands with the Mandoan nobles, and uttering bright captions in a friendly tone.

" My God," Bill cried to his wilting heart. " What does one talk to these men about ? What does one say ? "

He asked them what sort of a journey they had had. He

wished he had cigarettes left to offer them, and was immensely relieved when Nicholson pulled out his case.

He explained, tentatively, that they all were expected to dine that evening with Talal.

" A sort of public welcome, you know. He's the big noise here so far as Prince's is concerned. This is a kind of Lord Mayor's banquet, don't you know."

He heard himself talking like the fool they probably thought him.

" Quite safe if you only eat what I eat—I'm acclimatised by now. Not that there's any fear after the rains that they'll serve you with stewed baby or any tricks like that ! Still—their notion of hanging game is not ours."

" Indeed ? " Jordan's sallow face brightened. " Have you experienced much dietetic difficulty here ? Personally, I always find that meat *once* a day, and for the rest a little fish, or game perhaps, or a small dish of chicken and some kind of salad, and a decent savoury, is *quite* enough."

" I suppose you have your own ' boys ' to cook for you ? " asked Mason. " D'you have any difficulty in getting hold of good ' boys ' ? On the west coast I found that, when properly handled, niggers could cook quite decently."

They were wandering in a little solid European block towards the new Rest Hut where they could deposit their things before attending the banquet.

" You'll change, of course ? " Mason said. Bill was given the impression that only by changing for dinner could the prestige of the British Empire be preserved.

" What sort of fellow is this Talal ? "

" Do we have to eat with the natives ? "

" What's the drinking water like here ? "

" Very few signs of real cultivation as we came over— I suppose—— ? "

" Splendid physique those fellows." That was the genial Nicholson. Bill's heart, which had contracted at his florid exuberance, warmed to his appreciation.

" Look here, Durrant." This was a little fellow called Cooper. " There's something very important I feel I ought to tell you—while we have the chance—in confidence, you know. If Walton asks you to play bridge with him—don't. That's all. 'Nuff said. Don't."

The Rest Hut was, like Bill's bungalow, a rough box of red mud, thatched, and pierced with holes for doors and windows. Veils of muslin had been pinned behind the windows. A cotton curtain hung before the door.

The porters were running in and out like ants, carrying kit.

The box became filled with civilisation. Bill looked at it. "Inside there," he thought, "is Europe, Culture, Home."

He called Mutt to his side.

"Listen," he said. "Go and tell Safi Talal, with my greetings, to be surprised at *nothing* the white men say or do. And tell him to fill their glasses often."

He watched his servant lope off into the darkness.

"Well, they may be tolerable drunk," he said to himself. "But, my God, they're awful sober."

He returned to the hut where the Englishmen were making their hasty toilet.

"There's a drink that will be served to-night called sispri," he announced. "It's a sort of native spirit. It's absolutely necessary that you take some. Like eating a man's salt. It's not nearly as fierce as it tastes—a bit fiery, but not more intoxicating than beer unless any one has a particularly weak head."

He hoped that that would suffice. None of them would like admitting to weak heads. Or would they ? How long was it since he had met men like that ? Years and years. And he had always hated them.

"You can't hate people wholesale," he told himself. "Well, after to-night, I shall be perfectly good. It's their damned superiority I can't and won't stand."

These were the men whom he was bringing to build Talal's new world. And neither for himself nor for his friend would he stand patronage.

But it was a marvellously brushed and polished party which he escorted through the town.

They marched surrounded by torch-bearers in yellow tunics. The flames spluttered and roared. Little boys ran among the legs of the escort, agape with curiosity. Between the huts the cooking-fires died low. Drums beat ; slaves sang ; the smell and noise and tumult of the city bore down upon them.

" Think our tourist friends will like this ? " asked Mason, handkerchief to nose. " Shall we be expected to kiss the hand of this potentate, Durrant ? Because I'm damned if I will."

" Picturesque, brilliant, unique," Nicholson murmured, composing advertisements for the " Come to Mandoa " campaign as he stumbled through the sand.

" It's rather important to be polite," Bill suggested.

" All right, *all* right."

They halted outside the stockade surrounding Talal's house. A band, blowing horns and banging drums came out to welcome them, and they were led into a great fiery circle.

Around it stood twenty-five negro slaves, their naked bodies oiled and polished. Each held high over his head a spluttering torch.

In the centre, a circular table had been spread with cups of wine and bowls of fruit. Beside it stood Talal, with a score or so of nobles and archbishops.

The meal was terrific.

Scattered among the Mandoans, the Englishmen endeavoured to keep a vigilant eye on Bill, but he was so placed that he could only observe Mason's progress.

The engineer sat next his host and endeavoured to demonstrate at the same time his broad-mindedness and his superiority.

At first he presented a flushed and frigid dignity to Talal's cautious questions. Then, with the braised fowl—a really excellent dish—he began to thaw.

" D'you play polo here ? " he asked. " I saw some pretty useful ponies you had out there, didn't I ? "

" Polo—pardon ? "

Happily Mason was an enthusiast. He explained the intricate technique of the game, its profoundity, its exclusiveness. He told tales of his own prowess in India, and of his extraordinarily bad luck at Ranelagh. The monologue lasted all through the third, fourth and fifth courses of the banquet. The attendants continued to fill Mason's cup.

Talal listened with exquisite attention.

" Ah," he said at length. " That is most highly important sociological information. English amuse kiddies with horses. Very kind. Very paternal."

" Kiddies ? Amuse ? "

" Games ? Play ? Children ? "

The engineer flushed an even deeper red. Then, after taking a long breath and making, Bill believed, a prayer for patience, he proceeded to explain that polo was an exceedingly adult and aristocratic occupation, played only by soldiers and gentlemen. Talal still frowned.

" On horses you hunt a ball ? "

" Yes—you see . . ."

" The ball is very valuable ? "

" Valuable ? "

" Fight for possession ? Finding's keeping ? "

It was only after quarter of an hour of entangled cross-purposes that Bill intervened to explain that the Mandoans had not yet learned to regard competitive pursuit of balls as an adequate entertainment for adult men.

" Oh, we must soon alter that," laughed Mason. " There's a quite decent soccer team on the west coast now. You'd be surprised how well some of those natives play. Make men of them. I'm sure we could find a couple of useful half-backs among you."

" Half backs ? "

By this time Mason was ready to explain anything. So were his companions. The frigidity of their manner had completely melted.

" Games are the chosen instruments of civilisation to make men," muttered Bill, *sotto voce.*

" Ah, you play men and women together ? "

" Good Lord, no—except in mixed doubles."

" I see. Mixed doubles is the game played by men and women to make men—like the love dance ? We in Mandoa need no such prelude to sex-relations. I have myself thirty-seven children. How many have you, Mr. Mason ? "

Five minutes of explanation and the intervention of Bill were necessary before this misunderstanding could be cleared away. But even then, the notion of character-

building seemed impossible to communicate. According to
Mandoan ideas a nobleman was born noble, a slave was
born base, a freedman was somewhere between the two.
That anxious effort should be directed towards the ac-
quisition of a higher morality seemed not only peculiar but
superfluous.

" It's a question of character." Mason was no longer
quite sure of his pronunciation, but his principles were
sound. " Self-discipline, public spirit, self-control."

" Ah ! Pursuit of rubber, leather and gutta-percha balls
necessary to give British gentleman self-control ? "

Mason accepted that, but his host observed :

" In Mandoa every gentleman must be self-controlled
without games."

Then the conversation drifted to other topics, and it was
only after a considerable interval that Bill heard the
melancholy-eyed young noble on Mason's other side,
inquiring of the engineer, politely :

" Are you a great lover ? "

Mason stared.

Then he coughed. Then he looked round the company
and decided that no other white man was listening. Then
he took another draft of sispri, and said airily, " So, so. Or
—shall I say I am fortunate ? "

" Boys or girls ? " asked the Mandoan.

Mason was thinking of the previous question about the
number of his offspring. " Oh, boys," he said.

" I could send you some very fine boys to-morrow,"
said the youth. " I could come myself perhaps one
day."

Even well laden with sispri, Mason would have found this
situation difficult, but happily at that moment a diversion
was created. One of the yellow-girdled runners broke
through the circle of slaves and panted up to the table. In
each hand he carried a short spear, on the end of which had
been impaled a small object. He gasped out some account
to Talal, who commanded him to present the offering to
Mason and to Nicholson.

The two chief guests accepted with adequate grace the
proffered gifts. They were still both passably sober ; but
neither was quite sufficiently sure of himself to trust

without confirmation his own eyesight. And in the flickering torchlight, what Mason thought he grasped was a
severed human hand.

He looked at it.

He saw Talal glance at it, nod carelessly, and continue
his conversation.

Nicholson, equally horrified, looked at Mason, saw Mason
lay his prize quietly beside his plate, and reply with
nonchalance to a remark of his host's.

Then perhaps it was not—what it seemed to be. Perhaps.
" Am I ? Is it ? Is it ? Am I ? "

Very cautiously the commercial adviser followed the
engineer's example.

" Discipline, imagination, self-control," murmured Bill.
" Thank God I had them well oiled."

" Bad men," Talal announced affably, " have tried to
practise incendiarism and arson in aerodrome. The law has
taken its course."

It was Nicholson who recovered first.

" Wha' you want," he hiccoughed cheerfully, " is a nice
set of handcuffs. We could do them splendidly at cheap
rates. Cutting off hands a bit gruesome—what ? "

Talal expressed his gratitude for the kind suggestion.
To Mason he remarked, when the conversation became
general, " Your noble friend Mr. Nicholson has very high-
pepped commercial sagacity, yes ? "

Mason could only agree.

By this time the feast was going splendidly and Bill
looked round the table with satisfaction. The white cotton
cloth was stained and crumpled. A bowl of fruit had over-
balanced, scattering mangoes and pomegranates between
the cups. The Englishmen, no longer stiff, but flushed and
talkative, were conversing freely with their brown, bearded
hosts. Mandoan conversation was not wholly familiar.
The anecdote was unknown, the Tabu unheard of. Death,
sex, God, personal feelings and hereditary prestige were
freely discussed, and in this atmosphere conventional
reticence was discarded.

" What I feel," affirmed Jordan, " is that if my wife
really understood me——"

" Of course, I'm no snob—but there's no denying that

a gentleman *is* a gentleman," Mason declared, plucking at his neat blonde moustache.

" If I had my *rights*," cried little Cooper. " That man always took an unfair advantage of me. I should have been number one, d'you see ? It was never just . . ."

The deep Mandoan voices rumbled among those shriller revelations.

" . . . So I said to her," Nicholson concluded, " my dear lady, it makes no difference to me. Put them on, or take them off, I said. . . . It makes no difference."

Courteously, benignly, Talal regarded his guests. " The English are a verra' verra' sociable A.1 race, yep ? Sympathetic ?—sure. This is the beginning of a verra' verra' happy partnership. We exchange our goods. We exchange our conversation—O.K. And now we will tell the world."

He rose. His followers rose. The Englishmen rose.

They could all walk. They could all smile.

" Let no one think," Bill observed to himself, " that the British empire-builder abroad immediately whirls himself into orgies of dissipation. No, no. Many a Rotary lunch, a Masonic dinner, a buffalo love-feast, has been far less temperate than this. But thank the Lord, thank the Lord, for sispri."

In a broken procession they followed the Lord High Chamberlain behind the huts ; and there they found themselves on a platform of clay banked several feet high above the Market Square. Below them waited silently a vast concourse of people.

" Good Lord ! " muttered Mason. " We're in the Town Hall."

It was like the negative photograph of an English election crowd. There, the faces were white and the clothes dark. Here, the faces and arms were dark above light robes ; or the whole figure was naked, black and shining in torchlight. Hot corporeal smells fierce and terrifying, swung out from the crowd. The torches roared and hissed, spluttering grease, and maddening the insects that seemed to be part of the hot stinging atmosphere.

Safi Talal was speaking to the people.

" He's telling them," Bill explained, " that we are the angels of prosperity. Too long Mandoa has been poor—

hoarding a few grains of corn—burning dung—suffering from harvests that fail and floods that drown the cattle. We come from the west. As locusts come, first one, then four, then a whole army, devouring and destroying, so white men come, first one, then four, then a whole army, trading and enriching. . . . We shall bring tourists, who will purchase ivory and bead-work. We shall bring engineers to hold back the floods—and to mine jewels from the hills. Then we shall irrigate the cotton fields. And make a road across the marshes. And tunnel through the mountains. Our doctors will heal the sick and cleanse the lepers. Our teachers will instruct Mandoans in the arts and sciences of the west. . . . All this is because Mandoa *is* Mandoa, and the spirit of the machine has descended upon the holy land."

" Mandoa is Mandoa ! " shouted the crowd.

The Lord High Chamberlain took the hands of his two chief guests and drew them forward. Flushed and animated, Mason and Nicholson gazed down upon the crowd.

" Do we do anything ? " whispered Nicholson hoarsely.

" Say something," Bill prompted. " All together now— Mandoa *is* Mandoa—it'll please them."

Huddling in a little group the Englishmen came together. Gratified and warmed and only the merest trifle fuddled, they shouted " Mandoa *is* Mandoa ! " crossing their arms and clasping their hands as though about to sing "Auld Lang Syne."

It was an immense success.

The Mandoans on the platform shouted. The hydrid crowd of slaves and freedmen in the dark square shouted. The Englishmen yelled their response.

Only Bill knew that thus, painlessly, and unconsciously, the officials of Prince's Tours, Limited, had been presented to Mandoa as slaves of the Lord High Chamberlain and were secured for ever as his property.

It had been the only sensible thing to do, and it pleased everybody ; and it was twenty to one that they would never know.

CHAPTER VII

SIR JOSEPH PRINCE LOSES AN ILLUSION

Tᴅʀᴇᴇ months later Sir Joseph Prince, travelling southward towards Khartoum, sat up and for the third time refolded the light travelling rug about him. The window was shuttered, but from a loosened slat two bars of light fell like hot iron across his legs, from which the rug had slid.

If only he could sleep.

All day the train writhed and twisted along the frizzling plain like an eel on an oven-shelf. The earth seemed to act as a huge reflector to the ferocity of the sun. Even the Sudanese attendants, efficient and polite, dripped perspiration on to the trays they carried.

It was too hot, too hot.

He turned his head away from the carriage wall to breathe more freely, but the electric fan brought little more relief than the whirring of a gnat.

He would cool himself by day-dreams. He would remember years when he had not travelled luxuriously through Africa, stretched prostrate on the seat of a private compartment in an excellent government train, but stumbling, sweating, groaning, tormented by thirst and insects and doubt as to the way, haunted by the hideous fear lest he should struggle in circles till he fell.

It was then he had learned that even in the hottest desert comes an hour when the inexorable march of the sun seems to pause, and the long day turns towards the evening. Then the heat wanes, however imperceptibly, and the round copper sky cools slowly from the centre, till only its burning rims scorch, as they touch, the far horizon.

He had earned his right to travel comfortably. This journey was child's play, tourist's play. He was going by train to Sennar, and from there by the new Prince's air line via Nasser to Lolagoba. The intermediate air port ought to be Gambeila ; but the Air Ministry had been firm about using British territory as far as possible. That was one of the things he wanted to discuss with the authorities in Khartoum to-morrow.

Khartoum to-morrow : well. That railway itself was a fruit of adventure. He shut his eyes and imagined the march of British soldiers pressing through the wicked, hideous, desert towards Omdurman. He had been right to build his faith on youth and courage. The spirit of to-day was still the same keen courage that had sent Raleigh to Guiana, Drake to the Pacific, and Sir Hugh Willoughby, vainly, to seek the north-west passage.

The Sudan was a fine memorial to that spirit. He thought of those cheerful, inarticulate youngsters who applied themselves to master difficult languages, and came out here to these grilling, baking wastes, to build dams, irrigate cotton fields, found hospitals, plant gardens, and administer justice until the wilderness and the solitary place were glad for them and the desert rejoiced and blossomed as the rose.

He liked to think that some of these fine young fellows had first been bitten by that desire during one of Prince's Junior Tours.

By God ! He had been right to trust youth. The old race was not dead. Boats stealing up the River Plate. A better Indies than the King of Spain hath any—gold rods in Moscow—the swaying elephants of India. He dozed and wakened and dozed again.

That fool of a doctor who told him not to go to Mandoa was an old woman. As though he did not intend to see for himself this last and finest experiment of all.

Last ? He jerked himself wide awake at the drowsy thought. Why last ? He was not old.

He stretched out a slender, freckled hand, ridged by a soft network of protruding veins. The nails were well-groomed, the skin smooth. But once, the fingers had been torn by the wet ropes of a sailing ship driven towards the Horn ; the skin had been cracked by frost, handling logs in a Nova Scotia lumber camp.

Oh, it was a hand that had learned to grasp things firmly ; and if it trembled now, that was only because of the heat and the motion of the train. It was none the less virile because now it endorsed cheques and signed orders. With his cheques and his orders he could make dreams come true ; he could build hotels, send aeroplanes roaring through the sky, draw safaris through the great bush-veld, and enable other young hunters to recognise through the yielding tawny grasses of Bengal, the stupefying smell of wild-animal and hot blood from a wounded tiger.

It was the hand of a man who held authority—the man who was going to make Mandoa.

Mandoa, Mandoa ! The name was music to his ears. The wheels as they rumbled beneath him sang it. This was the biggest achievement of his life—to take a place so small, so isolated, so obscure, that not half a dozen men in Europe knew it, and to make it overnight, as it were, a centre of interest. Ambassadors and foreign secretaries, publicists and princes, tourists and contractors—they were all coming. He was drawing them, as by a spell, to this fantastic region. He was putting Mandoa on the map forever. A country was greater than a business-firm, even a firm like Prince's Tours, Limited. If he died now he would go down to history, not as the man who had made Prince's but as the man who made Mandoa.

It had been a good idea to travel incognito—worth the sacrifice of his characteristic beard, and the appearance which he had once so carefully cultivated. As Mr. Allen, visiting a married daughter in Khartoum on the overland route to Kenya, he could do as he pleased, mix with his fellow-passengers, and get into touch again with the Young on whose spirit he had gambled, in whose future he so confidently believed. Since the war he had not seen nearly enough young people—except at occasional parties, or among the picked members of his staff. On this same train were two or three groups bound for Mandoa. He wanted to talk to them, to learn again his justification, to refresh himself by their young enthusiasm. He wanted to re-capture his own youth from their reactions to his experiment.

Indeed, it was something to quicken the pulse of youth —this deliberate introduction of an almost virgin state to all that was best in western civilisation. In its way, it was a higher form of adventure than the Elizabethan voyages. For in Mandoa, the British sought enterprise, not ownership, influence, not government. They held a natural mandate there for western culture.

He had spoken first along those lines in his broadcast talk last month.

Memories of unpleasant criticisms concerning that broadcast, he brushed aside impatiently. There were always unpleasant criticisms of any outstanding effort.

He turned his mind—always a willing servant—to think of happier things.

This business had made the Durrants, Maurice, whom he loved, and William, whom Maurice in some way seemed to fear. No. Maurice had feared Bill's failure, as one did, with an unsatisfactory brother. Well, Bill Durrant was made for life. He, Prince, had restored to him his reputation, his immortal part. He was doing a good piece of work now. That was what the young needed, the opportunity to do good work.

It had been a risk for them both. Coming at a time of financial crisis, it might have ruined Princes' if he had not pulled it off so well ; and it had nearly cost Bill Durrant his life, several times.

But that was how men ought to live—unafraid of consequences, or, if afraid, determined all the more to defy their fear.

Only it was too hot, too hot. He couldn't stand hardship as he used to do.

Nonsense !

He was beginning to whine and mew like a sick woman, lying alone and brooding over his discomforts. He would go and seek out his fellow-passengers. He would refresh himself at the fountain of their youth. While talking, he would forget that the pulses on his temples thumped like drums, like sinister warning drums heard through the rustling African night.

He sat upright and began a meticulous, heroic toilet, smoothing with eau-de-cologne his silver hair, his fierce eyebrows, his hot and pricking skin. He forced himself into a stiff collar and tie, and took from its hanger his clean linen jacket. A beautifully groomed, deliberate, courteous old man made his way to the dining car of the train.

There he found, seated over iced drinks, the American

sculptor Marlow, whom he had met before, with three other
men and two women.

Marlow at once beckoned to him.

" Ah, Mr. Allen. I'm glad you've joined us. I want you
to meet my wife."

The soft, rounded, pretty creature smiled, dimpling. She
had her country-women's gift of preserving an almost
miraculous daintiness when travelling. Sir Joseph, enchanted by all feminine beauty, responded, his pleasure
overcoming his fatigue and his vague sense of illness.

" How do you do ? I'm so verra' verra' pleased to see
you," she cooed. " My husband told me what a wun'nerful
talk you had with him about tiger shooting in India. I'm
always saying to Ivor we just *must* go to India. Now I want
you to meet my friends—Mr. Watson, Mr. McLeod, and
Julian and Felicity Cardover. At least "—her teasing,
bubbling laughter mocked her formality—" I'm not sure
they all *are* my friends. I only met Mr. McLeod half an
hour ago, and he's already tried to wreck my life."

" Shame, shame," murmured Sir Joseph. " What has
he done ? "

" Well—my husband's told you he's a sculptor, I think.
And we're out after Negro types. We're going by boat up
the Nile to Juba, looking for Dinkas and Shilluks and
things, and *then* to the royal wedding at Mandoa. And this
man "—she indicated with mock indignation the big
ruddy-faced, unhappy-looking Scot—" wants to stop us."

" I've been trying to persuade Mrs. Marlow and her party
to keep out of that plague spot," growled McLeod. " It's
no place for a white woman."

" Then I say it's no place for a black one," murmured
the thin, fragile youth called Cardover.

" Then it's no place for a man either, white *or* black,"
said Mrs. Marlow. " So there you are."

" So there you are," echoed Cardover.

" Do you know these parts ? " asked Mrs. Marlow,
appealing to Sir Joseph as to an opportune arbiter after a
long argument.

" Not so well as I know South Africa, and the west
coast," said Sir Joseph truthfully.

" Then you know something about colour." McLeod

seized on him. " Look here—I've farmed in Kenya since 1904, and I fought in the East African campaign during the war, and I consider I've seen the best of Africa—and the worst—so far."

" You think there's worse coming? " inquired Sir Joseph, ordering an iced seltzer for himself and offering drinks all round.

" Worse ? Look here. You say you know South Africa. Tell me—do you think it's in a healthy state ? "

" Healthy? Economically? Politically? Just how? "

" Any way you like to look at it—but most of all, the native question. Isn't it true that the blacks are getting to know too much and to ask too much ? What's this trouble about immigration from Portuguese Angola, and from the Protectorates ? Why is the Chamber of Mines jumpy as a cat ? What's all this delay over the land-bills, labour bills and franchise bills for ? I'll tell you—the whites are losing nerve. And a lot of help they get from the home government ! Eh ? Well—what about us ? "

" You ? "

" In Kenya. I tell you, I've farmed since 1904—I've made by my own enterprise and skill, if you like—I'm not boasting, mind you—I'm just stating facts—it's no more than we all do—I've made a barren hillside yield good crops of coffee and fairish crops of tobacco. I've levelled roads *myself*, mind you, before the railways came ; I've built a decent house ; I've raised a family ; I've stood by my kind and I've harmed no man. And what thanks have I got for it ? The name of a Kenya settler is mud to your English press. We're derided, distrusted, insulted by government commissions, given no credit for the good we have done and abused right and left for a whole lot of things we never thought of doing."

" That's real bad luck, Mr. McLeod." It was clear that Mrs. Marlow had heard this tale of woe before, for the Scotsman was raw and puzzled with his grievance. " But I can't see why we shouldn't go through Lolagoba."

" Because there's bound to be a mess. Look here, Mrs. Marlow, you know your niggers in the southern states, surely ? "

" Oh, Mr. McLeod, don't mistake me for the usual

negrophobe southerner. I acknowledge I was reared with prejudices. But when you have learned science you have to forget some of your cradle-wisdom. My husband specialises in negro-types and I confess they make wun'nerful models, and I know . . ."

" Forgive me, Mrs. Marlow. All this artistic detachment may be all right in America but it does a lot of harm here. This business of admiring Negroes and cracking them up and painting them *puts ideas into their heads.*"

" But, Mr. McLeod, don't you feel that we have a lot to learn from the African ? " asked the sculptor. " His magnificent physique against our effete civilised urban type. His strong, original, instinctive life. The African has miraculously preserved those faculties we have lost. We have to turn again and learn from him."

" Learn from him ! That's just where you artist fellows come up against the ordinary man. I'm a Philistine. All right. I'll plead guilty. But I have to control blacks, work with blacks, manage blacks ; and I tell you, in Africa, it's a question of govern or get out. We don't want to learn from them ; and we don't want to teach them too much. We want to see that they do their work and do it decently and are properly housed and fed ; I grant you that. But they're good servants and damn bad masters. What price the slave raids last summer ? Who sold nigger kids for three rifles apiece to Arabia ? Black men or white— eh ? What's wrong with Africa to-day is that there's been too much of this humanitarian nonsense, and even worse, of this detached scientific and artistic pose. ' We've got to learn from the Africans.' The deuce we have ! Look at Liberia. Look at Abyssinia. Look at the Sudan before the British took it. Well—what have we to learn from those? 'Cruelty, corruption, slavery, disease. An African state is nothing but a filthy, treacherous, lecherous *mess*." The Scotsman brought his fist down with a thud on the table, and set all the glasses jingling.

" I don't quite see, though, why we shouldn't go to see the royal wedding at Mandoa," persisted Mrs. Marlow. The girl called Felicity raised an eyeglass on a black ribbon and put it to her eye. Mr. McLeod went on.

" I can tell you why ; but you won't listen. Mandoa's

like the rest of them—only worse. It's the world's hotbed of slave-trading, vice, ignorance, filth and disease. Yet here is the *imbecile* idea of recognising the government, marrying off some wretched princess at a great song-and-dance attended by half the nit-wit foreigners of Europe—aeroplanes, hotels, God knows what ! And what will happen ? Jim Crow all over Africa will get an idea he's the Lord's own little brother. Wages will go up. Servants will be sulky. Orders will be ignored ; passes neglected. Then a hut will be burned somewhere. Then a raid on a house. Do you know what happened in the early days of Rhodesia ? D'you remember the tales of the Matabele War ? Do you realise that all over East Africa are white women in lonely bungalows protected only by the white man's prestige ? And what's going to happen when European ambassadors kow-tow to a black princess ? News travels here uncannily. Don't think you can hide your idiocy under a bushel. Before we know where we are, I shall be expected to walk backwards from the presence of my own house boys ! After all we've done to build up an empire, to keep the flag flying, to carry on ; it makes me sick ! "

"Well, I'm real sorry you feel so bad about it, Mr. McLeod. But I do assure you it's all error."

" Error ! "

" You'd realise, Mr. McLeod, if you only followed science, that what these child races need is love."

"Science ? Love ? " gasped the Scot.

" She means the science of Mrs. Eddy and Christ—Christ Scientist," drawled the Cardover boy's bored yet emphatic voice. " Sophie is charming. She must have her little missionary kicks."

" Mr. McLeod, you're marvellous," said the girl called Felicity. She was slim and white as a wand, a flower princess. Sir Joseph watched her, adoring the wisdom of virginal youth. " Isn't he marvellous, Julian ? "

" Look here, Watson," Marlow declared. " You're going to Mandoa too. You defend us from this wild Scot. As an artist, I'm suspect. But you're a business man."

Sir Joseph took comfort, looking at the firm, well-built figure of the middle-aged man in the corner. The Scot's denunciation of the Mandoan affair had troubled him all the more because he admired that hardy settler type. But bronzed, laconic, and of sensible appearance, Watson might prove a useful advocate.

The business man puffed his pipe.

" Oh—I'm not going to contradict McLeod," he said at length. " I'm perfectly well aware that it's probably all a pretty rotten show. But as you say, sir, I'm a business man. I'm going to Mandoa because there's a possibility of opening up a railway there, and my job is to sell steel rails."

Sir Joseph nodded to himself. Probably one of the men from Brinley, Morn & Co., of Sheffield.

" Steel rails ? How spectacular," breathed young Cardover.

Watson snorted. Clearly he thought the Cardovers half-witted. He explained with patience.

" I'm out to sell my goods, not to dictate morals to other people. It may be true that this Durrant in Lolagoba is a rotter. Drugs, drinks—I've heard all that. It may be true that the only money in Mandoa's got from selling slaves. That's not my business. Safi Talal's one of the nastiest bits of work in Africa. Portuguese-Abyssinian stock with a dash of Arab. That's your Mandoan noble. Cruel as a Turk and treacherous as an Abyssinian. They're all a slave-owning, slave-raiding, sispri-soaking crew. Sorry, Mrs. Marlow, if he's a hero of yours, but that's the bare truth."

" I think he sounds *too* exhilarating," sighed Felicity.

" Felicity *adores* monsters," her brother explained proudly. " Inherently perverse."

" Monster—you've hit it," said Watson. " But that's not my business. The people I've got to consider are the British workmen at home, who'll be unemployed if a German or a Yankee gets in first with the contract. You can't serve two masters, that what I say. Either I'm fair to my own people or I'm fair to Mandoa. And if I were fair to Mandoa I should go straight up to the Foreign Office or whatever it is, and ask for the whole lot to be wiped out. There's no curing them. As for Prince's—Prince is an old fool—must be about in his second childhood by now. He used to be quite a decent chap, I believe. But I wouldn't like to have the justifying of *his* dividends before a shareholders' meeting, if the truth were told. Blood-money, that's what it is."

" But you'd take it ? " asked Sir Joseph.

" Well, as I say, he's opened up the country. It's not for the rest of us to be too particular, with the steel trade in the state it is. But you "—Watson looked at the American and his wife, and the two young English people— " you needn't go—I agree with McLeod. I'd say keep out of it. There'll be a really rotten scandal one day—like the Congo affair—and the name of Mandoa will stink in the nostrils of decent people."

" But I adore scandals," crooned Felicity. " Personally I think a little murder and what not might brighten the proceedings. I've always longed to see Safi Talal ever since we met that comic little man—what did you say his name was, Sophie ? "

" Rollett. We met him first at the Lufton's. You re-member, Ivor."

" Oh, yes—Rollett told us that Mandoa was positively *reeking* in blood, and Talal a perfect *prince* of sheiks. So I said to Julian, ' My dear, we *must* go, at once.' I've been four times round the world, and I've hardly seen an *inch* of really *pure* wickedness, unsullied by a taint of virtue."

" I don't like to hear a nice white girl—young lady— talking like that," grunted McLeod.

" Oh, don't you ? How too sweet of you, Mr. McLeod. The *real* he-man. Didn't I say he was marvellously true to type, Julian ? "

" I'm not playing, Miss Cardover. It's no place for a decent woman," the Scotsman said.

" But I'm *not* a decent woman, dear Mr. McLeod. And personally, if you mean rape—these he-men always *really* mean rape, don't they, Sophie ?—I always think the inconveniences of rape are grossly over-rated. A spot of rape might even make a journey over to Aberdeen tolerable."

" Excuse me. I'll take myself off, Miss Cardover. This is no talk for me." And McLeod, followed by the equally disgusted but less tempestuous Watson, withdrew.

The chairman of Prince's sat still, watching and listening.

" Aren't they perfect, Mr. Allen ? " said the girl.

" Felicity, dear, I believe poor Mr. Allen's taking you

seriously," cautioned Sophie Marlow. The discomfort of
the psychological atmosphere had penetrated even her
armour of love and science.

But the girl stared at her with wide, innocent, blue eyes,
lovely and imperturbable.

"But I am serious. You know I am, Sophie. Personally
I hope that every *word* Rollett said about that Durrant
man is true. I hope he's drugging and drinking and living
with native women and taking blood-money from Talal.
It would be too wonderful to meet a real degenerate. I've
met so *many* false ones. They never get further than
homosexuality and absinthe. That's why we're all going
to Mandoa. Teddy Ffrench and the Collinsons, and Rex
Leamington and Piggy Fanshawe and the Gessingtons.
Half Hampstead's going and *all* Bloomsbury and quite a
lot of Chelsea and some of Boulevard Montparnasse and
even Greenwich Village. I met Sir Joseph Prince once at a
party—a perfect pet. No girl safe with him for a *moment*,
I should say. He only got as far as squeezing my knees
under the table. I tried to tell him I was a Lesbian,
but of course he's so antiquated I shouldn't think he'd
even *heard* of H. S., poor lamb. All got up like a kind
of buccaneer. Utterly gaga—but quite sweet. Of course,
led by the nose I should say about Mandoa—a statue
ought to be put up to him when he's dead."

"He is dead," murmured Julian. "A walking corpse
left over from the romantic age."

"The only man who gave the twentieth century a *real*
scandal," sighed Felicity fondly. "Julian, dear—I must
have another drink. Let's drink his health, poor pet. Sir
Joseph Prince!" She stood, slight, graceful, debonair,
her eyeglass swinging on its black ribbon.

It was then that the elderly man who called himself
Allen gave a choking sob and fell forward across the table.

"My dear. Mr. Allen does not like your stuff," Julian
observed ; but the Cardovers were more efficient than
Ivor Marlow at procuring brandy, laying Sir Joseph along
the seat, loosening his collar, and gradually restoring him
to unwelcome consciousness.

Mrs. Marlow stood aloof, practising science.

Their combined efforts were successful. Sir Joseph

opened his eyes, coughed at the neat spirit, and sat up, apologising.

" It was the heat, the appalling heat," he said. He was sometimes taken like this. It was nothing.

He insisted upon struggling back to his own compartment alone.

As he went, he thought he heard the girl Felicity's high-pitched emphatic drawl, pursuing him. " My dear, I *thought* I recognised him. What a marvellous gaff! Superb."

He waited for no more. He lurched down the corridor and into his own carriage, white and shaken.

The shutters were up. Across the desert stretched a meagre tropical sunset, dropping from the unbroken sky behind the earth. The evening had come without his noticing it.

He fell into his seat.

He had always refused to believe in the decadence of modern youth. He had championed the young in lectures and interviews. He had built for them ; built on them ; believed in them.

And here they were.

The scandal raised against his firm he could deal with. Was there anything in the suggestions about Durrant ? He'd soon see to that. Was the whole transaction bloodstained ? By God, he'd show them.

Memories of the slight discomfort and evasiveness of Maurice Durrant came back to him. What if there was dirty work going on ? He was an old campaigner. He could put it right.

But the nightmarish horror of these young people who had no moral sense, who did not *care* if a great British enterprise were dishonoured, who showed nothing but wide-eyed curiosity in shame and ruin and beastliness—that was not to be borne ; that was intolerable.

Nor did the Cardovers stand alone. There were those detached and offensive Americans. There was the pedestrian and opportunist Watson.

These were the people for whom he made Mandoa.

Only McLeod, its declared enemy, showed proper feeling.

And instead of standing up to them and telling them what he thought, he had fainted like a sick girl.

He was too old.

That was the truth of the matter.

He had outlived his age. The world had gone beyond him.

Sick, dizzy, faint and shaken, he dropped his head into his hands and wept, hating himself, as the sobs shook him, for his unmanly tears.

CHAPTER VIII

MR. BLACKER DEFIES HIS CONSCIENCE

SIR JOSEPH was really ill when the train reached Khartoum and had to go into hospital instead of continuing his journey. He kept his head, however, and cabled for Blacker, one of his most efficient emergency managers, to take his place at Lolagoba. He also indicated that he would be glad to see Maurice directly he could leave his parliamentary duties. Then he lay back and abandoned himself to the miseries of paratyphoid.

Blacker, grim, taciturn, a demon for work, flew out in six days. He stopped for two nights in Khartoum and listened to his chief's reiterated complaints about the Mandoan Scandal.

" But there *is* no scandal, sir," he tried to reassure him. Durrant was a public school and Oxford man, and Blacker thought well of such.

Sir Joseph refused all reassurance.

" You've got to get to the bottom of this slavery business. Just how far has Durrant committed himself ? What are they doing ? Who'll draw up a reply to these busybodies ? I won't have a scandal at Prince's. We never have had a scandal."

He was pathetic, but he was also obstinate, and Blacker enjoyed neither obstinacy nor pathos. It was many years since he had grown from a solemn self-defensive child with adenoids into a solemn, Puritanical, self-opinioned, enormously efficient man, guarded and armour-plated all round against onslaughts upon his sensibility.

He sat beside Sir Joseph's bed and promised to "look into" things, to "keep an eye" on things, and to perform other prodigies of vigilance and judgment.

"I'd rather nothing happened at all than that we had a scandal," repeated the old man, who looked an old man at last.

Blacker said, "Yes, yes," and "Of course I understand." And squirmed on his chair hoping for the nurse to come and tell him it was time to go. Yet he disliked, even to himself, admitting his impatience with a sick old man.

There was no doubt that he found sick visiting tedious. The old and the sick are not rational. Blacker disliked all forms of unreason.

Fortunately delay was inadvisable.

On the third day he was off again to Lolagoba, now a centre of unprecedented activity. The white hotel and Princes' Tourist office were already built. Aeroplanes landed on the new ground three times a week, bringing furniture, pottery, tin-ware, gramophones, cooking stoves, fountain pens, soda water syphons, bicycles, cocktail shakers, opera glasses, patent medicines and perambulators for the offspring of Nobility.

Every Mandoan who possessed gold or ivory exchanged it for watches, horn-rimmed spectacles, or ukeleles. Every archbishop who had slaves attempted to turn all he could spare into cash. For the first time in Mandoan history, isolated groups of slaves were sold privately into Arabia, without waiting for that great annual ceremonial harvest at the beginning of the drought. Every one outside Ma'buta's party of fanatical Conservatives had succumbed to the fashion for possessions.

The very aspect of the streets had changed.

The control of affairs had passed out of Bill Durrant's hands. He wandered about the streets, inspecting alterations, or he dined with different families, teaching young sprigs of nobility how to play the gramophone. Or he sat on his verandah dispensing cocktails to whichever members of the staff cared to visit him. Because, after his first panic, he was really interested in people, they became interesting. He learned not only about Jordan's gastric disabilities, but about the shop assistant with social aspirations whom he had carelessly married when he was a student. He knew the secret disappointment of Cooper's soul, and the religious fountain from which sprang Nicholson's eternal optimism.

It did not occur to him that any one could think him supernumerary, for it seemed as though his work was as important as any. He had so many people to keep in a good temper, so many crises of misunderstanding to evade, that though he spent most of his time in having a drink, first with Mandoans in a stockaded courtyard, and then with Europeans in the Rest House or hotel, his activities seemed indispensible to the Mandoan renaissance.

When Blacker appeared, Bill regarded his bald and polished head, his solemn face and official manner with mild uneasiness.

He was informed that Mr. Blacker wished to Go Into The Whole Business with him, so invited him to lunch at the bungalow.

It was after lunch that Blacker suggested an interview at the office. Bill sighed, and accepted the necessity. There were some people who liked offices. But his worst suspicions were confirmed when the manager produced also a notebook.

He did not know that he was entitled to a certain measure of self-confidence, because Blacker respected his year at New College.

" I understand," the manager began, " that you now think you really can be ready for February 28th ? "

" Accidents apart, I hope so. But *are* accidents ever apart ? " murmured Bill. " The arch-archbishop and his lady—you know *their* romance of course—not unnaturally want to hurry things on. She's a pathetic creature—our Royal Princess. You know the point is that directly her daughter's married, this breaks the tabu laid on her and her arch-archbishop. She's expecting him to rush her to the altar at once and they'll live happily ever after. But I'm rather afraid that he's a bit bored already. Nice look out for their married life. That's the worse of true-life romances. Then, of course, there's Talal."

"Has he been making difficulties? I understood that he was anxious to have the whole affair carried out as well as possible?"

"Yes, but on the other hand it's all costing him a Hell of a lot. I suppose you know about this blackmail business by Ma'buta. I don't know what Talal's having to pay for every week we linger here in safety, but I understand he'll be a ruined man if it goes on much longer. And *then* Ma'buta would double-cross us if he could. Oh, this date business has been as complicated as a fixed Easter. There was the ecclesiastical difficulty too."

"What was that?"

"It appears," drawled Bill, "that marriages in March and April are tabu here—for reasons utilitarian rather than sacred; though like so many antique traditions, its common-sense justification has been lost in time. You see, Blacker, I've worked it out; marriages in the spring mean, as a general rule, babies during the next dry season, just when new additions to the community would be most inconvenient, and the ritual ablutions and purifications almost impossible. The older ecclesiastics are not really liking this business at all, though the arch-archbishop's got them pretty well in hand. But he told me he simply dare not add insult to injury by breaking the spring tabu."

"I see."

"So February 28th was the last possible day."

"Unless you had waited until May."

"Yes—but May means the beginning of the wet season —and the whole affair would be impossible. Blinding rains, ground a swamp, ceremonies *drowned* in torrents. You can at least count on fine weather in February. Then there are the princes. The Mandoans *insisted* on royal representatives. I understand my brother had to persuade the Foreign Office to put a little diplomatic pressure to induce those two mangy Balkan specimens we have procured. But even so they wanted to fit their visit in with a big-game expedition they'd planned somewhere on the Congo. That meant March at the latest for us. . . . Of course, it complicates the Bath question."

"Baths?"

"Oh, yes. Didn't you see in my report? Honestly,

those baths have given me more trouble than anything."

"Perhaps," said Mr. Blacker frigidly. "You would
bring my defective knowledge up to date."

"Well, they were Talal's idea, really. I thought that hip-
baths might do. After all, what's good enough for us, said
I, is good enough for an Italian ambassador, or a couple
of Bolivians. But Talal remembered the complaints of
American tourists at the Abyssinian affair, and apparently
had noted the word Baths in his mind. He saw the plans
of the hotel and demanded baths. Nothing else would
satisfy him. The national honour of Mandoa, it appeared,
depended upon seventeen porcelain baths, with taps, waste
pipes, plugs and all other modern conveniences. So there
they are. But, of course, we can't use them. It simply is
not possible to get an adequate water supply in February
for anything so extravagant as baths. However, I calmed
both parties down in the end by persuading Talal that a
Balkan princeling was hardly accustomed to baths even in
his own palace, and that honour would be satisfied if the
visitors were shown the bathrooms and then given notices
explaining that owing to the exceptional conditions of
drought, the authorities of Lolagoba had been reluctantly
forced to ration water. Guests could be notified *directly*
water was available. So *that* was settled ! "

"I am not at all satisfied with the question of the
water supply."

"Well, Mason's report on the newly found springs and
water holes seems pretty good to me. Of course, we'll
have to be careful. That is why we settled on three weeks
as the maximum period for visitors to stay. It just gives
us time to show them the place, and yet won't of itself
exhaust our reserves. I told Talal that whatever happens,
there must be no real hardships. None of these Mandoan
devices of cannibalism, or killing off a few more slaves
when supplies run short. *Definitely* bad form, I suggested,
cannibalism. And three weeks somehow has an exciting,
familiar sound. Do you read Elinor Glyn ? "

"No. I don't."

"You should. By the way, speaking of her, you know."
Bill sighed, for it was lonely work making jokes all to

oneself. " We had rather an amusing time, with the *beds*. I found that Talal had ordered five hundred bed-steads to be sent down the Nile from Cairo, to be trans-ported overland during the dry season. But they got stuck in the Sudd and there we were. After a perfect feat of engineering, Mason got the iron frames and what not across, but the mattresses were completely dished. Must have been rotten material. So we had a frightful business getting the rest out by air. I think we've got about a hundred. Should be enough to go on with. And I've put local talent on to making a few. We'll get more over in a week. . . ."

" I hope so." Mr. Blacker's prim fingers played with the papers before him.

The office in which the two men sat was a very different place from the little room in which Bill had pounded his typewriter while moths blew against the lamp. Here, in this bright whitewashed apartment, waved two fans, jerked by Dinka slaves crouched on the verandah. Tables, desks, files and shelves were all conveniently placed. A tray with siphons and bottles stood on the table. Through the thin partition came the sound of duplicators and typewriters. Business was business nowadays in Mandoa.

Mr. Blacker, however, appeared unaware of the energy and organisation represented by the change. He sat frowning with dissatisfaction at one of the papers he had been examining.

" I have here," he said at length, " the programme which you appear to have drawn up. I notice that the day after the wedding is marked ' Saint Gregory's Festival.' "

" That's a popular and most convenient saints' day—originally, I suppose, in honour of the good Catholic Gregory. But Mr. Guerdon introduced Gregory Powders, and, as usual, the two ceremonies have been combined. Gregory's day is celebrated after any great feast—and feasts here *are* feasts, I assure you—raw meat, high game. If you knew just what the festive menu consists of as a rule, you'd realise the beneficent influence of St. Gregory. The Holy Fathers of this church had almost as keen a sociological insight as Moses. I hadn't been in the country long when I came across Saint Matthew Arnold. It appears that Mandoa had always known a Saint Matthew, but when the Reverend Robert came, he was always quoting Arnold, and the Mandoans put two and two together. The prophet Jeremiah, I understand, is Jeremy Bentham. You see, there is no real difference between the secular and religious life in this country. I hardly like to tell you of the confusion I found between the Gloria and Gloria Swanson—and I do believe that Mary Pickford is worshipped quite sincerely by country people who come up to the talkies."

" Worshipped ? "

" As the Queen of Heaven."

Mr. Blacker, a fervent Protestant, did not like jokes about religion. " Indeed," he said.

" I thought a few saints days might amuse the visitors. The Arch-archbishop's quite ready to oblige by shifting them about a bit. Considering what he has to gain. . . . There are processions and public games, and so on. All very picturesque. You'll have to see the Stadium. We're awfully proud of that, Mason and Talal and I. We scooped it clean out of the earth on the hill. The trouble—*one* of the troubles, I should say, is to arrange for the archers, spear-throwers, etc.—they are marvellous marksmen here —to aim everything *away* from the spectators. I heard of a plot of Ma'buta's to have his picked athletes hurl their lances right into the Royal Enclosure. Most awkward."

" Most."

" We've got to be fearfully careful about the big game hunting for just the same reason. I'm doing all I can to find out which are Ma'buta's men, and what he's driving at. But it's not easy, and Mandoans love intrigue."

" I understood that your arrangements for the hunting expeditions were completed."

" So far as the Safaris and the game itself is concerned, we're all right."

" The game ? "

" That's been one of our triumphs," Bill declared. " You know, owing to over-population and drought and so on, big game is scarce here. The Mandoans unfortunately have no traditions of sportsmanship. I simply couldn't make them see that though in matters of agriculture, industry and building, Europeans cultivate every possible mechanical labour-saving device, they employ mass destruction by machine guns only on one another. They can't see why, if Reading biscuit-makers, and American flour-millers produce food by mass productive methods, they can't do the same with their food that runs about on four legs. So when I arrived I found that even in the south-east near Lake Rudolph, game was scarce on this side the border. I had to do something. Ever since the rains let up a bit I've been offering rewards for live beasts driven on to those estates to which we are taking parties. Of course, we've had some trouble. A couple of lions brought from Uganda ran amok among the imported antelope on the next estate, and at Bodak, just this side the Sudanese frontier, three elephants from the Budongo Forest trampled down a whole village. The people demanded compensation, and I was terrified lest they'd kill the beasts and eat them before we could hunt them. They tried to bring hippo, but these died on the way, and we hadn't water enough. Giraffe can't live here. It's a great problem—how to combine sporting and climatic needs."

" I have met that difficulty before."

Bill clutched at this first sign of sympathy.

" Then, of course, there are all the solid and worthy preparations—fields tilled, drains made, and roads of a kind up to the escarpment."

" Where they have not yet found minerals."

" No ; that Scotch fellow had a hope of copper."

" And the telegraph line is not up'yet ? "

" No ; it's the lust for adornment that's to blame No sooner does Mason put up wires than some Mandoan belle appears with them round her ankles. What's international communication to one who relies upon the universal language of sex appeal ? "

And what, indeed, thought Bill, was humorous exposition to this grim, bald-headed man who turned over his admirable reports as though he handled dirt ? He told him of the reconstruction of Hollywood Hall, the repairs to the Royal Palace, the heroic instruction of the Royal Band in the " Marseillaise," " God Bless Our Pope," the Fascist anthem, and the even more complex strains of two Balkan royal hymns.

The all-British railway line, planned from Khartoum via Sennar, Singa, Roseires and Nasser had attracted the attention of an enterprising firm of engineers, but an experimental stretch of line only proved the fatal attraction of steel rails and sleepers for a population newly required to keep hippopotami and elephants as pets for the sake of white sportsmen. The gift of free fencing material was all too opportune. The rails disappeared by night almost as fast as they were constructed by day.

"Then there's the hospital. It's only a beginning. Twenty beds for Mandoans, a ward for slaves, a maternity wing, and an annex for European visitors. The real asset, of course, is Doctor Macduff. What a name ! But a stout man, very. Enormously well liked here. He found his patients rather queer customers at first. . . . Oh. By the way. I must warn you. The Mandoan idea of etiquette is not quite Cheltenham-Winchester, if you take my meaning. I have circularised a list of Anglo-Saxon tabus, but I can't guarantee that there won't be *faux pas* I forgot to mention. Perhaps you'd better have a look at it."

Mr. Blacker lifted the type-script with the disdain of one handling a scurrilous anonymous letter, and read :

"RULES FOR MANDOANS.

"For use during the ceremonies of the Royal Wedding. Passed by the High Council of Nobles and Archbishops.

"1. Never spit on to a visitor's person or possessions. Preferably do not spit at all.

"2. Never answer the calls of nature while talking to a white lady. Even gentlemen prefer this to be done in private, except the French, who don't mind.

"3. Love-making in public should never pass beyond verbal compliments. Even for these, be careful, when alluding to parts of the body, to observe European tabus. Notwithstanding the evidence of the Bible (a misleading social document), remember that Europeans prefer to call the belly ' the waist,' and the breasts, ' the figure ; ' the loins should not be mentioned ; all more practical demonstrations of affection should be referred to as ' kissing ; ' and it should be taken for granted that the parts kissed are confined to the hand, brow, or, very intimately, the lip.

" 4. Never kill, nor even beat, a slave, donkey, dog or wife in public ; Europeans dislike it.

" 5. All public games of skill—*e.g.*, lance throwing— must be practised at inanimate targets.

" 6. Witchcraft, especially the examination of entrails for auguries, should be suspended for the entire three weeks, except for one organised demonstration, to be shown to anthropologists by ticket only.

" 7. The same applies to the customary sexual rites of adolescence, circumcision of both boys and girls, and initiation ceremonies to secret societies. These should not be even alluded to in detail before :

" (*a*) Ladies.

" (*b*) Military or diplomatic authorities.

" (*c*) Ecclesiastical dignitaries.

" (*d*) Christian scientists.

" 8. *At Least* a loin cloth should always be worn by both sexes.

" 9. *Never* de-louse, nor pursue any other type of personal small-game hunting in public, either upon one's own person or another's.

" 10. The following classes of food should never be offered to Europeans :

" (*a*) Dogs (unless effectively disguised).

" (*b*) Mules, ditto.

" (*c*) Human flesh—in any circumstances.

" (*d*) Excrement, human or animal.

" (*e*) Entrails ; except cow's liver and kidneys, sheep's sweetbreads, goat's sweetbreads (if they have them ?).

" (*f*) Insects—Europeans unhappily are *not* acclimatised to locusts. The French will eat snails, but better inquire first.

" (*g*) Uncooked blood—except when it emerges as juice from undercooked beef steaks. Probably this proves that Europeans like it, but do not like to think they do.

" (h) Fruit containing maggots or worms—if maggots must be eaten, please serve separately in stews so that they are unrecognisable.

" (i) Game Well Hung. Even though some Europeans may *say* that they like game ' high ' they do not mean what you mean, and are, indeed, very squeamish about it.

" 11. Remember that though Europeans like to slaughter their own meat on Shooting, Hunting and Fishing expeditions out of doors, they do *not* consider it a compliment to have goats or fowls slain before them at the dining table. This prejudice is inexplicable but strong.

" 12. Remarks about a visitor's age, figure, clothes, probable potency of the sexual organs, whiskers, and other personal details, are, even if intended as compliments, better avoided. European standards of beauty, grace and strength are not the same as yours and are, in any case, mostly under tabu. So are questions of parentage, income, the number of servants habitually kept, whether the visitor has ever been imprisoned or otherwise inconvenienced by the State, wife beating, copulation, intestinal functions and disorders, and personal hygiene. Indeed, most types of Mandoan small-talk being tabu in Europe (or at least in England, which is more important) it would be safer to leave the choice of conversation to your guests.

" 13. *And most important.* Remember that though the Europeans know you keep slaves, and though they will be glad enough to take advantage of the comfort their service gives, they never themselves refer to slavery, nor will they be happy if you do so. Therefore, *Slaves Are Tabu.*"

Mr. Blacker read the document through to its final word. Then he re-read the thirteenth point. Then he put down the paper and looked at Bill.

Bill had risen and stood looking out of the window, at the confusion of mules and dung-sellers, warriors in finely dressed skins, their hair piled high over clay discs, girls in bright cottons, fowls and curs scratching about the doorways. He enjoyed half-consciously this shifting pattern of colour.

He drummed his fingers on the white-washed wall. His lips were rounded in a silent whistle.

He turned at the sound of Blacker's voice and came slowly back to the table.

" You intend to publish this—ah, document ? " asked the organiser.

" I have sent it round to every one who can read."

" With this final clause ? "

" Certainly."

" Perhaps you are not aware that there have been press campaigns in England," said Blacker with so obvious a restraint upon his feelings that Bill felt quite sorry for him. " Prince's has been accused of conniving at conditions of slavery here. There is even going to be an inquiry made by a commission sent from the International Humanitarian Association. It is due here within ten days."

" Well ? " inquired Bill. He really did not see what the fellow was driving at.

" I have noticed during this morning that you have made several references to slaves."

" Unavoidable. Sorry. They swarm here."

" So I observe. Perhaps you don't know that no breath of scandal has ever before touched a branch of Prince's."

" It's wonderful how much a firm can live down——"

" Mr. Durrant—I am serious."

" When I come to think of it, so, of course, am I. Look here, Blacker. You have to take things as you find them."

" I understand that you have permitted a species of blackmail . . ."

" Permitted ? How on earth could I stop it ? Do you imagine *I wanted* to see Talal bled white ? He's a friend of mine. But I couldn't help old Ma'buta's tricks."

" You've used slave labour."

" Of course. Don't you understand that *every one* in Mandoa who is not a Mandoan, is a slave ? *No* Mandoan will do manual labour. I had work to do. So I had to use slave labour. Q.E.D. But I paid the contractors for every hour's work done. It was not my business to see who got the money."

" I should have thought that precisely this was your
business. Do you realise that your irresponsibility may get
the firm into very serious trouble ? "

" Look here, Blacker. I don't know what you mean by
irresponsibility. I've been responsible enough to do all
the things I was sent out here to do. The aerodrome, the
hotel, the stadium—I've got them going all right, haven't
I ? And I've persuaded the court to break its oldest
tradition and get a princess married, haven't I ? And I've
managed the whole affair with precious little friction and
practically no loss of life, haven't I ? But it's perfectly
true that I haven't tried to reform the damn country as
well as exploit it."

" Exploit ? "

" Well, isn't that what I was sent here to do ? Rails
from Sheffield ; engines from Doncaster ; gramophones,
work-baskets, sewing machines—good British labour—
haven't I sold them all ? Aren't the tourists coming in
British planes ? Did you want me to be head nurse as well
as commercial agent to the country—or what ? "

" It hardly seems to me a matter for levity, Mr. Durrant."

" Levity ? I don't know if you think it a joke ; I don't.
I thought we'd made a darned good job of the thing in
none too easy circumstances, and you say we ought to have
taught the Mandoans humanitarian conduct from the
Boy Scout's Manual as well. Do you imagine they'd
have listened to us for a *moment* ? As a matter of fact,
they're extremely proud of their local customs and morale
and so on. They think that we're no end barbarians with
our unemployment and trade cycles and what not. To
say nothing about wars. My dear Blacker, you start
trying to teach my friend, Talal, and you'll soon learn where
our British civilisation falls down pretty flat, I can tell
you. I think Mason came out here thinking that he could
run the whole show quite, quite differently. And he found
he couldn't. He agreed with me in the end that we'd gone
too far to stop. And he just had to let things take their
course. They do, you know. Now a fellow like Guerdon
could preach to the Mandoans, and they listened. He
introduced English literature, and a sort of Christianity,
and what not. So did the American talkie crowd—petting

parties, and machine guns, and Yankee slang, and all the culture of Hollywood. But neither had any possible thing to gain out of the whole business. We have. So we'd better lie low before criticising Mandoan morals. You can either make a profit out of people, *or* you can lecture them for their own good. But you can't do both with any effect at the same time."

Mr. Blacker was drawing little figures on his blotting paper.

Bill came and sat on the table.

" Look here," he said. " You talk about slavery. Has it ever occurred to you that we're *all* slaves ? "

" My dear Durrant, that quasi-metaphysical quibbling doesn't go down with me."

" I don't mean that—though there might be something in it. I'm no good at philosophy and what not. What I mean is perfectly concrete. So long as we're here, we each of us belong to somebody. I'm Talal's slave, of course. I believe you're Bun'dodo's—you know—the big old fellow who wears sock suspenders. We had to be slaves or outlaws. There's no place in Mandoan society for the stranger who is not a slave. It's a legal fiction. But so is most slavery or freedom in Africa. It's the economic and political facts that really count. If Bun'dodo chose to thrash you to death for refusing to carry an umbrella over him when he went courting his new lady-love, he'd be within his legal rights. But he'd be taking such unpopular action that society would revenge itself upon him within an hour. So he'd never do it. And your safety is secured without endangering your liberty of action."

" Do you mean to say that you—you *permitted* this insult to British prestige ? I don't understand you, Durrant. Your whole conduct of this affair seems to me inexplicable. You're an officer. You're a university man. Yet you seem to have no—no *standards*." Blacker sighed. He was really troubled. " Don't you *care* about letting down your people ? "

Bill thought for some time, then he said, " That's too difficult. First, who *are* my people ? Prince's ? I haven't let them down so far as I can see. I've done everything I was sent to do. Talal ? I'm *his* person. Well, I've done what he wanted. My family? I believe that I have more than justified its hopes."

" Oh, don't pretend you don't know what I mean," sighed Blacker wearily.

" I do know. In a way, I suppose. You mean that I don't faint with horror at the notion of a white man being by legal fiction the slave of a black one. I don't, because I've gone far beyond caring a damn about words. Facts are what seem to matter—the war—unemployment —poverty—boredom. Boredom matters the hell of a lot, Blacker. Well, we're giving Mandoa what it wants. We're getting something out of it that we want. We're doing no one any harm. Why all this fuss about words and names, and fictions? They seem to me childish. They don't deal with reality."

Yet he looked with sympathy upon the official to whom they mattered so much. He saw Blacker's moral universe, all neatly arranged according to definitions and categories. He saw his spiritual discomfort and his practical dilemma.

Out in the street a troop of porters were carrying great bundles of withies to thatch the new dispensary. They were lean, wretched creatures, suffering from skin diseases, tuberculosis, syphilis, and a number of other scourges.

" What are you going to do about it? " Bill asked.

" You could stop the whole thing, couldn't you? Have a sort of public trial and confession, make me the scapegoat, acknowledge that I let the Lord High Chamberlain raid British territory for slaves to pay blackmail to Ma'buta to keep me here—that the money, both private and governmental, which Prince's are getting, is blood money made on the sale of slaves, and that you'll have no more to do with it. There'd be a grand bust up. We should all be turned out. The others here, Mason, Nicholson, Jordan and Cooper would be implicated. However clean a sweep Prince made, some dirt would stick. Besides, contracts would be broken. In Sheffield, Manchester, Guildford, Leeds, the men making this stuff you're bringing here would be unemployed again. The British Government which has been encouraging recognition of Mandoa, would have a nasty little knock on the head. For all I know, a dozen complicated and exceedingly beneficent diplomatic games would all be spoiled. I don't know, and I don't suppose you do, what bargains about disarmament, tariff reductions and what not, don't depend upon the Mandoan situation. If you throw it up now, what sort of a mess are you going to make? You'll break the heart of little Umb'ola, and you'll break the lives of Yorkshire steel workers, perhaps, and Washington clerks and—heaven knows who else. You call me irresponsible, Blacker, but I've got enough imagination to see ' the altogetherness of everything.' And I know that you can't stop an affair like this once it's started without smashing more than the affair."

" That argument justifies almost every business fraud ever perpetrated—you must go on, because it'll cause such an upheaval if you stop."

" Of course. And which do the most harm—the detected frauds that result in a smash, or the undetected frauds that are concealed and put right when the boom comes? "

" You're clever, Durrant. But you're only proving the complete rottenness of dishonesty. I never said it was easy to stop once it had started."

" But when does it start? Are we given clean slates to begin with? Haven't we got to take life as we find it, and generally find it based somewhere upon cruelty or fraud? In this case, it's cruelty—cruelty of arbitrary power which now has an illegal name. If this were called contract-labour we could have a free conscience about it, but there'd be precisely the same cruelty involved. Slavery may mean everything or nothing. It's the fact of violence and oppression and bullying that matters to slaves, and the demoralising effect of irresponsibility. And so far as the facts are concerned, we may do some good by being here. You see, I *have* paid the contractors on the understanding that they pay their labourers, and though they may pocket the cash themselves, the idea has got into their heads that labour should be paid. And we are introducing medicine and tools, and a few appurtenances of civilised living. If we withdraw in horror, it'll all just slip back again."

" We should clear ourselves."

" At the expense of several thousands of other people."

" I cannot help remembering that it is to your advantage that we should carry on as though everything was perfectly all right, Durrant."

" Of course. I suppose I *might* think quite differently if my interests lay the other way. But I'm not sure. It's not as if I had a reputation to lose or anything. I've reached a stage when I don't care much what happens to me. One experience or another—they're pretty well all the same in the end."

Blacker shook his head slowly. Durrant was quite possibly sincere. But the others ? His wonder found expression.

" I admit that you may be exceptional. You say you don't care. I've got to take your word. But Mason—and Nicholson——"

" Oh—don't blame them. They came out as technical experts and found a system in full swing. Besides, like you and me, they're slaves. They really took to it very well. I had to get them a bit oiled on the first night, but after that it all went quite smoothly. It wasn't their business."

" But what shall we say to the commissioners of the I.H.A. ? "

" Tell them the truth. That we pay every one of our labourers a living wage ; that we have never accepted a penny in bribes ; that we have neither offered nor demanded blackmail ; that the morality of the Mandoans is no direct concern of ours, and that the worse it is, the greater the necessity for contact with the rest of the world. Show them everything they want to see ; answer every question they ask. And if they can find a case against us, they're cleverer than I think."

In the end, Blacker did nothing.

He talked over the matter with his colleagues, and found them absorbed, each in his special work. The thought of an immediate breakdown of their plans horrified them. They could not understand Blacker's trouble. Why should there be a scandal ? Everything was all right. Sir Joseph was ill, and sick men saw troubles that did not exist. Why couldn't Blacker go back to Khartoum and soothe him down ?

The preparations went forward.

The world's press, among news of shipwrecks, price fluctuations, divorces, war scares, epidemics and party quarrels, reported that the wedding of the Heiress Apparent of Mandoa to an Abyssinian princeling, would take place at Lolagoba on February 28. In magazines and on hoardings, in daily papers and on picture postcards, Prince's " Once in a Lifetime " appeal summoned the public.

" Once in a lifetime, don't you want to see something that has never been seen before, and never can be seen again ? The pageantry of the East, and the pomp of the Middle Ages ! A city to which, until you go, tourists have never penetrated ? A civilisation untouched by modern contacts since the days of Queen Elizabeth ? Then come to Mandoa——"

Still, Blacker was not happy. Durrant's cynicism did not content him.

The man was a gentleman and no fool, but he drank too much, was too unconventional ; he quibbled ; he compromised.

He was wrong about words mattering nothing. Words and principles mattered a lot. But where did righteousness lie ?

With an aching conscience, dogged, miserable, efficient, Blacker carried on.

BOOK III
MANDOA IS MADE

CHAPTER I

JEAN STANBURY DISCOVERS MANDOA

" Now I have left the earth ; I am in the air," thought
Jean, as the big passenger 'plane flew southward from
Sennar. " The earth with all that ever happened there
has fallen away like a garment. The huge silver knife
of the wing scoops out the blue sky in slices. The form
of the ground lies plastic to our will. We mould the hills
and the valleys. The red-haired pilot holds the world in
his stubby hands.

" I have left London. I have left Jean Stanbury somewhere beyond Sennar ; while we were in the train, she
disappeared, deserting her colleagues and her excellent
post as secretary to the International Humanitarian
Association's Commission to Mandoa. I left half a dozen
selves. There was the big girl, Jean, who brought up younger
brothers and sisters, sewing name-tapes on school clothes,
and bathing babies ; who banked up fires through nightmarish nights, when doctors emerged, rubbing their hands,
from sick rooms ; who propped Latin grammars against
the mending basket, agonising over Matriculation.

" I have left the assistant editor of *The Byeword* who
loved her paper and sat nursing it at the telephone, pro-
tecting each issue through incredible perils. I have left
the docile reliable niece, who could always be counted upon
to shut the chickens up for the night, or to make a fourth
at bridge. I have left the efficient organiser (at least, I
think she was efficient).

" I'm going to Mandoa. I'm going to have an adventure.
I'm going to enjoy myself."

" Of course," she thought, looking at Frau Von Schelden's
broad back just in front of her. " This won't last for ever.
I shall go back to Victoria Street. I shall recover all my
old selves again. But, just for the moment, they're dead.
I am dead, and I have risen from the dead. This feels like
being a spirit ; to swoop over Africa, into melting dawns

and star-pierced nights; to be flying towards Mandoa, Mandoa, Mandoa; to be no one; to be every one; a creature new-made, removed from effort and responsibility, loss and fear; to soar up, up, into the torrid noons; to plunge—ah, to what ? To whom ? "

Such lyrical ecstasy is not uncommon among excitable persons on their first flight over unfamiliar continents, but Jean could not be expected to realise that.

The passengers stirred and looked over their shoulders, and though Jean could hear nothing, she knew that they had said, " This is Mandoa."

She thrust her head through her window; the air seized her eye-lashes; they felt inches long, whipping her face. She saw the sharp pinnacles of the escarpment like toy ridges on the relief map in the old science room. She saw the burned yellow plain speckled with mole hills, that were perhaps native huts. She saw the frail green of cultivated patches, and the soft silvery fur of the Sudd grass over the marshes, and she held her hands tight on her crumpled, shantung lap, because this moment could never come again in the whole of time. Never again would she see her first vision of Mandoa.

Other moments might be hers, but never again this wonder of speed and power and strangeness, snatched from the streets and clocks and files and tea-shops that made her London life.

It was the first time that she had ever been outside England.

The opportunity to come had been completely unexpected. She had urged the Mandoan expedition as good business. She had written reports and notices and memoranda. She had soothed Mr. Beaton's fears, and Frau von Schelden's too easily ruffled feelings. But only at the last moment had they invited her to go with them as their secretary.

The past fortnight had vanished in a dream. She had interviewed associations. She had prepared minute instructions for the London office. She had made rapid raids upon shops to buy herself an outfit.

" For abroad, madam ? "

" For Africa. As a matter of fact, I'm going to Mandoa."

" Mandoa ? Really, madam. *How* interesting." For
every one had heard of Mandoa nowadays.

All her life Jean had so resolutely pursued duty rather
than excitement, that shops and travel bureaux and time
tables were glorified for her. The choice between doe-skin
and canvas shoes, and silk or cotton dresses made an
exciting spiritual problem ; and all these new luxuries of
choice and of adventure were the background to her
enchanted observation, as she watched the brown floor
of the aerodrome rise up like a wall against first one side
of her and then the other, when they landed at Lolagoba.

She felt the machine touch the earth and spring along
the ground. She climbed out stiffly, behind Frau von
Schelden. She staggered, rather dizzy and deaf, across
the great enclosure, while her cases bobbed precariously
before her, with the cases of other passengers, on the
heads of green-clad porters.

She replied to Dr. Beriot's kind inquiries, that she had
loved the flight, that her head hardly ached at all, only
she could not hear well, and that she did not mind the heat.

She entered the dazzling white hotel, Mandoa's pride,
in which were to be found Private Suites with Bathrooms,
Hot and Cold, and All Modern Conveniences.

She sank down upon a narrow bed with a pink silk
quilt in the hot little room, where everything, even her
luggage just brought in by the porter, was overlaid with a
light powdering of sand. She said to herself, " Well, I'm
here. This is Lolagoba. This is Princes' Hotel. I am in
the middle of Africa." And remembered about ants, and
read in a notice that guests must be sparing in their use
of water, and washed, in spite of that, and changed her
dress, and braved the fierce heat of corrugated iron
corridors, and found herself in the pathetically fragile
" garden " of the hotel.

Here a row of lilies drooped, their long shadows like
blue pot-hooks scribbled across the grass. A quaint green
lawn of artificial turf, such as sports shops spread below
cricket bats in the window, encircled the white building.
Immense white waxen trumpets, hanging from a bush of
glossy green leaves, almost startled her with their perfume.
She lifted her head and saw, beyond the lilies and the lawn,

the brown space of the aerodrome, its hangars crouched like sleeping beasts to her right, the little black figures of men running about, their shadows flying behind them. And beyond the plain, the evening sun balanced like an orange on the edge of the table that was the world, as though a touch would push it over.

She stood looking, breathing, tasting, gathering to herself the rapture of this first evening in Mandoa. So it was true, that she had left the world, herself, and all that she had ever known.

And then she saw Bill Durrant.

He was coming up the red path from the city, bare-headed, the slanting light on his sun-bleached, golden-tinted hair. He carried a white helmet in his hand, and his clothes were white, so that she saw him in a white and golden glory, striding before two negro servants, lordly and preoccupied.

He did not see her. He was thinking only of his own business, withdrawn into himself as he had never been in London, where he offered his heart for any daw to peck at, and was ready to seek for sympathy at any window.

And suddenly she was swept by blind, unreasoning, melting, feminine, panic. Without a thought, she slipped behind the moon-flower bush, and stood hidden while he went past her up to the hotel.

As the door closed behind him, she felt a shuddering reaction, as though she had just escaped grave peril.

Her knees trembled ; her mouth was dry. Hurriedly she fled to the side door and round to her little room, amazed at her own conduct. To run away from Bill—of all people —Bill whom she had known so well, who had proved to be exasperatingly harmless. It was absurd. It was also most unlike her.

She sat down on the rosy quilt, and began to think.

Bill Durrant was Prince's agent in Lolagoba. She had known all the time that she must meet him.

She was determined to get her feelings straight about him.

There were, it appeared, two Bill Durrants, and she liked neither of them.

There was her old friend of London, Cynthia's husband,

the ne'er-do-weell, charming, lazy-minded wastrel, for whom one had to be making the excuse perpetually, " It was the war." If he had not had that air crash ; *if* Stephen had not been killed—*if, if, if.* . . . And against that little word his friends balanced the heavy weight of his short-comings.

He had exploited her shamelessly, shamelessly.

He had come—she could see him still—that evening after he and Cynthia had decided upon the divorce, and talked for hours and hours in front of her fire, arguing for it, against it, using her as a substitute for Cynthia, now complaining, now cynical, now humorous, while she, weary from a long day at the office, had rocked in an agony, a tornado of sleepiness, praying for nothing but that he would let her go to bed—with him or without him, she did not care.

For several times it had occurred to her that he was seeking for more than comfortable words.

But nothing happened. At four o'clock in the morning he had lurched off into the quiet streets ; he had dropped off, like a bee drunk with honey, nourished upon her courage, leaving her exhausted, drained of sympathy and feeling, enabled only from the sweet chill of night air through the open door, to find energy enough to crawl into her bed.

And so he had returned to her after failures, after distresses, after his one outbreak of jealousy over his lost daughter, after his conversion to Socialism, feeding upon her, demanding from her, yet always remaining just sufficiently detached to give her nothing in return, to place upon her all initiative for greater intimacy. He had interrupted her evenings, eaten her suppers, borrowed her vitality. And though she had not sent him away, she could never yield completely. Always, even while lending him her knowledge and her practical sense, she had felt the unsleeping clock of criticism beat in her brain, tick, tock, tick, tock, marking his faults, her withdrawals, the time that both were wasting, the energy they spilled.

And now here was this other Durrant, the agent for Prince's Limited in Lolagoba, a man of certain importance but doubtful honesty, who seduced business men, and made dark pacts with natives, and sold slaves into a living death for his own ambition.

The few qualities she had been certain of in London—his kindliness, his humanity, his instinctive benevolence, were doubtful here. For after her first reaction towards this creature of decision and initiative, she had recoiled from cruelty, and interpreted his old dependence on her in the most sinister fashion. The only really important virtue, she had decided, was benevolence, to wish well to the world, to love. All others, such as strength and power and cleverness, were nothing beside that.

And Durrant of Lolagoba countenanced, and perhaps encouraged, cruelty. He was one of those men who feel that a white skin justifies any breach of conduct. Never, never again could she be his friend.

The dinner gong boomed, and she went to join her party.

It was just as well, perhaps, that she did not see Bill for a week. Her days were filled with work and sightseeing and sociability. She had to take letters from the dictation of Mr. Beaton and Dr. Beriot and Frau von Schelden, for, with transport so costly, she had offered to do without a stenographer. She had to write reports and prepare agenda, to send messages to the aerodrome to be telegraphed from Juba, and letters to the offices in Victoria Street and Oslo.

She had to sympathise with Frau von Schelden, whose bed had been invaded by an army of ants, and with Mr. Beaton, who for two days suffered from a touch of sunstroke.

But she had her moments, exploring the city with kind, vivacious Dr. Beriot whose curiosity was as eager as hers, and whose erudite wit illuminated for her the cathedral, the Royal Palace, the market place, and all other wonders of Lolagoba.

Of course she heard of Durrant.

Every one discussed him. Rumours flew.

He had been forced to resign by Sir Joseph Prince, they said, who was aghast at his malpractices.

He was leaving Mandoa.

He could not leave Mandoa because the slave owners
were blackmailing him.

He was drinking himself to death in his bungalow.
No. He could not be drinking himself to death in his own
bungalow, because he had signed orders, improved arrangements, visited the hotel daily, seen Mr. Beaton. " Able
but dangerous. I could get nothing out of him," said Mr.
Beaton. " An amusing devil. I like him," said Dr. Beriot.
" I wouldn't trust him an inch. I should say drugs, not
drink," whispered Frau von Schelden ; " and they say
that his relationship with that greasy beast Talal is——"
She shrugged fat, but modest, shoulders, leaving Jean to
infer the worst. Which she found incredible.

She prayed, as she went about the town, that she would
not meet him unexpectedly round the next corner.

Yet she rounded her corners.

She shirked neither jot nor tittle of her official task
because she was afraid of meeting Bill. Nor did her joyful,
astonished interest in the novelty of Mandoa abate by the
lightest featherweight because she was afraid. Indeed, her
fear itself had a novel charm.

She told herself that for women nearing forty (thus she
had described herself ever since her thirty-third birthday)
the adventure of being in Central Africa was far, far more
exciting than any prospect of meeting a man who, when
all was said and done, had never been anything but a
rather doubtful friend to her.

She had been in Lolagoba just a week when she rode
with Frau von Schelden back from the new hospital which
they had been inspecting. Womanly women were always
supposed to be interested in new hospitals, and the I.H.A.,
Jean had observed, preferred its women womanly.

They clung insecurely to the saddles of small, wicked
donkeys, who scampered and slithered through sand and
over cobbles in the most hilarious manner, for all the world
like donkeys on Brighton sands. Jean found it exhilarating,
but Frau von Schelden, thumping breathlessly behind her,
found it *schrecklich*, and mingled her discomfort with her
dismay at the use of tinned milk in the maternity ward.

The broad street shot them into a narrow alley. The
naked children who had not yet learned to beg, but who

had run beside them all the way from the hospital offering dried dung and beads for sale, became more clamorous. Their shrill voices filled the alley. The sky, like stretched silk, closed down above the thatches, shutting them in with flies and heat and odours, stifling them. Frau von Schelden grew hotter and more exasperated. She shouted at the children in German. They skipped about her, delighted, crying, " Who's my cutie ? " and pressing the little balls of dung, in red cotton, against her voluminous linen skirt.

" *Ach, Gott !* " cried poor Frau von Schelden ; " shall we never be out of this ? "

But before they were out, there was a tinkling of bells, and a shouting of male voices, and four runners, black, shining men in yellow loin cloths, sprang down the alley, waving staves, and scattering the children right and left. Behind them trotted two men on handsome ponies, the big magnificent bearded creature whom Jean recognised as Safi Talal, and beside him Bill Durrant.

They drew to one side, leaving room for the ladies ; and Jean, who had the better control over her beast, pulled in behind Frau von Schelden. In the scurry of animals and flies and dust and servants, the riders passed. The children vanished too, and Jean and her companion continued their way to the hotel undisturbed.

So. He had not seen her. Or, if he had, he preferred not to acknowledge her. Which was just as well. For were they not in opposite camps, even though Prince's had offered every facility to the I.H.A. inquiry ?

But that night they were forced to speak. Bill came after dinner to an informal reception at the hotel, to welcome a party of American publicists, and Jean, who had not realised that he would be there, turned away from Sophie Marlow, to find herself face to face with him.

He said, " Hallo, Jean."

She said, " Hallo, Bill."

He asked, " And how do you like Lolagoba ? "

And she replied, " I think it's lovely." Which was quite untrue, for the city was devoid of beauty, being squalid, formless, hot, insanitary and chaotic, with only the vivid

life of its nobles, and the overhanging cliff of the escarpment
to commend it.

But even while the warning clock ticked in her head,
telling her that she was false, insincere, and a coward, and
that he was graceless and unkind, he offered her a cocktail,
he introduced her to an English business man called
Watson, who was, he declared, interested in steel rails, and
left her.

Mr. Watson said that Mandoa was becoming quite an
international centre of gaiety. He said that the heat was
very trying for ladies, who were also afraid of snakes and
insects. He said that the water shortage was tiresome—
especially for ladies. He asked Jean if she had been there
long, and what she thought of Lolagoba.

Next morning Mr. Beaton told his fellow-commissioners
that Prince's had offered them accommodation in the
hunting camps prepared for the tourists if they wished to
see something of the rural districts. Then they could make
their own inquiries about labour conditions. It seemed a
curious arrangement, but it certainly would save the
expense of a long safari—also they could make special
surprise visits to doubtful places afterwards, if they thought
it necessary.

Jean was delighted.

She was delighted to be off again, living on donkeys, in
camps, seeing, perhaps, lions and deer and elephants,
interviewing slaves by torchlight, free, marvellously free,
from all taint of personal emotion and responsibility,
abandoned to the incomparable joy of Africa.

So she set forth, riding her velvet donkey, charmed by
its gold-braided coat, its jingling bells, its mincing, ridiculous
gait. Everything charmed her. Even when she shrank
from the cruel monotony of the burned plain—when she
sighed over the tragic gardens, blasted by drought or the
lean goats, cropping their diet of thorns ; her sighs, her
regrets, were no more than the mechanical human reactions
of her body. In her heart sprang a golden fountain of joy.
She could almost see it leaping and falling, like those
fireworks called Golden Rain that she and her brothers
had loved when they were children.

They had set off in the early morning, and lunched and

rested by a green water hole, an artificial dam, almost dry now, but still crowded with vegetation around its narrowing rim, " as though," Dr. Beriot declared, " the plants had come jostling down to drink like animals."

There they interviewed and questioned numbers of Negroes. For generations, it appeared, these had been slaves. They felt no shame, nor, they declared, suffered any hardship. Indeed, they asserted several times that it was better to be a slave than a freed man, for slaves were valuable property, and, in emergencies, protected by this. Their masters would find rations for them when the freed men starved. They had seen freed men tramping the drought-stricken plain, trying to sell themselves and finding no buyer.

Frau von Schelden would have none of this. Evil was evil, slavery slavery, in her eyes. Grimly she noted the evidence. Grimly she questioned. Neither the beauty of the feathery rushes by the intense blue water, nor the discomfort of the insects playing about her head, could divert her heroic indignation at man's inhumanity to man.

Jean admired, but could not emulate her concentration. She watched strange birds swoop out of the sky on to the backs of the goats, and there engage in a solemn hunting. She watched the fish in the clear water, and the vivid magenta and orange of aloe flowers, drained by the hungry light.

She could not believe that she was really here.

It was not that she wanted to stay for-ever ; she knew that she would return to Victoria Street, and her desk, and the girls there, but she was seeing what she had always longed to see ; she was doing what she had always longed to do, and her sympathy for suffering Negroes could not drown her pleasure in the opportunity to see them—a state of mind for which she rebuked herself without avail.

But the day wore on ; the heat of the afternoon passed ; the halt by the dam ended, and once more they mounted their saddles. The little donkeys lolloped down the uneven paths, the running Negro boys hitting mechanically their flat buttocks.

Suddenly twilight came. Like rigid ghosts, the ant hills stood, six or eight feet high. The fierce kiss of the mosquitos pricked Jean's neck. She did not care. So far as she was concerned, this stumbling, blindfold ride might last forever.

Darkness had fallen as they climbed a steep hill, slipping on stones and winding in and out among big boulders. They reached and rounded the crest, scrambled over a rocky tableland, and stood, looking down into a valley.

In the valley lay the little camp.

Jean had never seen anything more extraordinary and more beautiful in her life.

For the nine tents had been lit from within, and glowed like opalescent flowers in the dark cup of the hollow. There were eight round tents, and one big oblong one, with a canopy stretched before it, from which hung swinging lanterns, and under the canopy, tiny and neat as a doll's feast, lay the table spread for supper. There in the night, they glowed and waited, the exquisite little tents, the brave, the beautiful. She had no words for her gratitude and tenderness. Her heart melted at this evidence of human labour and courtesy in the dark wilderness. She could have wept for joy.

They plunged downward.

Nearer and nearer drew the camp. They could see black men in yellow tunics hurrying about, and among the negroes, one white man. She looked and looked, and with a shock of recognition, realised that it was Bill Durrant.

He explained, as he helped them to dismount, that he was making a final tour of the camps, and had decided to visit their's to-night to see if they had all they wanted, especially as the Mandoan nobleman who was officially their host, had been unable to come.

His manner was easy and non-committal, but Jean was aware of a sudden bristling indignation among her companions. Bill was the villain of the piece, whose activities they had come to investigate ; and he had forestalled them. It was all very reprehensible, cynical and shocking.

She tried to share Frau von Schelden's anger and Mr. Beaton's scorn, but she could not prevent her thoughts from straying to the charm of her little tent.

It was made of dun-coloured silk, very light and clean. Its monastic bareness delighted her. She felt that she never wanted to sleep anywhere else.

At dinner they ate strange food below the lantern-lit canopy. There were sweetmeats in clay dishes, and meat served with sugary-salted fruit and delicious vegetables.

Perhaps this is not real, Jean thought, perhaps I shall find myself back in Victoria Street ; and she pinched her wrists under the table.

But there sat Bill, nonchalant and polite, and Mr. Beaton, stiffly suspicious, talking about the economic conditions of land servants—" agricultural developments," " feudal hierarchy," " labour tenancy." Dr. Beriot, intelligent and malicious, abetted him ; and Frau von Schelden, stolid and resolute, flung down her flat, thumping statements. The diet of children, the provisions for pregnant women, the prostitution of slave girls, fell like heavy challenges on to the table.

They were enclosed, Jean thought, in a little circle of morality and accusation and good citizenship, while beyond them rustled the huge anarchic darkness of the African night.

The coffee was good ; the liqueur was hot and sweet to the palate.

Two tall servants kept returning to their master with advice and direction and polite reproof. They seemed to be very anxious that he should do all the right things and offer the right foods.

Jean watched them closely. She thought that a man's attitude towards an alien race might perhaps be discerned from his manner to his servants.

She hated insulting comic names applied to natives. Mutt, Jeff, Sixpence, Uncle ; these seemed to her hideous —the expression of a boundless contempt.

But there was little contempt to be traced in Bill's manner. Indeed, he appeared to regard his servants with respect, paying attention to their advice, and delivering requests with courtesy.

When the other Negroes emerged from the kitchen-tent where they had presumably been washing up, Bill beckoned one, asking if they would sing.

The commissioners, lynx-eyed and critical, surveyed the entertainment.

The black men knew nothing of hesitation. They grouped

themselves about the dying fire, as though heat were native to them, and crouching on their haunches, began a low monotonous chant. Mutt and Jeff were not with the singers, who seemed to be men from a single tribe, the descendants, probably, of one group of villagers torn by raiders from their home in Kenya or Uganda, and enslaved to whatever Mandoan noble owned this particular estate.

Frau von Schelden sat with pursed lips, but Pierre Beriot moved closer to Jean.

" Are you also steeling yourself against insidious influences ? " he whispered mischievously. " I do not believe that you are at all safe. Take care. Take care."

She was not safe.

She was already seduced by pleasure and curiosity. The dirge, melancholy yet serene, of the singing Negroes, seemed to swell and die out of the air itself. It did not move her to ardour for reform, as it moved Frau von Schelden. It soothed and pacified her. She could sit there for ever.

" Beware, Mademoiselle Stanbury," the Frenchman murmured. " We are humanitarians and reformers. That has nothing to do with æsthetic pleasures. Observe this Mr. Durrant who seeks to divert our attention from gross injustices by romantic interludes."

The lamps grew dim. Cigarette tips moved like fireflies in the darkness. The song died away.

Frau von Schelden, censorious but self-controlled, aroused herself to deliver erudite comments upon the Bantu scale, and its peculiar modulations.

Mr. Beaton returned to a former argument in favour of the Hague rather than Geneva as a centre for international action.

In the oblong tent before which they were sitting, a lamp still burned. Jean could hear low murmuring voices from within.

Possibly these came from the two big Negroes, Mutt and Jeff, who had not joined the singers. But she found the persistent, unemphatic conversation a trifle sinister.

Pierre Beriot had now contradicted Beaton.

" Even so, if we accept our responsibilities as leaders

of a vanguard establishing civilised morals . . ." the Englishman was saying.

" But civilisation," the Frenchman repeated. " Just what do we mean by that ? "

There was a pause, while Beriot rolled over on his tongue and rejected first one good phrase then another. Through the silence the deep voices from the tent, growling like distant thunder, rumbled more clearly.

" ' C-A-T, cat—M-A-T, mat—the cat sat on the mat.' What the hell's a cat, anyway, big boy ? "

The three commissioners started.

" What's that ? " gasped Jean, turning instinctively to Bill Durrant.

He smiled, his maddening, non-committal, sideways smile, looking up at her between his long eyelashes, as he lit his cigarette, the flame quivering behind his cupped fingers.

" The answer to Beriot's question—isn't it ? What *is* civilisation ? A CAT sat on A MAT. The old educational classic, what ? "

" I don't get you, Durrant," Beaton said.

Bill shrugged his shoulders.

" My two servants are teaching each other to read, preparing, for all I know, to be my masters. They are acquiring that elementary education which is the basis of a common civilisation—or isn't it ? You specialise in these things ; I'm an amateur. Incidentally, you observed, they don't know what a cat is. Hi ! Mutt ! Jeff ! "

Two black forms rose as from a dive, from under the tent flap.

" Cats are small feline creatures of the tiger family. In England we think we have domesticated—tamed— them. They *do* sit on mats when it suits them. God bless my soul. There are cats in Egypt, aren't there ? " Bill appealed to the others. " You should know cats."

" The cat," began Dr. Beriot, " is a creature of exquisite sensibility and divine fastidiousness——"

Mutt and Jeff gazed placidly at their instructors, and Jean acquired the impression that they, together with Bill, were secretly amused at the commissioners. They probably knew that Mr. Beaton's party has come to

Mandoa to save them, and being individually fortunate, and without trained public spirit, they had no desire to be saved.

But happily, Frau von Schelden was tired. The commissioners had a long ride to face next morning. She said that she wished to retire. Instead of further explaining the nature of the cat, Bill ordered his servants to escort the guests to bed. The camp sprang once more to varied and animated life. Lanterns flitted hither and thither. As lamps were lit, the tents again glowed softly like opening flowers. Good-nights were said. The party separated.

But Jean sat on.

Bill was talking somewhere with his two servants perhaps giving them final instructions about closing down the camp. She heard their intimate and friendly laughter and their low, merry voices.

It was impossible to believe that Bill was really the man of calculating cruelty who would sell slaves and betray Mandoans for self-interest. A consummate villain might deceive a commission of inquiry by acted innocence, but all this was too easy. There was no strain, no affectation in it.

In the end, Jean considered, the test of sincerity lay in personal relationships. It was the feeling towards these African people that counted. If one felt their humanity, if it became an emotional as well as an intellectual reality, one was safe. Mistakes might be made and errors tolerated, but the mainspring of action was sound.

Jean, who had first been convinced of Bill's fundamental benevolence towards the world, and then feared her mistake, was reassured again. He was all right. He was the man she knew.

Prince's might still be a callous commercial firm, indifferent to everything but its financial interests. The Mandoan scandal might still be a scandal. Bill was careless and lazy minded. He left ill alone. He lacked the stuff that makes reformers and protestants. But he was sound.

She had no rational grounds for her assurance, but she was none the less assured, and her knowledge called for action. She had wronged him, and she must apologise.

She had thrust him away, and must return to intimacy.
She knew now that they were bound together in a relationship that depended upon old confidences and memories
shared. Such contacts cannot be broken without damage.
She must put herself right with her friend—at once.

So strong was her impulse, so deep her emotion, that she
said to herself, " Perhaps this is love. Perhaps I have always
really loved him. That is what this relief, this absence of
criticism means."

She sat on, smoking and waiting for his return, listening
to the sounds of her fellow commissioners retiring for the
night, and of the Negro porters closing down the camp.

Tranquillity like a blessing came upon her. The clock
that had always ticked in her active mind, marking off
judgments, choices, hesitations, now stood still.

She was sitting so quietly that she hardly seemed to
breathe, when Bill returned.

He came quite close to her in the darkness before he
said, " Hallo, it's you, Jean." And sat down beside her as
though their situation were the most natural in the world.

He produced his case, and lit another cigarette from
the stump in his mouth. Again Jean had the impression
of his sly, sidelong smile. But he did not speak. They sat
for some time in silence.

Then she said, trying to sound casual, " I suppose they've
all gone to bed."

" I suppose so. Unless they're routing about to see if
the porters sleep in chains or anything."

His bitterness tore a rent in her tranquillity. She had
been so completely convinced by his indifferent manner.
She drew back a little.

" I suppose you think we're spying on you ? " she said
at last.

" Oh, not at all. Naturally I know why you're here.
And naturally, you don't want to go home empty-handed
without a scrap of evidence. You needn't be afraid. This
is a lawless country. You'll find slaves if you know where
to look, and plenty of other evils."

" Bill."

" Well ? "

" Are you very angry with us ? "

" Why should I be ? "

" I think I ought to tell you that I was one of the chief instigators of this inquiry."

In low tones so as not to disturb her colleagues, she narrated as much as she felt free to tell of her part in the International Humanitarian Association's campaign. " It's all public property. We're not biased—honestly we're not. These are experienced social investigators and they don't *want* to find scandals where none exist."

" Quite. But it's to their interest to find some. And there are plenty. Good luck to you all, say I. By the way, I wouldn't talk too much to the Mandoans themselves about it. They're proud people and sensitive, and not used to criticism."

She could not get near him. He was miles away— amused, polite, a little scornful. She wanted to protest, " You've got no right to treat me like this," but she realised that her own conduct did not present a very pretty appearance, when judged on its personal rather than its official side. She had told him to go to Mandoa, and she had come to " spy " on him. The thousand and one complications separating those two facts were beyond all possibility of explanation.

Yet she was reluctant to let him go. She had grown so much accustomed to thinking of herself as the moral superior, encouraging, reproving and supporting her dependent friend, that this reversal of rôles shocked her. He was independent of her solicitude. He no longer needed her interest.

Because she was disconcerted, she said rather hotly, " You can hardly blame people for feeling uneasy about labour conditions here."

He said, " Who said I blamed them ? "

She sought another opening. " Why then, if you are so indifferent to what public opinion thinks, did you come down here to hang about us ? You must have seen it would create a wretchedly embarrassing position ? "

" I'm a man under orders. My employers tell me, come here and go there, and I come and go. I was told to see that you were comfortable."

" You know that's not true."

" If you know so much, why do you ask me ? "

" It's so obvious."

" Good. That's all right then."

" I don't understand you. I can't believe that you've really turned into one of those cynical——" She paused for the definition.

" ' It's terrible how a white man can go to pieces in the tropics,' " he grinned, laughing at her.

She would not be laughed at.

She leaned forward, urgent, explanatory.

" Look here, Bill."

She laid her hand on his arm.

That startled him. He clutched her hand, crying, " My dear—— ! "

She felt the strong shock of emotion flow through her.

For a moment, anything might have happened.

" Good heavens, he loves me. He feels . . ."

They waited.

Every instinct, every memory, hung between them. Their past and their future stood balancing on a breath.

Then long-trained habit intervened. Jean drew away.

" Well, of course, if your motives are really so innocent." Her tone, light and mocking, cut through the spell.

She felt his recoil.

" Innocent as a new born babe," he reassured her.

" Then we'd better go to bed. I'm tired. I don't know what *you're* doing, but *we've* got a long day's work before us."

Their division was complete.

She dropped her cigarette end and stamped out the spark with her heel. It was satisfactory to extinguish anything so completely.

" Very well. Good-night, Bill."

" I'll see you to your tent."

" No. Don't bother. I know which it is."

" You'll fall over the ropes."

He was teasing her in his familiar, gentle way.

" *Since there's no help, come let us kiss and part.* . . ."

The line came unexpectedly to her mind. But they did not kiss.

" Shall I see you in the morning ? "

" I don't suppose so," he answered. " I'm off early."

" Nay I have done, you get no more of me.
And I am glad, yea, glad with all my heart
That thus so cleanly I myself can free. . . ."

She groped her way towards her tent.

There it glowed in the darkness, single, solitary, a conventual chamber of inviolate order.

Behind her, in the confusion of shadow and firelight, Bill stood watching her go.

If she turned now—— ?

" Now, at the last gasp of Love's latest breath. . . ."

She went on ; she raised the flap of her tent, entered, and let it fall behind her.

She was shut in now, quite safe and free from interruption. If she still trembled, it was from reaction rather than pain.

What had happened ?

Nothing had happened, she told herself, pulling the whispering silk of her dress up over her shoulders. All this had been thought out and decided long ago.

Yet, as she carefully folded her clothes and laid them on the camp-stool, she felt that she was laying aside more than her dress and petticoat. She was laying aside physical and emotional adventures ; she was laying aside her husband and her children.

" And I am glad, yea, glad with all my heart. . . ."

Well, if not with all her heart, with a good deal of it. She had her work, and Africa, and a thousand human contacts.

" Settled by a majority vote," she thought wryly.

But even as she stretched her long body on the narrow bed, she knew that in life nothing is ever finally settled ; that the dilemmas recur, and the decisions have to be re-made again and again, and that only in death is finality.

Soothed by the thought of that final rest from criticism, from judgment, and from choice, she slept.

CHAPTER II

MA'BUTA ADVERTISES MANDOA

MASS was celebrated daily on Ma'buta's land. The local archbishop, a kinsman of the chief, offered flesh for bread and blood for wine, invoking the Holy Trinity, Father, Son, and Mother, while the obedient warriors worshipped. Ma'buta himself attended the ceremony, and, when it was over, sat before the altar to do justice.

He did justice with all piety, burning heretics, excommunicating usurers; and he did not suffer a witch to live.

He was thus sitting when towards the end of February, a week before the royal wedding, messengers came from north-west and south-east with news. From the north-west, he learned that a party of four Europeans, two men and two women, approached his camp. They had been travelling in the marsh districts. They were interested in slaves. They called Negroes to them and asked questions. They were friends of the Lord High Chamberlain, who had stayed one night at their camp. Of the women, one was fat and one thin. The thin one was the woman of Safi Durrant.

The messenger from the south-east brought news that a white man, travelling from Lake Rudolph, was inquiring for Ma'buta's land. He had fallen down a bank near the lake and hurt his foot. He was sick with fever. He declared that he must see Ma'buta, even if he died afterwards. For Ma'buta knew secrets which he must know. Ma'buta could tell him all about the slaves of Mandoa.

Ma'buta sat grunting and chuckling before the altar. All this was good. It was very good. The white men should be escorted to his camp. He was ready for them. If they came to buy slaves, that was good, for no one in Mandoa had more than he. While Talal sweated and laboured at the capital, Ma'buta had sat patiently demand-

ing and receiving tribute. Oh, he had slaves to sell in
plenty.

If they came to forbid the sale of slaves, that too was
good, for it was Talal who had sold and traded, Talal
who had conducted the raids, Talal who had crossed the
hills into white man's territory. Ma'buta had taken care
to send tales of Talal's infamy to white officers in Kenya
and Uganda. From time to time he had ordered a slave
to be thrashed by men in yellow, and sent him across the
frontier with his story. Yellow was Talal's colour. The name
of the Lord High Chamberlain should stink in the white
nostrils that now found it sweet.

And if the white travellers had neither purpose, if they
came interfering and spying and desecrating his land, and
disturbing his servants, Ma'buta still knew what he could
do. Talal had already paid blood-money for his friends
in Lolagoba. He could pay again. Let him pay. Let him
pay white men for their machines and Ma'buta for his
peace. All things work together for good to them that
love God.

" Though I have been young, who now am old, though
I have been strong who now am feeble, yet shall I see mine
enemy languish at my gate. I shall triumph over the
young and violent. I will become the ruler of Mandoa, and
white men shall serve me and my people unto the third
and fourth generation. Then will I drive out evil
from the land, and see righteousness done before I
die."

He gave orders for food to be prepared, for a hut to be
cleared within the camp, and for water to be carried from
the springs.

Then he sat at his gate, rocking gently backwards and
forwards on his haunches, picking his teeth with a polished
thorn, waiting.

The party of four arrived late in the afternoon. Ma'buta
saw a large, solemn, elderly man, with a round stomach,
who talked as though his mouth were full of rich fruits ;
a slight, dark, lively man whose eyes twinkled behind
round glasses, a fat woman with a red face, and a tall,
thin, younger woman with no breasts.

These were the questioners of slaves. The thin woman

belonged to Safi Durrant. The large man was chieftain of
the party.

Ma'buta rose and saluted them. God, he declared, had
sent them to him. He had heard of their noble work.
Their interest in his poor country flattered him.

He spoke as usual through an interpreter, though he
could understand more than half they said. He conducted
them within his stockade and had rugs spread on the
ground, beautiful rugs of antelope skin, zebra, giraffe and
buffalo, the hides kneaded till they were supple as silk.
He himself sat on a carven throne, his feet on the pelt of
a lion that he had slain.

Broiled goat and chicken and fruit and cakes of pounded
grain baked in the ashes were carried by warriors—each
a pure-blooded Mandoan—and set before the guests. It
was a feast of honour. Ma'buta offered sispri in clay vases,
and beer in vessels of reeds so closely plaited that no
liquor escaped. He declared that his heart was warm
towards the white men, and that he understood the purity
of their bowels, for all were Catholics together. (Blessed
be the most Holy Trinity.)

The commissioners of the International Humanitarian
Association were very tired. Mandoan travel was interesting, but it was strenuous. To reach Ma'buta's camp
they had climbed from the plains up the steep foothills
across a devastated country, where boulders big as a man's
head blocked their progress. When they rode, their donkeys
stumbled and slithered over the cruel surface. When they
walked, it was like treading on stoney skulls.

Their feet were blistered, their faces tortured by insect
bites, their bodies aching.

Their physical discomforts had been increased by
psychological incompatibility. There was no doubt that
the combination was unfortunate. Frau von Schelden's
obstinate pedantry exasperated Beriot. A pacifist and a
Socialist, she loved all Frenchmen by duty and hated them
by instinct. His flippant manner shocked, though it did
not surprise, her. She could not believe him sincere, though
she felt bound to acknowledge his competence. She contradicted him on every possible occasion, and her triumph
when she put him in the wrong—which was not seldom,

for he took facts light-heartedly — galled others beside the doctor.

As for Mr. Beaton, he liked Beriot little better himself, but he had anticipated trouble between French and German, and prided himself on his ability to see both sides of a vexed question. It was the British destiny to act as honest broker in continental transactions, and Mr. Beaton conducted his conscience as a public institution, carrying diplomatic obligations into private life.

Jean, being his secretary, also was his confidante.

" Luckily," he would tell her, " I am a broad-minded man. I take no pride in it. I sometimes think it may be a weakness for one in my position, but I always can see both sides of a case. Frau von Schelden, mind you, is a good woman and a hard worker. But she is tactless, and the poor thing has no sense of humour. She never sees the point of my jokes. I am sorry for her husband. Extraordinary how these women without charm manage to marry. Of course she's very *German*. But I don't blame her for distrusting Beriot. Clever fellow of course ; a good doctor. Though I never know quite how far that superficial brilliance *goes*. I think you will not accuse me of boasting, when I suggest that no one could care more for the welfare of Africans than I, but this French absence of colour prejudice can be carried a little *too far*."

In the tent they shared together, Frau von Schelden, conscientiously folding her graceless undergarments, and sighing with relief at deliverance from their restriction, would confide in Jean. " I hope I am wrong. And I should hate to think that I were right. But I wonder how far our doctor is to be trusted *alone* with native girls."

And as they rode together, Dr. Beriot would pull his donkey beside Jean's, and bump over the stones beside her muttering, " *Mon Dieu*, give me patience with that woman ! "

Frau von Schelden lost no opportunity to compare the German record in East Africa with conditions on the French Congo. She found pleasure in retailing grim stories of Somaliland. She admitted no concessions to frivolity or speculation in her unflinching rectitude of judgment.

Yet if Frau von Schelden did not spare others, she did

not spare herself. Jean, provoked to defend her, found a hundred arguments in her favour, but the little French doctor listened, his eyes twinkling. Weighing Jean's reasons against her motives, he teased her with gentle malice as a hypocrite. He obviously found a mild pleasure in her company. He even made love to her in an absent-minded fashion, which Jean, unaccustomed to such flattering attentions, found pleasant, though not at all disturbing.

During these long rides she learned a good deal about his personal history. She knew that he had travelled as a boy down the Congo to visit his father, a colonial official, and that the things he had seen there inflamed his adolescent imagination with a passion of pity for the helpless Africans. She learned about his years as a medical student, his service in a government hospital in Senegal, his publications on tropical diseases, and his early enthusiasm for the I.H.A. He told her also of his wife's death, three months before the commission had left Europe ; and Jean, whose expectations and experiences were insular, learned with surprise that conjugal devotion is not an Anglo-Saxon monopoly. It became clear to her that Dr. Beriot had adored the tragic, gay, deported Italian Socialist whom he had married, cherished, and been unable to save from the tuberculosis that was her legacy from three years' penal servitude.

Daily Jean grew to like and understand him better ; his society soothed her and helped her to endure with equanimity the constant friction and uneasiness of the commissioners.

Yet, however little happiness the commissioners found in their personal relationships, at least in their official business, they had found success. Everything was going well. Their conclusions were developing just as they had anticipated.

They found in Mandoa ample evidence of an old-established system of traditional slavery, and saw signs of a flourishing international trade in slaves. But no proofs directly implicated Prince's Limited. The agency had perforce made use of existing conditions, but it had paid the contractors who supplied its labour ; it had made some effort to improve the lot of the labourers, and it was possible that, by bringing Mandoa into contact with civilising influences, Sir Joseph himself might initiate the process of reform.

This was just the conclusion that Beaton wanted. He was anxious for justice, but he hated scandal. In his heart he longed to find his own countrymen incapable of the greater villainies of commercial exploitation. Dr. Beriot, more anxious to concentrate attention upon the necessity of introducing modern methods of treating leprosy and sleeping sickness, than to grind any political axe, was inclined to agree with him. And Frau von Schelden, having discovered a new mine of information about initiation ceremonies among girls, was prepared to sign a conciliatory report, but she insisted that no acre of territory should be left uninspected, and that the final and dangerous visit to Ma'buta must on no account be omitted.

So here they were, at the last stage of their adventure, physically exhausted, nervously irritated, but moderately content with their conclusions, and hoping within two days to set forth on their return to the capital.

Thus they ate and they listened to Ma'buta with the perfunctory interest of a committee which had already made up its mind. They sat on the beautifully sewn fur rugs; they ate the delicacies handed to them by Mandoan warriors, who in turn received them from Negro slaves, observing a rigid and decorative etiquette of precedence.

Ma'buta was cautious. Still ignorant of the hidden purpose of this visit, he conversed only on non-committal topics—the weather, the hunting, the hills, the floods, the journey. He asked questions about the forthcoming ceremony in the capital, and professed an objective and unconcerned interest in Mandoan development.

Then, when the meal had continued for an hour, and the travellers tried in vain to suppress their yawns, the sentinels at the entrance to the stockade lowered their weapons in salute, and a middle-aged Mandoan nobleman entered with ceremony.

Ma'buta introduced him to the visitors as his son, Ma'keela, and listened to his long message in Mandoan. He nodded several times during its recital, and finally issued an order, after which the younger man withdrew.

Ma'buta turned to his visitors.

" We are about to have the honour," he told them, " of a visit from a fellow countryman of yours, Safi Beaton— perhaps also a member of your party, though coming from another direction. His name is Safi Arta' Rollett."

Rollett ! The four Europeans stared at each other with surprise that was not without amusement. So this was what had happened to Rollett ! Dear me. Well, well. Even Frau von Schelden perceived the humour of the occasion. Here was so completely proper an end to their adventure.

For Rollett had, of course, quarrelled with the International Humanitarian Association. He had hoped to be appointed a member of the commission, and understood the reason for his exclusion perfectly well. He was an extremist, a fanatic, a dangerous man. He recognised it, and was proud of the indictment. In the end, effective reforms, he had told Jean, could be achieved only by unpleasantness. The Beatons and the Beriots of the world did nothing, because they refused to offend even the offenders. The I.H.A. desired justice as their end, without admitting denunciation as their means. A commission consisting of a British prig, a French cynic and a German philanthropist of the patronising *de haut en bas* type, would get nowhere.

Rollett had stormed and raged at the executive committee. He had tackled Jean in private, accusing her of cowardice, compromise and irresolution. " I am disappointed," he had written in his last letter to her. " Can't you see that you are only wasting time and money ? Those three may mean well, but they will do nothing but soothe consciences that ought to be aroused."

He had almost convinced her. She hated violent measures and extreme opinions, but he shook her faith in the commission. Only her reflection that he had a personal grievance, saved her from complete conversion to his views, and once she had accepted the invitation to go herself to Lolagoba he had had little opportunity for further influence. Just before leaving Europe, the commissioners had heard that he had broken away from the association, repudiated in advance whatever report they might make, and had formed his own group of irreconcilables, obtaining a financial grant from the Leatherbite Trust. He had issued a statement to the press declaring that he was himself visiting Mandoa on behalf of the Crusader's League, but that unlike the I.H.A. commission, he would make no compromise with the Mammon of Unrighteousness. He would not travel by a Prince's aeroplane ; he would not sleep in a Prince's hotel.

The commissioners had smiled to each other at this characteristic statement, and thenceforward forgotten about its author.

Now they smiled again with lifted eyebrows, and congratulated themselves upon their wisdom in reaching Mandoa first.

Mr. Beaton began to explain to his host, suavely and laboriously, the nature of Safi Rollett, his admirable qualities and his slight weaknesses of intellect and position. But his words failed in effect, as Ma'buta had become absorbed in orders and preparations, and was still speaking to his lieutenants when the warriors at the gate again withdrew, and admitted Ma'keela Ma'buta, followed by Negro porters, who carried on a sling between two poles, the emaciated figure of Arthur Rollett.

His khaki shirt was tattered and filthy, for he had been dropped from his stretcher into a swamp, and the porters carrying his kit had deserted. His leg, broken just above the ankle, had been roughly bandaged, but dangled agonisingly from the sling on which he lay. His eyes were bright with fever, his beard unshaven ; he had lost his sun helmet and tried to protect his aching head by a large leaf that now fell limply on his neck.

But here at last he was in Ma'buta's camp, the goal which he had sworn to reach or die. He was here at the fount of evidence against Prince's Limited. He had triumphed over dangers and miseries and torturing discomforts. Neither fever, nor fear, nor broken bones, nor absconding porters, nor the hideous journey from Lake Rudolph, nor the poverty of his resources, nor the malignity of the natives, could deter him. If he died to-morrow he could at least to-night verify his references, and learn his justification.

For, ever since he had written his first article for *The Byeword*, his underlying terror had been lest he should have exaggerated. His source of information had been the rumours spread by Ma'buta's emissaries south of the frontier. They had been caught up by an enterprising and gallant mission teacher and sent, after many cautions and hesitations, out to Rollett. And now Rollett could know at least that he was right and had been right from the beginning.

He sat up, blinking his eyes, steadying his waltzing head with one tremulous hand, and thus he saw, coming towards him, not an aged Mandoan chief, but Mr. Beaton, genial, pompous, placid, and behind him, Frau von Schelden, beaming through her smoked glasses, the French doctor and Jean Stanbury.

He did not believe his eyes. They had failed him before. In so many nightmare visions they had deceived him. Fever, he knew, could play these tricks on men, and he had both malaria and dysentery.

He smiled uncertainly, blinking into space, and saw, beyond the mirages of fever, Ma'buta squatted upon the ground in his white robe and leopard skin, just as he had imagined him. He saw the old chief raise his hand in salutation, and he raised his own. This was recognisable experience. This was reality.

He turned his head resolutely from the mocking phantoms of his enemies.

In his ears still rang that hearty voice :

" I'm afraid you've had rather a bad time, old fellow. Well, what a good thing we're here to look after you, eh ? Dr. Beriot—I think we've got our first real casualty for you."

But Rollett had heard other voices. At night in the poisonous marshes near Lake Rudolph, listening to water sucking below the raft and live creatures stirring in the reeds, he had lain shivering with fever and excitement, listening to his father's enormous voice scolding, shouting, denouncing, telling him that he was no good, no good, no good, a milksop, a mollycoddle, a mammy's darling. He had known again his horror because, through his short-sighted eyes, the towering figure grew to immense proportions ; because his mother's beloved face grew whiter and stranger ; and because, though he defied tyranny, and always had defied it, his recalcitrant body cringed and shuddered, his heart felt as though it must burst with fear. And his father had told him now that he was no good, no good, no good—an ineffective, explosive, violent little man ; that his passion for justice was no more than a complex from his furtive childhood ; that he cared more to prove himself in the right than to free Africans from slavery ; that he could not manage people, could not understand them, could not be in the same room as another man for two minutes without fighting him, and that vanity alone had prompted this final, futile, ridiculous adventure.

That voice had been as real, as clear, as these.

The ghost of Beaton was mouthing unctuously, " Tell your master that this is our friend. He is ill. We should like to take him to our tents, where Dr. Beriot . . ."

But even the ghosts of delirium must be defied by one to whom defiance is a duty.

" Tell your master nothing of the kind," cried Rollett. " These are not men, but spirits. Don't listen to them. They are evil."

The interpreter growled his Mandoan, rolling his eyes from one disputant to the other.

" Come, come, Rollett. Pull yourself together, old chap," the big man said.

" I am Arthur Rollett—the white man who sent you messages from Kenya. It is I who for more than twenty years have worked to free your people."

" You see our friend is ill—I am distressed, but——"

" I am not ill. I know you for what you are. Ma'buta, I implore you not to listen——"

" Perhaps Miss Stanbury——"

" I am not ill, I am well enough to tell the truth. These are not real——"

" Look here, Rollett," Mr. Beaton laid a large, kindly hand on the little man's shoulder. " You're obviously over-wrought and ill. Pull yourself together. Let me get you a drink."

" You think you can shut my mouth, but you can't. You can't silence me. Not all the ghosts——"

" No, no. We're not trying to silence you. But we can't wrangle here in front of the natives, old chap."

" And why not ?   Why not in front of the Africans as well as behind their backs ? It's time that they learned the truth. They've been deceived too long. All Europeans do *not* think alike, and it's wicked and dangerous to pretend they do. Until they realise that we have differences of opinion, they'll never be able to grasp the even rudiments of their own position."

Mr. Beaton believed in sweet reasonableness. No one could say that he was an intolerant man. He smiled indulgently at Rollett's extravagance.

" You may be right. You may be right. I've always respected your sincerity, Rollett. But this isn't quite the time or place for discussion, is it ? What about waiting for to-morrow ? "

" Oh, to-morrow—to-morrow—it's always to-morrow with you and your kind. And, meanwhile, men suffer injustice and oppression."

Dr. Beriot, dark and slim and graceful, moved forward and began to remove the bandage from Rollett's leg.

" Keep away. Oh, go away. Leave me alone ! You can't stop me by kindness ! "

Frau von Schelden shouted slowly at the interpreter, as though he were very deaf as well as alien and a little hostile.

" A sick man is not responsible—does not control. *Hein ?* His words—words. Our friend is ill—fever—sick."

Rollett leaned forward and plucked at the interpreter's arm.

" Listen. Do you understand ? These are spirits—the ghosts of evil men and women—the worst kind of evil. Men who mean well but act wickedly in all good faith. Take no notice of them. You see ? They're not real."

Ma'buta had been more confused by the altercation than his sardonic immobility conveyed. He did not know what made the sick man in the chair so angry ; but he knew about spirits. In spite of the fortifications of the Catholic faith, he was not prepared to give to ghosts the benefit of any doubt. If the four Europeans were indeed spirits, he was taking no risks.

" I've always known you, Beaton," Rollett cried. " One of the people who grow fat on reform. Always polite. Travel round the world in the cause of charity. Nice articles in papers that pay well—yes, using facts collected at the risk of their lives by other fools. You once said that I had no sense of humour. What a pity ! A sense of humour is so handy, isn't it ? It lets you see both sides of a question so that you never need *do* anything. You'd never hurt any one's feelings. You never need fear the dear duchess won't ask you to tea again."

His voice trailed off. The effort was exhausting him.

It was Jean who saw the warriors near the entrance, quietly, at a gesture from Ma'buta, close the bars of the stockade.

Dr. Beriot spoke rapidly in French to Beaton. Mr. Beaton turned to Ma'buta.

" Now, please—you see how our friend is ill. He does not know what he is saying. We ask you kindly to let us carry him to our tents, if you will excuse us." Jean saw that he was determined to get Rollett away before he made even more of a fool of himself.

What followed seemed as much like a nightmare as Rollett's insistence that they all were spirits.

In order to waste no time, Beaton and Beriot laid hands on the stretcher and ordered the porters to carry it from the yard. But, as they turned, they saw that the gate was closed against them. They saw the ring of warriors, their white tunics motionless in the rising moonlight, their dark hands clasped upon their spears. They saw the silent menace of their posture, and knew at last that they were in a trap.

Jean admired Mr. Beaton then.

Turning to Ma'buta, he smilingly thanked him for his offer of hospitality, but explained that in order to cure their sick friend, they must have air and freedom and access to their equipment.

The chief's answer was a grunted command. The porters carrying Rollett's stretcher knew who was master here. They turned again towards the empty hut, and marched slowly forward.

The warriors broke their circle, forming an armed guard

down to its black entrance. Between their lines, Rollett was borne on his stretcher. The darkness swallowed him. The porters reappeared. The warriors moved again, closing the space behind the four commissioners. They were shut in completely. There was only one thing to do, and that was to follow Rollett into the hut.

They walked slowly, a fence of spears at each side of them. The only sounds were the whine of the insects and the grating of a weapon on the hard earth.

" One day," Jean told herself, " I shall sit in front of my gas fire in Chelsea, and tell people about this and make it sound very funny. I always asked for adventures. Well. Here I am in the middle of one."

When Dr. Beriot touched her arm and murmured kindly, " It's all right," she snapped, " Of course it is ! " and felt relief at her outburst of bad temper. He could not help her. He had only given himself the pleasure of demonstrating masculine superiority, and it pleased her to snub him.

Then they were in the hut. The curtain of hides flapped back against the door and shut them into darkness—a hot, muffling stench of darkness, like a hood thrown over her face. She stood to one side, and when her bare arm touched the wall she felt it move beneath her flesh. It was alive with insects.

Then horror leapt upon her. She wanted to scream. She felt that the walls were too fragile to protect her from the peril without, from the malignant silence of those waiting spears ; yet they shut her in to a horror no less intolerable, and were themselves most horrible of all.

" Why did you come ? Why couldn't you keep away ? " groaned Rollett from the ground.

" Has any one got a light ? We shall have to see to that leg," said Mr. Beaton cheerfully.

Dr. Beriot struck a match. The flickering light danced for a moment on the ring of anxious, careful faces bent above the sick man's tumbled figure ; then it failed.

" I fear that I have only got two more," observed Beriot. " We shall have to make a torch."

" No, no. Leave me in the dark. Why can't you leave me alone ? For God's sake get away. Isn't it enough . . ." Rollett's voice trailed off. He vas subdued at last.

"One should be careful in lighting torches to avoid firing the hut," said Frau von Schelden. "In such cases it is customary to permit prisoners to burn." Her encyclopædic knowledge and good sense did not fail her. "On the other hand, if we survive ourselves, it is not customary to kill prisoners. We are technically slaves and can be sold back to those who claim us."

"I do not think there is any need to take this—ah—predicament too seriously," Mr. Beaton declared. "It is quite possible that by the morning we shall be released."

"With the utmost politeness," the Frenchman added.

Jean wanted to do something, anything, helpful and practical.

Suddenly she had become desperately sorry for Rollett, struggling among his nightmarish delusions, shut in among his enemies, and forced to submit to their laborious kindness. The only tolerable relationship to one's enemies, she thought, for such a man as Rollett, is that of generous superiority. And instead of that he had brought danger upon them ; he was himself a burden ; he was dependent upon their help and skill.

Her maternal habit, her instinctive assumption of responsibility, goaded her. She drew reeds from the thatch to plait into a torch, shivering when she shook down dust and insects into her hair, yet grateful to their loathsomeness, desiring punishment.

With infinite care the doctor struck his penultimate match. The strands of reed flared up for a moment, but died down again and dwindled into a spark.

"Oh. It must live ! It must live ! " prayed Jean, yearning over the little living light. It seemed that if this failed, everything failed.

Frau von Schelden said something intelligent about loose textures and air currents, but, as though her earnest breath had killed it, the spark quivered and died.

"I have one more," Dr. Beriot said.

"For God's sake, let's stay in the dark ; I'm perfectly comfortable. I can't——" protested Rollett.

He'd rather die than be touched, Jean thought. It was her fault that the torch had failed. She was clumsy. She always failed people. She had lacked courage towards

Rollett and tenderness towards Bill. Her vaunted competence was a brittle, worthless virtue. This might be her last hour, and she had done nothing, nothing. Her whole life had vanished in smoke, expended on futile effort. The brothers for whom she had toiled and sacrificed her youth and her ambitions, were dead; *The Byeword* had failed. And the I.H.A.—what was the I.H.A.?

She did not know. Her head ached. Her pulses throbbed violently. Her breath came in shallow gasps. She thought, " Is this suffocation? I suppose if we die, we shall be called martyrs for our principles. They'll say we died because of our common belief in—what? It's a funny thing to be facing death for a cause and not be certain what the cause is."

She thought of all the paragraphs she had written as publicity secretary for the I.H.A. There was a sentence of Olive Schreiner's she had copied out so often that she knew it by heart—"*That deep conviction, buried somewhere in our nature, not to be eradicated, that man as man is a great and important thing, that the right to himself and his existence is the incontestable property of all men*"—that was the case against slavery. That was what they all believed—Mr. Beaton and Rollett alike—and the seven hundred and ninety-six thousand members of the International Humanitarian Association. "*And above all, the conviction that not only we have a right and are bound to preserve it ourselves*"—her hand nearly always slipped on the typewriter keys there. It was so hot and sticky. So hot. She must stretch her legs. "*But that when we come into contact with others we are bound to implant it or preserve it in them.*"

Into contact. But who ever came into contact with others? " Why, we aren't even in contact with each other," she thought drowsily. " We don't like each other. We don't understand each other."

She had not really liked nor understood Bill. When she was with him, she had always thought of herself, rather than of him, of her integrity, her kindliness, her position. She had trained herself for so long in detachment that she had become a miser of herself; she could not give herself away. She had served and served, laboured for her family, for *The Byeword,* for the I.H.A., but never once had she really surrendered herself, never once had she lost her life to find it.

" In order to know any person, to serve any cause, you must give yourself completely, holding nothing back. Perhaps if I die now——" But no! Death would not liberate her from the protection that had become a prison.

When it came to the point, they were all lonely, lonely. Not one of them knew what the others were thinking. " We live by ourselves. We die by ourselves. We are prisoners inside ourselves." She thought of herself, of her mind imprisoned within the hot constricted pressure of her skull, just as her body was imprisoned within that horrible hut. Her right foot touched Frau von Schelden's cushiony thigh ; if she bent her elbow, it prodded Beriot's lean ribs. If she moved her left foot she might kick Rollett's tossing body. She was cramped and squeezed almost beyond endurance ; but she was utterly alone. " Each of us is isolated. There's no solidarity because there's no liking, no friendship, no love. What's the use of being martyrs together if there's no love ? " her spirit protested.

Pierre Beriot, fumbling in the darkness, tried to turn the folded coat that Beaton had placed as a pillow under Rollett's head. The poor Rollett ! What bad luck that human endurance should depend so largely upon physical accidents. Rollett was probably the bravest of them all, and they all were trying to behave most beautifully. But, because he was by now quite unconscious from pain and fever, he had broken into the high sing-song chant of delirium, " I can't, I can't. Oh, I can't, I can't, I can't ! " His voice ranged up and down, filling the hut with sound more stifling than the heat.

" If Rollett had not come," thought Beriot, " we might all be safe now. Does it matter much ? " He saw before him floating on the rancid darkness, his wife's face. He had tried to snatch her back from death, to keep her for himself. Her head had been brown and smooth like a bird's. Her heart under his hand leapt like a bird's heart, so quick, so wild. He had watched her, caressed her, held her with such eager, agonising, tender love that each curve, each movement of her body had been known to him. But his passion had never been without fear of loss. His seeking hands had never reached towards her in happy confidence, for death had always been her true possessor. Death had claimed her before Pierre even saw her. Death came between his mind and her's. She dwelt apart in a shadowed country where those who are young and doomed can know only each other. " I never knew her," he thought, now feeling with firm, kindly fingers the leaping pulse that was not hers. With hands to which his love for her had taught gentleness, he tended, as well as he could in the dark hut, the sick man, thinking, " What's the good ? We may all be dead by morning. And why not ? What is there to live for ? I never knew her. I have never known any human creature. We can touch their bodies. We never reach their minds. What are we doing here in Africa ? Recognising our responsibilities ? Showing kindness ? Ah, but we only know kindness towards those whom our bodies love. If I never really knew my love, how can I know a Negro ? How can I save these strangers of alien race when I could not save her ? There is no real companionship. We each live in a private, distorted, individual world— stars turning in space, warmed for a moment by each other's light, then lost in infinite distance. God ! How I hate lice. This is like the war. And now, as then, I think I'd rather die than endure bad smells."

He felt again, skillfully, gently, along Rollett's swollen leg, and realised that, since he had no splint, since the man tossed and turned with fever, his only hope was to hold the fracture still until the morning. He cursed Rollett for causing him this discomfort. He cursed the heat, the lice, the bitter stifling stench, his cramped body and his aching arms, but he held on, from time to time making an arid joke, his mind sick with the sense of isolation.

Frau von Schelden heard his unhurried careful movements, and they irritated her. She could have wished to show some generosity herself to this fanatical and tactless Rollett who had most certainly endangered all their lives. Yet one had to yield to the medical profession.

She was very uncomfortable. " I am no longer a young woman," she admitted at last to herself. Travelling had tired her. The heat, the stench of the hut, the darkness and the oppression of suspense made her feel physically ill. She thought, " If Franz saw me now ! . . . Thank God he can't see me. Will he be able to persuade Rosa to go on living with him if I die now ? " She did not want her little husband to live alone. She thought, with a piercing pang, " Perhaps he'll marry again. . . ." She knew Rosa. She had never been deceived about her daughter's character, about her frivolity allied with dogmatism, her extraordinary notions of social morality, which shocked and hurt her parents. Rosa had taken lovers. She refused to marry. She treated her mother with a hard, fierce independence, mocking her ideals of service. " I never knew her," thought Frau von Schelden. " Do we never know our children ? We put them into the world with pain and anguish of anxiety. When they are children, we guard their bodies, their souls. But when they grow and should become companions to us, they close their minds. They become strangers. They will not let us serve them. Is that why I must turn to Africans, to this association ? It is true that some of us must serve or perish. That is why this is so solemn, so important to me. That is why I cannot endure the Frenchman's flippancy, or that English girl's lack of real interest. She is in love with Durrant. She is, I think, a little in love with the Frenchman. Does nobody care ? Is nobody quite sincere ? Oh, God, how alien we are. Not two people in the world share the same thought, the same mood. Not even a mother and her child."

She made a final effort.

" Dr. Beriot, I imagine from what I can—er—feel myself, that you should find ample opportunity here to continue your attack on my countryman, Fahrenholz's, sub-divisions of the *Pediculus Humanus*."

" I shall be delighted to deal later, when I can get to my microscope," replied Dr. Beriot politely, " with any specimens you can give me."

" Eh ? Eh ? What's that ? " Mr. Beaton was anxious to join in this circumspect but sub-acid discussion.

" We are talking about body-lice," the doctor explained. " Frau von Schelden has kindly offered me some of her's. There's an old quarrel about whether different human races

breed different specimens of louse, or whether lice simply
change colour according to what they feed on."

" *Are* they different ? " asked Jean, acutely conscious of
the alien race exploring her chemise.

" The English and French authorities think not. A
certain German professor thought they were. It's a nice
ethical as well as biological question. If even the parasites
we breed are different, there's another nail in the coffin
of any theory of human solidarity."

" This is the end," thought Mr. Beaton. " Very soon they
will surround the hut, dancing their war-dance, waving
their spears, prepared to drag us one by one out to our
death. As I am the leader of the party, they will take me
first. No, they may leave me till the last. I shall have
to hear the shrieks of the women. It will be a noble death
—though horrible." He tried to adjust his cramped limbs
into an attitude of dignity. At least this was some consolation, that if death came now, it came in an heroic
manner. They would be martyrs for a cause. There would
be an end of compromise, of never being quite sure of one's
own rectitude. Rollett's accusation had cut more deeply
than he knew. To grow fat on reform—never to offend
the dear duchess. How true was that ?

Mr. Beaton had always intended to be noble. Saints and
reformers were his models. When he had struggled through
Keble College and decided finally, after three years of
uncertainty, against ordination, it was only that he might
serve God outside the Church. And if his efforts had been
recognised, if he had made friends above the station in
which he was born (his father had been a chemist in
Grantham), if he had made a reputation for himself, was
that. so blameworthy ? Was it not just a little to his
credit ?

But this expedition had been uncomfortable from the
start. Dr. Beriot laughed at him ; he knew it. Miss
Stanbury never understood him. She was a good secretary
but lacked womanly softness. Frau von Schelden was a
German, and though Mr. Beaton approved of Germans,
he could not love them.

" I have tried to administer trusteeship. I have fought
the good fight—yes, indeed, I have—in spite of what

Rollett says. I have kept the faith. Fanaticism is not
the only way. A statesmanlike attitude is necessary to
effect reform. At least if I die now it will set the seal on
my sincerity. I have always been misunderstood. I have
always stood alone. Even Edna, though she believes in
me, cannot understand political issues. That girl on the
boat called me a pompous prig. They don't understand.
I've never really been sure of myself. I've always wanted
to do good. There'll be obituary notices in the *Times*
perhaps. George Beaton, O.B.E.—if I'd lived I might have
had a knighthood. But that isn't vanity. Oh, God, Thou
knowest my inmost heart. Thou seest my desires. I have
tried to serve Thee. Forgive my unworthiness. But
nobody else has ever understood. We're strangers. We're
cruel to each other. Rollett was cruel. Forgive us our sins
as we forgive those who trespass against us. I do forgive
him. But he will never know now. We none of us ever
know."

In the darkness his face assumed a look of calm and
noble resignation, but nobody could see. Nor could the
five in the hut read each other's thoughts, nor hear the
unspoken cry which rose from each of them as they
crouched together.

All that they heard were the impersonal phrases of four
adults behaving beautifully, giving nothing away, on
guard against each other, and Rollett's reiterated protest
against pain and failure, " I can't, I can't, I can't," and
the unshod hoofs of a mule galloping away from the
stockade, striking the hardened earth. The silence from
the courtyard grew more sinister. As though a ring of death
drew closer and closer round the hut, they felt the pressure
of advancing peril.

They did not know that the hoof-beats came from
Ma'buta's swiftest messenger, hurrying to demand from
Talal their ransom. They did not know that the oppressive
silence rose from Ma'buta's warriors happily asleep. The
spears had been laid aside. The knives were sheathed.
The fires died down to powdery ashes. Only the sentinels,
guarding hut and courtyard, stood wakeful at their posts.

CHAPTER III

SAFI TALAL ADVERTISES MANDOA

SAFI TALAL came by night to the hotel.

It was as he had seen it in his dreams.

Here shone the beauty, the order, the proof of man's dominion over material things, for which he was risking life and property. This was his son's memorial.

When David Copperfield Talal died, his father had observed the etiquette of stoicism. David had fallen during a raid ; therefore, he had died gloriously. For those who perish fighting, there is absolution. Absolution means immediate entry into Paradise, and everlasting communion with the saints.

Here was no cause for tears. It was well with the child. Ma'buta had been tamed, his silence bought by ransom. All was well.

Unfortunately women could not discipline themselves by reason. Talal's first wife, the mother of David Copperfield, still mourned for her son. Whenever Talal went to her dark hut—she refused to abandon primitive ways—she reproached him, she wept, she protested. Everything that he was doing now was wrong, since it had cost her son's life.

In the civilisation which he was about to build, thought Talal, something would have to be done about the women. His own wives were well enough, but they made a modern home life quite impossible. They threw refuse all over the courtyard ; they insisted upon employing witches secretly at child-birth. When his fourth wife had been taken to the new hospital, the other five had wailed for three days without stopping.

In the American books that he had read, men loved women as he had loved men. They thought of them in absence, felt tenderness and longing and desire for their presence. Talal had only known such feelings towards the men who were his friends. He had desired and taken women ;

he had loved men. But far more than any man or woman did he desire this new world that opened out before him in the hotel, the aerodrome, and the office of Prince's Limited.

The garden was lit by stripes of even light from the tall windows. Light flowed across the level lawn, touching to gold the lilies and the moonflowers. The whine and beat of a jazz tune from the immense new gramophone drowned the chuff, chuff, chuff of the engine driving the electric plant. These two competing sounds, with the high-pitched drawl of European voices, the rattle of type-writers and the buzzing summons of bells, meant to Talal the music of civilisation.

Within those walls were baths and clocks and dictaphones. There was an ice machine. There was an electric re-frigerator. There were ministers and generals, and an admiral. There was a Catholic cardinal and a Hindu saint. There were two French deputies and an Italian hair-dresser, fully equipped for the service of the ladies. To-morrow there would be the Balkan princes. There was a chef who cooked foreign dishes, an American sculptor and his wife, a crowd of tourists, and a Scottish doctor who had refused to remove Talal's appendix. This annoyed Talal. Dr. Macduff had insisted upon extracting from his fourth wife's despised interior, with spectacular apparatus of instruments, anæsthetics, and trained nurses, an in-significant tumour. Yet he refused the lavish fee offered by Talal, saying, forsooth, that there was nothing wrong with him. The Lord High Chamberlain rubbed a muscular abdomen, exasperatingly innocent of pain or rigidity, and frowned. He regretted the loss of any civilised experience.

But after the frown, he sighed. His mood was pensive rather than angry. He had his hotel, his visitors, his garden. And though the imperishable, fadeless, synthetic lawn had proved neither fadeless nor imperishable, and had to be rolled up and placed in tin-lined cases during the three hours of fiercest noon-day heat ; though the electric lighting apparently suffered from St. Vitus' Dance ; though the telephone service from the hotel to the aerodrome and Prince's office was not yet in working order ; and though an entire consignment of foodstuffs, bed linen and stationery had been devoured by ants, Civilisation had carried out the first part of its bargain.

Yet something had gone wrong. The gifts had been offered, the payment not accepted. Talal's intention of teaching political wisdom in return for telephones and aeroplanes had been frustrated. What was worse, doubts had arisen in his own mind. He was losing confidence in his power to teach.

The door opened, and a tall fair women who had spoken to him on several previous occasions came out into the garden. She was very thin. Critically he observed her long-legged, breastless body, swathed tightly in white satin. Her shoulders were hunched forward and her sight was evidently defective, as she wore a single eyeglass hung on a silver cord. The poor thing, Talal decided, was diseased.

The mosquitoes also were troubling her. She rubbed her bare arms, and Talal saw that her nails were pointed as claws and painted scarlet. Possibly she was imbecile as well as sick, for no sane woman would walk half-naked among Mandoan insects after nightfall.

Or was there some law of compensation by which those bred among porcelain baths, ice-machines and spring-mattresses, had to create deliberate discomforts for themselves ? For instance, this taste of white men for embracing female skeletons, of white women for stripping their bodies precisely at that hour when insects became most ferocious —were these reactions against an unnatural immunity from pain ?

The girl sauntered towards Talal, extracting a cigarette from the jewelled case that swung on a slender chain from her wrist.

" Good-evening," she said pleasantly.

" Good-evening."

" Won't you have a cigarette ? "

" Thank you."

He was already accustomed to the extreme impropriety of white women. She handed him the little case. He helped himself. She rubbed her thumb across a minute gold box, and it put forth a flame as a flowering plant might bud.

" I like that," said Talal.

" My lighter ? There's nothing special about it. I rather hate gold myself, but some poor fish gave it me, and I haven't another."

" I should like to have it." Talal turned the toy solemnly in his fingers. In Mandoa one asked for what one admired, and the owner accepted the compliment, though he withheld the gift.

The proper response would be, " It is unworthy of you," but Felicity Cardover said, " Then for God's sake take it. And in exchange tell me how to stop being devoured alive by these damned bugs."

Talal handed the toy back to her, with a bow, saying, " You should wear a shawl."

" I haven't got one."

Talal clapped his hands, called for his slave, and ordered him to bring a scarf immediately. The soft running footsteps pattered away.

" What did you say to him ? " inquired Felicity. She had sunk down on the garden bench and sat there smoking.

" I told him to fetch a scarf."

" For me ? "

" Of course."

" Do you keep wardrobes full, just in case ? "

" In case, yes. I have ten cases. Scarves, shawls, robes, veils. Wardrobes I do not know."

She laughed. " How very convenient."

" No. Perhaps not. Tell me about wardrobes." Here at least was an opportunity of acquiring information. But the girl put the round glass into her eye, and stared at Talal.

" I wish I knew whether you were very innocent or very clever."

" Clever of course," replied Talal, slightly affronted. English women were much less easy to deal with than white men.

" Do you think I am beautiful ? " She turned her lean snake's body towards him.

" Oh, no. Not at all."

" What, as bad as all that ? "

" Perhaps you, too, are very clever. A lady missionary ? A teacher ? Yes ? "

The girl's body shook, whether with fear, rage or laughter he could not guess.

"Do you think all white women are ugly then?" she asked.

"No, no. Clara Bow, college cuties. Some beauts. You are perhaps ill."

"I see." She paused. Then, "Tell me why you are giving me a scarf," she said.

"You need one. I am your host."

"Is that all?" She leaned back on the seat and clasped her bare arms behind her head. He found the scent of her powdered flesh exceedingly unpleasant. Unaccustomed to flower perfumes, he did not know that Lalleul's "Numero 8" had been composed with meticulous and highly expensive art to titillate the senses. He moved away, averting his nostrils.

"You know," her drawling voice continued, "I find Mandoan men extraordinary attractive."

Of course she did, poor thing, thought Talal.

"Is it true that you have killed a man?"

"Eight."

"How marvellous! And did you really bury your daughter alive with your own hands?"

Horrified, he stared at her. "With my own hands? I am a nobleman. Naturally I employed slaves."

She thrust back her head, and now was the time when an experienced lover should bend to kiss the golden sickle of her lifted throat. Talal did nothing of the kind. Her musical, practised laugh sounded strangely in his ears. He was disliking her heartily.

"I am tired of European men," she said. "They are so self-conscious. All either direct or inverted Puritans. The old tricks, the old excuses, the old limitations. A woman does not want apologetic lovers."

Talal looked tactfully away from her to the hotel. In his opinion what a woman wanted mattered very little. Her function was rather to satisfy the wants of men.

"You are a strange man," this remarkable creature continued. "I suppose I'm an entirely new type to you. But there's a charm in novelty, isn't there? Or isn't there?" She leaned forward now, so that her rope of pearls swung against his knee, and the scent from her hair almost sickened him. She laid her red-taloned hand on his bare arm.

" Or am I quite out of the running ? " she whispered.

" Oh, run by all means," said he, and left her. He had no notion that he had just snubbed Hampstead's most fascinating and corrupt success, who had hitherto thought herself irresistable to both sexes.

He only knew that he was vaguely depressed, because the poor emaciated creature appeared unhappy as well as unhealthy. She said that she was tired of Europeans. What worried Talal was that most Europeans seemed tired of themselves and of each other. Was it possible that even their civilisation failed to content them ?

He entered the hotel.

The Sudanese porter saluted him. The Egyptian clerk at the bureau bowed as he passed. He was accustomed to salutation ; it meant nothing to him; but he drew satisfaction from the wicker chairs, the ash-trays and glasses on the little tables, the palms, the mats, the polished metal spitoons.

He was well known there. From several tables groups of visitors greeted him. He turned to one, in a remote corner, and sat down in a chair vacated for him.

These were, he understood, all men of culture, Fanshawe the anthropologist, Marlow the American sculptor, and young Julian Cardover, who was some sort of a poet.

" *Dominus tecum*," said Cardover, in whom long habit had perfected the technique of picking up catchwords. " How's tricks, baby ? "

Talal smiled. He knew now, of course, that the slang of the earlier Californian talkies was not the language of gentlemen, but he humoured the Englishman.

" Tricks," he observed, " are good. I hope you gentlemen are enjoying my poor country."

" Far from it," laughed Fanshawe. " At least, Cardover and his sister aren't. You've disappointed them."

" Please why ? No bath water ? A temporary inconvenience of the drought and unusual visitations."

" *And* no water pipes. We know all about that, Talal," said Philip Fanshawe, he whom his intimates called

Piggy. " No, no. It's the absence of excitement and vice that disappoints them."

" So ? " This was the talk of children, not of men. Let them come to the serious philosophical conversation for which Talal's soul still yearned. " I too am disappointed. I am sad. I had hoped for much interchange of wisdoms. You should give us the fruit of your hands, you, whom God has gifted with craftiness—engines, automobiles, ice-cream sodas. And we would have offered you fruits of mind-experience; but when we meet, we say nothing. Compliments. Pshaw ! Listen. The English say ' Good sport.' ' Are there birds to kill ? ' Yes. We have provided for you birds and lion, and hippo. Even elephant, at great cost. All very, very valuable. And at once, what does your Sir Malcolm Devizes, K.C.M.G., ask us ? ' How many slaves killed on last year's march to Abyssinia ? How many died under lash ? What proportion of death in child-birth ? ' William Durrant very particularly warned *us* against asking ' What is your income ? Were your parents married ? ' Such questions are indelicate. Yet your Sir Malcolm and your Mr. Beaton and your German lady most indelicately are all mad about slaves. We had hoped to instruct you in wisdom of selling surplus population, also polygamy. Your own populations are very, very surplus, yeah ? But you will not learn what we would teach you. No ! "

His deep voice rumbled among the shriller voices, delivering his grievance. Fanshawe called for more drinks from the Sudanese waiter. From the next room, where the younger people danced, the gramophone blared :

" I gotta little puppy, and I gotta little cat,
  I gotta little kitten sittin' on a little mat,
        But I ain't got you-oo."

" Precisely," murmured Fanshawe. " We all of us can get the puppies and the kittens, when what we really want is ' just you-oo,' whatever ' just you-oo ' may be."

" Talal's ' just you-oo ' is our admiration and adoption of his political and social system," observed Marlow.

" But we *are* appreciative, and we admire like anything.

Even though it's all less exhilaratingly licentious and barbaric than we had hoped," Cardover said.

Talal turned on them.

"That is so," he said. "You admire the cathedral, because is is quaint. And the archbishops because they are many. You like our processions, our clothing, our statues. We are all funny, primitive ; too, too marvellous. Oh, yeah ; I know. I have heard."

"And beautiful. Surely you must admit that we admire your beauty, really genuinely admire it," Marlow protested.

"And your dances," said Fanshawe. "We have written columns and columns about your dances."

"You are the worst, Mr. Fanshawe." Talal bowed politely but sternly to the anthropologist. "You would prefer to keep us quaint and unique. You would always wish not to spoil our culture. I have heard that many times."

"Of course. I can't tell you what resentment I feel against these damned talkies and your wretched Mr. Guerdon. I hoped we were finding an indigenous civilisation, as unspoiled as Southern Arabia or Thibet. And look— look at it now—with its mixture of Catholic and evangelical, medieval and modern, and complete African-pagan. It's no *use* to us any more."

"Don't let him depress you, Talal," cried Cardover in his high, excitable voice. "If you could know how we envy you ! We, who are the victims of an effete in-tellectualism. You, who still dare to retain the—shall we say ?—purity of primitive sensation. You, who lose your individual consciousness in your corporate dances. My dear Talal, if you *knew* what anguish we have suffered through the loss of our power of spontaneous and corporate ecstasy."

"Oh, come," muttered Marlow. "In the States we still have ball games and lynchings—and you in England have cup finals and community singing."

"What are they," cried Cardover, "compared with your natural, sinless, cool, lustful completion of bodily bliss ? Unselfconscious, unafraid. Your wholeness with the community ! Your deep tranquil blood-unity ! "

The glass doors between the lounge and the dancing-

room swung apart and a couple of waiters fastened the
bolts to hold them back while they carried through trays
of used glasses. From their corner table Talal and his
friends could see a triangle of brightly-lit floor across
which the couples walked face to face, body to body,
clasped in lethargic embraces. The gramophone blared :

> " I gotta little sherry an' I gotta little gin,
>   I gotta little flat an' that to put my sweetie in :
>   But I ain't got you-oo ! "

" Negro rhythm exploited by a Polish song-plugger, with
American words, sung by a Canadian-Jew, and reproduced
on a German record—and that's our civilisation. God ! "
groaned Fanshawe.

" Compared with the beauty, the audacity, the magnificent traditional ritual of that hunting dance we saw last
night," sighed Cardover. " The bare feet stamping the
hard ground, the brown limbs tossing, the passion and
pageantry of the motion, every gesture as it had been
for four hundred years, and every flicker of the eyelid
significant. Think of that profundity, that splendour, that
deep religious emotion, compared with this shallow, manu-
factured *mess*."

The Lord High Chamberlain, with narrowed eyes, was
watching the locked embraces of the dancers.

The tune had changed to the Mandoan waltz-song which
had taken London by storm after Clotilde Nuxhaven sang
it at the Royal Command Performance at the Palladium—
an effort which ensured her future banishment from the sun
of majesty for ever. The dancers took up the nonsensical
refrain :

> " ' Mandoa, Mandoa, Man-*do*,' she said,
>   And *that* was the reason why
>   We saw all the Princes fly.
>   Though the ship might sink
>   And the car might skid,
>   (And I rather think
>   That she hoped they did)
>   She said, ' Step in when you're passing by ! '
>   And Mandoa, Mandoa, Man *did* ! "

" *That*," groaned Cardover. " *That* is all that modern taste can make of your enchanting country."

" Complete nonsense," Fanshawe added.

Talal looked at them despairingly. Was it possible that these men understood so little ?

" Mr. Cardover, Mr. Fanshawe, Mr. Marlow," he began. " You are very clever, artistic, cultivated men. But you know nothing about us—nothing. Since you came, you have all the time said, ' How terrible to have machines, cinemas, jazz. How fine to be isolated, unique, primitive.' Do you think it is nice to be isolated ? To be isolated means to be poor. No trade, no travel, no cultural contact. To be unique means to be lonely. To be primitive means to sleep in dirty huts, to ride on donkeys, to do the same things day after day. It means to live in a very little world where nothing changes, to suffer from droughts and diseases and tapeworm and lice. It means to have very little choice what one will do. All is fixed, settled. This corporate ritual that you like so much. . . . Listen. Would *you* like to know just what you must do to-morrow— hunting song, spring dance, rain blessing ? On this day you must eat this food, wear this garment—everything settled a hundred years ago ? Would you *like* to have no books, no photographs, no motor cars ? If these were such evils, why did your nations make them ? Why lid you stop being a primitive people if it was so nice ? But I will tell you—I, who am what you call primitive person. I will tell you this about primitive life. It may be good as you say for bodies—though leprosy and blindness are surely bad, and we have these—but it is *not* good for the soul. There is just this against it, that for men of intelligence like self, primitive life is one hundred per cent a bore ! Yes. That is so. A bore."

" That's an interesting theory. Interesting, but not wholly convincing," Marlow said. " You see, the trouble is that even when one has—er—books and photographs, and motor cars, the boredom continues. This new fashion for Mandoa is partly, you know, the outcome of our fatigue with just these instruments of pleasure that you desire. We want to return to that simplicity that you find so tiresome."

" The romantic reaction," Fanshawe said ; " the appetite for the unknown, the remote, the thing that's different."

" Escape—the eternal flight from the present, from the familiar, to the past and the remote," murmured Cardover. " Man's protest against the ennui of existence."

" You are as much a romantic as we are, Talal," Fanshawe said. " You, too, have revolted against the classic and traditional culture of your race. You and your young bloods we see travelling round in bowler hats, with their slaves carrying typewriters behind them. They, too, are rebels, cherishing a hope that whatever is strange will be better. When we said we were disappointed in your country it was just because it is not strange enough for us. This hotel, the stalls in the market, and the aerodrome and so on ; they are almost familiar to us. You've made us *too* comfortable. Your people are *too* polite. Everything has gone so far without a hitch."

" Ah. You desire hitches ? " Talal caught eagerly at any hint of what could be truly desirable.

" Yes. I suppose we do. Adventure—that's the thing."

Talal lay back in his chair and looked at them. He admired these people—the intelligent and melancholy anthropologist, who smiled sadly through horn-rimmed glasses at a world too rapidly becoming standardised ; the restless, mobile American sculptor with his strong, clever hands ; the strange, emaciated, shrill-voiced poet. These men constituted the flower of civilisation. And they wanted all those things that he was striving to avoid.

He wished that Durrant was there to advise him, Durrant who was the only man he had yet found with understanding of both Europe and Mandoa.

But at that moment his attention was caught by Felicity Cardover's progress through the lounge. She was wearing his scarf swathed about her arms, and she walked between the little tables smiling her remote, unhappy smile, her short-sighted eyes seeking for somebody or some thing. She had suffered a bad quarter of an hour among the mosquitoes after Talal had left her. But when his slave returned, panting and perspiring, with the gossamer scarf, she had decided not to let a trifle like wounded vanity stand between her and anything so unique and beautiful. She had returned to her bedroom, smoothed her platinum-blonde hair, re-powdered her neck and arms (thank heaven the bites could not swell until to-morrow morning !), and gone down to the public rooms. Whatever Talal might think of her, she knew her appeal to European tastes, and glided across the tobacco-clouded room, slim as a pillar, smooth as a hazel wand, all white and silver, save for her crimson painted lips and finger nails and flaming drapery.

She saw her brother, but Talal, leaning back beyond the palm, murmuring to himself, " Mandoa, Mandoa, Man *do*," she did not see.

" Hallo, Fell," her brother greeted her. " Where *did* you get that garment ? Quite improperly exquisite ! "

" Quite improperly won," she murmured, watching the dancers to see whether Rex Leamington or Sophie Marlow were there—though it was her brother always whom she desired to impress.

" Perfect ! " exclaimed Marlow. " Surely not European ? "

" Genuine Mandoan, I believe," she said negligently.

" Oh, where did you get it ? And when ? "

" The answer to the first question," she said, " is—in the garden. To the second—half an hour ago."

" And I dare not ask—for what ? " murmured the sculptor.

" Felicity would not mind telling you. She glories in vice," cried Julian's high-pitched voice. " Is this the price of virtue, Fell ? What ? Lost your nime agine, pore gurrl ? "

She sank into a chair, draping the scarf across her arms. " If I said yes, my dear ? "

" I should ask with whom ? "

" Well, Safi Talal gave me the scarf. You had warned me of his reputation. I shall say no more."

" The lady's virtue is immaculate," boomed Talal's deep voice from behind the palm. He rose, chivalrously saluting the company, and went to watch the dancing. Lovely, he thought it, with its tunes that changed every five minutes, its shining floor, its unconcerted movement, its individualism and intimacy.

But others apparently thought otherwise. Two American

tourists leaned against the wall, a plump middle-aged lady and her younger companion.

"Really, I didn't spend two thousand dollars to see *this*," the plump one declared. "And I went all through the market to-day. There's absolutely *nothing* to buy. A few little bits of embroidery—we got *far* better in Malta— or was it Cairo?—and some glass beads."

"The whole place has been picked over. There's nothing to *do*, that's what I say," the younger woman agreed.

"I suppose it's worth waiting for the royal wedding?"

"Prince's did tell us it would be the last of its kind. Africa's changing every year. And I'm scheduled to lecture to our literary and philosophical society on 'Ancient Mandoa as I saw it.' If it wasn't for that, I'd take the 'plane for Egypt to-morrow."

"Oh, I'm doing Central Africa and the tropics after this. I dote on jungles. One might meet with a little excitement there."

Talal shifted his tunic.

Depression hung heavy upon him.

He had done the wrong thing.

The hotel and the ballroom, the stadium and cinema, were not what Europeans and Americans wanted. His arrangements had been too good, his people too docile.

All that he had planned, all that he had paid for, was unnecessary. He had drained the resources of his country. He had aroused dissatisfaction among the younger men. And at the end of it all, the visitors were disappointed. For the men, it appeared, desired violence, and the women expected rape. They had wearied of their well-conducted cities. These dancers, who rocked together so decorously in each other's arms, were really yearning for assault and bloodshed. It was exceedingly confusing.

He must talk to Durrant.

He must talk to Ma'sull.

"'Mandoa, Mandoa, Man *do*,' she said," bleated the giant gramophone.

But what should man do? Talal wondered.

Grave, dignified, appearing immensely sure of himself, he walked back through the lounge to the foyer, and out into the garden, the Sudanese attendants bowing.

" Queer beggars. You'll never get to know what they're thinking," said little Cooper to the architect, Jordan. And Jordan, who impatiently awaited the return of Frau von Schelden, the only woman who had ever really understood him since his mother died, assented mechanically.

Felicity Cardover, seeing Rex Leamington, hailed him to her table. She wanted to sooth her ruffled vanity by rousing the dormant jealousy in her brother's light-blue eyes.

She began to be exceedingly polite to Rex.

Talal stood in the garden. He needed Durrant ; he wanted him, and, though well-used to unsatisfied desire for things, he was unaccustomed to deprivation of desired persons.

But Durrant was in Khartoum with his brother and the sick chieftain, Sir Joseph Prince. Talal had to make his own decisions. He was not afraid of acting on his own unsupported judgment. Born with the right of life and death in his hands, a statesman-warrior-aristocrat of strong will and passionate temperament, he never doubted his authority ; but he enjoyed consultation. Durrant understood him. Durrant was useful. Durrant always had ideas for transforming vague wishes into concrete action.

Talal felt a grievance against Durrant for his absence, and grievances made him impatient.

Irritably, he reviewed the position.

Four days remained before the royal wedding. The Cathedral already was hung with coloured cottons. Garlands of paper flowers festooned the streets. The mud walls of the palace had been distempered blue and peach colour. From the stockade to the Cathedral spears with saffron and emerald pennons, point downwards in the ground, made a crazy and fragile fence for the royal route. Every possible attraction had been offered to the visitors—games in the stadium, processions of archbishops, jazz dancing in the hotel, and traditional dancing out on the aerodrome.

But the tourists, it appeared, were not amused. Even the prospect of fireworks did not excite them, though a wire entanglement stood ready for the catherine wheels which, after the ceremony, would whirl, in a blazing spinning lion, twenty feet tall, before the stadium.

They wanted blood and wounds and high adventure. Like young warriors training for a feud-war, they were in love with peril, vexed by the discipline of safety. The pace was too slow for them. Ice water, glass tumblers with straws and wicker tables gave them no satisfaction. The American women were even contemplating departure.

Talal plucked his beard.

What if they all grew weary of Lologoba and, like a flock of birds, rose into the air and vanished, before the Heiress-Apparent had married Prince Anjak, and the Royal Princess and Arch-archbishop become man and wife, before the isolation of Mandoa had been broken?

Backwards and forwards paced the Lord High Chamberlain, his hard feet silent upon the artificial grass.

What if he had risked his power and fortune for nothing, bribing Ma'buta to keep an unwanted peace?

Only insecurity could hold these people, and he had given them security. He had misunderstood. No, since Mandoans never made mistakes, Durrant had misunderstood. It was all Durrant's fault. Durrant knew nothing of these white men. He had misled his friend. His advice was all wrong.

But to effect a sudden change was not easy. Mandoa *was* Mandoa. Laws, once made, could not be lightly cancelled; commands once issued could not be withdrawn. The policy of orderliness and co-operation that he had forced on the High Council, bribing, intimidating and persuading nobles and archbishops, could not suddenly be retracted. He could not acknowledge that he had been misguided. Acknowledgement of mistakes was fatal in Mandoa.

Only a change in the facts of the situation could help him. If a white man were murdered, an aeroplane mishandled, the hotel burned, or a foreign representative kidnapped, then anything might happen.

These people wanted the old, fierce, terrible Mandoa— and Talal had sworn to exact vengeance to the third or fourth generation from any man, woman or child who broke the peace.

Curse Durrant for his folly! Curse Mason and Jordan and Nicholson for their insistence that peace and prosperity

must go together. "The good will essential for trade,"
Nicholson had bleated. Nicholson was so clearly no man
of breeding. A freedman at best. Vulgar, noisy, aggressive,
artificial. If Talal had not set a fashion in gramophones
and wash-basins, bicycles and sock suspenders, not a
Mandoan would have traded with the creature.

It might be a good idea to put snakes in Nicholson's
room. Or cut his throat. Or kidnap him from his office.

The soft scuttering pad of two runners hurrying together
possibly saved the British trade commissioner from instant
death. Talal listened. He heard an oath, quick breath in
the darkness, and the click of the gate.

He moved quietly to the bush of transplanted moonflowers, and through its screen saw his young kinsman,
Ma'haldi, binding to the gate-post a reluctant prisoner
as though he were a refractory horse.

He went to the gate.

"What are you doing here?" he asked sternly, for
Ma'haldi was supposed to be in charge of his household
during his absence.

"Oh, Safi, I sought you. A messenger has come from
Ma'buta to say that he has taken prisoner the European
Commissioners, Safi Beaton, the doctor, the German lady,
and Miss Stanbury. They are in his stockade. He demands
five hundred pounds each person, paid in silver or gold,
immediately, for their ransom."

Talal's first impulse was of dismay. He had paid too
much. Prince's Limited must provide this money.

Then he uttered an oath of exultation.

This was just what he wanted.

He asked, "Who else beside yourself has seen this
messenger?"

"Many have seen, but to none has he spoken."

"Who else beside yourself knows this news?"

"None, O Safi. I brought him straight to you."

"Good," said Talal.

He went to the gate and saw the exhausted messenger,
half-suspended from his bonds, choking and retching.

"Good," said Talal again. And with his sinewy hands
drew the ropes higher and tighter. His kinsman helped him.

Within a few moments the body slumped heavily to the

ground. Ma'haldi knelt on one knee and felt his heart.
" He is dead."

" Good. Leave him there. Go home. Say nothing of
this—ever. Even to the women."

Talal returned to the hotel.

He asked at the office for Mr. Blacker, and was told that
he had gone to bed.

Talal nodded as though he already knew this. He said,
" Tell him that news has come. It is important. I shall
be in the lounge." And went on through the swing doors.

The dancing had almost ended, but round the bar and
at the little tables sat and stood the visitors to Mandoa,
drinking their final whiskeys, saying " Good-night," or
lingering, bored and hot, reluctant to go to bed.

Talal's entry, his swinging stride up the long room,
white tunic flowing, scabbard striking the little tables,
roused their jaded attention. Mandoans were trained in
significant gesture. They knew how to walk, how to
stand, how to speak. The Lord High Chamberlain, gathering
to himself all the eyes of the company as he went, made
for the doors through to the dancing-room. The circling
colours and noise and lights and gaiety, froze behind him
as he raised his arm and called for silence. He stood
between the light and the shadow, his heart warm with
triumph and irritation. He had listened too long to Durrant.
Who was a Lord High Chamberlain to take advice ? The
advice had been wrong, been wrong, been wrong. He would
act for himself now. Very well.

" Friends and brothers ! " his deep voice called, rever-
bating among palms and basket chairs. In the dancing-
room, Rex Leamington turned off the gramophone.
" Colorado Roses " died with a rasping whir. " You are
men of sense and civilisation. There will be no panic."

Julian Cardover took a step towards his sister. She
met his look with dark, insatiable eyes. " The worthy ladies
and gentlemen sent by the International Humanitarian
Association have been kidnapped. Somewhere they are
imprisoned in the mountains." A smothered oath from
Jordan broke a silence that was now most satisfactorily
tense. " I do not know where. The messenger unhappily,
having suffered ill-treatment perhaps from those whom

he met on the road, died before he could give his message.
I tell this that you may know that the High Council will
right now take action to recover respected philanthropists.
Also ransom may be demanded. Also it is important to re-
affirm that, while safe in city, no one can leave capital
except at own risk. Hunting parties should be escorted by
armed guards. Oh, yeah ? We do all we can. *Here* we are
civilised men. But southerly mountain people are *not*
civilised. Oh, no."

He ceased. His brown arm fell.

He gazed round upon his hearers with dignified
melancholy.

Immediately the groups broke ; the listeners surged
towards him. There was, as he had requested, no panic,
but a heightened interest, a tension, an expectation,
stiffened the languid vitality of the people.

" Is there any real danger to them ? "

" Which direction did the messenger come from ? "

" How long have they been captured ? "

The questions beat upon his happy mind.

He saw the American ladies, visibly demonstrating
courage. Felicity Cardover clutching his scarf about her
lean body, murmured inadequately, " I do think he's
rather a blossom-face."

Cooper, pink and agitated, on behalf of his suffering
friend, Mr. Jordan, began with an awkward assumption
of authority, " Look *here*, Talal." And down the lounge
walked Blacker, solemn, responsible, reassuring, assuming
the perfect poise of an English gentleman controlling an
awkward situation.

Ripple after ripple of reaction spread through the hotel.

The special correspondent of the enterprising *New York
Dispatch* began immediately to collect opinions on the
catastrophe. The cardinal legate, sent to safeguard Catholic
interests, was interrupted after he had removed his teeth
and settled down for the night. He snapped at his secretary,
protested against disturbance, but finally realised the
importance of a pronouncement, and declared, " Tell
him that this outbreak of pagan barbarism confirms
my appeal for the need of a re-awakened faith in Mandoa.
The Church must draw this strayed child to her bosom."

The Italian delegation suggested French influence ; the French, grieving for the possible fate of their distinguished countryman, Dr. Beriot, hinted at Bolshevist propoganda among the natives. The Germans delivered a panegyric upon Frau von Schelden ; and Sir Malcolm Devizes declared that the whole rumour was violently exaggerated, and that Beaton would in all probability turn up to-morrow.

Safi Talal sat with Mr. Blacker in his office. The whir of an aeroplane engine drowned for a moment the droning of the insects. It was Houghton, the star pilot, flying to Khartoum to tell Sir Joseph Prince, of the first misadventure to break the unruffled calm of the Mandoan affair.

CHAPTER IV

SIR JOSEPH PRINCE IS JUSTIFIED

PARATYPHOID is a long and troublesome disease.

Sir Joseph Prince, unaccustomed to ill-health, took it hard. He tossed on his bed like a sick and irritable child, at one moment complaining about the whole hospital equipment, at the next, pathetically grateful for every small attention. Five times a day he would abandon himself to death ; five times he would insist that too much fuss was being made of an insignificant disorder, and protest against enforced seclusion. He should be at Lolagoba. The devil alone knew what they were doing there without him.

He took an intense interest in all his symptoms. A nurse, incautiously leaving a thermometer near him, found that he had been taking his own temperature every quarter of an hour. He thought that each change in his condition signified hideous developments. He blamed the brusque young doctor for his light-hearted manner, and displayed deep resentment when told that, with his fine constitution, he would live to fly the Atlantic at eighty-five.

After Blacker's visit, he fretted more than ever.

He could not forget the conversation in the train. The Cardovers haunted him. In feverish dreams he sometimes saw Felicity Cardover, young, fair and beautiful, turn slowly into a snake before his eyes, spitting out the poison that had made him ill.

After nearly a month's illness, he sent for Maurice Durrant. He was, he felt certain, about to die, and immortal longings stirred him.

All round him the world seemed to be drawing disaster upon itself. Human idiocy appalled him. Conferences were summoned, delayed, cost thousands of ill-spared pounds, and melted away having accomplished nothing. Politicians were impotent, business firms indolently blind. There was not one man in the world who showed the true spirit of adventure and initiative. " We need courage, audacity," moaned Sir Joseph. " Oh, sister, I feel so ill ! Are you *sure* the doctor's coming this afternoon ? " Prince's Limited was going to pieces. Blacker and Bill Durrant between them were messing up Mandoa. He must have Maurice. Maurice had sense and kindliness ; he was good to look at ; he concentrated ; he was not afraid of work nor ashamed of his affection for Prince's. Maurice would come—neat, cool and competent, and put everything right for him— his aching head, his exasperation with the headquarters office, his anxiety about Lologoba. Maurice could deal with his brother. The interminable days might stretch out weeks long, ages long. The nights might linger to infinity. But if there were a date on the calendar, an hour on the clock, that he could mark with his finger, saying, " Then Maurice will be here," time would lose its terror.

So Maurice came.

His coming meant considerable sacrifice. He had to apologise to his constituents. He had to present adequate excuses to his party whips. He had to buy a tropical outfit, and make endless arrangements about his work at Prince's. But he enjoyed these inconveniences. They meant that he was needed, that the old man liked and trusted him, that even if his mother had never wanted him, Sir Joseph Prince, who was a great man, a man of experience and authority, had chosen him from all his army of friends and colleagues, to succour him in his hour of need.

The journey exhilarated him. He felt himself to be a person of importance. The destiny of more than a distinguished invalid lay in his hands. He would probably have to take over the Mandoan affair. He would certainly have to make himself responsible for Sir Joseph's comfort. He would probably have to over-ride Blacker, to deal tactfully with Bill, and to face the authorities in Khartoum.

Power and benevolence soothed him.

In Khartoum he found a gratifying concern about the distinguished invalid. Sir Joseph Prince, after all, was one of the great British characters. Flowers and fruit from the governor-general's palace, wines that he could not drink, birds that he might not eat, arrived daily at the hospital. In the hotel the same agreeable interest encircled Maurice. He drew from his relationship with Sir Joseph an acquired glory.

In her private office he interviewed the matron, who assured him that Sir Joseph was in no immediate danger. " These strong men are all alike, Mr. Durrant." She smiled. Her arms were soft and round, and little beads of perspiration spangled her upper lip. It was very hot. Maurice could imagine himself when ill, abandoning his exhausted body happily to her care. " They're all alike. Like children. Wanting you all day long. He's been asking for you, I can tell you. Marking off the days on his calendar. He sets a lot of store by you, that's easy to see."

That was certainly pleasing, yet a little distressing too. Maurice's innate romanticism hated to think of the mighty fallen. He loved power and dignity and the splendour of strength. A feeble and childish Sir Joseph, surrounded by the apparatus of the sick room, was even a little repulsive.

The private ward in the hospital was not reassuring. Dazzling platinum-coloured bars of light struck through the slats of the blind on to the bare scrubbed floor, the bed, the clean white wall. A scent of eau de cologne and lysol reminded him of his school sanatorium.

He went forward, a little shy, a little stiff, to receive the old man's almost rapturous greeting.

Sir Joseph pulled himself upright and held out claw-like fingers.

" It's good to see you, my dear boy. It's good to see you."

To Maurice's horror he thought he saw tears sparkle in the rheumy eyes, but he could not be sure, for the face was striped with shadow.

He said heartily, " Glad to see you looking so fit, sir. Your female dragon down below says that you'll be up in no time."

" Oh, I don't know. I don't know about that. I am a sick man. A very sick man'"

" Oh, now, sir. Not so bad. You've had a thin time, I know."

What the devil did one say to old men who were ill ?

Why did illness make people so confoundedly emotional?

Fleeing emotion as though it were the plague, Maurice talked of his journey, gave messages of condolence from the headquarters office, spoke of the directors, and made the excuse that he must not stay too long at a time, to escape. But Sir Joseph recalled him.

" There's so much to discuss, my dear boy. I've missed you so. Don't go yet." The voice trembled. Sir Joseph was an old man.

Maurice was both repelled and pleased.

He murmured an inept reply, feeling his nerves bristle with their habitual warning against the surrender of self-possession. He had repressed his own hunger for love so long that the springs of human tenderness had frozen within him.

He was glad to be wanted, proud to feel himself needed and loved, but the demonstration of gladness was too difficult. He invented a promise to the matron, and broke away leaving Sir Joseph limp on his pillows, tears of self-pity and weakness on his cheeks.

But walking down the cool, carbolic-scented corridors, Maurice recovered his own confidence. Indeed, the interview left him with a heightened sense of superiority. He had been self-controlled when the head of Prince's Limited had been emotional. He had been in a position to withhold or protract his desirable presence. He had confronted weakness with strength and self-abandonment with dignity. This happy experience fortified his pride.

He returned to the hotel and changed for dinner, whistling as he drew the fresh linen over his newly-bathed flesh. He went to the bar and ordered a cocktail. The spirit cheered and exhilarated him.

A very pretty woman, sophisticated, elegant, strolled up to the bar and demanded a dry Martini. Her green dress was swathed so tightly that it showed the tender curves below her delicate breasts. Her body was sweet and yielding and her eyes held a promise of audacity and amusement. She cast an appraising, critical glance at Maurice, observed his slender precision and well-groomed correctness, and permitted her soft lips to tremble into the faintest indication of an approving smile.

The hotel, the cocktail and the smile did their business.
Maurice made for the restaurant with fine masculine
assurance, ordered a table placed so that he could watch
the pretty woman, and a discreetly expensive dinner with
admirable wines.

When he travelled with Sir Joseph, women had always
looked first at the handsome and picturesque old man.
His own more commonplace good looks infuriated him.
He had once heard a young girl sneer, " Our Mr. Durrant
of the made-lace department." He looked like a confounded
counter-jumper.

But here in Khartoum he definitely was some one—a
Member of Parliament, a director of Prince's Limited, a
young man with responsibilities on his capable hands,
and a future before him.

These pleasant reflections enabled him after dinner to
come forward, with the easiest manner in the world, when,
in the lounge, he saw the pretty woman looking for matches.
He had a cigarette lighter ; he found a chair for her. They
drifted into delightful conversation. Her husband was an
engineer called Maybury-Jones. He had gone off to look
at dams or something. She was lonely and bored in
Khartoum. It was altogether too opportune, too pleasant,
this encounter with Mr. Durrant of whom, of *course*, she
had heard in England.

Her smile was flatteringly intimate, her conversational
tone exactly right.

Maurice went to bed some time after midnight, feeling as
though the world were at his feet.

Five days later, he walked from the hospital to the
hotel and saw Bill sitting in the lounge, drinking cocktails
with his lady.

The tableau was so much like his worst forebodings, the
leit-motif of his nightmares, that Maurice stood for a
moment by the entrance, watching them, trying to persuade
himself that he saw only a mirage of infantile apprehensions.
But then Bill laughed his deep, amused, ironic laugh, in
which dwelt the whole secret of his superiority, too deep
for doubt.

Maurice knew then what he ought to do. He should go
forward, greet the lady with gay, possessive assurance,

ask Bill, "Hallo, old fellow! What are you doing here?"
and seize control of a situation that still was rightly his.

But he did nothing of the kind. He turned on his heel,
went off to his room, bathed, changed, rang for a whisky
and soda, and sat awaiting dinner, angry, spiteful, chewing
the cud of jealousy. Of course Bill was here. He would
be here, he would be. The world was so small, there
was not room for them to live apart. The only person who
ever wanted Maurice was Sir Joseph. At that moment
Maurice hated his chief for being old and sick.

"Your own fault. You introduced Bill to Prince's.
You got him here. Fool! Fool!" he told himself. He
heard a knock on the door.

At first he perversely refused to answer, but after its
third repetition, he called gruffly, "Come in," and was not
surprised to see his brother. Bill came in smiling.

"Hallo, old son! And how's the world? They told me
you'd arrived."

"Quite a gathering of the clan," observed Maurice
dryly. "Have a drink."

"How's the old man? No, thanks. I've had several
downstairs, with Mrs. Maybury-Jones. She tells me you're
a friend of her's."

"Friend? Heaven preserve me. I've paid for the
lady's drinks on two occasions," said Maurice treacherously.

Bill sat down on the bed.

He had grown thinner than ever, browner, more graceful,
lazy and corrupt, Maurice considered. The drink story
might be a legend, but the whites of Bill's eyes were a
trifle yellowed. Maurice handed his cigarette case, asking
with a creditable show of carelessness, "When did you
arrive?"

"About four o'clock. Your strenuous friend Blacker
sent me here with papers for the chief, and a spot or two
of other business. Really an excuse to get rid of me.
I think I've done pretty well, myself; but, on the eve of
the great event, as it were, Blacker finds me an embarrassment. The truth of the matter is that he's a fine fellow
and all that, but he doesn't know how to treat Mandoans.
I do. It's my one talent—a poor thing, but mine own.
Blacker thinks I take too much upon myself, so sends me

off to draw a few last words of advice and what not from the big noise here. Well, I don't mind." Bill flicked the ash from his cigarette, as the hotel gong boomed officiously. "He can't do much harm now. Everything's as well fixed up as things in Mandoa ever are. They'll have a frightful scurry at the last minute, of course. What Beaton does not understand is that the High Council looks upon the place as *it's* own country—not a sort of newly acquired British mandate." He yawned. "But as a matter of fact, I don't mind a few day's holiday. It's quite good to know that no one will disturb my beauty sleep to-night by the information that the screens put up to hide the worst slums from European eyes have fallen down and obliterated about ten families, or that Um'bola has gone into hysterics again."

His flippant manner fretted Maurice. "Have you been round to the hospital yet ? " he asked.

"No. I put off that pleasure till to-morrow. One ordeal is enough for one day, thank you. I'm for food and bed." He yawned.

Maurice rose, straightening his tie before the mirror, instinctively reproaching his brother's lazy abandonment. "How did you get here ? " he asked.

"Flew. Straight through. Only stopped to refuel at Roseires. With that mad fellow Lancing. Was that the gong ? "

Bill pulled his long limbs drowsily from the bed. He had not changed from the shirt and shorts in which Maurice first saw him, and these were crumpled. He smiled indulgently at his brother. "You're very grand and all. Should I be? I'm too tired. Had a bath when I landed," he drawled, picking up Maurice's neat ebony backed brushes and beginning to smooth his hair.

Then Maurice saw that Bill's hands trembled violently. His lean face, when in repose, twitched with nervous exhaustion.

Drink ? Drugs? Fever? Flying ? wondered Maurice. As though in answer to his unspoken questions, Bill said, with a sort of bravado, "I piloted the damn bus from Roseires. Lancing deserves a putty medal." He laughed rather drunkenly, knocking a bottle of expensive brilliantine, unobtainable in Khartoum, on to the floor. "Sorry, old son," he said. "Made a bit of a mess. Tired and so on."

He did not offer to pick up the broken pieces, but continued his toilet, coolly appropriating Maurice's excellent equipment.

Maurice watched him, noting his uncertain movements, and his jaunty recoveries. "He's drunk, of course," he reflected grimly, but the observation brought him no satisfaction.

For nothing could ever balance the scales between them. Bill funked flying, but he funked because of a crash during that war which Maurice had not shared. If Maurice had been two years older, he, too, might have lost his nerve, his health, and his power.

And if Bill funked, at least he flew. He had piloted the bus from Roseires.

Oh, God! Would nothing ever compensate for that original handicap? Must the curse of immunity always rest upon Maurice? The bitterness of the unlucky was nothing to the suffering of the fortunate.

Prim and composed, Maurice watched his brother, then gathered his scattered coins, cigarette case, gold pencil and note-book, from the dressing-table, and dropped them into their respective pockets. "Dine with me?" he asked.

"Thanks," said Bill.

They went down the corridor together.

The next day Maurice took Bill with him to see Sir Joseph. He reserved to himself at least that satisfaction. He was Sir Joseph's confidant. He could assume proprietory rights in the sick-room, ordering Bill away at the first sign of the invalid's fatigue. Familiarity had reduced his own embarrassment and he looked forward to the temporary discomforture of his usually unselfconscious brother.

But Bill apparently saw no occasion for embarrassment. He greeted Sir Joseph as though they had met in a smoking room. He told a couple of stories (good ones—Maurice noted the second for repetition at the House. Good stories were rare), and he plunged into a very vivid, yet practical account of progress in Mandoa.

Of course, thought Maurice bitterly, he's accustomed to sick rooms.¹ A man who's had a wife and baby, damn him, has not the same fear of squalid intimacies. He'll be giving the old fellow the bed-pan in a minute.

Sir Joseph was enjoying Bill's company. He had roused himself and resumed a ghost of his old debonair, dictatorial self. " I wasn't even worth impressing," grumbled Maurice secretly, too much in love with his grievance to reflect that the sick man's self-abandonment in his presence had been a form of compliment.

Bill was so clever with Sir Joseph, consulted him, rallied him, even teased him a little. What was it, what was it, that gave him his damned air of ease, that enabled him, nerve-racked, shameless, degenerate as he was, to greet so easily a hostile world ? Maurice had always fought hard for popularity, ploughing his way against storms and clouds and headwinds, only to find Bill sailing gracefully into harbour before him.

The situation was intolerable.

For the next three days Bill spent hours in consultation with Sir Joseph, amusing, interesting and pleasing him. Maurice wanted the doctor to curtail Bill's visits, but the doctor had the impertinence to declare that they were just what Sir Joseph needed. They lifted him out of his lethargy, and gave his admirable constitution a chance to assert itself.

Then on the fourth day, Houghton arrived with his news of the capture of the I.H.A. commissioners " somewhere in the mountains."

The three men sat together in Maurice's pleasant room. Houghton was blunt and brief—also extremely tired, for after several long flights he had been summoned, just as he was getting off to bed and sent, non-stop, to Khartoum.

Talal had told every one in the hotel. The guests could talk of nothing else. There had been some explosive noises among the various political missions. Fortunately the I.H.A. was not over-popular.

No. Talal could give no details. The messenger's body had been found at the hotel gates. He had dropped dead while telling his story to Talal.

"Are you sure it's not a plant?" asked Maurice.

"That's what we want *you* to tell us," replied Houghton, turning to Bill.

Bill was playing with the cords of the venetian blind.

"It's a bit queer," he said. "The queerest thing is Talal's public announcement before even telling Blacker."

"What do you *think*?" Maurice asked impatiently, for Houghton's direct consultation of Bill had turned a knife in his heart.

"Don't know till I've seen Talal."

This irritated Maurice more than ever, for the airman's red, perplexed face was still turned to his brother.

"Do you realise," Maurice asked, "that if the story's true, Jean Stanbury's one of the prisoners?" For he knew that the Stanbury girl was a friend of Bill's, possibly one of his many mistresses.

But probably she had grown tired of him, for Bill only said, "She was certainly in the party when it started. I told them to be careful. I suppose they went poking their noses tactlessly into what didn't concern them."

He spoke ungraciously.

He was indeed worried, but not about Jean.

He did not know if the story were true or untrue, but he knew that Talal had betrayed him. He had impressed upon Talal the need for order, or at least for its appearance. And Talal had turned the hotel into a nest of gossip and speculation.

The announcement to the guests was a deliberate defiance of Bill's policy, a repudiation of friendship.

"This isn't the man I thought I knew," Bill told himself. "I suppose the Kenya colonels and so on are right. We never can understand these people."

He felt betrayed in more than his *amour propre*, hurt and deserted. He must see Talal at once. He must find out exactly what had happened.

"The point is, we can't possibly judge anything from here," he said aloud.

"Where do you *think* they are?" repeated Maurice obstinately. He wanted to make Bill give himself away.

"I can't possibly tell," Bill snapped.

Really, thought Maurice, nothing could be worse than

this. Attention once more was concentrated completely upon Bill. His own impotence maddened him.

He held the key to one position alone.

He suggested that they had better tell Sir Joseph.

He rang up the hospital. He ordered a car. He roused the nodding Houghton, who, when the vehicle started, promptly fell fast asleep again. He went first to the private ward and told the news lightly and amusingly, before Bill and the airman were allowed admission.

Sir Joseph pricked up his ears at the suggestion of kidnapping. Here was adventure. Here was excitement. Here was a break in the dull monotony of the sick-room. Here was an opportunity for youthful daring.

He fired questions at Houghton. He put forward a hundred alternative suggestions. This was life. This was like the old days.

Bill had only one plan, but he urged it eagerly. He must start for Lolagoba at once—within the hour. He must see Talal. He must learn the truth. He understood the way in which these people's minds worked. Only he must be there among them.

Sir Joseph nodded approval. His beard positively bristled with excitement. Youth on the train might have let him down, but that was an old nightmare. Here was the world as it should be, with three young men, all ready to do or die. Splendid. Splendid.

Maurice stared at his brother, hating him; then went and rang up the aerodrome. Houghton quite obviously could not start to-night. What pilots, what machines, were ready?

It was all unfortunate. One man had a broken wrist, another was down with fever. A third was expected in the morning. A fourth had only just come in, like Houghton, exhausted.

They would have to wait until the morning.

He came back, half-triumphantly, to the bedroom. If Bill were a man now, he would pilot himself. But he could not do that. Dual control with Lancing was one thing. Flying alone at night, another.

He gave his report.

Bill glanced up. " Is there a machine ? "

" Yes, they could fix up Houghton's. But there's no pilot till to-morrow."

" All right I'll go and speak to them." Bill turned to Sir Joseph. " That'll be all right, sir. I should be able to get off to-night." And went to the telephone.

" I thought your brother had objections against piloting 'planes ? " asked Sir Joseph.

" He has." Maurice's heart was boiling and thumping. Bill was going to win out all ways. Bill was going to make the dramatic gesture. He would rush off into the night to an heroic death and live for ever in Sir Joseph's memory. In his mother's memory. This was like the war again—a trap set for the secure, the stay-at-homes.

Maurice could see the invalid's eyes glittering with excitement. He had lost ; Bill had won, damn him, damn him, damn him !

Bill returned.

" That's all right," he said carelessly, though his face twitched again. " I'll start in half an hour."

" Good lad," cried Sir Joseph.

Without any pre-meditated intention, Maurice heard himself say : " Good. We'll get through by to-morrow then. Make it an hour. There are one or two things I want to clear up first. You can spare me for a few days, can't you, sir ? "

" What ? You off too ? "

Maurice could read, behind Sir Joseph's surprise, his pleasure. It infuriated him. The old man was rapacious. He sucked joy from vicarious peril as vampires suck blood from living veins. He wanted Maurice to risk his life as a passenger with an unreliable, neurotic pilot, flying by night over impossible country. He wanted it. He pretended to love Maurice, but he wanted him to face death.

Bill said nothing to Maurice. A single look, surprised yet self-assured, had been his only comment.

There followed some discussion of detail. Houghton twice fell asleep and had to be roused to give Bill further instructions before going down with him to the aerodrome.

Sir Joseph blazed into renewed vitality. Maurice wrote at his dictation a letter to Blacker ; he made notes of instructions about ransom , publicity and the attitudes to be assumed towards the various political missions. He would not let his thoughts touch his future fate. Correct, polite, efficient, he interviewed the matron, left instructions for further communications, and motored back to the hotel.

An hour later he drove up to the dark aerodrome. In a white stretch of floodlight lay Houghton's monoplane, the engine quivering, the propeller lazily ticking over. Bill, one foot on a step, waited, talking to a Sudanese mechanic. He turned as Maurice drove up, and climbed to the ground again.

" So you really intend to come ? "

His voice was thick, and he swayed a little, grinning stupidly.

" Good God ! He's drunk," thought Maurice.

But Bill was not too drunk to say : " Well—I can't chuck you out. But your blood's on your own head. You could have waited for Houghton in the morning."

Houghton, drugged with fatigue, came round from the tail of the plane.

" She's all right now."

" Good."

Bill lurched forward and climbed up into the cabin.

The mechanic was hanging on the side, bawling something in at the window.

" You going ? " Houghton asked Maurice.

The propeller began to spin more rapidly. The noise rose in a humming crescendo.

Maurice looked round the striped darkness.

He could still get out of it. He could still leave ill alone. He would be as useful at Khartoum as at Lolagoba— as anywhere.

The solid earth seemed to tug at his feet. In a minute the machine would move forward, run along the ground, and vanish into the night, leaving him there, safe and sensible, and with no harm done.

Leaving him there—as he had always been left behind by Bill. Left in safety and comfort and ignominy to face his mother's nervous explanations and her apologies for his omissions.

No, by God.

He stepped forward. He placed his foot on the metal step where his brother's had rested, and heaved himself into the dark cabin. The mechanic dropped off, and a door closed, shutting him into a little prison of noisy darkness ; a prison which began to run forward slowly, taxi-ing along the level beam of light. The faint glow from the lighted instruments showed him hands and feet moving beside him. The machine swung easily round. Bill opened the throttle. The noise crashed into a roar. And now they were dancing over the hummocky ground against the wind, leaping, sinking, bounding, then climbing steadily into the solid ink-blue air.

Maurice let out a deep breath.

Here they were. Here he was, driven by a crazy and probably drunken man, southward over the Sudan, into the darkness and the night, and heaven knew what sand-storms, cyclones, and air-pockets. (Were there such things ? Maurice thought he remembered reading somewhere that they were a myth.) Perils by wind and air and rock threatened them. He knew that somewhere near Lolagoba were cliffs called the Escarpment. These might be the final danger—if they survived so long.

But they were together. Whatever chance Bill met of death or of disaster, Maurice met it too. He had outwitted Fate. He had taken upon himself his brother's destiny. If Bill had been brave, Maurice had been even braver. Deliberately he had committed himself to a neurotic fool. Now he indeed deserved Sir Joseph's, " Good lad ! Good lad ! " Now, if Bill died, he would not wretchedly live to face his mother's unuttered reproaches. He had done with all that. His unheroic safety humiliated him no longer. He had never felt so free, so happy in his life. Winning North Donnington, sitting at the mahogany table in the Kingsway office, pouring out whisky for under-secretaries in the Knightsbridge flat, had never really redeemed him from humiliation.

But now he was happy.

The monoplane, entering a bumpy patch of air, dropped suddenly.

This is the end, thought Maurice, and looked round at his brother with a triumphant grin.

But the engines roared again ; the pace steadied. Bill, his gaze concentrated upon the instruments before him, his lips drawn back from his clenched teeth, sweating, green about the gills, drove on into the night.

CHAPTER V

BILL DURRANT STAYS BEHIND

NEXT morning, while having breakfast at Nasser, the pilot and mechanic of one of Prince's air liners, carrying goods to Lolagoba, put down their cups at the sound of a strange tumult in the heavens. Leaving the shaded verandah of the rest-house, they gaped up into the sky and saw, prancing and circling above them, a small monoplane. Now it swept in a large circle round the aerodrome, making as though it would land ; then, with a bursting roar and splutter of the engines, it lifted itself, belching black smoke, and fled into the upper air, like a soul released from Hades. Again, it cautiously descended, all but hit the roof of the rest-house, then rose yet again in eccentric spirals.

It took the spectators a little time to decide whether the monoplane's behaviour was due to deliberate stunting or to the indecision of a novice who wanted to land and had forgotten how. After about three minutes the pilot thought the second probability likely enough to act upon, and, running out on to the aerodrome, began by signals and gestures to guide the wayward machine down to the earth.

At last, after a circuit in which they nearly touched the waiting liner, the wheels hit the ground, sprang up, and leapt in a series of bounds like a Russian dancer, right to the southern limit of the field. There, a wing struck the iron fence, its fabric crumpling like paper. The machine swung round in a circular skid, and, with a grinding jar, came to rest.

Groundsmen, rest-house staff and pilot scurried across the field, but before they could reach the wreckage, a cabin door opened, and first one figure, then another, dropped out stiffly, and the Durrant brothers, blinking and grinning, surveyed with rueful satisfaction their achievement.

The piloting had been Bill's, but the luck was Maurice's. He had not been, so Bill declared, born for violent death. The monoplane having developed engine trouble after leaving the line of the Bahr el Astrak, Bill decided that he could not reach Lolagoba, and circled round looking for Nasser. His landing had been his final effort, but, though shameful, had done no human damage except to his brother's looks, for Maurice, anxiously watching through the cabin window as the wheels struck earth, received a bump on the forehead that slowly swelled and blackened to interesting proportions during the afternoon.

Still, there they were, walking across the field on their own legs, escorted by the questioning crowd, both slightly intoxicated with reaction and relief.

The meal that followed was one of the most hilarious Maurice had ever known. The adventure had been justified. Through the tumult of his roaring ears and throbbing bruises, Maurice listened to Bill's skilfully edited account of their ridiculous flight, no longer jealous of his easy manner. He even became talkative himself. It seemed as though his night's adventure, the bang on his head, and two whiskeys and sodas had, for the first time in his life, relaxed his nerves, and freed him from self-consciousness. He heard himself contradicting Bill, not with the priggish dogmatism of valiant fear, but easily and laughingly, as equal to equal. And Bill, with perfect friendliness and ease, gave him back joke for joke.

When the brothers boarded the air liner, they both felt more than a little drunk. But they were sober again before landing at Lolagoba.

It was mid-afternoon, the hour when the city was usually at its quietest. But to-day, though the white hotel, the hangars and the offices drowsed below the quivering light, an air of expectation hung about the place. It did not come from the scurrying gait of the black groundsmen ; they always scampered across the hard-baked earth. The inevitable little boys risking their lives by scuttering like tadpoles in the path of a landing aeroplane, were no livelier than usual. But perhaps the unusual number of machines in the hangars, perhaps the flood-lighting apparatus squatting before the hotel, perhaps the expectation in the faces of the porters, gave Maurice the impression of a place on the eve of great events.

From the air, he had seen the big shapeless mass of huts and courtyards, sprawling along the plain below the eastern hills. On the ground, stretching stiff limbs, he reflected that this was actually Lolagoba. The flag on the great map in Prince's, the discussions round the board-table, the " Once in a Lifetime " advertisement campaign —they meant this, this place.

Bill advised Maurice to go straight to the hotel.

" You may find Blacker there, resting. If not, he'll be at his office. A boy will take you round."

Bill's friendly tone gave Maurice the courage to ask, " Where are you off to ? "

" To see Talal."

" Right-o. I suppose you prefer to deal with him alone ? "

Bill nodded. They were no longer driven by mutual suspicion and irritation to facetiousness. They were able to discuss practical arrangements with ordinary regard and courtesy.

Watching his brother striding along the road leading to the town, Maurice wondered what exactly it was that had put them both at ease. Bill certainly seemed in Lolagoba to be a different person, more responsible, more simple. But he himself ? Something had happened to him too.

He followed the porters carrying his cases towards the white hotel.

Bill walked in a dream to the Lord High Chamberlain's palace. A new gate, glittering with gold paint, closed the gap in the stockade, which was itself garlanded with flowers, concealing small electric bulbs on hanging wires.

The sentries wore new uniforms, no longer the easy saffron-coloured tunic or loin cloth, but real uniforms of yellow and scarlet cloth, with coats and trousers, and buttons and cords, and pockets and silver braid, and boots and spurs, and even gloves. They strained and sweated, in proud and dignified discomfort.

At the sight of Bill they grinned and saluted, pleased to see him back, glad to display their finery, showing off their whistles and swords and braces. Yes ; the safi was in. Yes ; half Lolagoba was there. Yes ; Safi Durrant must enter.

In the big courtyard Bill found, not only the Lord High Chamberlain and three or four of his friends, but Ma'sull the Arch-archbishop and three Mandoan priests. They sat together beneath a canopy, drinking sispri and smoking the cigarettes that Lolagoba had found almost the most delightful gifts of civilisation. A cabinet gramophone, solemnly tended by two Negro slaves, flooded the court with the luscious sweetness of Richard Tauber's voice, singing " You are my heart's delight."

When he saw the Englishman, Talal rose, and flung up his arm in salutation.

But Bill was still stirred by indignation. He hardly wasted a look upon the others. Going straight up to the Lord High Chamberlain, he began, " Just a moment, Talal. I want a word with you."

They went apart, to a little private court between the blank wall of a hut and the stockade.

Then Bill spoke his mind.

" Look here. I went off thinking that everything was all right. I'd discussed every detail with you. I wouldn't have put it past Blacker or Mason to make a mess of the whole show, but what the hell did you mean by stirring up this mare's nest over the kidnapping business ? Walking into the hotel like that and turning the whole place upside down ! You knew the kind of commotion you'd cause."

He was really angry. His feelings had passed from fury against betrayal to the terror and effort of his flight. Then the cathartic release from a broken tabu had soothed and healed him ; then, walking through streets already transfigured for Tuesday's ceremony, his indignation had re-awakened. He watched Talal withdraw his cigarette, spit meditatively, then smile his slow, rich, triumphant, gentle smile.

" What the hell, my friend ? *The* hell ? Oh, yes. Now I have to ask what the hell you meant by telling us here to be so careful. No guns fired, no knives in street, no violence. No, no, no. All behave like children at their best. I tell you *you* nearly bust up whole show with your Rules for Good Mandoans. Do you know what *I* found ? Your fine visitors were pleased with our good boys—oh, yeah ? They were bored, I tell you. Bored. Ready to quit. It was toss-up if they stayed for wedding *at* all."

"I am afraid I don't understand you," Bill said, more calmly, the impulse of his emotion failing before Talal's unexpected counter-attack. "What exactly do you mean ? "

Talal told him. With dignity and precision he narrated the events of two nights ago, his encounter with Felicity Cardover, his talk with Fanshawe, Marlow and Julian, and the conversation of the two American ladies.

"So when Ma'buta sent that message, I thought, ' Here is the thing. Now we will give them something to think about.' You see, Durrant," he concluded, " you do not understand these white people. I do. Now they are happy. All places in safari taken; all 'planes engaged; six search parties out ; that Mr. Jordan who built the hotel has gone to look particularly for Frau von Schelden. Oh, yeah ! But in wrong direction."

" Then you do know where they are ? "

" Sure. Ma'buta has them safe. That old fox will never kill live goods. His motives strictly financial. All *very* fortunate. Europeans love hunting. Yes. But hunting lion and rhino, *nothing* to hunting for lost white ladies. I tell you, Durrant, this is a great game."

" Game ! My God ! Do you suppose the commissioners think this a good game ? "

" How can I tell ? It is good advertisement," said Talal solemnly.

It was.

Bill, reflecting upon the situation, saw it more and more with Talal's logical vision. Beaton wanted advertisement ; he would get it. The visitors had wanted excitement, they had found it. The Mandoans loved intrigue, bribery, ransom and the whole paraphernalia of brigandage. They had it. Every one ought to be pleased.

The sanity behind the absurdity almost convinced Bill. He stared at the inscrutable countenance of his friend, then broke into a shout of laughter. It was a mad world, a mad world, but Talal was probably as sane as any one.

Then he pulled himself together.

" Look here ; have you told Blacker that Ma'buta's got them ? "

" Certainly not. It would spoil fun."

Bill calculated.

" My dear fellow. It's Saturday already. There's plenty going on without butchering the wretched commission to make a tourists' holiday. We've got to get them safely away as quickly as possible. You'd better come round to Blacker's office with me, and let's see what we can do."

They returned together through the streets that were no longer empty. Negroes, Arabs and Mandoans jostled European gentlemen in khaki shirts and shorts, ladies in flowery chiffon frocks and sun-helmets, and members of the Royal Bodyguard in stiff new uniforms. It had been a good joke, to let the tiresome and interfering Beaton and his commission provide the fillip of uncertainty needed for Mandoan entertainment. A kind of rough Kiplingesque justice, Bill thought ; a schoolboy trick, funny. Poor old plump Frau von Schelden shut up in a native hut !

He knew vaguely that somewhere beyond the joke lay more serious considerations, but he did not feel capable of dealing with them while the sound of engines still roared in his ears, and his head throbbed, and the garish colours of the streets swam in the slanting light.

In Blacker's office they found an unofficial committee, consulting together with deep earnestness. Beside Blacker, who, solemn and anxious, was scribbling on his blotting paper, were Sir Malcolm Devizes, authoritative and laconic, Mason, the engineer, and Maurice playing his part of director beautifully, with just the right shade of deference towards these older men and just the right suggestion of importance in his manner.

They had been discussing the possible fate of the prisoners, and the wise information to give the press. The advent of Bill and Safi Talal aroused them to that sense of expectation, restrained by the knowledge of their own dignity, commonly displayed by Englishmen in such crises.

The story told by Bill was not quite the whole truth. He declared that the Lord High Chamberlain had discovered that the imprisoned Europeans were probably held up in Ma'buta's camp. Ma'buta, the enemy of all European influence, was the largest slave-owner in Mandoa, the implacable opponent of emancipation. The story was not merely plausible—it was welcome. It turned a casual accident into a political manœuvre. It also reflected well on Prince's Limited, which had given every facility to the commissioners, offered escorts and advised caution. Beaton, independent and obstinate, had ignored the firm's warning and insisted upon " seeing things for himself." And this was the result.

There remained only one further step to make the episode complete. Prince's must perform the rescue. " The Firm Which Is Never at a Loss," according to its advertisement, must lose no opportunity here.

Maurice saw all the implications of the situation at a glance. His mind was not naturally quicker than Bill's, but it was less confused by side issues. While Bill was thinking of Beaton's feelings, Sir Joseph's ambitions, Talal's possible motives, the effect of the incident upon the reputation of the I.H.A., and a hundred other things, Maurice went straight for the main point and announced his intention of leading the rescue party himself.

" You ? Mr. Durrant ? " gasped Blacker.

" Of course," said Maurice.

He was aware of Bill's slow sidelong glance, sweeping over him. He felt Sir Malcolm's approval and Blacker's relief. He explained his realisation of the need for Bill's presence in Lolagoba to deal with Mandoan psychology. He explained his promise to Sir Joseph that he would be personally responsible for the safety of the commissioners.

With every argument he felt power and decision flowing into him.

This game was between him and his brother.

He was tired of ignoble safety. He was tired of staying at home while Bill dashed off to the war, to South Africa, to the Argentine, to face death and poverty, the hazards of marriage or the fear of failure. This time the risks should be his. He would reverse their rôles. If he were

killed, Bill could bear the burden of immunity. If he
succeeded, they would be quits for ever.

It was Talal who really decided the matter.

He listened to Maurice's hurriedly improvised argument,
nodding his head.   Then he said quietly, " That is right.
That is O.K.   Mr. William Durrant needed here ;   yes,
Ma'buta knows him. Ma'buta hates him. Would be no
good as mediator.   No one here knows Mr. Maurice
Durrant. Strangers are good. You will have Bun'dodo
with you—yes ? "

Bun'dodo was Talal's blood-brother, foster-brother and
friend. A shrewd, experienced man.

" Bun'dodo—yes—a very able fellow. He'll understand
the Mandoan side of the business."

So it was arranged.

They planned to send a small scouting 'plane over
Ma'buta's camp at once, to drop messages announcing
that ransom would be paid, if the prisoners were safely
delivered, but threatening to bomb the camp if any hitch
occurred.

A larger passenger 'plane, in which Maurice would
travel, could land five miles away, and he would march
from thence with an armed guard, to hand over the ransom
and meet the prisoners half-way between the camp and
the landing ground.

A statement was prepared for the press, announcing the
probable location of the prisoners, and the immediate
departure of the rescuers led by Mr. Maurice Durrant, a
director of Prince's Limited, and the well-known Conservative M.P. for North Donnington.

Walking from the office, Bill drew Maurice away from
the others.

" You want me to keep out of this ? " he asked.

Maurice took a deep breath.   " Yes, I do," he said.

Bill seemed to consider the situation, not hostile to
it, merely contemplative.

" Of course you know it's risky ? "

The newly heroic Maurice could laugh.

" As risky as your piloting ? "

Bill accepted the hit.

" They may try to bargain," he continued.

" I'm used to that. It's in my line of business. Don't
forget I've got a commercial mind," said Maurice. The
phrase was an echo of an old taunt of Bill's.

He dared to joke now. He dared to expose his old wounds
and laugh at them. He was free, free, free. Free from old
fears, old inhibitions, old inferiorities.

" All right," smiled Bill. " Don't say I didn't warn you."

" What message shall I give Jean Stanbury ? " asked
Maurice.

But Bill, absent-minded and friendly, did not even rise
to this. " Oh, give her my love," he said casually.

And that was all there was to it.

A hundred details had to be decided.

This rescue business was to be done in style. The hotel,
the offices, the aerodrome, hummed and buzzed. Reporters
appeared out of the thin air ; cameras clicked and whirred.
A talking picture was made of the Lord High Chamberlain
of Mandoa, statuesque and noble, wishing good luck to
Mr. Maurice Durrant and Safi Bun'dodo. Then the engines
of the 'planes throbbed their impatient crescendo. Maurice
and Bill shook hands, and the rescue party roared off into
the evening leaving the white population of Lolagoba
seething with excitement, and Maurice the hero of the hour.

During all this time, Bill had moved in a dream. His
mind was an aching confusion of memories and speculation.
While Blacker and Maurice and Mason discussed the
details of rescue, Talal had been pouring into his ears the
problems of Mandoan politics.

" My God ! Devils are to pay here. Um'bola says her
daughter wears high hat already, and she will not be
bullied in own palace. Ma'sull says he does not want to
see Um'bola after wedding—wants to retire and hunt.
All the High Councillors say they are ruined already. No
more money for State banquet. *Can* we charge foreign
delegations for their own entertainments ? I say no. It
is not done. But they—they will not pay. Now, if Prince's
will arrange another loan—I tell Blacker we must have a
loan, but he has *no* imagination."

The whirl and sweep of Mandoan grievances engulfed
Bill ; the empty treasury, the ambitious little princess,
the emotional Um'bola, the horses for the royal carriage

that nobody dared to exercise, kicking their mud stable to pieces in excess of well-fed, well-bred high spirits—all these woes flooded his ears, still half-deafened with the ocean-like roaring of the engines.

He stood on the aerodrome after the rescue party had left, trying to collect his thoughts.

If all went well, the 'planes should be over Ma'buta's camp in half an hour. It was only forty miles away. Allowing time for the walk from the landing ground and possible negotiations, they might all get back that same night—unless they chose to wait till morning.

It was no use worrying. There were a hundred things that must be done immediately.

He ought to see tiresome little La'gola, and bully her into decency to her mother. He ought to pay a ceremonial call on Prince Anjak. He ought to interview Ma'sull.

He felt deadly tired. The strain of the flight was beginning to tell upon him now, but he forced himself to set about his business of propitiation, explanation, and cajolery.

The Heiress Apparent, La'gola, was spoiled and capricious. She insisted that Bill should stand in her presence, spoke through an interpreter, though she knew English quite well, and demanded that several details of Tuesday's ceremony, already rehearsed, should be altered. The little Abyssinian prince was alarmed and childish. He was very young. Life to him had been an affair of escapes and imprisonments, waiting for news of life and death behind flimsy curtains ; long, tedious ritual, endured through overwhelming fatigue, and terror after terror. His small, cowed person promised little majesty, and Bill could not help sympathising both with the lad who quailed before his coming ordeal, and the girl-bride who regarded her bridegroom with contempt.

It was very difficult. He looked at the children sorrow-fully. They were to be married on Tuesday to advertise Prince's enterprise in Lolagoba. They were puppets in a complex political intrigue. Their personal feelings mattered nothing.

But their personalities appeared to Bill with poignant individuality. When the little Abyssinian princeling held

his lean body straight, aping Mandoan pride, Bill felt the
effort in his own nerves and sinews. He felt in himself the
defiant courage of the scared child.

"Those children ought to be kept out of this," he
muttered. "They're too young."

The Royal Princess had sent word that she would see
him. He left the future bride and bridegroom together
and followed a guide through the maze of huts and paths
in the palace enclosure.

Already evening was darkening into night, but the
aeroplanes had not yet returned. Bill lifted his head and
listened. Far off, a drum was beating; its reiterated,
sinister cadences rumbled below the high bird-like
cries of pedlars in the market place. A dog howled. Babies
wailed in the stifling huts. Somewhere, a woman mourned
her dead with monotonous, unrelenting sorrow. These
sounds pierced the twilit seclusion of the palace quarters,
but no noise of engines hummed on the quiet air.

Bill entered the lace-hung room where he had first met
Um'bola. It had been transformed for some reception.
The soiled curtains still veiled the broken walls, and
crumbling plaster still showed the bulging thatch, but a
cheap Axminster carpet covered the uneven floor. Small
gilt chairs of a flimsy, vulgar pattern, and a really exquisite
table inlaid with mother-of-pearl, had been set in a stiff
circle. The inevitable gramophone stood on a treadle
sewing machine, its crimson trumpet, like an immense
metal convolvulus, flowering among the lace and gilt.

Um'bola herself was sitting alone, Mandoan fashion, on
the floor when Bill entered. She sprang up gracefully.

The impulse driving all her actions, Bill reflected, was
merely a biological function. She was in love with Ma'sull.
She wanted another child by him. What else was that but
an animal desire? Why should he serve the biological
instincts of a Mandoan woman?

But he could not sustain the brutality of his cynicism.
Whatever the origin of her emotion, its effect was something more than a gross animal hunger. Her spirit had been
refined to extraordinary sensibility by her long purgatory
of suspense. Her grace of movement, like a mystic's grace
of soul, seemed to spring from the harmony and concentra-

tion of her entire body, mind and spirit, drawn to one end.

Bill watched her with growing uneasiness. What right had he to interfere, clumsy and blind as he was, with human wills and destinies ? What right had he to expose this delicate creature to the shock of disillusionment ?

His old sense of responsibility recurred to him. He saw Prince's Tours Limited breaking in upon the gossamer-fine web of human fortune, and changing its entire pattern. These were people, people. The brave, quailing spirit of the boy, the girl's untried arrogance, the woman's yearning loyalty—these were the pawns in a commercial game. No ; they were figures in Sir Joseph's romantic dream of adventure. No ; they were, to Sir Malcolm Devizes, favoured units of an inferior race to be handled with protective justice.

Bill's fevered perception showed him the nerves, veins, skeletons and tissues of flesh and blood and bone behind brown and black skins. Their fragile organisms raced towards death, pumping the liquid blood, opening and shutting the pulses, observing an appointed dance of destiny. Then mechanical hands reached out from engines called Policy, Profit and Reform, to clutch them, jerking them from their ordered course.

The interference might be good ; it might be evil ; but in neither case was it negligible. In some heaven of absolute justice, he, Bill Durrant, would have to answer for what he was doing to Prince Anjak, to the Heiress Apparent, and to the Royal Princess. Yes ; and where did it end ?

Out into the streets he went, driven by his imagination. The full significance of the past twenty-four hours was upon him now.

Last night he had set out from Khartoum upon the flight which he had always intended should be his last. After Stephen's death he had told himself he would fly once more, and only once. He would take his 'plane up into the air, higher, higher, higher, until Stephen's hands seized the joy-stick, Stephen's heel kicked the rudder, and round they went, round, down, in a whirling spin to death.

But he had not met Stephen. He had not died. He had taken enormous care to preserve his life. Maurice's presence had had little to do with it. If Stephen had demanded Maurice too, who was Maurice to divert the ends of justice ?

No. He had been spared for something. What ? What ? His aching head provided no answer to the question.

He found himself wandering between huts hung with paper flowers, and stockades festooned with flags.

This was Lolagoba. This was Mandoa.

Bicycles bounded round corners at him. Gramophones brayed above the human noise.

It was to bring bicycles, gramophones and Gillette razor blades into this city that he laboured. La'gola and Anjak must marry ; then Um'bola must be delivered from her dream of love ; Talal must hand over his entire fortune to Ma'buta, in order that British firms should employ cutters and piecers and packers ; in order that sewing machines from Doncaster, lace from Nottingham and pottery from Leek should adorn these alleys ; profit, profit, profit ; that was what the sewing machines sang as they whirred.

No, no. That was not right. This city was hung with flags for a noble reason. Sir Joseph's high vision of adventure must be realised. Sir Malcolm's yet more valuable, yet more constructive, ideal of good government and British influence must be fulfilled.

But even that was not all. What of Jean, with her notions of equality and brotherhood, and reform, illumined by mercy ? Would slaves be freed ? Would hospitals be built, and lepers cleansed, and the appalling wastage of infant mortality checked ? The babies wailed in the night. Their mothers mourned them. Somewhere among the mountains Maurice was even now liberating Mr. Beaton and Dr. Beriot and Frau von Schelden that they might continue their work of salvage.

Profit. Power. Pity.

Surely these were good ?

Surely he, Bill Durrant, agent of Prince's Limited, walking through the streets, deserved the grateful salutation of these people ?

He was a god. He had shown mercy on them. He had delivered them from the darkness of stagnation and barbarity. He was bringing them the three great gifts of civilisation—Profit, Power, Pity.

He had killed Stephen Stanbury.

He had saved his own life.

This had happened for a purpose. Payment would be demanded from him.

The ultimate justice must be served. His gifts to Mandoa themselves were not enough. They cancelled out each other. He was interfering with destiny. He was giving in exchange Profit, Power, Pity.

That was right. That was fair.

But that did not solve the problem of his own fate. He was still in debt to Stephen for a life.

With the lucidity of unreason he calculated his spiritual arithmetic.

" Mandoa cancels out. But I ? "

He had reached the outskirts of the city, not far from his own bungalow. The huts no longer crouched side to side, but were scattered over squalid areas, foul with refuse, where skinny goats browsed among the garbage, and hens scratched on the filthy thresholds.

Again he stood and listened for the aeroplane. He was shivering now with reaction and fatigue. This time he almost thought that, if only the city would cease its multitudinous sounds, he would hear something.

" Safi Durrant ! Safi Durrant ! "

" Be quiet, Bindi ! Hush ! "

" Safi Durrant ! "

A little old man stood before him, bowing over clasped hands. Bill knew him as an ex-archbishop, unfrocked for some ceremonial offence, who was now practising with no great profit, as a magician.

" You have come back. In the flesh," announced the old man solemnly.

" Yes ; and in the spirit, haven't I ? " asked Bill.

" No, no. The spirit is absent still."

" Good." Bill tossed him a shilling, that flashed in the flickering light from a near-by fire. " Good. Good."

From the dark doorways, figures stole towards them. " Read me my riddle then," cried Bill. " What should a man do who is in debt for a life ? "

This was the kind of question the wizard liked—vague, portentous, solemn.

He spat four times, north, south, east, west. He span round on his toes and dropped down between the spittal.

A little boy, then a woman with a child, then a young man, moved nearer to watch. This was a common street entertainment—a minor public questioning and divining —not a private, terrible, important magic, a death-wishing or life-saving or child-getting.

" You must pay your debt," said the wizard to his client.

" Precisely. But how ? " asked Bill.

" With another life, another life, another life ! "

" Whose ? That's what I want to know. Whose ? "

" A life you love. A life you love. A life you love."

Bill shouted : " That tells me nothing. Come along. A shilling's a shilling in these days."

He tried to imitate the careless, unconcern of Mandoan custom.

But the wizard, whose vocabulary was as limited as his imagination, could only roll his eyes, so that their whites turned in the ghostly dusk, repeating, " A life you love."

Down the street came cries of donkey-boys, the thwack of whips, and the high-pitched voices of Europeans. A little party of tourists, led by Felicity Cardover, galloped towards the group surrounding Bill and his wizard. "What's this ? Hi—guide ! What's this ? Oh, Mr. Durrant ! I say, he's having his fortune told. . . . Captain Durrant, have you heard any news of your brother ? . . . *Do* tell us what's happening." Their shrill voices closed in upon him.

" This is a witch. He was an archbishop. He will tell you your fortunes if you like."

" How much should we pay him ? "

" Oh, I *must* hear my fortune ! " cried Felicity.

" You can give him a shilling—but he's not worth twopence," said Bill, and turned away, unable to endure the noisy company.

He continued his desultory stroll, muttering drunkenly to himself, " A life you love, a life you love," and stopping to listen for the throb of an aeroplane that did not come.

CHAPTER VI

THE MANDOAN AFFAIR GOES FORWARD

BLACKER, Jordan and Mason between them had done their best for the press bungalow at Lolagoba. No member of the staff of Prince's Limited undervalued the power of publicity. But local circumstances were against them.

Four separate attempts had been made to connect telegraph wires with either Juba or Nasser. Four times Mandoan ingenuity had found better uses for the wire. "When I see my scoop about Prince Anjak's night-shirt walking around the market place on a cutie's ankle," said O'Flane of the *New York Despatch*, " I could blaspheme my God."

True, the air service to Khartoum left three times a week, but if Lolagoba acquired first-class news value, what was that but adding insult to inconvenience ?

Hitherto, the news value of Lolagoba had been nothing to boast about—a primitive and insanitary city, a peculiar constitution, an odd ecclesiastical system, and certain picturesque details of costume and manner were unlikely to find their way into front pages. Geography arouses less public interest than history, less than sociology, and far less than individual sensation. Times were bad. Advertising revenue was not what it had been. There was no single fortunate correspondent in Lolagoba unburdened with instructions to cut down expenses. Lolagoba was not the centre of the world, and no incident, however dramatic and unexpected, was likely to make it so. February, 1933, was a bad month in which to turn the thoughts of the world to Central Africa.

Something indeed might be made out of the story of the kidnapped I.H.A. commissioners—if they had been kidnapped. But it was in no very hopeful mood that throughout Saturday night the pressmen dozed in the too fragile wicker chairs of their bungalow, wandered about the aerodrome, and sat in the hotel bar, bored and sleepy.

Early on Sunday morning, O'Flane and his friend, the correspondent of the *London Morning News* escaped from the smell of stale tobacco and whisky in the bar, and strolled out on to the level stretch of sun-cracked earth.

" The liner's leaving for Khartoum at seven-thirty, isn't it ? " O'Flane asked the porter, not because he did not know, but because his instinct to ask questions never deserted him. He turned to Fox, the English journalist.

" I've gotten a picture of Jean Stanbury here," he said, producing a blurred and unflattering snapshot of Jean, riding a donkey. " Would you say that on this evidence I was justified in reporting ' Beautiful English Blonde in Hands of Savages ? ' "

" Every white female under sixty, when in an unconventional situation outside Europe, or the U.S.A.," sneered Foz, " is always beautiful. Her virtue is always in danger. Miss Stanbury's a sensible, well-set-up woman in the thirties, with no nonsense about her and as much sex appeal as a dining-room table. Personally, I should think she's better able to look after herself than most of us. But, academically speaking, there's always strong human interest in the rape motive. When Selby got back from Kenya, he told me he had made over two hundred quid out of articles all based on one idea—the Brave White Woman dining in the Wilderness, dressed, as at Home, with bare arms and jewels, Silver and white Napery. (Don't forget ' Napery.' It's a good word. Damn sight better than table-cloth.) Heroines of the Jungle—you know—English Home Life in Darkest Africa. It's not that the public cares twopence whether Mrs. Tiddleypush uses a table-cloth or eats out of the tin. The real fascination lies in the thought of white virtue exposed to hordes of lusting savages. *All* the hidden passions are touched ; biological, race purity, sex jealousy, respectability." Fox yawned. " Prestige too. If she were a charwoman, now, it wouldn't matter. It's the thought of that white skin—manicured nails—perfumes—you know the kind of thing. They never mention mosquitoes, and heat rash and perspiration, by the way. God ! What a climate."

" You haven't answered my question." O'Flane bit off the end of a cigar and spat it out.

Fox, who was fastidious and disliked the habit, snapped at him : " Oh, exploit Jean Stanbury's virginity and its dangers by all means. She won't thank you, but from such ideas are empires made. What our empire builders would have done without the fear of rape, I hardly know."

" Aren't you going to send a story ? "

" I've done something. But thank God we go slow on the I.H.A., and all kindred bodies. My old man's on the economy stunt, and this is not the time to spend the nation's money on humanitarianism. Sentiment's sentiment, you know—but home's home—and first things come first. And so on. If young Durrant pulls off a picturesque rescue, that'll be a different matter. Prince's are among our best advertisers—we can go all out on them . . ."

" The Germans'll have a hard time to make much out of the von Schelden woman."

" Oh, no. Home and mother. She's got a husband and a damn good-looking daughter. She showed me a photograph of her. Incidentally—I wonder . . ."

The sudden extinction of a light in Prince's office told them that others beside themselves had been up all night. They saw Blacker's tall figure walking, rather drunkenly, as tired men walk after lonely vigils, towards the hotel.

They strolled out to join him, trying to fancy that they found some refreshment in the tepid morning air.

" Well ? Salaams, Blacker. How are things going ? Is Lolagoba going to make history to-day ? "

" If you gentlemen will help her to do so," replied the manager, in whom fatigue increased solemnity. He was genuinely anxious about the fate of both prisoners and rescue party. " We're sending another 'plane in half an hour, I don't mind telling you. Of course, we count on your discretion as before."

But at that moment all three men stopped and listened. Faint and far away they thought they heard a soft thrumming.

" It can't be . . ."

But it was.

Clearer and clearer grew the noise of the engine ; then O'Flane caught sight of the growing black speck of the scout machine.

A quarter of an hour later, Lolagoba learned that the rescue party had arrived safely at Ma'buta's camp ; that it had seen the indubitable evidence of the commissioners' baggage outside the chief's stockade ; that it had dropped the note ; that Ma'buta had condescended to appear, without his prisoners, and ask for an interview with the rescuers ; that Maurice Durrant and his guard had landed and spoken to Ma'buta who, blandly ignoring the evidence of the baggage, protested his complete ignorance of the prisoners' whereabouts, and offered to do all in his power to help the search party if his expenses, which would be heavy, were guaranteed.

" In other words," said Maurice's hastily scribbled note, " he's holding us up to heavier ransom, and we haven't found out yet whether the commissioners are really alive or dead. I'm making a shot to get through into the stockade to find out what has really happened. Meanwhile, I'll use bribery up to any tolerable extent, and trust to Mandoa doing justice afterwards."

Blacker's wan face grew greyer at the news. " Gentlemen, gentlemen," he repeated. " I count upon your discretion."

The pilot of the scout machine was fed and sent back to report progress. Blacker summoned Bill Durrant and Safi Talal, and once again the group of consultants assembled, this time in Sir Malcolm Devizes' room at the hotel.

Sometime before midnight, Bill Durrant, after his pilgrimage through the streets, had found himself near Talal's house and had gone in to see him, spending the rest of the night dozing, waking, talking, drinking a little and dozing again, till Blacker's message came.

It seemed to him that the meeting in Sir Malcolm's room was a congregation of the mighty. There they met, self-controlled, honourable, able men, helpless before the laws of political etiquette and the agility of the feudal-tribal-mystical mind.

" All the arrangements for to-day, sir, surely should go forward ? " Blacker suggested nervously to Sir Malcolm. " We ought to preserve a sense of proportion."

They all wanted to preserve a sense of proportion. After

all, the I.H.A. commissioners had gone into the country
at their own risk. Mandoa was not Manchester nor Berlin.
The slave trade boasted strong vested interests, and its
exposure could never be as safe as croquet.

The government and order of the country were not in
Prince's hands. It was not even in the hands of the foreign
visitors—difficult though it might be for Sir Malcolm ever
to think of himself and his countrymen as foreigners.

" Of course, you can never tell what these people will
do *next*," Mason repeated irritably, ignoring the impassive
presence of Talal.

It was the ingratitude of Mandoa that moved Blacker.
Here he was, doing everything for these people, and the
Mandoans repaid him thus.

" I suppose we can count on the support of your government ? " Sir Malcolm asked Talal gratuitously. He found
it hard to realise that the Mandoan High Council in 1933
was as helpless in dealing with over-mighty subjects as
the English High Court of Parliament in 1455. " Naturally
you will bring the kidnappers to justice."

Talal smiled benignly. He knew perfectly well that no
Mandoan tribunal could bring to justice the man who had
already brought him to the brink of ruin. But he answered
Sir Malcolm as he felt that gentleman expected and desired.

Cross purposes, thought Bill. Justice is to be the remedy
for torture. A nice soothing remedy. Supposing Jean
and Beriot—nice chap, Beriot—had had been thrashed
to death for fun. That was the kind of thing Mandoans did.
Justice would heal their torn sinews, soothe their twisted
nerves, and place them safely back in their various homes.

He thought of Jean's cottage in Chelsea, where she
bullied him into laying tables or making omelettes and
·treated him to long moral disquisitions. The curtains
bellying out on the night wind were filled with justice.

Oh, justice could do anything. Justice would demand
from him a life in payment of Stephen Stanbury's life. A
life he loved.

Justice would make Sir Malcolm feel happy. Sir Malcolm
looked to Talal to do justice.

Bill sat twisting tobacco-stained fingers between his
knees. After his night with Talal he looked dreary, dis-

sipated and unshaven. "Not a satisfactory type," Sir Malcolm was thinking. Blacker's judgment, glancing at him on his way to more serious considerations, registered disapproval. It was a pity that Durrant, though a gentleman, lacked backbone. Blacker had expected Bill to volunteer to go to his brother's assistance. Not that he could do any good, but it would have been the natural thing to do. It was all a very awkward business.

". . . So, of course, everything must go forward as arranged," Sir Malcolm concluded.

They all agreed.

The little conference was closed.

Everything must go forward.

This, thought Bill, is the watch-word. With our backs to the wall. . . . But that was fighting against the Germans. Haig's despatch, wasn't it? Well. The only Germans here were the officials, distracted by the possible fate of their distinguished countrywoman, and suspiciously unconvinced that all conceivable steps had been taken to ensure her safety. Perhaps they thought that if their government still held Tanganyika Territory, the whole of Central Africa would now be safer for white women in general and for Frau von Schelden in particular. . . .

But there were other enemies against which commonsense was now arrayed—the natural cruelty of untamed human nature, the lust for possession, the desire for power, the intrusion of uncomprehending philanthropy, and Talal's uncertain hold on his own colleagues, already fretting against their burden of taxation, and the ecclesiastical disputes ranging round a successor to Ma'sull.

Yet they must go forward with the celebrations, the royal wedding, and the introduction of Mandoa to civilisation.

At half-past seven the air mail left for Khartoum. Those visitors who were not breakfasting in their rooms strolled down to the restaurant. Little groups discussed the possibility of rescue. Dr. Beriot grew in fascination, Frau von Schelden in benevolence, Beaton in integrity, Jean Stanbury in youth.

Bill, drinking a cup of tea before going to interview Ma'sull and all the difficult church dignitaries, heard a description of innocent loveliness, ardour, and doomed ability, which he hardly recognised as a portrait of Jean Stanbury. The greater became the anxiety for the commissioners, the higher their value rose in popular estimation.

At half-past nine a religious procession was scheduled to march to the stadium, where the Cardinal Legate would celebrate High Mass, in recognition of Catholic influence upon Mandoa. Its motive was purely official, political and strategic, but now it borrowed from the rising tide of personal emotion an entirely unplanned significance.

Visitors who had had no intention of leaving the comparatively cool shelter of the hotel, now declared their desire to attend Mass. A religious service suited their solemn mood.

" It is like the war," observed the plump, comfortable wife of a French deputy.

" *Is* it ? " murmured Felicity Cardover, to whom the war was little more than an excuse for the aged to indulge in senile drivelling. She cared not a button for the fate of the commissioners. But Julian wanted to see the show, so she too joined the party. The Marlows went because they hoped to see Types. The Balkan princes went, because the service was part of their programme. The pressmen went, because this was one of the sights of Mandoa. Princess La'gola and Prince Anjak went, riding in carven chairs beneath jewelled canopies, and the Royal Princess Um'bola went, shrouded in her veils.

Bride and bridegroom had both been received into the Church, in order that no accidental irregularity should mar their Catholicism. The cardinal could marry them. They would set an example of true religion to their nation. The Holy See was gratified.

The cardinal's suite had provided one of the most ticklish problems of accommodation. A private chapel where he could say Mass, rooms for his purple-robed attendants, rooms for his guard, whence they could emerge in trunk hose, ruffs, and Elizabethan tunics, and rooms for his peculiarly sacred self, had been hastily constructed from boards and corrugated iron, and formed a little group of hutments behind the hotel.

The iron reflected the heat and had to be covered with

thatch ; the cardinal could not mix with the visitors and required a separate staff to wait on him. His diet nearly sent the chef distracted, and a special aeroplane had to be sent to bring salted fish for his fast days.

" I'd rather cater for Gandhi—goats and all," said the stores clerk. " My God, I wish they were all Quakers ! "

But on the Sunday, at the time fixed for the procession to start towards the stadium, the cardinal and his suite were ready. It was the Mandoan Church which created the problem now.

The cardinal should have been greeted by the Arch-archbishop and his subordinates at quarter-past nine.

At ten o'clock Bill Durrant, in the church hall behind the cathedral, faced the ranks of dissatisfied archbishops.

They had sent word that they would not carry a cross nor intone a response, until the tax of nine dollars, three pounds, or one slave per head had been remitted.

Arch-archbishop Ma'sull, silent and helpless, sat in the great chair of ceremony, looking down upon his colleagues. If they struck now they might ruin all his schemes, and he would die imprisoned in honourable dignity. But he had no eloquence to stir them, for already he was a man doomed to loss of authority. His forthcoming marriage and retire-ment had stripped him of prestige. And his prospective successor was a leader of the malcontents.

Archbishops were exempt, as a rule, from poll tax. They enjoyed a blissful excess of privileges over responsibilities. They had lands and slaves and gardens, and they took women without the tedious elaborations of Mandoan marriage. But now they were taxed and sore, and driven. They had been forced to rehearse the complex ritual for the wedding festival. The conglomeration of saints' days, rearranged for the benefit of alien visitors, had quadrupled their duties. They were far less eager than the nobles for the supression of heresy, and their submission to Holy Church had been purely verbal. Bitterly they protested, rising one after the other in their white robes, to speak their grievance.

Bill listened to the long-drawn-out complaints. He knew that it was of no use to send for Talal now. The

Lord High Chamberlain had no influence over these
gentlemen. Indeed, they regarded him as a cause of their
misfortunes. He could not send for the cardinal, whose
impressive figure might have subdued disaffection, for it
was part of his scheme that Mandoa should preserve an
appearance of steadfast and religious unity.

He had to find some argument himself.

He was tired. His head ached, and he was racked with
anxiety for his brother, for the commissioners, and for the
success of the whole enterprise. But he must do something.

He began quietly :

" Well, now, do you want Mandoa to be as it was before
I came to you ? "

Some did ; some didn't. Bill sensed the ripple of
questioning.

" Because it can return to what it was. Will you have
yesterday for to-morrow ? " Bill asked. " We would go,
taking with us the gramophones that make music, the
bicycles that bear the body as by magic, the aerodrome,
the telegraph."

" We are not children," they answered. " We have no
need to play with toys."

" You are men who can suffer," Bill pressed. " Would
you prefer that we go away, taking our hospital with
ointments and medicines ? You, Shan'tango, whose leg
was broken ; you, Your Grace Bar'muta, whose wounds
were closed silently in a sleep ; would you prefer to suffer
again, without the help of white doctors ? "

" We are not cowards. We are men who can bear pain,"
they grunted.

Bill tried other tactics. " What is the price of a slave ?
Nine dollars, three pounds, not the price of a rifle ! My
lords, do you set against civilisation a sum less than the
price of a rifle, or an inconvenience lasting less than three
weeks ? "

" What is this civilisation ? What good do you bring
us ? " cried Shan'tango bitterly. " We are ground by
taxation, worn out by marchings and processions. You
tell us it is worth it. Then—worth what ? "

When, indeed, Mandoa was civilised, thought Bill, what
would it bring these men ? What did it all amount to ?

The chorus of deep voices rumbled round him, asking, protesting. What had he brought to Mandoa ?

He thought : A group of men with an air of authority and habits of decision, like Sir Malcolm Devizes ; a custom of keeping carbon copies of correspondence ; gramophones and sewing machines ; a money currency ; a fashion of not taking bribes, so incomprehensible to Mandoa that hitherto it had had no influence ; a hospital ; and dis-approval of the slave system.

What was there among all these blessings to please these passionate and secretive men ? He spoke again.

" We bring you power," he said, " the power of the Catholic tradition." For, when all was said and done, contact with Europe meant this also. You couldn't ignore it. " We bring you a more elevated and authoritative conception of the priesthood. You are priests ; you are churchmen. Out in the hotel, a Prince of the Church Universal awaits you. Go with him, and contact with him will bring you holiness. You will learn how to make people obey you because they fear eternal damnation for their souls ; how to gather to yourselves gifts of money and positions of power . . ." Bill's imagination, fed upon memories of Protestant histories and denunciations of Popery, supplied him with visions of a dominant priesthood, a universal church, and Rome, built upon seven hills, to which all the roads of the earth should lead.

The archbishops now listened, fascinated. He gave them good, heady stuff, opulent with unreality, that sang itself into a magic rhythm.

Two hours after the procession should have started, the archbishops consented to take their places. They had been convinced that Prince's Limited gave them full value for their money.

For a mile and a half through the city, wound the great snake of ceremony. All Mandoa moved forward, led by the Prince of the Catholic Church, to recognise the source of all authority. Nobles, archbishops, warriors, freemen and slaves, tourists, officials, secretaries and reporters, marched in the sweltering sun towards the stadium, to honour a god who appeared variously to them as a captain of warriors with supernatural powers, as a chief magician, a compensating justice, a holy terror, an historical anachronism, or an impersonal force.

It was half-past twelve before the first banners actually reached the stadium ; it was one o'clock before the service itself began.

The arena of the stadium was thronged with a multitude no man could number, in robes of white and green and yellow, scarlet and blue. But the midday sun drained the crowd of colour. The walls of the stadium and the earthen arches, were black shadow and white gleaming light. The brazen crosses and points of the ceremonial pennoned spears, caught and held the quivering sun. Dazzling and glittering above the wedged ranks, they swayed and tilted. The curdled, stale, ancient smell of sweaty cotton hung on the windless air, stirred only by the vibration of eight thousand voices as the Mandoan Processional rolled up to the blazing steely sky.

This was the company, thought Bill, that was about to pray for Maurice, for neat, meticulous Maurice, the perfect clerk ; for sober, admirable, evangelical Mr. Beaton ; for Frau von Schelden, and the witty free-thinking Beriot—for Jean.

" Oh, Trinity, Glorious, Ineffable," cried the Mandoans, nobles, archbishops, freemen, while the Negro slaves straightened their limbs, stiff with a hundred bruises, " Oh, Mercy Incomprehensible ! "

Bill had work to do. He had seen the recalcitrant procession to its appointed end. He turned his donkey back to the hotel and offices, scampering over burning sand and slippery shale. But while he was still half a mile from the aerodrome, he heard, faint and far away, the vibration of an approaching aeroplane.

Was it from the north, a late-comer from Nasir ? From the west, a messenger from Juba ?

It was from the south. Like a silver midge, catching the sun, dipping, glittering, rising, he saw it now.

Bill halted his donkey, shading his eyes against the ferocious glare, and watching as out of emptiness another shifting diamond point, smaller and more mobile, flitted gnat-like round the first.

The big passenger 'plane and its escort. They were returning together.

Either the prisoners were safe, or rescue was despaired of, and the pilots were cutting their losses by bringing at least their machines away in safety.

Hitting his animal an undeserved thwack, Bill bounded forward. The groundsmen, the clerks from the offices, and the staff from the hotel were already out on the aerodrome before he reached it. Moreover, from the town, bare feet were running, sending up the dust in powdery clouds. If Bill had thought that all who knew of Ma'buta's treachery, the commissioners' capture, and the intended rescue, were a few chosen nobles and the foreign visitors, he was much mistaken. All Lolagoba had heard that some event of great importance hung upon the arrival of a sky-machine from the south. Rumour ran riot. God was sending in it a new and powerful prophet ; it carried treasure to buy slaves free for ever. . . . So those who had not followed the crosses and banners to the Stadium ran now from the city to the aerodrome.

But it was not only in the huts of the half-deserted city and on the road that the aeroplanes had been sighted. Out in the stadium as the sanctus bell tinkled and, like a tulip bed in the wind, the congregation bowed forward, the droning crescendo of the machines broke the silence and the prayer for safety received immediate answer.

The guards held back the crowd until the blessing had been spoken, but even so, seventy-four women, children and old men were trampled underfoot and crushed to death or stifled during the exit, as the flood of humanity poured out of the arena.

So when the big aeroplane circled over the aerodrome and dropped gracefully and easily into the runway, Bill, shouting, ordering, and even threatening to clear a passage with machine guns, had all he could do to make a landing possible.

The door of the cabin opened and Maurice, white-faced and crumpled but perfectly composed, appeared above the bobbing, pressing heads.

Hardly aware of the significance of that appearance,

yet conscious of tension relaxed and excitement released, the crowd opened its mouth and roared at him.

But Maurice had turned and, half-way down the steps from the cabin, held out his hand for Frau von Schelden.

She was obviously in no state to disembark unaided. Dr. Beriot from above, Maurice, Bill and half a dozen groundsmen from below, got her down the steps. Then Dr. Beriot himself came, turning back, as Maurice had done, to give his hand to an ugly middle-aged woman whom Bill, looking up from his attentions to Frau von Schelden, saw emerge, stooping, from the cabin, then straighten herself on the steps. She wore a soiled green frock ; her face was grey with fatigue. She uttered a direction to some one behind her in the cabin, then climbed awkwardly to the ground.

It was Jean Stanbury.

The crowd shouted, unintelligently exulting. Two youths had picked up Maurice and, in spite of his protests, were carrying him shoulder high away from the 'plane.

Bill saw Jean's desperate signals. He left the German woman with Beriot and pressed towards her. She clutched his arm, not for support but to prevent their separation in the surging mob.

" Beaton—he's in there—ill. We've got to get him to the hospital at once."

" What's wrong ? "

" We don't quite know—a sort of fever. Rollett's dead."

" Rollett ? "

By speaking straight into each other's ears their voices were just intelligible below the noise of the singing, shouting crowd.

At every moment fresh reinforcements were approaching from the stadium. The guard, which never left the field, managed to keep the mob from wrecking the big aeroplane, but it could not also clear a path for a stretcher.

Maurice no longer protested. His one hope of safety lay in acquiescence. He was the hero of the moment, exposed to a hero's hardships, and his triumphal progress to the hotel was as unpleasant an honour as any hero might expect.

But Bill, watching from the steps up to the aeroplane,

saw its convenience. He bent down to Jean. " It's all right.
They'll follow Maurice. We'll get through towards the
hospital."

He was right.

In another seven or eight minutes, before the Royal
Guard had returned from the stadium, a way to the hospital
was practically clear. In quarter of an hour, Beaton, flushed,
dazed, only half-conscious, was borne away. Dr. Beriot
took Frau von Schelden with him.

Bill turned to Jean. " What are you going to do ? "

" I ? I'd better go and see if I can help."

" Help ? You can't help any one. You're worn out."

They were lifting another burden from the cabin but
this time the face was covered.

Jean watched for a moment without speaking.

" Is that Rollett ? " asked Bill.

She nodded.

Bill gave instructions to take the body to the hospital.
" That's all ? "

" Yes," said Jean.

" Bun'dodo ? "

" We had to leave him behind as a hostage."

" *Did* you ? "

Bill raised his eyebrows. He had a notion of the sanctity
and significance of hostages in Mandoa, and Bun'dodo
was Safi Talal's blood brother. But this was not the
moment to question Jean. He took her arm.

" Come along. We'd better follow the conquering hero
to the hotel," he said.

" He's been splendid," Jean murmured mechanically.
She spoke with the difficulty of extreme fatigue, and Bill
had almost to drag her across the field.

They went round to the hotel by a side door, and he
took her straight to her room.

" I can't rest yet. I must see Maurice. I must see Dr.
Beriot."

" You'll do nothing. You'll lie down now." She looked
vaguely about the familiar room.

The last time they had met was in the darkened camp.
Magic had dwelt then in the hour, the place, and in their
heightened vitality. Now, the body that slumped heavily

on to the bed might have been a sack of coals for all Bill cared ; the arm that supported Jean, as another pulled pillows under her head, might have belonged to a Negro porter, for all she knew. Bill made her comfortable on the bed, brought her a drink, and left her ; then, for the third time since he returned to Lolagoba, he sought Blacker in conference. He found again Maurice and Sir Malcolm assembled with him. Some one had sent for Talal.

" A kind of yellow fever, you say ? " Sir Malcolm asked.

" Beriot says its more like that than anything. But yellow fever's a west coast and Mexican disease."

" Infectious ? "

" If it's yellow fever, it's carried by mosquitoes. He's isolating Beaton and Frau von Schelden. She may be only tired, or she may have it too."

" That's bad," said Sir Malcolm.

Maurice described the ruse by which he had penetrated the stockade, his dealings with Ma'buta, his bargaining over the ransom, and his final consent to the abandonment of Bun'dodo as a hostage.

" After all, it's only a native . . . " he was saying, when Talal, summoned by messenger, walked in.

The Mandoan's face was impassive. He stood, very tall, slender and sinewy, before the white men who had rescued their kind, leaving his blood-brother in his enemy's hands.

Bill, who was still a little vague about Mandoan etiquette, knew that something was wrong, but could not be certain what it was.

" Was Bun'dodo quite willing to stay ? " asked Blacker, after the usual courtesies had been exchanged.

Maurice laughed. " Not at all," he said. " The poor beggar made the most fearful fuss. But naturally, when I saw how ill Beaton was, I had no alternative. It was a matter of life and death to get away quickly."

" Of course," said Blacker.

Bill watched Talal's face.

The three Englishmen were exceedingly pleased with themselves. The rescue had been effected. Rollett's death was unfortunate, but no fault of their's. It was to be hoped that poor Beaton would soon recover. The official pro-gramme could go forward. Talal, or somebody, would soon ransom old Bund—whatever his name was. . . .

Talal listened courteously. When asked questions, he answered them. He made no comment upon the action taken.

But when the conference had broken up, he went quietly over to Bill and spat on his foot.

" What the devil do you mean by that ? " Bill cried.

Talal smiled. He drew his stiff lips away from his white teeth, as an animal snarls.

" Your brother," he said, " has given my brother into the hands of mine enemies. There is a feud between us now for ever."

" Don't be a fool, Talal. You know there's nothing of the kind."

" Oh, no ? To dishonour me, that is nothing ? To betray me, that is nothing ? To spit on the face of my ancestors, nothing, nothing, nothing ? "

Bill sat down again beside the ink-stained table. Round him were the implements of office work—files, typewriters, desks, a duplicator, pens, blotting paper. He picked up a pencil and balanced it across his finger. Talal's furious voice rang in his ears.

" Look here," Bill said at last. " Do sit down and be reasonable. I haven't done anything to you. We've often said that a time would come when a difference between our points of view would make things blow up between us. I've had the deuce of a business with your archbishops already to-day. I've always reckoned that I could deal with you as with a civilised man."

" You are always ready with words," growled the Mandoan.

" Then listen to a few now. I'm not responsible for what my brother did or did not do. That's the first thing. Secondly, who suggested that Bun'dodo would be a good person to accompany the rescue party ? You did. Thirdly, did Maurice know that Bun'dodo was your blood-brother ? Of course he didn't. And even I haven't a notion what it means, anyway. Maurice's business was to get the commissioners safely out of Ma'buta's camp. When he found that the old beast would take Bun'dodo as hostage, naturally he jumped at it. I can't see why it was such a frightful thing to do. I thought you all rather liked being in a ticklish position."

"All Mandoans are brave men and warriors. To have killed my brother was nothing. To die fighting is to reach Paradise. But to hold a man's body is to hold a man's honour. Ma'buta knows now that he holds me. My blood-brother is a hostage for more than a ransom. While he is held, I can do nothing. If I let a blood-brother be sacrificed, I am dishonoured."

"There is no sense in that. It has nothing to do with facts."

"There is no sense, but there is honour."

"But Bun'dodo's in no danger. We can ransom him."

"It is I who am in danger. It is you who are in danger. All Mandoa is in danger. I am bound by honour to rescue Bun'dodo—whatever Ma'buta demands. And he will demand freedom of action, to kill, to destroy, to drive out the foreigners, to do what he will. You know what it has cost me to keep Ma'buta quiet."

"You said you would get it all back."

"But I did not know I would be called upon to rescue my blood-brother."

"This is all so far-fetched."

So far-fetched, thought Bill, in this tidy office, with the typewriters clicking through the thin partition, and the electric bells to summon clerks and office boys.

"So long as you tolerate a barbarous superstition," he said, "you can't be civilised. What's the good of all these engines and things you're so keen on, if you risk the whole affair for an arbitrary point of artificial honour? Those blood-brotherships are only remnants of a dead magic."

"So. . . . So."

"Talal. You know it. You can't play at living in the twentieth century while you bind yourself by codes belonging to the fourth or fifth. What does it *matter* if Bun'dodo is held prisoner for a few days?"

"If I do not go now, at once, and offer all in my power to release him, I am dishonoured."

"But you can wait till the Wedding's over."

"I am dishonoured."

" But can't you see that this point of view is not *real* ?
It's not a *fact* ? "

Fanshawe and Cardover deplored the fading of the
tribal myth. Marlow sighed for picturesque and unique
customs, producing pure " types." Here were myth and
custom active, and Bill could make no headway against
them.

He held his aching head in his hands and strove for
mastery of the position.

" If you go now to Ma'buta, you think that he will offer
Bun'dodo's safety, in return for release from his oaths not
to interfere with us in Lolagoba ? "

" I know it."

" If he were released, what could Ma'buta do ? "

" Fire, sword, rapine, murder."

" There are the Royal Guards, the High Council, the
army."

" What, against him ? He owns half the slaves in
Mandoa. The archbishops and nobles are already dis-
contented."

That was true.

" We have the transport and so on."

" He could convert the people."

" Preach a crusade against us—a holy war ? "

" Sure."

There they were, between two forces.

On the one side, stood the foreigners with their machines
and offices, their knowledge of sanitation and amusement,
their offer of varied experience and contact, their rational
arguments and reverence for facts. On the other side,
the Mandoans, with their hereditary traditions of magic
and honour, their secret codes, their high, lustful arrogance
of courage.

The two were not compatible.

" After all, only a native . . ."

" It was an accident," insisted Bill, but magic takes no
account of accidents. " It was one life against five." But
magic takes no account of numbers, no account of reason,
no account of facts. There was no intelligible story that
Bill could tell Blacker and Sir Malcolm and the Cardinal
Legate, and the Balkan princes.

"What are you going to do?" Bill asked.

"I am leaving Lolagoba now. I shall go by aeroplane to Ma'buta's camp."

"Oh, no you won't. If you insist upon preferring your old magics to our science, you must leave aeroplanes alone." By road across the mountains, Talal could not reach Ma'buta's camp till Monday night. The wedding could be over before the chief, released from his oaths, could take any action. Bill reckoned time, and smiled amiably. Talal reckoned too.

They faced each other across the table.

"You stop me, eh?" asked the Mandoan.

"You want me to stop you!" cried Bill. "You don't want me to wreck the whole business for a damn punctilio! You're a coward, Talal. You want to break away, and you daren't."

"You call me coward! You . . ." Talal's wrath passed into Mandoan invective, which he delivered with calm and deadly precision, spitting out the words. But Bill was irrepressible.

"You want me to stop you. And if you don't want me to, you should. It's what you *should* want. I know what you want better than you do."

He heard his hoarse voice cackling out the watch-word of superiority down the ages, the high excuse of imperialism. "I know what you want better than do you!" And, springing to his feet, he rounded the end of the table, and spat deliberately at Talal's sandalled feet.

As a spit, it was a bad effort. His mouth was dry, his lips stiff. But as a challenge to action, it was adequate.

He saw Talal's hand flash to his sword hilt. Bill flung himself forward, and the next few seconds became a confusion of physical violence and tumultuous sound and piercing pain, at the end of which Bill found himself with his head propped on the maternal knee of an Egyptian clerk, while seven or eight members of the staff encircled the once more dignified and impassive Talal.

Bill summoned his failing strength. A pang from his left shoulder made him feel sick; but, "It's all right," he said. "In a way, I was the aggressor. You'd better put us both under arrest. But especially Talal. He's broken his own injunction of non-violence. We're absolutely within our rights to arrest him." He propped himself up on his right arm and crowed jubilantly. "You can't have this kind of thing going on in a civilised office."

Then he returned to the shelter of the Egyptian clerk's supporting knee, and the sleep which he had warded off since leaving Khartoum descended upon his senses like a curtain.

CHAPTER VII

FELICITY CARDOVER SINGS A FUNERAL SONG

THE Egyptian clerk came nervously down the lounge from group to group, asking, "Has any of your ladies or gentlemen got a Prayer Book?"

Felicity Cardover looked up from the cigarette she was lighting and laughed. "Search me! Who wants Prayer Books? My good soul, I should have thought this place had had religion enough to last it for a thousand years."

Rex Leamington spoke to the clerk, who went puzzled and unhappy upon his way. "They want to bury that wretched missionary—or whatever he was—that Durrant picked up on his rescue party."

"Well, why not bury him? Are they afraid his bones won't rest properly unless the right words are said over them?"

"Magic. *Un*sympathetic magic," murmured Julian.

Felicity protested. "But why a Prayer Book? Why not the cardinal? My dear, the place positively pullulates archbishops. Why not make use of them? Personally, I *adore* the cardinal. His little lace petticoats are *too* divine."

"Cardinals or what," complained Julian; "I cannot endure this odour!"

It was Monday evening, and Lolagoba prepared to celebrate the Wedding Eve of its Heiress-Apparent in the traditional manner. From every square and open space, great fires flickered, and round them on spears for spits roasted the marriage meats, dripping their fats into large bath-like dishes, five feet across. Goats' flesh lay boiling in milk with figs and raisins, scrawny saddles and legs of mutton fried in butter. Dough cakes, like suet dumplings, sizzled in the fat. From end to end of the city the smell of cooking burdened the evening air. Even in the hotel lounge it was overpowering.

After Sunday's excitement, Monday had been rather dull. The games and sports in the stadium lacked the corporate thrill of the Papal Legate's Mass. The prisoners having been rescued, the interest of suspense was over. Only official delegates from the foreign missions had been invited to the bride's reception at the Royal Palace. Bill Durrant and Safi Talal were absent. Rumour declared that they had been discovered in a drunken brawl, and incarcerated in guarded rooms till after the royal wedding.

So Felicity and her friends were bored. They sat together, drinking cocktails and complaining of the smell.

"I should say," Felicity observed in her high, silvery voice which sounded so clearly in the hotel lounge, "that Bill Durrant and Talal are homos. Wouldn't you? Maurice, poor pet, was shocked and shut them up apart. I *love* Maurice. Such a little Empire builder! The *world's* handy man, my dear. Orders carried out *more* than punctually. I've never felt so well organised in my life. Dear Bill believed in live and let live, but Maurice makes us all feel *divinely* disciplined and what not. Oh, God! This smell."

"The best thing to do with smells, I always heard," said Leamington, "is to face them. If we try to run away from them, they pursue us. If we go out boldly and sniff them, we become acclimatised."

"But we can't go out yet," Felicity sighed. "Those two American dears have just come in and said that nothing's happening yet except the cooking. I've stopped in bed all day on purpose to keep awake to-night for the *real* fun. I'm dying to see nameless orgies. My dear! How tragic for then to be nameless! Shall we all go out to-night and give them names?"

"Well, I can't sit here much longer being forcibly fed on suburban Sabbath dinners," moaned Julian. "Come on, Fell."

"Yes, my sweet. But where? I've been positively everywhere in this God-forsaken city."

" God-forsaken ? No, Fell. Too—*too* much God about
it, I should say. If the band plays ' God Bless our Pope '
again I'm going to brain the leader with his own cornet."

" Let's go to Rollett's funeral," suggested Rex. " He
won't have many mourners, poor chap. All his little
friends are in quarantine, and, anyway, they don't love
him much, I gather. He spent his life denouncing the
I.H.A."

" My dear, Sophie Marlow knew him. Let's get hold of
her. She doesn't believe in death, either. Let's make her
come and explain to us *why* what's in the coffin isn't really
Rollett, and exactly how he ' passed over.' "

" She's in her room, practising science against The
Smell," Julian said. " But it *is* rather a bright idea. I
wonder if any one's found a Prayer Book." He saw the
sculptor drifting listlessly into the lounge. " Hi ! Marlow !
Have you heard if they've found a Prayer Book, and what
time they are going to bury Rollett ? "

Ivor Marlow strolled towards them.

" I don't know about Prayer Books," he said. " But
I've been talking to Sir Malcolm's secretary. Apparently
the trouble is that Rollett was violently anti-Catholic,
and though the place swarms with parsons, they're all
Greek Church, or R.C. or something—except that German
fellow, who's a Lutheran. Old Beaton was a deacon or
something, but he's sick—pretty bad, to-night, they say.
So Cooper's going to read bits of the funeral service if they
can find a book, and Prince's and the British delegation
are sending official wreaths. (They've got to be made of
paper, I hear, because the real flowers are needed for hotel
decorations till after to-morrow.) They'll pop him quietly
away to-night while the feast's on."

" Why didn't they do it last night ? Beastly unhygienic
I call it," grumbled Rex.

" Because they wanted a post-mortem or something to
see if they could find out exactly what *had* killed him,
in case we're all doomed to sudden death."

" That *will* be jolly," Felicity said. " Well, what time is
the interment, dear brethren ? "

" Any time now, I think. But they may put it off till
after dinner."

" As if any one could eat dinner in *this* atmosphere.' The air's solid food. Let's *all* go. It'll fill up the time till the orgies begin. Root out your wife, Ivor, and make her come along. It's her duty to pay her last respects to a fellow Anglo-Saxon."

Felicity produced her shagreen and platinum case, and added a deeper petunia to her lips. Her mirror gave her an idea. " Shall I put on black ? Yes, I think I'll wear black. After all, I did meet him once, didn't I ? *I* thought he was rather sweet. Let's get Teddy French and the Collinsons and Piggy Fanshawe, and that *sweet* man who sells steel rails or something—Watson. I'll go and put on my black chiffon. You get hold of some donkeys, or other form of transport, children."

She rose. She floated from the lounge. The other visitors, as usual, watched her progress with the glances of disgust or admiration which were meat and drink to her.

Half an hour later, the funeral procession started.

First went the coffin, borne by eight Negro porters. They wore white tunics embroidered with " P.T." in scarlet letters, the uniform of native employees of Prince's Tours, Limited. Prince's had arranged the details ; Prince's had provided the coffin ; Prince's had even bought, for a high price, the land outside the city for Rollett's grave. The firm that was never at a loss could be generous to its enemies. Rollett had slandered and libelled it, had denounced its methods, its profits, its personnel. But dying alone in Mandoa, he had placed himself at its mercy. His dead body rode in the aeroplane which his living spirit had disdained. Alive, he had refused to enter a Prince's hotel, but now his resting place, his shroud, his mourners and his wreaths, were all the gifts of his magnanimous enemy.

Mr. Blacker, with quiet tact, saw that the newspaper correspondents should not remain unaware of these trifling benevolences.

Behind the coffin walked Sir Malcolm Devizes, the representative of the British Government. His secretaries had told him of Arthur Rollett. He knew that the man had been a dangerous crank. Rollett had held subversive and pernicious ideas. He had talked a lot of perilous stuff about the empire. He was tiresome, malignant, a gadfly pest, but he was dead, and death, especially death in foreign places, is respectable. It would do British prestige no good to emphasise his shortcomings. An Englishman had died here in Mandoa, and died, fortunately enough, poor chap, before he could do much harm among the natives.

Sir Malcolm ordered a wreath from Prince's Limited, and announced that he would do honour to the dead. He stirred to a similar sense of obligation the German, French, Italian, Jugo-Slavian and Japanese representatives. A Mandoan archbishop and a Mandoan noble withdrew themselves reluctantly from the wedding feast for an hour, to walk with the official mourners, courteous and discreet.

Mr. Blacker, Maurice Durrant, and little Cooper who was to read a shortened form of the Anglican service, represented Prince's.

" Sir Joseph was always generous. I know he would like us to show that we bear no ill-feeling to the poor fellow," Maurice said. And the other members of the staff appreciated his chivalry.

After all, if Rollett had not tried to reach Mandoa without the help of Prince's, he would not have died. His death was, in one sense, a tribute to the efficiency of Prince's, an involuntary advertisement of its indispensible utility. The firm could not do less than show its appreciation of this accident.

Behind the unofficial mourners walked the visitors. Sophie Marlow had refused Felicity's pressing invitation, but her husband came with Fanshawe, the anthropologist, and Rex Leamington, Teddy Ffrench, Nita Collinson, and the Cardovers. Felicity had amused herself by dressing from head to foot in black. Veils of sable chiffon clouded her dazzling fairness. " My dear," she said, " I represent the man's widow—all the women he might have had, and hadn't."

" How do you know he hadn't ? " Teddy asked her. " Probably he was bigamously married and had illegitimate twins in Ipswich."

" Then Julian and I represent the twins," she answered, and mounting her donkey, prepared for a charade more entertaining than any improvised in Chelsea drawing-rooms.

Rollett's funeral procession entered the city itself.

By this time the feast had started. The market square blazed with flaring light from the great fires. There, in the centre, sat the aristocracy, nobles and archbishops, land-owners from the country, warriors from the mountain districts. They crouched in exclusive circles, according to rank, round the great dishes. Between them walked the slaves carrying jars of sispri, bowls of mutton broth sweetened with dates, platters of whey, and butter rolled in balls. Beyond the men sat the women, beyond the women sat the slaves, the poor, the strangers. Not a pot-bellied child, not a flea-bitten cur, that evening failed to secure a bone still sweet with flesh, or a handful of dough-cake, dripping, rich with grease. The fires leapt, scattering ruddy light over the darkening crowd. The puddings frizzled in the boiling fat. Mouths and fingers were burned on roasting meat, and healed with tepid sispri. Shouts for drink and food, cheers for the royal bride, drowned the purposeful munchings and gurglings of the feasters.

As the funeral cortege crossed the northern end of the square, the city band of ex-slaves broke raucously into its newly acquired masterpiece, " God Bless Our Pope."

" Ought we to see the feast before the funeral ? " asked Felicity. " In this case the marriage feast may be set forth as funeral baked meats."

She fastidiously drew her scarf away from a huge Nubian woman who, with twin babies strapped to her bosom, straddled past them, tearing flesh from an ox bone long as her thigh. The fat glistened on her black skin, and streamed down to the babies who reached up to the food with clutching hands.

" Didn't you say," inquired Felicity, " that our dear departed friend preached the equality of mankind ? Wasn't he always trying to persuade us that we were blood-brethren of these people ? " The rings on her slim petunia-tipped fingers glistened in flickering firelight as she pointed to the Negress. The Negress saw them and grinned for pleasure, waving her bone and giggling joyfully, her elephantine flanks quivering with laughter.

" Really," Felicity's limpid voice continued, " *such* perversity almost *justified* an unpleasant death. Of course, he was trying to stop the commissioners from publishing their report, wasn't he ? If he's infected them all with some murderous disease, he'll do that quite effectively, I should say, wouldn't you ? Not wasted effort after all."

She checked her donkey and beckoned to the Negress.

" You should not be feasting," she told her severely. " Don't you know that Arthur Rollett—Rollett, you know, your champion—the Englishman who discerned in you the dignity of human worth, is dead ? We are going to his funeral, to see his body put underground where worms may eat it—decently—out of sight. You should be weeping."

The Negress, not comprehending the words but delighted by the attention, grinned and chuckled.

" You see ? " Felicity shrugged her shoulders. " Ingratitude, *I* call it."

" Rollett hated Prince's, didn't he ? " she asked later. " How his soul must enjoy its final rites !—performed entirely at the firm's expense. And to be nursed by the commissioners while they were shut up in that camp. Dear me, isn't life too *wonderful* ? "

The sounds of feasting in the square grew fainter, but Lolagoba celebrated in every doorway. The whole procession had to walk in single file down one street where a herd of Dinka slaves sprawled, snoring voluptuously, dead drunk on sispri, beside the women whom they had enjoyed.

" Thus do slaves mourn the untimely end of those who die to set them free," observed Felicity. Her funeral oration spilled itself in little crystalline sentences along the pilgrimage. " These are the human beings whose dignity he extolled. Our brethren. Well, well, well. No wonder orgies are left nameless. There is, after all, only one name for them, and that, rarely mentioned in polite society."

They passed beyond the city. Here was the land Prince's had bought, in which to give its enemy a Christian burial —a strip of waste land, pierced by the gaping grave. The slaves halted. The wreath-covered coffin stood under a twilit, fiery sky, lit by the uncertain glow from the market square half a mile away. Shouts and screams and laughter, gusts of brazen music, snatches of song and squeals from scalded slaves, made sound as fitful as the flickering light. Like a pall upon the air hung the smell of roasted flesh.

Little Cooper came forward and stood uncertainly by the open grave, holding his Prayer Book. With trembling fingers he opened it at the service for the burial of the dead, but the small print faded to a grey blur. He could see nothing.

Desperately he turned to Maurice Durrant.

" I can't see. Has any one got a light ? "

Felicity heard, and had one. She moved forward in the black draperies of her mock mourning, her beautiful face frozen to acted gravity.

She held the jewelled cigarette lighter which Talal had admired and returned to her in the hotel garden. Its tiny delicate flame trembled across the printed page as she held it between her painted fingers.

" We brought nothing into this world," Cooper began, " and it is certain that we can carry nothing out. The Lord gave and the Lord hath taken away. . . ." Then the flame quivered, leapt, and died. Felicity finished for him :

" Blessed be the name of the Lord." She had spent some years in a High Anglican school, and was well instructed.

They produced matches, but the wick refused to light.

" Damn. Petrol's given out," Felicity said.

It was Maurice Durrant whose presence of mind never failed him.

" The Lord's Prayer," he prompted, and Cooper recovered his nerve.

" Our Father, which art in Heaven, hallowed be Thy name . . ." They all joined him, glad of activity in the fantastic scene. No voice was clearer and sweeter than Felicity's, leading the congregation as she stood, the pure outline of her perfect profile white under the livid sky, upturned to Heaven.

The Negro orderlies lowered the coffin into the grave, and shovelled earth in after it. The dry stones rattled upon the wooden lid.

Rollett was buried. His inconvenient voice, refusing to leave unpleasant facts alone, insisting upon reiterated principles, denouncing stupidities, castigating greed, spoke its unwelcome messages no longer. Dying, he had provided an advertisement for Prince's, an excuse for official British complacency, and an entertainment for Felicity Cardover.

Felicity, dimly aware of these circumstances, enjoyed them.

As the group about the grave began to separate, she turned to Fox, the journalist, and asked, " Will you have to write obituary notices ? "

" No. I send the news of his death, but they do all that in the office. I doubt if they'll think it worth it—except that there's a certain news value in his death out here. But for himself, he wasn't really important. He never quite came off. He could write, I know. I remember his book about the drug traffic. Carter believed in him, but Carter's gnats were all dragon-flies, and he could never see the camels for the gnats."

" Was Rollett a bit off it ? " asked Felicity.

" Mad ? No. Unless a belief that people will forgive insults because you tell the truth, shows madness. You see, he never really understood why people objected to him. In season and out of season he said the same things ; he castigated the men who differed from him, and he was always surprised when they showed their annoyance."

" You think he told the truth, then ? " she asked.

" My dear Miss Cardover—to repeat a celebrated question —' What is truth ? ' As a pressman of many years' experience, I have come to the conclusion that no statement, however outrageous, can be stranger than fact, and that probably all statements are tinged with a little truth. I shouldn't be surprised at anything—except to hear that Rollett died a rich and successful man."

But Felicity was not the only mourner who had been thinking of the dead man. Julian, as so frequently and irrationally occurred, had been sharing her mood and her fancies. He also considered that she had talked to Fox quite long enough. Fox ? Who was Fox, pray ?

Julian beckoned to the slave-boy holding his sister's donkey, and led the beast up to her.

" Your funeral coach, Fell. Sorry there are no plumes. I've been thinking, Fox ; wouldn't this make rather a marvellous story? *Even* for the press? 'Liberator of slaves buried during a native feast,' and all that? Personally," he turned to his sister, " I have been composing a poem about it."

He knew this to be an unfailing bait for her attention.

" Oh, Julian! Have you really? Tell us, tell us! " For Julian's habit was to improvise in *vers libre*, and chant his lines, improving as he repeated them.

They turned again towards the city, and Julian intoned slowly as they went :

> " The funeral cortège winds between the bones,
>   Knuckle-bones, shin-bones, gammon, gristle, fat !
> The city is a charnel house
>   Where these mortal worms,
> These worms of humanity, gnaw the roasted bones,
> Being yet above ground,
>   Rotting under the sun.
>   But we
> Commit our brother to the undying worm."

" Oh, go on, Ju. That's pretty foul, but quite pleasing." Julian went on.

As he went, his shrill voice gained confidence and intensity. The little group about him marched to his rhythm.

> " Bones," he cried.
> " The bones that were men,
>   Bones that were beasts,
>   Bones that were he—
> He, the man of fire, the man of truth,
> The idealist.
> We,
> Who shut his bones down in the darkened earth. . . ."

Jean Stanbury, rousing herself from a half-drugged coma, in the quarantine camp beside the hospital, thought for a moment that she was back in Highgate, having slept late on a Sunday morning, and that the smell of cooking came

from the Sabbath joint. Conscience-stricken, she sprang
out of bed, and stood dizzily, trying to summon her drowsy
reason as she heard, passing along the barrier beyond the
tent, a shrill voice that cried :

> " So we buried the martyr, the Prophet,
> The Man who declared humanity to be sacred.
> We
> Committed him to the feasts of ants and jackals,
> The corruption that ceaseth not, the immortal worm.
> He
> Goes victim, masochist, to the endless feast ;
> While We
> Gnaw marrow-bones here on the merry earth.
> Did he say we were men ?
> Did he say that we
> Were a little lower than the angels ?
> Then
> *Absit Omen !*
> Let us give him the lie !
> What care we for angels,
> We, who are beasts and worms ?
> We, who crawl on our bellies,
>   like Napoleon's armies,
> We, who live for our bellies,
>   sucking the juicy fat,
> The gravy, the lean, the roast, the boiled, the raw,
> We, who sprawl in swinish satiate sleep
>   Over his grave ? "

Jean's befogged brain gave her no clue to the song's
intention; but, clutching feebly at the tent-pole, she
remembered the black fœtid air of the hut, the tossing
unconscious body on the ground, Beriot's gay weary
voice, the slow sickening of Beaton, the hope of morning
as the night stretched itself out, each hour a thousand
minutes, each minute a thousand seconds. She remembered
that Rollett was dead, that Beaton was ill, that Frau von
Schelden had collapsed. She remembered that she must
be brave ; she must hold out to the end, be stoical, be
helpful.

" Did he say all men
    Were equal ?
    Then,
    Absit Omen !
    Let us give him the lie ! "

The strange refrain was taken up and repeated by a
chorus, one high, sexless, flute-like treble singing above
the rest.

She did not know what it was, but she remembered now
that they had been rescued ; Maurice Durrant had come
and carried them back to Lolagoba in an aeroplane ; she
was in hospital in quarantine, and the need for fortitude,
helpfulness and presence of mind, burdened her no longer.

All sorrow for death, all pity for frustration, all reflection
and all memory, were drowned in that soothing mercy.
All that she knew of Rollett now was that she need succour
him no longer. Responsibility had been taken from her.

She slid back gratefully to the narrow bed, and turned
her face towards the canvas wall. Before the Cardovers
and their party had passed the quarantine camp, she had
plunged fathoms deep into sleep again, and was dreaming
that Maurice Durrant descended into the garden at Highgate from a silver aeroplane, and told her she had passed
matriculation.

From the hospital towards the hotel went the mourners,
passing Bill Durrant's bungalow on their way.

Bill lay, also half-disabled but wakeful, listening to a
highly inaccurate account of the day's events from Jeff.
(Mutt was feasting with his friends in a neighbouring alley.)

" Did He say all men
    Were equal ?
    Then
    Absit Omen !
    Let us give him the lie ! "

sang the revellers.

" A pretty song," Bill commented. " Who sings it ? "

Jeff looked from the window.

" It is the Safi Cardover and his lady. They just gotten
away from Englishman's funeral."

" Englishman ? What Englishman ? "

Bill's memories of the last twenty-four hours were still confused. In his struggle with Talal, a struggle so unequal that it involved little but one deft wrestling turn by the Mandoan, he had dislocated his shoulder. He was physically and nervously exhausted ; his malaria had returned to him ; and the ubiquitous Macduff, who had already that evening dealt with suspected yellow fever, cholera, dysentery, nervous prostration, and quarantine expedients, ordered him to bed in his own room with sleeping draughts and quinine.

Jeff was only too pleased with his master's return to consciousness and curiosity. He sat down on Bill's bed and proceeded to give him a genially inaccurate account of Rollett's career. Rollett had been a conspirator against Prince's Tours, Limited, against Mandoa, and against the Durrant family. He had tried to influence the negroes against their masters, thus dooming them to certain retribution. He had spread misery and suspicion wherever he went, like a poison weed trailing infection through a forest.

Jeff was an enthusiastic supporter of Prince's enterprise in Mandoa, which had brought him into the service of Safi Durrant, and he was the implacable enemy of its opponents.

" May his soul rot in Hell as his bones rot in the earth," he concluded piously.

" I don't think I should go quite so far as that," said Bill lazily ; " but you may be right."

The name of Rollett conveyed to his mind only the vaguest suggestion of fanaticism. He had no notion that he was listening to a sentence passed by his servant on the man whose theories, perhaps, best justified his own conduct. He was much more concerned about his own relationship to the Lord High Chamberlain.

He did not know how far his conduct had mortally insulted Talal. He feared lest the breach between them should be final, and the thought distressed him, like a physical pain above his heart—a heavy constriction. Only now, when he had forced himself into violence against the Mandoan, did he understand how much this incongruous friendship had meant to him. Talal's courage and subtlety, his intelligence, his directness, his cool imperturbable simplicity of desire, had healed Bill's wounded imagination, and soothed his taut nerves. He had made the Mandoan accept him as a man of ordinary human luck, not doomed, not haunted. He had acquitted himself passably well in Mandoa, because he borrowed strength from Talal's conception of him. And now he could not be bothered by thoughts of a dead Englishman called Arthur Rollett, because he was obsessed by the need for restored understanding with the Mandoan.

> " Did he say all men
> Were equal ?
> Then
> *Absit Omen !*
> Let us give him the lie ! "

The chorus faded down the street. It was lost in the shouts of Lolagoba celebrating the wedding eve. It was a sound of revelry among other sounds. It meant nothing to Bill Durrant, tormenting himself over his alien friend.

The procession returned to the hotel garden, and singing, passed the windows of the room where the Lord High Chamberlain, bound and guarded, lay, a captive of Prince's Limited.

Talal, indeed, far from retaining his wrath against Bill Durrant, was grateful for his solution of a delicate problem of behaviour. He had sent messages to his kinsmen that he was unwell, and they, believing that he had gone to rescue Bun'dodo from Ma'buta, accepted his noble absence without comment. The whole court accepted it. No member of the High Council suspected that its brightest ornament, at that moment, sat drinking himself calmly into oblivion on Prince's brandy, guarded by four stout Arabs sworn to secrecy, in an otherwise unused part of the hotel.

Talal, too, heard the Cardovers' funeral dirge for Arthur Rollett, and, between his potations, murmured sleepily :

> " Did he sh'awl men
> 'Requal ?
> Then——"

He returned to his good brandy.
The Cardovers sauntered on to the hotel garden.
The high song was over.
Julian repeated the final stanzas :

" For what are men better than sheep or goats
    Who belch, gorge, copulate and sleep again ?
For what are men better than worms that turn
    Through the eye sockets, though the corrupting brain ?
    We are worms, we are worms, feeding on human pain ! "

The chorus joined him :

    " Did he say all men
    Were equal ?
    Then
    Absit Omen ! "

" Come on now. All together."

    " *Absit Omen !*
    Let us give him the lie ! "

Maurice Durrant, having returned by a shorter route
to Blacker's office, heard the song also, and frowned dis-
approvingly. He stood, tapping his fingers on his desk,
and thinking.

He would have liked to send for the young Cardovers
and tell them what he thought of them.

Since his rescue of the commissioners, he no longer
shrank from using his authority. Being no longer frightened
of himself, he was afraid of nothing. Having outdistanced
his brother in every direction, he sloughed off his inferiority
complex, sent Safi Talal and Bill to bed like naughty
children, took the direction of affairs into his own hands,
and found control easier than he had dreamed.

Because he thought matters in Lolagoba simple, they
were simple. Seeing no difficulties, he over-rode them.
The labyrinthine complications of Mandoan politics were
invisible to his naked eye. He saw an official programme,
for which certain preparations had been completed, others
had not. Certain items were in the hands of Prince's ;

others had been left to the natives. All natives were natives
in the eyes of Maurice. Natives obeyed orders. In twenty-
four hours he had put the High Council in its proper place,
and the High Council, without Talal, without Ma'buta,
divided against itself, unaccustomed to subordination,
accepted, for the moment, its position.

> " Did he say all men
> Were equal ?
> Then
> *Absit Omen !*
> Let us give him the lie ! "

sang Felicity, on the hotel verandah.

The Cardovers were detestable young people. Their
behaviour was detestable.

" I ought never to have let them go to the funeral,"
thought Maurice. " They can't be trusted to behave with
decency."

On the other hand, their mother was a daughter of
Viscount Broxholme, and he had great influence in the
Conservative party.

Still, these aristocrats sometimes liked a touch of
asperity. What they disliked was the humble sycophancy
of the clerk.

One had to think of so many things at once.

Though Mandoa was simple, for there one had only to
deal with natives, England and a political career were
very, very complicated.

Maurice pressed an electric bell.

A clerk appeared.

" My compliments to Mr. and Miss Cardover, and will
you ask them to be good enough to make less noise, as some
of the hotel visitors wish to sleep," he said with satisfaction.
Viscount or no viscount, his hotel should not be disturbed.

But the Cardovers, having found pleasure in the sound
of their own voices against the tumult of the city, refused
to be suppressed.

They flocked to the bar, with eight or nine fellow spirits,
fortified themselves with alcohol, and set out again to see
the sights.

By this time the feast was well in progress. The city roared with flame and feast and singing. Quarrels flared fiercer than the flames. Knives flashed. The bandsmen having wearied, their instruments had been seized by willing friends, and trumpets brayed and grunted, cornets squealed, drums thundered, above the human sounds.

Marlow and Fanshawe had accompanied the party from the hotel, hoping to curb Felicity's rash experimentalism. They continued to lead her now away from the most crowded squares, towards the Royal Palace.

Her black draperies streaming, her seat unsteady on her donkey, she still raised her high voice in Julian's song. The royal bride heard it, stretched placidly on a pile of cushions as her maids rubbed her brown skin with perfumed oil, and brushed her abundant black hair. Her marriage should be attended by cardinals in scarlet, and silver aeroplanes. She had no doubt that it was the fame of her attractions which brought strangers from all the corners of the earth to Lolagoba. She had enjoyed a splendid day, bullying her sixty-nine new slave girls, and ordering three handsome Negroes to be thrashed to the bone in her presence. She had given a reception to the Balkan princes, attended by the finest of the officia strangers and the highest dignatories of Mandoa; and she had made her mother cry twice about the Arch-archbishop.

Her mother, the Royal Princess, was absurd. She thought herself in love with Ma'sull. She was an old woman, old and ugly. La'gola could twist Ma'sull round her little finger. If her mother thought that the Arch-archbishop wanted her when he could have her daughter. . . . All Arch-archbishops gave daughters to the Royal Princesses of Mandoa. Even Ma'sull, even if he were old, would prefer soft lips to dry, and young plump limbs to thin and weary ones.

" I told her," recounted the Heiress-Apparent to her slaves, " that if she thinks she can keep Ma'sull to herself after I am married, she must be mad. I shall be Royal Princess, and I shall command the ex-Arch-archbishop to visit me—and she knows he will come."

The slave girls, bending in rhythmical movements above

her back, giggled their approval. It was their duty to
applaud her, as it was their duty to rub the oils and
perfumes into her slender body. The fact that Ma'sull
was her father impressed them no more than it impressed
her. She was a child of divinity. The Arch-archbishop
was a priest who prayed.

" What is that music ? " then inquired La'gola.

" It is the foreigners from the hotel singing your praises,
O Light of a million eyes," said one of the slaves.

" Is that all ? " La'gola lay back on her pillows.

> " Did he say all men
> Were equal ?
> Then
> *Absit Omen !*
> Let us give him the lie ! "

" I'm getting sick of this. Let's go home," said Julian.

" Ju's well oiled, poor mutt. He's drunk with his own
verse," Felicity mocked him, but she stopped singing, and
the final repetition of their hymn was heard by the bride's
mother, who, in her own part of the palace, sat waiting
for the dawn.

She had no duty this wedding eve save that of prayer
for her daughter's happiness. But this she neglected, lying
face downward, weeping bitterly. She was not thinking
of God, but of her lover. Ma'sull found her old. La'gola
said so. Ma'sull wanted to retire and live a hunter's life
among the hills. Ma'sull thought nothing of the court and
the cathedral. He thought only of wild places and wild
animals, and she could no longer follow him over stony
tracks. Her muscles were soft with living in dark huts and
sleeping on silk cushions. She had been carried on litters ;
she had sat on thrones, wrapped in her veils. And now she
was unfitted for other ways of life. She was bound by
habit to the comforts that had been hateful to her, while
he was living only for masculine enjoyment. She could not
leave the court. She loved him alone. After to-morrow,
they would be free to marry, to live together, to bear sons
and daughters, while La'gola and Anjak reigned in Lolagoba.

But it was too late. His desire and her strength had

faded. Their ways lay apart for ever. She was helpless.

She had seen the Mandoan affair as a miracle from Heaven, arranged to grant her illegitimate desires. The aeroplanes, the hotel, the tricking of the High Council, the strangers and the wedding, had been designed that she might find freedom in her lover's arms. And she was not free. She was bound by the needs and limitations of her body. She could take no advantage of the miracle.

" Did he say all men . . ."

She heard the shrill senseless voices and sat up to listen. The words to her meant nothing. She did not know they were a funeral dirge. But the startling sound steeled her faint resolution, and the final repetition of Julian's song drowned her choking cry as she thrust into her mouth the poison beans clutched in her sweaty hand, and fell forward, dead from fear before the venom worked.

CHAPTER VIII

THE ROYAL WEDDING APPEARS IN THE NEWS

EARLY in March in 1933, at the foot of the fourth column of the foreign news page of *The Times*, between " Proposed Restrictions on Norwegian Timber Trade " and " The Spanish Railway Strike," appeared the following paragraph :

" ROYAL WEDDING IN MANDOA.
From our own Correspondent.
Lolagoba, February 28.
" The Marriage between Princess La'gola, Heiress-Apparent of Mandoa, and Prince Anjak of Abyssinia, was celebrated this afternoon in the Cathedral at Lolagoba by Cardinal Gapruzzi. His Majesty sent as his representative Sir Malcolm Devizes, K.C.M.G., and the ceremony was also attended by Prince George and Prince Ferdinand of Jugo-Bulrania, together with representatives from France, Germany, Italy, Portugal, the Spanish Republic, Czecho-

Slovakia, Japan and the Irish Free State. The festivities, which have been prolonged since Saturday, were somewhat overcast to-day by the death of the bride's mother, the Royal Princess Um'bola, titular sovereign of Mandoa, who was found poisoned early this morning in her private apartment at the palace. But the official programme was carried through unaltered, except that after the marriage Princess La'gola was crowned with the Veiled Crown of Mandoa by Arch-archbishop Ma'sull, the head of the Mandoan Church. During the coronation ceremony, a disastrous fire broke out in the eastern part of the city, which spread rapidly, doing extensive damage. No British are reported missing, and loss of life has been confined to natives in the poorer districts. The conflagration is believed to be the work of disaffected Negroes who have recently been disturbed by Communist influences."

Fox of the *London Morning News* sent a descriptive column about the fire, together with a reported rumour that it had been deliberately started by the agents of Safi Ma'buta, the leader of the opposition to foreign influence, who had recently held up for ransom the commissioners of the International Humanitarian Association.

The *Manchester Guardian* published not only a brief though graphic account of the wedding and fire, but also a leading article headed " Slavery in Mandoa," suggesting that the fire was a final protest by the dark obstructionist forces of vested interests in this evil, and looking forward with confident anticipation to the report of the I.H.A. Investigatory Commission. It also stressed the need for granting further powers to the Permanent Slavery Commission of the League of Nations.

The *Daily Herald* discovered sensation in the thought that " Princess Marries by Mother's Death Bed." The *Daily Mail* rejoiced in the level-headedness shown by the British visitors to Lolagoba during the city fire.

Next day, *The Times* recorded, among " Telegrams in Brief " that " the number of casualties in the Lolagoba fire is now estimated at between nine and ten thousand. No Europeans were hurt, and the disaster was confined to the poorer parts of the city."

The Dublin papers gave several photographs of the Cardinal and the Free State representative, emphasising the significance of this restoration of an old Jesuit colony to the bosom of the Church, also applauding the independence which had hitherto preserved Mandoa from absorbtion by imperialist powers.

The *Corriere della Sera* described the magnificent physique of Mandoan warriors, the pageantry of the Sunday Mass, and the Catholic and military nature of the state. *Vorwaerts* concentrated upon the humanitarian mission of the I.H.A., and the tyranny exercised by the Mandoans over their subject races. *Angriff* enlarged upon the sinister fact that a French doctor had been unable to prevent the kidnapping of Frau von Schelden.

The name of Mandoa cropped up from time to time in the world's news, but as the correspondents gradually returned to their former occupations, the reports drifting through from Khartoum or Addis Ababa became less and less direct. On April 2, the *Morning Post, Daily Mirror* and *Evening Standard* each published photographs of Mr. Maurice Durrant, M.P., on his return from Lolagoba. The *Morning Post* declared that he had been investigating the persistent Red allegations of slavery in Mandoa ; the *Daily Mirror* recorded that he had conducted himself with conspicuous gallantry during the city fire ; and the *Evening Standard* suggested that his most important occupation there had been his courtship of Miss Jean Stanbury (photograph inset), the handsome and adventurous Englishwoman who had been acting as secretary to the International Humanitarian Association's commission, and whom Mr. Durrant had rescued from ferocious bandits.

The superior sagacity of the Beaverbrook Press was demonstrated by an announcement appearing on the following Monday in *The Times*. To Mrs. Durrant's overt pleasure, and to the prospective bridegroom's secret satisfaction, it was placed at the head of the column called " Forthcoming Marriages."

" MR. M. DURRANT, M.P., AND MISS STANBURY.

" The engagement is announced between Maurice Peter

Durrant, M.P. for North Donnington, younger son of the
late William Peter Durrant and of Mrs. Durrant of 170
Brompton Mansions, S.W. 3, and Jean Letitia Stanbury,
only surviving daughter of the late Mr. and Mrs. Moreton
Stanbury of Highgate. The marriage will take place
shortly."

On April 17, the announcement of the marriage
itself appeared. It was celebrated quietly at St. Mark's,
Knightsbridge, and the honeymoon was to be spent in
Scotland.

    .   .   .   .

O'Flane's experience of " putting Mandoa across " was
most unfortunate. On March 1 he decided that, what with
kidnapping, a murder, a suicide, a wedding and large-scale
arson, the news from Lolagoba justified expenditure.
Defying editorial injunctions, he chartered one of the air
taxis that were now in great demand, and flew to Juba,
in order to cable from there to New York a really magnificent piece of descriptive reporting, together with tele-
graphic photographs of the fire, the procession, and the
coronation of La'gola by her mother's lover.

" . . . Dancing firelight beneath an African moon, black
shadows whence break gusts of drunken laughter, snatches
of song, and sudden screams ; goats and sheep roasted
whole on dripping spits ; lambs seethed in butter ; jars
of flame-like spirit ; a hundred thousand dusky warriors
feasting together in a city square, squatting thigh by thigh
round the piled dishes. Drums throb with maddening
rhythm ; knives flash in firelight, pulses beat high, and
hearts are stirred. Wine, women and song beneath the
African moon.

" This is Lolagoba at midnight on February 27, in the
year of grace, 1933.

" Twelve hours later—is this the same city ? Streets
thronged with men in gala tunics. Houses wreathed with
paper flowers. Sunlight glittering on brass and silver.
Vivid as butterflies are the Mandoan nobles, gorgeous in
emerald and scarlet, their brown bearded faces solemn.
They stand splendidly upright. They march in order.
The scabbards holding their swords sparkle with jewels ;

the hilts of their daggers are of carven ivory. They stand like sentinels along the square from which five hours ago their slaves removed them—limp from their festivities. Behind them crowd the less privileged orders, negroes from the farms, slaves with bared shoulders, traders, women. . . .

"They are quiet, hushed to solemnity; for this is a solemn hour. But now a thunder of drums, a burst of trumpets.

"Here comes the bride!

"Out from the Royal Palace, beneath a canopy of gold and ivory, waving with ostrich feathers, rides Princess La'gola, the fabled beauty whom no Mandoan man has seen, on a litter borne by forty slaves. (The horses trained for the coach were, they say, uncontrollable.) Round her are warriors with drawn swords; before her march church dignitaries bearing crosses. These are the six hundred and more archbishops of Mandoa—the strangest ecclesiastical hierarchy in the world.

"And immediately behind her walks the Arch-archbishop, whom etiquette does not allow us to call her father, who will crown her as Royal Princess, in succession to her mother who was found dead—of poison—early this morning.

"What dark secrets, what mysteries of cruelty, lie behind the ordered splendour of this marriage ceremony? They are well hidden. The procession takes its appointed way, the people singing, the archbishops lifting their jewelled crosses, the nobles their high-tempered steel.

"Under a canopy sit the foreign visitors on raised seats. A wall of the cathedral has been knocked down for their accommodation. This is no sacrilege; the wall is of mud and can be built again. We hear the cheers, the singing, the beating of the drums. We see emerging from the northern entrance to the square another procession—the Cardinal Gapruzzi in his scarlet robes, attended by Vatican officials in purple, and ecclesiastical guards in such ruffs and hose as Columbus wore when he sailed the Atlantic. This is the gesture of Rome towards her straying children; for the Mandoan Church, though heretical, is docile, and the Royal Princess and her boyish consort have been re-baptised for the occasion.

"Without, cobalt blue shadows and the blinding sun, the huts, the drums, the Negro slaves—the pomp and cruelty of an African town ; within, the dim religious light of a cathedral and the solemn beauty of the Catholic ritual.

"This, again, is Lolagoba.

"But the marriage has barely been solemnised, the Veiled Crown of Mandoa barely placed upon the head of the unseen sovereign, when the acrid sinister smell of burning straw strikes on our nostrils. Far away, cries are heard, and through that vast, packed throng, runs the undying horror, ' Fire ! '

"Then we see triumph turned to terror, solemnity to blind, unreasoning panic. Every Mandoan child in that city of drought and congested huts thatched with loose straw, carries from childhood one unsleeping fear—Fire ! Pandemonium in the great cathedral ; pandemonium in the square beyond. Some rush towards the oncoming cloud of smoke, to rescue and to warn ; some flee before it— anywhere out of the now perilous city. Old men and children, pregnant women, slave girls with their babies, are trampled underfoot. I see a handsome nobleman, who two minutes before, had been the embodiment of stately immobility, gird up his robes and run, thrusting aside whomever checked his flight. I see an old woman, one of the court ladies, hurl herself at an archbishop imploring him to save the Royal Palace. I see priests, swinging their jewelled crosses as cudgels to clear a passage through the wall of shrieking, jostling humanity before them.

"We, the visitors, accommodated in the special stand, sit still. There is nothing else to do. All ways of escape are blocked. But one slim figure springs upon a barrier and, using a megaphone, cries, ' Please keep your seats. There is absolutely no danger. The fire is quite a mile away and under control.'

"It is Mr Maurice Durrant, English Member of Parliament and director of Prince's Limited, who recently flew from Khartoum to take charge of the arrangements here. He is our saviour. His calm words checked the rising fear of panic.

"Out in the city, his brother, William Durrant, and other employees of Prince's Limited, are checking the spread of the fierce, devouring flames, by tearing down thatches, dragging away carpets, clearing a gulf that the great flames cannot leap, beating out fiery straws that fly upon the wind. . . ."

And so on, for another column.

Unhappily, during February, the advertising manager of O'Flane's paper had quarrelled with the publicity agent for Prince's Limited in New York. The point in question was the rate to be charged for a series of displayed, half-page, illustrated advertisements. O'Flane could hardly know this ; but his eulogy of " The Firm which is Never at a Loss " and its employees, came at an unfavourable moment. The manager was displeased at the heavy expenses incurred to boost a concern of Prince's. The editor found his space overcrowded with scandals about a senator suspected of rum-running, the murder of a film star, and the disputed paternity of a child born to one of last year's Boston débutantes. All that finally appeared was a half-column giving news of the marriage and the fire, and one photograph over the caption " Dusky Beauty Weds."

.   .   .   .

On March 11, Hubert Hailebury Carter, living in retirement in the country after the failure of *The Byeword,* supporting himself precariously by free-lance journalism, sent in to the *New Statesman* an unsolicited article entitled " In Memoriam, A.R."

It opened with a paragraph describing the death of Arthur Rollett, founder of the Mandoan Crusaders, in Ma'buta's kraal, north of Lake Rudolph. It continued by stating that this champion of liberty and justice had received too little recognition in his life-time.

". . . His tongue was the pen of a ready writer, and his pen was a sword," Carter concluded. " He waged untiring warfare against the cynicism of corrupt capitalist interests, against the blind egotism of imperialism, against oppression in high places.

" He made enemies ; he was persecuted ; he died alone in a far country, imprisoned by the representative of a corrupt slave-owning aristocracy whose activities he had

denounced, attended only by the patronising kindness
of philanthropists whose compromise with evil he had
endeavoured to forestall.

"He never understood the policy that plays for safety, the
mental indolence that comes to terms with cruelty, nor
the self-protection that makes friends with Mammon. He
never understood the children of this world whose wisdom
in their own generation appeared to him like treachery. In
his flame-like innocence, his loyalty, his single-heartedness,
he was a child, and like a child, too often mocked by his
inferiors. It has been said by his deriders that he accomplished nothing. The tyrannies he denounced still flourish ;
the evils he indicated still exist ; his spear-like denunciations fell back blunted against the stone wall of
man's complacency.

"But let no profiteer from human suffering, let no
trafficker in human liberty, no sordid speculator in the rights
of man, suppose that he has done with Arthur Rollett.
Such purity of passionate pity cannot be defiled ; such
burning intensity cannot quite be quenched. The flame
he lit is not wholly extinguished. Here and there in valiant
hearts untrained to the meannesses of compromise, it
flickers ; and one day it will break forth in triumphant
conflagration, cleansing and illuminating. And in that day
it may be written of Rollett, as it was written of another
idealist whose work seemed, to contemporary eyes, a tragic
failure : ' Because he believed he was believed. We may
smile at the simplicity of the believers. We no longer hope
that any individual, however heroic, will make all things
new. . . . But if men had never promised more than it
was possible they should perform, society would be the
poorer, for the achieved reform is the child of the un-
achieved ideal.' "

Arthur Rollett had, during his lifetime, frequently
written insulting letters about the *New Statesman* and its
policy. Carter's article was very long, and, owing to his
increasing habits of intemperance, a little incoherent. The
editor, justifiably, refused it.

.   .   .   .   .   .

On May 7th, an executive meeting of the International
Humanitarian Association discussed the draft report on

Mandoan Slavery prepared by Frau von Schelden and Dr. Beriot, with the assistance of Miss Stanbury. Mr. Beaton was not yet well enough to take active part in the proceedings, but the committee passed unanimously a vote of sympathy in his illness and good wishes for his recovery—wishes which were eventually fulfilled. In the Birthday Honours List, Beaton received a knighthood.

The report was moderate, sensible and graphic. It gave a brief account of the constitutional and economic peculiarities of Mandoa ; it described the extent to which it was a slave state, and the difficulties of reform owing to the weakness of the central government. It mentioned the unfortunate circumstance of the fire accompanying the royal marriage. This accident, the commissioners explained, resulted in a widespread superstition that the gods were displeased with foreign influence in Mandoa. The wedding and its association with international trade and contacts, had become identified with the policy of the Lord High Chamberlain, Safi Talal, the chief sponsor of innovation. The sudden death of the Royal Princess Um'bola, the accession of her more aggressive daughter, and the ascendancy in the High Council of the Conservative leader, Safi Ma'buta, complicated an already difficult situation.

The commissioners recommended, among a number of other practical suggestions, that copies of their report should be forwarded to the League of Nations before the September assembly, with urgent representation that the League should use its influence to support those agencies in Mandoa already favourable to reform.

The executive passed the report, and resolved to carry out the recommendations. It also congratulated Miss Jean Stanbury, not only on her able work as secretary to the commission, but on her marriage to Maurice Durrant, M.P., director of Prince's Limited. It declared itself gratified that Mrs. Durrant would continue her work for the association.

.   .   .   .   .

Lord Lufton, a member of the council of the I.H.A., read the report and felt highly gratified. On several occasions since Rollett's explosive visit, he had felt uncomfortable. Little gusts from the high winds of idealism disturbed the new tranquillity of his thought.

But this report reassured him. It proved that his attitude of caution and moderation had been right. He felt himself to be freed from a nagging responsibility, and he returned, justified, to the cultivation of tulips and begonias.

. . . .

At the May meeting of the Board of Prince's Tours, Limited, Sir Joseph resumed his accustomed seat at the head of the famous table, and a considerable period of the time allocated to business was occupied in congratulating him on his return to health and London, and on the successful conclusion of the Mandoan affair. These latter congratulations he passed gracefully on to Maurice Durrant who, blushing modestly, received not only praise for his conduct in Lolagoba, but good wishes for his romantic marriage.

The Mandoan business was, like all other businesses in 1933, not an unmixed success. So far as the accommodation of the visitors, the stage-management of the wedding, and the arrangements for continued air transport, were concerned, everything had gone admirably. It was true that the more solid results hoped for from the magnificently conceived and executed publicity campaign had not yet materialised. The railways and roads remained unbuilt. The contract for reconstructing those quarters of the city destroyed by fire, had not been signed. The heavy expenses incurred by Prince's for the wedding, had not yet all been met by the High Council. The country, it must be understood, was poor ; trade was still precarious and badly organised. If the slave traffic to Arabia, hitherto the main source of national income, was checked—" and," declared Maurice with fine courage, " it will be our business as civilising agents to see that it *is* checked"—then for a time at least the state finances would be more chaotic than ever.

" At the moment," said Maurice, " it is only honest to admit that the psychological tide in Lolagoba is against us. The fire may or may not have been deliberately lighted by Ma'buta. Personally, I believe it was. But on the other hand, during the previous evening the whole city had been ablaze with bonfires, and it would have been little short of a miracle if some such accident hadn't happened. Still, whatever the cause, the temporary results have been unfortunate. The Mandoans think that it was a warning from God against foreign influence. The nobles are a bit fed up with high taxation. And, at the moment, the party most unfavourable to our influence has full control of the High Council.

" But, personally, I think it's merely a question of hanging on. As you all know, our agent, my brother, has remained behind to keep an eye on things. In spite of our personal relationship, I think I am entitled—I think Sir Joseph will support me. . . ."

" Hear, hear. Hear, hear," growled Sir Joseph.

". . . In saying that the experiment of sending him to Lolagoba has been justified. He may lack certain practical qualities, but he has shown considerable capacity to get on with the natives. And in rather delicate circumstances like these, I hope that you will think that we were right to renew his contract."

" Hear, hear ! Hear, hear ! " A low thundering rumble of " hear, hears " round the table gave assent.

" Thank you, gentlemen. It only remains to tell you that when the tide turns—as we are sure it will turn— our agent will report to that effect. We shall then ask your leave to grant a substantial loan to the Mandoan Government, in return for which we shall naturally expect Prince's Limited to have pride of place in that work of reconstruction and modernisation under the civilising influence of European contacts, and, we hope, the paternal guardianship of the League of Nations, which is, we believe, surely dictated by the logic of world progress to be the future history of Mandoa."

" Hear, hear. Quite, quite. Yes, yes," ran round the table, with only Lord Woodcock left to grumble :

" What's it all to cost ? That's what I want to know. What's it all going to cost ? "

. . . .

Ten days later, Maurice Durrant invited H. M. Warrington to lunch at the House and told him of his intention to ask the Foreign Secretary whether His Majesty's Government would undertake to raise the question of the Mandoan

Slavery Report by the International Humanitarian Association, at the League Assembly.

He did not ask H. M. Warrington ; he informed him.

Warrington, the tactician, looked down his cigar and said cautiously, " Don't give the impression that your wife's going to run you, Durrant."

Maurice, immune even from that fear, replied promptly, " I shan't. In the first place, she doesn't. We discuss the Mandoan situation on terms of complete equality. I was in the place, but she actually took part in the investigation. She knows a good deal more about it than I do." He could afford to be generous, and to triumph in his generosity. " In the second place, between ourselves, a good deal of mud has been slung at Prince's, one way and another. That old *canard* about our profiteering from slave-labour is not absolutely dead. I propose to kill it. We are going to make slavery in Mandoa impossible within seven years."

" Good ! " said Warrington.

He thought that on the whole Durrant was right, and that, in any case, he looked so well, behaved so vigorously, and appeared so sure of himself, that marriage clearly suited him. The journey to Mandoa had done him good, and he wore an air of success which brings justification in its train.

    .   .   .   .   .

In Dublin, Florence, Brussels, and Jugo-Bulrania, subscriptions were collected for a short time from devout Catholics for the reconversion of Mandoa, and prayers were offered even in Westminster Cathedral for the Royal Princess and her Consort, who were piously endeavouring to lead their country back to the True Faith.

Two Dominican fathers eventually departed upon a mission of teaching and preaching among those innocent heretics, who had strayed from ignorance rather than from perversity of heart.

Prince's Limited, aware that trade frequently follows the cross, offered free transport to the missionaries, but privately, to avoid offending clients of different denominations.

    .   .   .   .   .

In September, the chief representative from Abyssinia

informed the League that His Majesty, the Emperor of Ethiopia, aware of his international obligations, and actuated—as ever—by considerations of humanity, had refused rights of transit through his territory to all slave-traders from Mandoa. The new alliance by marriage between his country and the Mandoan crown would, he hoped, mitigate national resentment, and, by this means, communication between Arabia and Lolagoba being checked, the iniquitous traffic which all civilised men were so anxious to prevent, would be effectively terminated.

Charmed by the opportunity to appear as the champion rather than as the penitent of Humanity, the Abyssinian enlarged upon his theme with some eloquence, regardless of the notes passed to him every few minutes by the president. It was a hot day, and the interest of the spectators hardly equalled the enthusiasm of the speaker. The subject, however, had been opened, and after the assembly, lecturers on the humanitarian activities of the League of Nations felt entitled to add one more work of mercy to their list ; though on the precise nature of the League's action in Mandoa, they were a trifle vague.

    .   .   .   .   .

Meanwhile, in Lolagoba, recruiting agents from the Belgian Congo, Kenya and South Africa, were enrolling contract labour for mines and roads and bridges. The Mandoan nobles, suffering from the slave slump, were quite pleased to let their possessions go in return for the cash bonuses offered in advance of wages by the recruiting agents, and handed over without question by the slaves to their old masters. Safi Ma'buta, determined to preserve the ancient customs, instituted a valedictory service from the cathedral doors, similar to that which had bidden farewell to the adventurers of the slave train. After all, so far as Mandoa was concerned, the two expeditions differed very little.

    .   .   .   .   .

Mandoan tradition made its own interpretation of the events of February, 1933. Several versions of the story, varying according to the tastes and interests of the story-teller's patron, were told at night round the fires, and by day in the shadow of the roofed stockades. That chanted

by Ma'parma, poet and historian to Safi Ma'buta, ran
somewhat thus :

" In the name of the Father, and of the Son and of the
　　Holy Virgin,
　　Most glorious Trinity of the Most High God :
　　There were two chiefs in Mandoa.
　　The one was Ma'buta, old and wise and honourable,
　Friend of the Saints, Father of Warriors, Son of the
　　Blessed Trinity.
　　He dwelt in the mountains ;
　　He tended his cattle ;
　　His goats and oxen grazed in the green pastures ;
　　He hunted lion ;　he hurled stones at waterfowl ;
　　The fish slid into his hands from the deep waters.
　He knew the wells ;　and pools along the streams hid not
　　before him.
　He was a Father to his people, and a great chief in the
　　High Council.
　Fire and flood were his servants ;　winds and waves
　　obeyed him ;
　Because he was a child of the Most High Trinity
　And a protector to his people.
　　·　　　·　　　·　　　·　　　·　　　·　　·

" Safi Talal was a light man and dishonourable.
　His bowels lusted after forbidden pleasure.
　He crossed the frontier. He went to Addis Ababa.
　He saw vessels of glass, weapons of metal, houses of iron.
　His belly was enlarged within him ;　his heart was
　　narrowed,
　He went whoring after strangers ;
　He betrayed his country ;　he polluted his people.
　He sent to white men messages
　That they should come in sky-machines,
　That they should raise great houses,
　That they should bring strong boxes
　　　　That made music,
　　　　That made pictures,
　To seduce men's hearts from righteousness,
　And their bowels from manly virtue.
　Safi Talal corrupted Lolagoba.

He seduced the hearts of the High Council.
He cast spells upon the Arch-archbishop.
He pierced the wall of the Cathedral with a wound.

    .   .   .   .

" But Safi Ma'buta was a protector of his people ;
He was more cunning than serpents ; he was stronger
    than lions ;
He made Safi Talal pay tribute to him.
The white men came before his stockade, travelling ;
They came, bringing their women ;
Safi Ma'buta was afraid of nothing.
He exacted tribute ;
White men drew near to pay him.
They flew in sky-machines.
They scattered money,
Gold and silver and cattle and slaves and ivory,
All these, all these, for the honour of Safi Ma'buta.

    .   .   .   .

" The Heiress-Apparent wed an alien consort ;
The Royal Princess slew herself from terror ;
The white men over-ran the holy city.
Where was Safi Talal ?
Drunk in the hotel,
Drunk with sispri. Shameful. Dead to honour.
His blood-brother Bun'dodo was a prisoner,
A hostage in the hands of the Mountain Dwellers ;
Did Talal go to his rescue ?
Did he leap to pay his ransom ?

    .   .   .   .

" Safi Talal lay drunken with the white men.
He, the Lord High Chamberlain of Mandoa.
While the crown was placed on the head of Our La'gola,
While the Royal Princess lay dead in the palace,
He lay helpless, drunken, dead to honour.
    Shame, shame for ever,
    Shame on Talal, the Light Man.

    .   .   .   .

"' But Safi Ma'buta was a father to his people.
When the wrath of God descended on Lolagoba,
When the flames roared and the fire raged and devoured,
Safi Ma'buta came from his high mountains.

He was swift as an eagle ; he was strong as a lion.
He drove the white men out of Lolagoba,
And the fires fell ; the wrath of God departed.

  . . . .

" Now is there peace and righteousness in Mandoa.
Corruption is purged.
In the white men's resting place
Grass grows and green herb in the rainy season.
Ants crawl unhindered where their women slumbered,
Jackals devour ; sun and sand and tempest
Blow through the roofless halls.
Serpents and dragons
Mate where the strangers feasted with their women.

" Now, though the sky-machines fly from the North and
   land there,
They depart again as soon as they have landed.
Now, though white priests stand in our congregations,
They are but two, and their words are dust and shadow,
Sand blown before the wind, soon to be scattered.
Now though Safi Durrant hunts on the mountain,
His footsteps leave no mark on Mandoan pathways,
His words arouse no echo in the Council ;
It is as though he were a shadow walking,
It is as though he were an echo fading,
A call in the hills which fails and is not remembered.
But the homes of the righteous are in the hands of God ;
The Blessed Trinity has enriched Ma'buta.
His flocks and his herds, his slaves, his wells, his women
Grow rich with the tribute of the false ungodly.
Mandoa is saved ; evil is driven forth ;
Corruption is overcome ; and folly perishes.
And that servant of the Most Holy God, Ma'buta,
Shall be remembered till the desert withers,
Till the stars fall, and the waters clamber backwards,
And Mandoa, Mandoa,
No longer *is* Mandoa.

" In the name of the Most Glorious Trinity,
   We speak the Truth.
     Amen."

RECESSIONAL

CHAPTER I

RITUAL IN LONDON

In their Knightsbridge flat, the Maurice Durrants, with a small group of friends, were lunching about Mandoa. It was late July, a lovely summery day, with bees bumbling among the geraniums in the window box, and the curtains drawn back to show the roofs and chimneys and green trees of London stretching far away into a golden haze. So high was the flat that the traffic down the Brompton Road sounded no louder than the hum of bees—a pleasant sleepy summer sound.

"A marvellous day," said Lord Lufton, gazing appreciatively at the colour symphony of smoked salmon and delicate green lettuce on his plate. "In some ways, you must be glad to be back in England, Mrs. Durrant. What has Mandoa to offer compared with this?"

"The rainfall in July," Frau von Schelden informed him, "is 8 point 7779 per diem." Her little husband looked at her admiringly through his thick glasses. He had come to London to be with her while she attended the summer executive of the I.H.A. He felt that he never wished to let her out of his sight again.

"This, I suppose," said Selena Lufton, "is the middle of the rainy season? How does that poor brother of yours like it, Mr. Durrant, stuck there all by himself through the rains?"

"Ah, but he's not all by himself now," smiled Maurice gently. "There are Dr. Macduff and his assistant at the hospital, and the two Catholic priests, and his own clerk, you know. And he had a holiday in Egypt before the rains began."

Jean, watching her husband, satisfied herself that Bill's name no longer aroused in him a ghost of old jealousies and repressions.

That, at least, she had done. By marrying Maurice, by

so promptly fulfilling Maurice's desire for fatherhood, she had set things right between him and Bill for ever.

She loved Maurice. She loved him with a passion of tenderness for the lonely, vulnerable little boy he had been. She loved him with admiration for the competent, decisive, successful man he was. But most of all she loved him for the need that he had brought to her, the raw, naked, hungry, human need, which was their buried secret. Bill had never needed her. God alone knew what he needed ; he was not human, not natural, perhaps not quite sane. But Maurice was really quite a simple person. And if sometimes he irritated her; if she failed to share his overwhelming reverence for the The Right Wines, The Right Company, The Right Ritual of social amenities, if she sometimes regretted the lost privacy of her spinster life, she set against these disadvantages the enduring satisfaction of her affection and respect.

Fanshawe was airing his favourite theme.

" What I felt most on coming back to London," he said, " was the isolation of modern English life. Drive down any street in—say—West Kensington or Maida Vale. Every little room or flatlet contains its own unit of individual private life shut up as in a sealed box. You'll find that Miss Brown and her young man, playing jazzy music on their gramophone, have no idea of its effect on Mrs. Jones upstairs, crying over the loss of her third baby, or on Mr. Smith downstairs, preparing to put his head in the gas oven, because he's cooked the books of his firm and doesn't know how to put 'em right before the annual audit."

" But in Lolagoba," asked Lady Lufton, " would they know, or care ? "

" They would know. Lolagoba is a social unit—although its society is separated into castes. Every one in a street knows what is happening to every one else. A baby can't have a wart on its back, without twenty other mothers repeating charms over their own infants. And what you are going to do, Durrant "—he turned with amiable ferocity upon his host—" is to destroy that corporate, sociable, spontaneous life, and substitute the ' I keeps myself to myself' attitude of the respectable modern household. That's what I can't forgive."

But Maurice only smiled, giving an order to the head parlourmaid, sure of himself and of Prince's, and of his life-work.

"No, no, Mr. Fanshawe," said Frau von Schelden. "You forget the cruelty, the misery, the driven slaves—those poor little girl prostitutes. It is those we want to help."

"I forget nothing. But has our own civilisation no victims? Frustrated human appetites, perversions, miseries? What you are trying to do, forgive me, is to substitute one form of evil for another."

"But what I do not see," Dr. von Schelden said mildly, "though my wife all day she tells me 'Yes,' is the good of this reform for Mandoa, when all time our civilisation totters, yes? In Germany, revolution perhaps; war, perhaps in six months. We heal others but ourselves we cannot save."

"You know, Dr. von Schelden," cooed Selena, "I don't feel somehow that the revolution is really as near as people think it. Not in *England*, anyway. We somehow don't *have* revolutions here. We're always fearing the worst, you know. But the worst never happens." She beamed.

Jean, toying with her excellent chicken soufflé, felt less secure. The worst, she reflected, did quite often happen. She thought of the war and of her brothers' death. She thought of Rollett dying alone among his enemies, conscious at the end, not only of suffering, but of humiliation, aware that he was defeated and his work confounded, and that not even with his mortal agony could he buy success. She thought of the thousands of men, women and children, killed or crippled for life in the fire at Lolagoba. It seemed to her that life was a very precarious affair, a delicate treading over brittle ice that might at any moment break and plunge one down into black, ice-cold water, beyond the reach of any human solicitude or indifference.

She looked across the table at her husband. He was happy enough, enjoying his vantage point as host, his position as a man of the world, as a junior statesman and director of Prince's Limited. He dreamed of virgin markets, big business and world influence, of power which he would wield with justice, of profit which he would gain with equity, and of responsibility, which was his privilege.

" If revolution comes," Dr. von Schelden said, "Crash! go your plans for nothing."

Would the ice open beneath Maurice? Jean had little faith in divine justice. Poverty and wealth, opportunity and frustration, she had decided long ago, were accidents. She deserved no better now that she was rich, secure and satisfied, than when she had been lost and defeated, dismissed from *The Byeword*, unemployed and most unhappy.

" You're a cynic, doctor." Selena Lufton laughed coyly. " Would you have us do nothing to help this poor, distracted world, because a revolution might come ? "

Lady Lufton was a stupid woman, Jean thought irritably ; and as though in response to her irritation she felt the child within her stir—a strange, intimate indication of its vitality, a secret communication between them.

No ; we cannot give up, she thought, though civilisation may end to-morrow. The voices at the lunch table went on, though she was withdrawn into private communion with her child. The busy traffic flowed along the Brompton Road, though the group in the Knightsbridge flat lingered comfortably over their admirable food. Outside in the great world, the politicians discussed, quarrelled, bluffed, rushed across continents and back again ; ships reached their ports, and disgorged their cargoes of wheat and steel rails and rolls of silk. Letters were written, speeches made ; aeroplanes roared out of the summer sky ; the " freed " slaves from Mandoa marched to forced labour on the Congo ; life went forward inevitably, implacably.

We must do what we can, she thought. The world does not end to-morrow. Life goes on.

" Rollett," she said to herself, aware of his vibrant, emphatic, sensitive, pugnacious personality as it had been at Stoney Ridge, when he told her that she had beautiful hands, but that her values were more important. Her beautiful hand fingered the stem of her untouched wine glass. Her values? " We've got to go on," she said suddenly aloud. Her guests started a little and turned to her with polite attention.

She blushed, for she had spoken involuntary.

" All I meant was—it's no good thinking of what *may* happen. We have to work for the world we know as best we can. Committees, reports, bills, conventions—all rather dull and slow. We play for our own hands—we advertise our own societies. Our motives are never, I suppose, quite pure." Lord Lufton thrust out his heavy, puzzled underlip. His motives, he knew, were always beyond reproach. Fanshawe smiled, thinking about the earnestness of good women. " But we have to go on," Jean repeated.

She looked round the table, a big, handsome woman, strong and maternal, a little humourless, the seed sown in her mind by Rollett, growing as surely as the seed sown in her body by her husband. What she did not recognise was that third influence which had quickened her imagination and drawn her towards Africa, towards Maurice, and towards the work which she saw stretching out before her down years of patient, fruitful effort. Yet it was of Bill, her lost lover, her lost friend, the man who had tried to make Mandoa, that she was thinking as she said to Dr. von Schelden, " After all, a great deal has been done already. The reforms have been started, we are only waiting for the signal to go forward."

She rose and gathered her guests' attention.

" Shall we have coffee in the other room ? " she said.

CHAPTER II

THE SATISFACTIONS OF A LORD HIGH CHAMBERLAIN

DIRECTLY the rain stopped, they left Talal's house and wandered eastward through the steaming city.

The tide of human life had flowed away from its ruined streets, where the brittle shards of the burned-out huts stood roofless, their blackened poles like fingers pointing to Heaven, or crumbling in feathery ash to the moist earth. But throughout the rainy season, the tide of vegetable life had been flowing in. Tlagi-vines slung on succulent arms from wall to wall; passion flower and bougainvillæa billowed in purple foam above the stockade and overflowed across the empty compound. Immense fuchsias drooped heavy swelling buds down streets where once the donkeys minced and ambled. Lizard and chameleon, snake and scorpion, took up their dwelling in the bowers of foliage that had been human habitations.

The city itself had spread southward and westward. Amorphous, chaotic, it sprawled across the plain. Huts could be built within a week. They rose like ant hills from the ground as though from their own volition. The clamorous, sociable life of the streets continued. The intricacies of convention were still observed. The nobles still rode on jewelled saddles, their attendants thrusting aside the impish children. The married women kneaded dough cakes beside the evening fires. The slaves still carried gear and food and fuel. The goats still butted and pissed upon the threshold.

But the traffic avoided the ruined city. It was accursed. Safi Ma'buta, Lord of the High Council, declared that this was because the white man had polluted it and made of it a stable for all evil spirits.

The three wanderers skirted its unholy jungle, and stopped at the choked entrance to a green alley, now almost solidly blocked with woven vines and huge bloated fungi, round as cartwheels, spotted with white and scarlet.

" Really, I suppose we shall have to do something about that eventually," murmured Bill Durrant. " After the rains are over. It's a nasty sight."

" When I come back from Paris," replied the Lord High Chancellor.

The ex-Arch-archbishop, Ma'sull, had just returned from fishing in the great shallow flood that annually invaded the marshes during the wet season. His handsome face brooded over his memories of gleaming silver fish in the brown water, of sudden perfectly timed movements, and the sharp satisfaction when a spear struck home. So he said nothing.

" You don't care, either of you," grumbled Bill, but

without rancour. " Nobody here has any public spirit."

" Ma'buta ? " suggested Talal with friendly malice.

" Oh, by the great Trinity, Ma'buta ! " scoffed Bill.
" He will hold office until he dies—at longest. And he is
an old man."

" May his bones rot ! " murmured Ma'sull mechanically.
Now that he was no longer a guardian of magic, he enjoyed
indulgence in these innocuous curses.

" You say the Eiffel Tower is of metal, one thousand
feet ? " Talal pursued a former catechism.

" Can't even remember if it's still standing. Yes, it's
a radio station or something," Bill replied, hacking with
his cane at a particularly offensive trail of tlagi-vine. A
shower of raindrops drenched his sleeve. Every flower
and leaf was laden with water.

" I shall drink sirop at the Café de la Paix, and wear
trousers, and sleep, every night, with a white prostitute,"
announced Talal contentedly.

" Then you will return, instructed in the ways of
civilisation, to find Ma'buta failing, the High Council
bored with reaction, and Prince's Limited waiting with its
loans. And then we will rebuild the streets——"

" With shops and cafés."

" And drains and water pipes."

" And five theatres."

" And roads that will bear motor lorries instead of
porters."

" If you spoil the hunting grounds, I will kill you both,"
declared Ma'sull simply, spitting out the tobacco that he
had been chewing. " And my successor will lay a curse
on you for ever. Amen."

It was the evening Anthem of these three. On rare
occasions they were joined by the humble figure of Mr.
Byron Wilberforce Gish. He kept his place ; he knew his
subordination. But he longed passionately for their return
to power. He yearned for the proprietorship of the first
garage in Mandoa, for a chain of talkie theatres, and a
repair shop for wireless instruments.

Directly the rains ended, Talal had planned to start
on a lecture tour in Europe and America arranged by
Prince's Limited. He would visit the cities of his dreams ;

he would make money, and, when he had seen all that he wished to see, and collected as much money as he could, he would return. Then he would bribe the court, and sue Ma'buta for wrongful detention of his slaves, and the court, sick already of the old chief's tyranny, would give him his case. He would thus be ready to take up his old leadership. He would win the approval of the civilised world by hurrying through a decree of emancipation of slaves, and would win the approval of his colleagues by arranging for full compensation of the owners. The compensation would be paid from taxes levied on the entire population, including freed men, who hitherto had contributed nothing towards the upkeep of slavery, and the emancipated themselves, whose wages would be mortgaged throughout their life-time, to the government that declared them free. Thus all was perfectly easy and correct, and Talal had every reason for satisfaction.

"You will not come with me?" he asked Bill for the twentieth time. For the twentieth time Bill shook his head.

"No, no. I prefer Mandoa for the moment."

"That is so odd. I will never understand. If you hunted, if you made love to boys, if you were even like your funny friend, Mistaire Fanshore—and believe it is nice to be primitive, I would say nothing. But you know what I think. You see I am right to wish for culture, for art, for civilisation—yess? *Yet* you will stay in Mandoa when you could go to Paris!"

"I'm a paid servant of my firm," Bill reminded him.

"What? Do I not know you could be exchanged to Scotland?"

Bill laughed.

"I happen not to like Scotland. Ma'sull might. It's full of fishing and golf."

"Golf?"

"One of the most distressing defects of civilisation. Never mind."

"Is it because of golf you will not go to Europe?"

"No, no. It's not as bad as all that. One can avoid it."

"Then—why?"

"If I knew that, I should know the riddle of my useless existence," Bill said lightly. For, indeed, he did not know.

Towards the end of the rainy season, there are sunsets in Lolagoba. The rich, humid days wane in a splendid riot of colour. But on some evenings when the downfall has been excessive, the whole town is bathed in vapours that rise like the smoke of sacrifice towards the clear night sky.

This was such an evening; and to escape from the warm steam-bath, Talal and his friends climbed up a rocky track that winds across the face of the escarpment. They climbed steadily for an hour, between dripping shrubs, till they emerged suddenly on to a narrow platform known as the Saddle Rock, and stood in clear star-light looking across the town.

Below them, the soft rolls of billowing cloud were round as sheep in full fleece and white as washed wool. They veiled the lights of Lolagoba, muffled its sounds, and stretched in a soft, vapoury sea towards the tranquil sky, a sea that had risen almost to the feet of the climbers.

Beneath the veiling cloud, the city might have been the metropolis of the Lord High Chancellor's dream. Its roofs might tower toward skies busy with traffic, its underground railways burrow below the earth. Down its streets, for all they could see, might ride in swiftly silent cars, the men and women who controlled the delicate interlocking finance and politics of two hemispheres. From its observatories might go forth climatic prophecies to the world's farmers, warnings to ships, guidance to air travellers. In its shops might be gathered merchandise from all the corners of the world, fashioned to suit taste exquisitely disciplined. In palaces glittering with light, or drowsed with soft harmonies of shadow, the citizens might take their sophisticated pleasures in ever more complex and refined delights.

Or, for all that they could see, these clouds might veil the plain of Ma'sull's dreaming, a happy hunting ground, alive with game : zebras, striped like sunlight between the rushes, giraffes swaying toward the trees with airy grace, wild stamping buffalo, liquid-eyed antelope, frisking wildebeest, and thundering lion. Flamingoes like rose-shaded lanterns, perhaps, glowed among its rushes; its deep pools were alive with silver fish, their brown waters stirred as the snorting hippopotami rose from the mud, or crocodiles like rolling logs flopped from the bank. It might have been a world where men lived lives of perfectly co-ordinated physical movement, their steel-fine muscles and unerring eyes, their sensitive response of nerve and limb, feeding with daily satisfaction their brooding minds, that remembered only the kill of yesterday, and dreamed only of the battle of to-morrow, of brain against animal brain, muscle against muscle, and the clear, savage, tranquillizing rapture of the chase.

But Bill's vision of Lolagoba saw it as it was—a muddled dirty confusion of squatting huts. Round-bellied children swollen with colic rolled in the dark doorways; fowls scratched and dogs nosed under their tails for fleas. In the wide market place the scrofulous potter dozed beneath his torn umbrella, and women crouched over their little piles of grain or dung.

He saw it as a place of poverty and squalor, without arts, or learning, or dignity, or discipline, or science, a place ruled by a corrupt and irresponsible aristocracy, a place where human effort was subject to a million accidents of nature, of chance, of man's unmerciful caprice. Honour was bound to irrational superstition and impotent in day-to-day transactions; kindliness was lost in lust, friendship in passion, and the god of master and slave alike was fear.

Yet—yet, he chose to stay.

Silent between his friends, he leaned on the stone parapet, still damp and warm from the day's soaking rain, and asked himself again Talal's reiterated question:

Why did he choose to stay when he might go?

Perhaps, he told himself, it is from cowardice. Here, he was somebody. Here, his place in society was unchallenged. He was the English agent. He had his own bungalow. His Negro servants, Mutt and Jeff, adored him with flattering familiarity. Talal and Ma'sull were his friends. It did not matter that at the moment he had no authority in the High Council, and could obtain permission to start no new enterprise. He had escaped from the ceaseless competition and effort and rivalry of Europe, where one man was as good as another, and most, more steadfast, more persistent, more competent than himself.

He had escaped from his pre-occupations with his own past, with the war, with his marriage, with his failure to find his appointed niche in the fabric of society. He was a fugitive from himself.

He acknowledged this, but knew that it was not the whole answer to the question. Beyond the huddled city stretched the aerodrome, with Prince's Hotel and offices and tool shops. By a persistent madness, completely unintelligible to his reluctant servants, Bill kept a runway clear for landing aeroplanes. He had the mosses scraped from the hotel verandah, cut back the vines, and daily wrestled against Mandoan lethargy to preserve his employer's property from ruin. Talal said, "But no one comes in the wet season." Gish declared, "It will be time enough after the rains. Weeds dry and shrivel of their own accord. Why struggle with work that the sun will do for you?" The small colony of Europeans, Macduff, the doctor, the Catholic fathers, and the engineer, found nothing remarkable in his efforts, and only grumbled when the chairs in the hotel lounge rotted with damp and split their cushions, when enormous slugs and fungi fat as hogs invaded the hospital, and when rain poured through the roofs of the mission house and bar.

Bill did not believe that if the Europeans left the city their precarious fabric of construction would survive for half a day. The hospital, the dispensary, the mission school, the store—what were these pledges of progress to the amiable indifference, the ferocious conservatism of Mandoan society?

And, should the promise be fulfilled, the pledge redeemed, what had Europe and America to offer these alien people?

Bill remembered the Labour Exchange on Armistice Day two years before; he remembered the election crowd at North Donnington; the unhappy animated marionettes at the restaurants where he had danced with his mother. The vision was not idyllic. People said that the fabric of civilisation was crumbling, even in its oldest centres. The flood of barbarism might pour back across the world as it did in the dark ages. The little fortresses man built for himself might vanish like abandoned huts in the Mandoan wet season, chocked and buried below the invading weeds.

Bill had no particular faith in his own action. He was upheld by no ideal of ultimate perfection. A series of chances had led him to Mandoa. He represented a firm that pursued its own profit, and a nation that considered its own prestige. Yet, while he stayed in the country, the runway would be kept clean and the office occupied. It was little enough; but it was something. It meant that he was not wholly useless; it meant that he had kept faith, though he knew not with what power; he had prepared the way, he knew not for what event.

The moon had risen and flowed in gradual silvery radiance across the floor of mist. The white flood billowed against the rock and curled softly round it, licking the damp stone. Then suddenly, a light wind from the mountains tore the cloud, and through the rent the three men looked down to Lolagoba.

They saw the red fires spangling its streets and squares; they saw the metal roofs of the hangars gleaming fitfully; they saw the black pool of darkness which was the city's empty, weed-grown heart.

Talal pointed to it, and laughed his deep, contented laugh. " Ha ! But we will build it again, Safi Durranta, eh ? By God, we will build it better. Elevators and factories and electric cars. We will make it a great city."

But the clouds swam together again, drowning both light and darkness. They closed in upon Lolagoba, like silence after a voice has spoken, like time after an episode has ended, like life, after a man has died.

THE END

SEPTEMBER 1930—SEPTEMBER 1932.